Operation Lionhearted

By Maribeth Barber

Copyright © 2021 by Maribeth Barber

All rights reserved. No part of this publication may be reproduced, distributed, or transmitted in any form or by any means, including photocopying, recording, or other electronic or mechanical methods, without the express written permission of the author, except in the case of brief quotations embodied in critical reviews and certain other noncommercial uses permitted by copyright law.

For permission requests, please contact Maribeth Barber at maribethbarber.com.

This is a work of fiction. Any resemblance to actual events or persons, living or dead, is entirely coincidental.

Cover design by Joshua Griffin

Ebook formatting by Elisabeth Grace Foley

ISBN: 978-0-578-93844-8

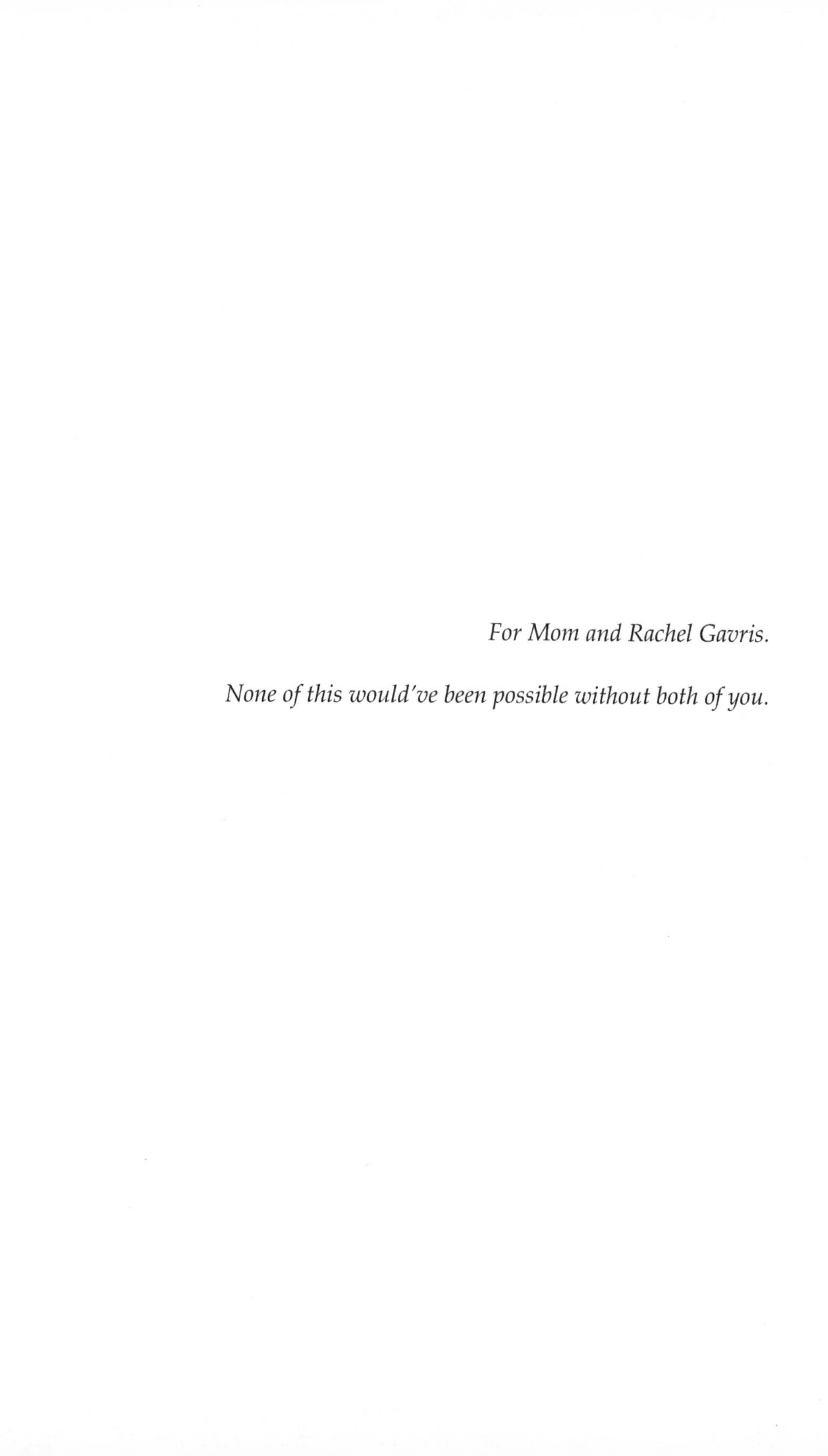

For Mom and Rachel Gavris.

None of this would've been possible without both of you.

Chapter One

The agonized groan of an opening door reverberated through Lin's skull, startling her from an uneasy sleep in her mother's lap. Fresh, icy air surged into the back of the hover-truck. The two dozen prisoners crammed inside moaned and stirred, stretching their legs and shielding their faces from a nearby floodlight. Lin rubbed her eyes.

"Mama?"

"Shh, baby, I'm here. I'm here."

Mama stroked Lin's hair back, her long fingers emanating reassurance and comfort. The guards hurled obscenities and ordered everyone out. Mama set Lin down on the floor and grasped one of her dark, tiny hands.

"It's all right, sweetheart. Let me get down first, and then I'll pick you up."

Lin shivered, waiting until Mama had climbed out of the truck before she locked her arms around her neck. One of the guards shoved Mama with his rifle butt, but she managed to stay upright and keep a firm hold on the little girl.

"Where are we going, Mama?"

Mama didn't reply. She simply held Lin close, twisting her head from one side to the other, looking for someone. Lin shivered again and tried to get her bare legs underneath her mother's coat.

"Mama, I'm hungry."

"Shh, baby." Mama pushed Lin's head against her shoulder, her palm making contact with the back of the little girl's neck. Through the contact, Lin sensed *Fear. Confusion. Desperation.* "Just let me think a minute, all right?"

Fog swirled. Soldiers bellowed. Off in the distance, Lin saw the twinkling lights of the city and heard the rumble of engines. The growing, fretful crowd tightened, huddling close like a swarm of bees in Papa's garden.

"They're just looking for a new home, little one." Papa's words, spoken in happier times, came to Lin like a piece of forgotten music. *"They must protect their queen from the birds that might eat her up, see? They make sure she stays deep inside the swarm where they can keep her warm and hidden..."*

Could Papa be in this crowd? Lin lifted her head, but Mama forced her head down again as a man's voice, too strong to belong to anyone in this disheartened crowd, rose above the hum. When Lin tried to fight her, Mama only pressed harder.

"A message from the Citizen!" the man declared. "'The Uprising is complete. Valya is free of the injustice that has so long plagued her people. From this day forward, all divisions between class and gender are abolished, to prepare the way for unparalleled equality the likes of which have never been seen in the Kellan Star System.'"

No one cheered. The speaker didn't seem to expect it.

"'This future, however, is reserved for those who've longed for it. *Not* for those who've done everything in their power to stop it.'"

"Oh, Elyon Above," someone gasped. Lin winced as her mother's grip tightened.

"Mama, you're squishing me..."

"'The continued existence of the tyrannical aristocracy and those loyal to them threatens our new order. While they live, Valya will never be free. While they live, she will never advance. Therefore, I, Rael Navorre, have no choice but to order their complete and utter annihilation—'"

The crowd exploded in bone-chilling shrieks before he could finish. People clutched each other; some tried to run. Lin screamed. Mama whirled away from the harrowing scene and dropped to her knees. Her fierce, burning love, so different from the quiet affection usually leaking out of her touch, made Lin's heart throb.

"I love you, my baby," Mama whispered. "I love you so much. Come on, let's say your prayers, all right?"

"What's happening?" Lin cried. "Where's Papa? I want Papa!"

The unmistakable pulse of laser rifles drowned out her wailing. The tone of the screams changed from terror to despair.

"Elyon Above, ruler of the stars," Mama whispered through chattering teeth. "Blessed be thy holy name. Thy realm divine—"

THWAP!

Mama went limp, crumpling over Lin like a rag doll. Her warmth—not her body heat, but the living, indefinable thing that made her *Mama*—vanished, like a candle snuffed out. Lin screamed and twisted free, scrambling to her knees and shaking her mother as hard as she could.

She never saw the plasma beam coming. It slammed into her shoulder. She flew backward, all the air leaving her lungs—and everything went black.

Chapter Two

Twenty-three years later

"Lindy! My holocam's gone wonky!"

Jo's panicked cry rang through the ostentatious hotel suite, so loud and shrill it made Lindy wince. It was too early in the morning for this kind of crisis. She hadn't even had her coffee yet.

"You said that would probably happen after all the gravity disturbance on the way here," she called back. "'It'll scramble all my equipment and ruin my lenses,' you said. I don't know why you're so shocked."

"Well, I thought fixing it would be a piece of cake, but it *isn't*! Blazing crackers!"

Lindy smirked sleepily, finished pouring pitch-black coffee into two mugs, and considered wandering back into the bedroom and offering Jo some assistance. Her best friend for ten years and her coworker for seven was normally laid back, but when it came to her professional equipment, Jo was *obsessive*. Lindy could still hear her swearing vengeance on their nova-cruiser's captain. It was his fault, after all, that they'd passed through that gravitational turbulence on the way here to Xandroa.

But hesitating halfway between the kitchen and the bedroom, Lindy decided against intervening. So long as she was distracted with untempered lenses, Jo wouldn't ask why she had slept in an extra thirty minutes...or why there were dark circles under her eyes.

Nor would Jo catch her flicking on the holovision and turning the morning news on mute. The subtitles would tell her everything she needed to know without the anchorman's voice. Setting the extra mug on the coffee table, Lindy folded her long legs on the couch, shot one last glance towards the bedroom, and peered at the holographic screen over her own steaming mug.

"Valya saw yet another day of rising tension between dictator Rael Navorre and his discontented countrymen. Claiming their living conditions haven't improved since the Valyan Revolution, the protestors have limited themselves to minor skirmishes with Navorre's Magnificent Army. But the mysterious demagogue known as 'the Renegade' has promised more acts of sabotage and rebellion if the former Prince of Valya disregards these latest demands for reform."

The sight of angry Valyans shaking their fists against armored soldiers made Lindy's skin prickle—but the projected image vanished into the holovision set before she could glean any more information. Startled, she spun around and found Jo standing behind the couch, lowering the remote control she'd found in the kitchen.

"Thought it sounded too quiet in here," Jo said, blowing imaginary smoke off the remote's rounded end. "Looks like I came in just in time."

Lindy pulled a confused grimace. "What are you talking about? I'm just catching up on the headlines."

Jo snorted. "On mute? I saw your face when we received that news bulletin yesterday. You got as tense as a cat on a hot hover roof. I know what you're trying to do, and it's not working."

Lindy bristled. "What do you *think* I'm trying to do?"

"Trying to keep me from worrying about you." Jo glared and folded her arms. "And maybe if you hadn't thrashed around in the middle of the night like you were being chased by a pack of wolves, you'd have gotten away with it, too. But you won't, so stop trying."

Heat flooded Lindy's dark, chiseled face. She looked away, slurping her coffee. Jo let out a heavy sigh and plopped to a seat beside her. She was so petite, the motion barely jostled Lindy from her own stiffened position.

"Wanna talk about it?" Jo offered, gentler.

Lindy tossed her thick, curly hair over her shoulder. "Not really."

"Okay. Do we need to scrub the mission, then?"

"What?" Lindy looked sharply at Jo. "No, *no.* Why would you even ask that?"

"Well, if you think you're emotionally compromised or something..."

Lindy groaned, set her mug on the coffee table, and pressed a firm hand over Jo's arm. She instantly sensed a quiver of anxiety. Jo, who knew what a Valyan could detect through a simple touch, didn't even try to suppress it.

"I'm *fine,*" Lindy said, forcing herself to sound as calm and confident as she could manage. "And you're right. The news did throw me off last night. But we're nowhere near Valya, and we've got a mission that needs our full attention right here, right now. I'll straighten up, Jo. I promise."

Jo said nothing for a moment; her brown eyes narrowed. Lindy held her breath. The Meridian Intelligence Department was brutally clear: if one member of a trooper team ever had doubts about the other's capabilities, the mission could and would be immediately aborted. In all the years the two of them had worked together, neither had had any reason to pull that card.

But Lindy's home planet had never gone up in flames during that time, either.

Nevertheless, when Jo sighed again, it was a lighter, relieved sound. She slipped a hand into her skirt pocket, the playful sparkle returning to her eyes.

"Well, then," she said, holding up a flash drive. "Guess we ought to go over our mission parameters one last time."

Lindy grinned, discreetly releasing her pent-up breath. "I guess we probably should."

When Jo placed the drive in the middle of the coffee table, a soft blue light pulsed around it for a moment. Then the apparently normal surface transformed into an interactive display pad. Four files appeared. Lindy touched one and opened it with a passcode.

"Step One," she said. "Senator Ralk picks us up here at the hotel. I'm his date. Cover story?"

Jo folded her hands and squeezed her eyes shut. "Miss Melinda Tremaine is doing a piece on Xandroan summer fashions for the *New Harvelle Ladies' Post*'s fall issue. Photographer Josephine Camrin will take pictures—with the ladies' permission—while Miss Tremaine interviews them about their selections."

"Good." Lindy swiped to an image of a white mansion. "Step Two. Get to President Sarkova's party at ten minutes till eleven. You've got the camera contacts, I've got the micro-cam in my hat, and we both have audio recorder gel. Objective..." She swept aside the equipment list. "Record *any* interactions between President Sarkova and Christopher Osborne. If we can't stay on them, we'll have to rely on the audio gel—which means we need to find a way to get it on one of them."

Jo tapped her chin thoughtfully. "We'll figure it out."

"The whole thing should be a piece of cake. I don't see how we can walk out of there without getting *something*."

"Even if we only get enough material about Xandroan fashions to keep the ladies of Meridian running riot with their husbands' pocketbooks, it'll be a successful mission, in my opinion." Jo frowned. "How long does that audio gel last, anyway?"

"Two hours. Plenty long enough for MID to listen in on any worthwhile conversations."

"I hope they're worthwhile. If they only get Osborne coming onto the ladies like a wild animal, all this hard work will be for nothing."

Lindy snickered. "True. Okay, backup plan. If anything goes wrong, the abort code is…?"

"'I'm not feeling so great right now,'" Jo recited quickly. "With all the appropriate fanning and gasping and one of us grabbing Mr. Ralk and letting him know that it's time to go."

"Emergency exit plan?"

Jo scooted forward, pulling up a bird's-eye view of Nikolass Sarkova's sprawling estate. "We take this shortcut back to town through the vineyards rather than out the front way."

"And if we can't get out?"

"Then we definitely won't be getting any invitations to tea and scones with Meridian's 'Most Likely to Stab You In The Back' businessman."

"Not *quite* what I wanted to hear…"

"Yeah, yeah, I know. If we can't get out, it's Operation Kitchingham."

"No matter what?"

Jo nodded without looking at her. "No matter what."

Lindy decided not to press her. Jo's mood swing was understandable. Operation Kitchingham had been named for a trooper who'd killed herself in a Zathrenalian prison, preferring to die by her own hand rather than allow her captors to torture her for information. Today's troopers kept needles hidden somewhere in their clothing. A single injection, activated by a spoken code, would put them in a coma that only a specific antidote could reverse. Your captor could always kill you anyway, of course, but there was a certain comfort in not having to do it yourself.

"We're not gonna get to that point, you know," Lindy said.

Jo glanced at her. "I do?"

"Of course you do. Have I ever *not* had your back in a dangerous situation?"

A slow smile spread over Jo's face. "No..."

"And has MID ever failed to find us when we needed an emergency evac?"

"No. I mean, we've had a few close calls..."

"Well, you expect those when you're a trooper." Lindy got up, downing the last of her coffee. "Better do a complete wipe of the table's display history. The last thing we need is for someone to snoop around and realize there's more to us than our journalist badges."

By the time Lindy strapped on her watch and gave herself a long, critical look in the mirror, it was 10 o'clock. Her sleeveless blue dress contrasted nicely with her dark skin and her wealth of black curls. More importantly, its wide shoulders concealed the hideous scar on her shoulder. Strapless dresses had been listed as a big no-no on her MID file from her first day on the job six years ago.

Behind her, Jo dressed in a motor-mouthed flurry—but Lindy knew her friend would become a picture of cheerful professionalism as soon as she encountered her photography subjects. It wouldn't matter if those subjects were haughty Xandroan ladies or a certain Meridian tycoon suspected of dangerous dealings with this planet's president. Jo had as good an eye for suspicious behavior as she did for trend-setting hemlines.

And you know your *stuff, too. Believe in yourself. You were made to do hard things.*

Lindy smiled at herself in the mirror. She could've sworn she heard her grandmother's voice in that bit of self-advice.

"Okay, how do I look?" Jo asked.

Lindy turned. Jo posed in the middle of the room, palms facing the ceiling. Her white dress, blue belt, white flats, and straw hat looked natural and comfortable. Her trusty and fully repaired camera hung around her neck, resting against her stomach just above the belt.

"You look like an incredibly innocent photographer," Lindy said.

Jo laughed. "Perfect. You look very sophisticated yourself if I do say so."

"Exactly the look I was going for. All I need now is my hat…"

A rap on their suite door startled them both. Jo started for the door, but Lindy reached her in two long strides and grabbed her elbow.

"Hang on a second. He's *my* date."

"Oh sure, like you *really* want to open the door for that potato dumpling."

Lindy smirked and hurried out. She found the short, stout Senator in the hallway, dressed in an impeccable suit and tie. The V-shaped ridge in his forehead, an unmistakable Xandroan characteristic, was the only thing about him that seemed remotely intimidating. He cleared his throat and adjusted his tie, allowing her a good look at his webbed fingers.

"Miss Tremaine," Ralk said, attempting a pleasant smile. "Are you ready?"

"I am," Lindy said brightly. "Just let me grab my purse. And please, come in. My grandmother would have a fit if she knew I'd left my date standing in a hotel hallway."

Ralk obliged her with a chuckle. Lindy shut the door behind him, but as soon as it clicked, she seized his arm. He jerked back, eyes popping.

"How many people are with you?" she whispered sternly.

Ralk swallowed. "J-just my bodyguards. I left them in the lobby—as we agreed."

"Good. Jo?"

Jo emerged from the bedroom with her bag and Lindy's purse over her shoulder. Lindy seized her purse and snatched out a tube of lipstick. While Ralk gaped, she popped off the top and moved the tube over him in a scanning motion.

"Sorry about that, Senator," she said. "Just have to make sure you're not bugged."

"Am I?"

"No, sir. The sensor inside the tube would've started beeping if you were."

"You *need* some of that lipstick, Lin," Jo said.

Lindy cut her eyes at Jo but grudgingly swiped it over her lips before tossing it back into her purse and giving Ralk her full attention. "Senator, I know MID promised you asylum on Meridian if this operation goes south, but I really don't think that'll happen. As long as we do this right, no one will ever know you tipped us off about your president's dealings with Mr. Osborne. I wouldn't be worried if I were you."

"Easier said than done," Ralk said, rubbing his hands together. "But I'll try to take your word for it. Are, uh…are you two armed?"

Lindy smiled. "The less you know about what we've got on us, the better."

"Right. Then I guess we'd better be going."

"I guess we'd better," Jo said. "If it takes us forty-five minutes to get to Sarkova's place and we're supposed to be there for eleven, we've got five minutes to spare."

Lindy jerked a thumb at her. "My walking, talking timekeeper. Who needs a watch?"

Ralk chuckled. He moved to open the door for them, then stopped and turned.

"Before we go, ladies, I have a question. How in the name of all that's good and holy did you two get involved in this…

ummm..." He gestured at the room. "This sort of thing? You're journalists, and yet you're also...intelligence agents?"

Lindy smirked. "Easy answer. It breaks the monotony of writing about the fashion industry."

Ralk laughed. Lindy cocked her head a little flirtatiously to the side, but as she caught the door out of his hand and sauntered after him, she glanced over her shoulder at Jo.

Her friend merely raised her eyebrows and pursed her lips.

Chapter Three

Unsurprisingly, since their planet was famous for its oceans and lakes and they themselves were well-designed for swimming, Xandroans loved the water. As soon as Senator Ralk's driver parked the hover in the crowded lot a few yards from President Sarkova's mansion, Lindy stepped out and looked around in sheer wonder.

A sparkling lake reflected sunlight and snow-capped mountains. The mansion, perched on a flood-safe hill, boasted a huge garden with fountains and roses of every color. Guests milled about under white tents along the lakeshore. Some of the younger ones had already changed into bathing suits and leaped into the water with giddy shrieks.

"If you choose not to swim," Senator Ralk said, "no one will think twice. We know you Meridians are not quite as comfortable in the water as we are."

Lindy glanced at the well-dressed couple stepping out of a nearby hover. "We'll have enough to keep us busy, Senator. Besides, we didn't bring swimsuits."

"And besides *that*," Jo muttered, crouching for a low shot of the house, "I hate swimming."

Ralk looked as if she'd just committed some kind of sacrilege. "You do?"

"Yep." Jo snapped a picture and jerked her head at Lindy. "Back when we were in college, she took me kayaking. 'It'll be fun,' she said. I fell in and nearly drowned."

"Oh, you did not," Lindy laughed, linking her arm with Ralk's. "I caught you before you were in the water for more than ten seconds."

Jo got to her feet, checking the finished photo. "Scariest ten seconds of my life, then."

After a short stroll through the garden, they reached the tents. Several of the guests hurried to shake Ralk's hand. Lindy and Jo stood politely to the side while he assumed a politician's practiced stance: a cool smile, a strong (but not too strong) handshake, and a deliberate focus on anodyne subjects. Discreetly, Lindy scanned her surroundings. Flirtatious squeals rose up from the swimming youngsters; the more dignified VIPs under the tent exchanged pleasantries over neon-pink Xandroan wine.

The two men she'd hoped to see were absent.

Where are you, *Osborne? I know you're on Xandroa. It's just a matter of time.*

"...and allow me to introduce my companion for the day," Senator Ralk intoned, "Miss Melinda Tremaine."

Lindy blinked, forcing herself back to her immediate situation. A handsome Xandroan in a three-piece suit stood in front of her, his dark hair slicked back until it hardly looked real. A blonde in a loose purple gown hung on his arm, her forehead ridge pierced at both ends.

"Melinda," Ralk said. "May I introduce Mikel Sarkova, son of our esteemed president, and his fiancée, Eva Korisima? Miss

Tremaine is a correspondent for the *New Harvelle Ladies' Post*, Mikel. She and her friend Miss Camrin are doing a piece on Xandroan fashion."

"Oooh, fashion journalists!" Miss Korisima cried, flouncing her skirt in such an unsubtle way, Lindy had to keep herself from snickering. "Well, Miss Tremaine, I think *I* could give you some help with that—if, of course, you're interested."

"Umm, absolutely, ma'am," Lindy said. "Mr. Sarkova, a pleasure to meet you."

Quickly but deliberately, she blocked the empathic sensitivity tingling beneath her skin and extended her hand. Mikel took it with a cool smile.

"The pleasure is all mine, Miss Tremaine," he said. "Pardon me, but you wouldn't happen to be related to the Meridian councilor of the same name?"

"I am, as a matter of fact. She's my grandmother—or rather, my adopted grandmother. As you can see..." Lindy gestured at her dark face with a rueful laugh. "We look about as much alike as apples and oranges."

Mikel chuckled. "It is inconsequential. You are both beautiful ladies."

Miss Korisima looked offended. Senator Ralk squirmed. Lindy cleared her throat.

"Well, I'm just sorry my grandmother couldn't accept your father's invitation," she said. "Last I heard, she was having what she'd call 'a political kerfuffle.' I know she was looking forward to meeting with the President and seeing his beautiful estate for herself."

"Yes, I heard about that 'kerfuffle,'" Mikel said. "Amazing, how this Valyan disturbance has so divided the Star System—*and* certain planetary governments."

Lindy hummed in agreement, but before she could change the subject, he leaned closer—a painfully obvious intimidation tactic. An amateur might've looked away. Lindy, however, kept her head up and met his gaze without flinching—and without acknowledging the Senator's rather conspicuous fidgeting.

"A word of Xandroan caution for your grandmother, Miss Tremaine," Mikel murmured. "Sometimes, it is better to let things unfold as they will, *without* the interference of bleeding hearts. And now, if you'll excuse us…"

Lindy raised her eyebrows, but he drew back with another frigid smile and said no more. Miss Korisima seized his elbow, raking Lindy with a withering, contemptuous glare as she fell into step beside him. Senator Ralk exhaled noisily. Jo sidled up next to Lindy and snorted.

"Good riddance," she muttered. "I didn't like that dress of hers, anyway."

"Uh, ladies," Ralk faltered. "How about some refreshments?"

Jo's eyes brightened at that, and she darted to the nearest table. Lindy followed with far less interest. Her thoughts were too jumbled. At least Mikel hadn't seemed to realize *she* was Valyan. Most people never did; they simply assumed she was a dark-skinned Meridian.

But had that part about "bleeding hearts" been a threat against Nana? Everyone in the Star System knew Councilor Margaret Tremaine supported Valya's exiled royal family, *not* the planet's dictator or the insurrectionist Renegade. But why would the Xandroans—or at least the Xandroan president's son—be offended or threatened by her involvement?

Stop. You can worry about that later. Focus on the mission at hand. Lindy grabbed a plate and glanced around again.

"Any sign of Osborne?" she whispered.

Jo gestured with her head. "There he is."

"Where?"

"Look straight ahead. Right there on the shore, chatting up the blue bikini."

Lindy dropped a mini-quiche on her plate just as she glimpsed the broad-shouldered man with the salt-and-pepper hair, his sports coat draped over one arm. The Xandroan woman in the water clearly enjoyed his attention.

"I hear he's a lady-magnet," Jo whispered, snatching up a pair of tongs.

"Well, he *was* 'Sexiest Man of the Year.'"

"Oh, yeah, sure, according to the *Stanhope Guardian*."

Lindy looked around. Ralk was engrossed in a group conversation about Torxallo's main highway, but he caught her eye and nodded before turning his attention back to the current speaker. Lindy leaned closer to Jo, who was still loading her plate with more sweet things than savory.

"I'm gonna try to talk to Osborne," Lindy whispered. "You keep an eye out for Sarkova. And remember to take pictures while you're at it. We've still got our normal job to do."

"Aren't you gonna eat first?" Jo asked.

Lindy answered by popping the entire untouched mini-quiche into her mouth. Jo giggled. Lindy grinned and turned away, grabbing a glass of the pink wine the waiters kept passing around. As she sipped, she tapped the brim of her hat and heard the faint, telltale click of a tiny recorder activating.

Keep it casual, keep it casual…

"*Oh!*" she cried, pretending to stumble. The wine sloshed over the edge of her glass. Her high-heeled sandals were awkward enough to make the fall a convincing one. When a strong hand seized her elbow, she knew she'd pulled it off.

But she'd also forgotten to shield her mind, and her rescuer's emotions barged into her head as soon as they made contact. *Concern. Interest.* For a brief, unsettling moment, Lindy couldn't think straight.

"Are you all right, miss?"

Lindy looked up, straight into the piercing grey eyes of Christopher Osborne, Meridian's most powerful and distinguished businessman. He cupped her other elbow in his hand, supporting her until she could stand upright. The wine had splattered on his white shirt.

"I—I'm fine," Lindy gasped, only half-faking it. "I must've tripped on something."

Osborne grinned, flicking his gaze down to her slim dark legs. "Oh, the hidden dangers lurking in Xandroan sand. Can I get you another drink, or…?"

Lindy laughed. "I hardly deserve another drink when I've got most of mine on *you*. Here, allow me…"

She reached into her purse and pulled out a handkerchief. With a demure bat of her eyelashes, she wiped at the pink stain on his sleeve.

"Oh, I'm afraid it's not coming out. Xandroan wine is the *worst*."

"Never mind that," he chuckled. "Christopher Osborne at your service, ma'am."

Lindy pulled a shocked face. "Osborne? *The* Christopher Osborne?"

"The one and only."

She thrust a hand towards him. "Melinda Tremaine, *New Harvelle Ladies' Post*. I'm doing a piece on Xandroan fashion—though I'm afraid I won't get much until the ladies put their clothes back on."

Osborne wiggled his eyebrows. "Well, why should they in this heat?"

Lindy concealed her disgust behind a smile as she returned the handkerchief to her purse and drew out her data tablet. "I hope you don't mind if I include an anecdote about your attendance here. My editor will be beside herself when she finds out I ran into the Sexiest Man of the Year, right here on Xandroa."

Osborne laughed. Lindy would've enjoyed the sound a lot more if she hadn't seen his file a week ago, bulging with evidence of extortion, embezzlement, money laundering, art smuggling… and now, quite possibly, a treacherous weapons deal with someone here on Xandroa.

"I don't mind at all," Osborne said. "And I'll tell you a secret you might like to include in your article as well. That goddess in the water is my date."

Lindy gave him another wide-eyed look. "The one in the blue bikini?"

"Mm-hmm."

"She must be quite a trend-setter. Is this your first time on Xandroa, Mr. Osborne?"

"Oh no, no. But it's the first time I've ever had such a fine stroke of romantic luck here. As a matter of fact—"

"Mr. Osborne?"

Lindy turned at the unfamiliar voice and froze. Two men approached. One was a young Meridian—Osborne's aide, she guessed—but the other was very old, his Xandroan forehead ridge already sunken from age. There was no mistaking him. Lindy clutched her tablet and willed herself *not* to look at the stain on Osborne's sleeve. The less attention it received, the better.

"Sir," the aide said. "May I present President Nikolass Sarkova. Mr. President, Christopher Osborne of Osborne Industries."

"A pleasure, sir," President Sarkova said, extending a frail webbed hand.

"Indeed, Mr. President," Osborne said. "I've been looking forward to meeting you for some time. You have a beautiful estate here."

Wait, this is their first meeting? But all the intel said—

The intel could be wrong. It's happened before...

Yeah, about once every fifty years!

Lindy started to back away. Osborne noticed and raised a hand.

"One moment, sir. Excuse me, I didn't mean to ignore you completely, Miss Tremaine."

Lindy waved. "Oh no, it's no problem. Still counting on that anecdote, though. I'll just catch you later today, okay?"

Osborne smiled and again let his gaze drift for half a second just below her hemline. "Deal."

Back underneath the cool shade of the tent, Lindy had to blink a few times to adjust to the darker light. She touched the brim of her hat; the camera clicked off. She looked around, but neither Jo nor Ralk were nearby. Maybe they'd gone to explore the garden. Or maybe they'd seen her get within inches of both Osborne and Sarkova and decided to keep their distance.

At least I got the gel on Osborne—and *recorded his apparent first meeting with Sarkova. MID's listening now. They'll figure out if that's legit or just an act.*

Meanwhile, I'd better switch roles and get some material for this article if I want to keep my other job.

Lindy squared her shoulders, approaching a plump woman in a royal-blue, sleeveless tunic. She'd just pried the stylus off her tablet and opened her mouth when the hidden communicator in her ear crackled; she turned away smoothly before the woman could notice her.

"Thorpe," Jo hissed. "Thorpe, this is Sparks—come in."

"This is Thorpe," Lindy murmured, snapping her stylus back in place. "Where are you?"

"Mansion, front porch. You need to get over here, *now*."

Lindy snatched up another quiche. "What's going on?"

"Sarkova and Osborne's guys are making some kind of exchange in the parking lot."

Lindy popped the rest of the quiche in her mouth and swiped her hands together. "On my way. Nimble, be ready to head out on my signal, got it?"

Thankfully, Ralk wasn't completely wasting his time on food, drink, and schmoozing. He responded more promptly—and firmly—than she expected. "On your signal, Thorpe."

Lindy trekked up the gravel walkway to the mansion as fast as she could until she finally saw Jo perched on the porch railing, flicking through pictures on her camera. To an innocent observer, she looked like an introvert who didn't want to socialize. Jo, however, wasn't the introvert on this team. Lindy saw her tilt her head towards the parking lot. One blink and the camera contacts would snap a picture. Lindy put a finger to her ear.

"I see you, Sparks."

Jo answered with a nod. Lindy headed for the parking lot. The closer she got, the better she could hear the voices behind the nearest row of hovers.

"Very delicate pieces of work, these chips. You must handle them carefully—and warn your contact that they must *not* expose them to light, whatever they do."

Someone—a Meridian, judging by the drawl—snorted. "What, they'll melt under sunlight or somethin'?"

"We have found extreme exposure tends to diminish the chips' effectiveness. The test subjects are not as easily...controlled."

Lindy held her breath. *Confirmed, then.* Osborne *was* illegally purchasing weapons from the Xandroans—and not just any weapons.

He was buying cases of Xandroan Chips.

It was cyberpathic technology. A single chip could control anybody who had one plugged into their brain stem—or rather, the person remotely operating the chip could control that individual. It had been such an alarming concept, the Interplanetary Council had slapped Xandroa with sanction after sanction until the planet promised to stop manufacturing them.

But that had been forty years ago. Somebody obviously wasn't abiding by that promise. Maybe no one ever had. And if Osborne was acting as a middleman for another "contact," then...

He could be shipping them to anybody. Namaria? Valya? Zathrenal?

Lindy picked up her pace, drew her comm out of her purse, and pressed it to her ear without unlocking it or dialing any numbers. She gripped the brim of her hat and marched into the parking lot, trying frantically to improvise a realistic, one-sided conversation.

Think about Owen. Remember his face and say all the things you were too afraid to say.

"You mean to tell me," she blurted, "that you've been lying to me this whole time?"

The voices on the other side of the parked hovers dropped a little. Lindy stepped out from between two vehicles and into the open, resisting the urge to look in the direction of Osborne's goons. *Not yet, not yet…*

"If you'd been listening to anything I've said over the past year, you'd have known I'd understand your decision to quit that job," she went on, raising her voice. "You pursue what makes *you* feel alive, not what a few snotty academicians or your parents dictate!"

Owen's plaintive whining—something she never thought she'd hear spewing out of that intellectual mouth of his—hurtled back through her memory. *"I was supposed to be the game-changing lawyer, Lindy—like my parents! I couldn't bear to look you or them in the eye—"*

"Oh, *come off it!*" Lindy screamed, whirling on her heel. She immediately found herself staring at seven Meridian thugs, six Xandroans, and three heavy grey cases passing between them. The men turned their backs to her, clearly uneasy. Lindy spun around again and kept her voice shrill.

"If you didn't want to be a lawyer in the first place, you should've said so. You could've gotten a job at a grocery for all I would've cared. I would've had your back, too—but no! *You* pretended for three months you were still at that firm when you were really just watching holovids in your apartment all day long, not even *looking* for work. And now you're broke, and you're shocked that I'm upset? You know what you did, Owen? You broke my heart. And you played me for a fool."

"I'm hoping that one day I can win your trust back, Lindy," she remembered him saying.

"Listen to me. If you can lie to me about this—and lie *this* well —you could lie about anything. I could never trust you again, Owen. Never." Lindy slammed her fist against her hip and turned to face the hover again. Most of the men still piled cases into the vehicle, but they paid her no attention now. One of the Meridians even had a comm to his ear. She started walking backward. "We're *done*."

"I'm sorry, Lindy..."

"Not as sorry as I am that I invested a whole year of my life in a fraud like you," Lindy snapped. With that, she jerked the comm away from her ear and pretended to hit the "end call" button. She felt breathless and flushed.

"You oughtta win 'Best Actress' for that performance," Jo deadpanned over the ear communicator.

Lindy ignored her. She flung her comm into her purse and turned back towards the lake, the party, and the puzzle of Osborne and Sarkova. Owen Roth could go to...well, to lots of unpleasant places. But she had evidence now, and if it took pretending she'd *finally* gotten the chance to chew that liar out and not just sit there crying like an idiot...

"Uh, Thorpe? I don't feel so great right now."

All thoughts of Owen vanished. Lindy whirled just in time to see a dark-robed house servant seize Jo by the shoulder and yank her off the porch railing. Lindy stifled a gasp and hurried forward—and nearly collided with the unattractive, massive man who abruptly sidestepped her.

She recognized him at once as one of the Meridians, the one who'd been on his comm.

"Miss Tremaine," he leered. "A pleasure to make your acquaintance."

Lindy opened her mouth, but before she could say a word, he jabbed a needle into her neck and everything went black.

"Mmmmmmph."

The groan scraped its way up Lindy's throat as she forced her gritty eyes open. For a moment, she saw nothing but blue and white and a couple of shadows looming over her. She groaned again. One of the shadows came closer.

"Well, Miss Tremaine, how was your nap?"

The voice jolted her awake. She blinked and lifted her head off a cold tile floor. She was in a bathroom, her hands bound behind her with a blue silk necktie. Her hat sat ignored on the countertop. Christopher Osborne squatted in front of her, his grey eyes narrowed. Lindy cleared her throat and looked at him as steadily as she could.

"Mr. Osborne." Her voice was hoarse. "What's this all about?"

He snorted. "Well, that's what *I'd* like to know myself. Perhaps you and Miss Camrin would be kind enough to answer a few questions for me."

Lindy stiffened. Jo sat a few feet away, her back against the toilet, her own hands tied behind her. Mikel Sarkova stood over her with his shirt unbuttoned at the collar, pointing a small black raygun at her head. Jo stared up at him, her jaw thrust forward.

"I hope," Osborne said, "you're not going to tell me you were simply in the wrong place at the wrong time."

Lindy glared at him. "What *am* I supposed to say? I walked into the parking lot to take a call, and the next thing I know, I'm waking up here!"

Osborne sighed. Lindy jerked at her snug restraints.

Time for Kitchingham? No, not yet. Not until I'm convinced we can't get out of here on our own.

"You say you were taking a call?" Osborne asked.

"Yes. My ex-boyfriend called."

Osborne reached into his pocket. Lindy's heart sank as he pulled out her comm, touching its screen with his thumb. The home display glowed to life.

"Miss Tremaine, I've accessed your comm log. Don't bother asking how—I think you're probably familiar with various hacking methods. You might as well admit you haven't received any calls since yesterday afternoon." He smirked. "Maybe you were simply *rehearsing* what you'd like to say to your cad, hmm?"

Mikel snorted. "And maybe Miss Camrin was simply taking a breather on my father's porch. It's an uphill walk, after all, from the tents to the house."

"I'm an *introvert*," Jo retorted. "I need my personal space every once in a while. All those highfaluting ladies were about to choke me with their perfume." She looked at Lindy for the first time with raised eyebrows. "We need to make a note of that in the article. Xandroan perfume is the worst."

"Oh, cut the crap," Osborne snapped. "Fashion journalists don't fake calls—unless, of course, they're chasing a bigger story than they're letting on."

Lindy started to speak, but before she could, he jerked her to her feet and slammed her against the locked door. When he clamped a hand against her throat, his emotions leaked freely through his palm. *Anger. Fear. Anger. Disgust. Anger, anger, anger...*

One-two-one, one-nine-one-eight. Rattle it off, and you'll be oblivious in seconds.

"You know," Osborne hissed, "you might be more convincing if you weren't Margaret Tremaine's girl. For all I know, she's roped you into spying on young Sarkova and me."

"My grandmother is a Councilor of Meridian," Lindy rasped. "Not a spy."

"You think I'm *that* naive? I know Margaret Tremaine. She's always cracking down on, shall we say, 'unconventional business ventures.' I've even heard *she* could be one of those blasted MID troopers." Osborne met her eyes with a seething glare. "You wouldn't happen to know anything about that, would you?"

"All I know...is that I'll have you...arrested...for assault...if you don't let me go!"

He sneered, released her throat. Lindy pulled in a wheezing breath and leaned against the door—only to reel with a cry when he struck her face with the back of his hand. He hit her so hard, her teeth rattled.

"Lindy!" Jo cried.

"Jo, just—" *Shut up, be patient, remember the audio gel!* Lindy coughed and spluttered as he pinned her to the door again. The hate thundering in his palm made her quail—*but you are a trooper, you've been trained for this, they're listening in, they know you're in trouble, keep it together, Melinda! Don't give up, and DO NOT RECITE THE CODE.*

"Now," Osborne snarled, "let's play a game of 20 questions, and if you aren't honest with me, I'll have Mikel disintegrate your friend into a clump of smoldering cells. How does that sound?"

Lindy struggled for breath and looked at Jo. Jo stared back, her dark eyes wider than ever, blinking hard and fast. Lindy almost reconsidered—and stopped short.

She's taking pictures. She's taking pictures of Osborne and…

Jo glanced up at Mikel and blinked again, drawing a nervous, shuddering breath as she did so. It was very convincing. The pictures were probably being analyzed at the Meridian embassy in Torxallo at this very moment.

They've got all the proof they need. They'll come for us. They will, they will, they will…

Osborne seized Lindy's chin. "First question, Melinda. Why did you fake that call?"

Lindy swallowed. "Because I needed to get back to Ralk's hover."

He raised his eyebrows, surprised by her admission. "Why?"

Lindy swallowed and discreetly tugged at her restraints. "I left my holocam in there and he…he wanted me to film your men making the microchip exchange. He promised it'd be a good story. I could sell it to another paper and break out of the *Ladies' Post.*"

Judging from the shocked fury on Osborne's face, the fib was close enough to the truth to pass muster. Mikel went white.

"He's on my trail, Christopher," he gasped. "He's on my trail…he'll tell my father…"

Jo's eyes widened. "You mean those weren't your *dad's* goons?"

"Shut up!" Mikel shouted, shoving the gun into her forehead. "You were watching longer than *she* was! I ought to just kill you right now!"

Osborne half-turned from Lindy, his grip loosening. "Mikel..."

"Shut up!" Mikel screamed, turning the gun on the tycoon. Lindy felt Osborne's emotions switch from anger to fearful surprise. "*You* know too much! What's to stop me from killing all three of you right here? I swear, I'll make it look like *you* killed them and then did yourself in, Christopher! And no one will be the wiser because no one will be left to incriminate me."

Lindy gave another quick tug of her wrists. The silk tie loosened. She held her breath.

"You forget about *my* men down there in the parking lot, Mikel," Osborne growled. "They'll track you down and string you up like a goose if you lay a finger on me. Besides, you're an idiot if you think you're the only one in this room with a weapon."

"Then *you* get rid of them," Mikel snapped. "And make it look like an accident."

"And Ralk?"

"Oh, I'll take care of Ralk. He's a bumbling fool, and if—*watch out!"*

Osborne whirled, but Lindy's fist slammed the underside of his chin before he could grab his raygun. He crashed into the countertop; one of the faucet handles snapped under his weight, spraying water. Lindy heard Mikel cry out again, this time in terror, but she was too busy seizing Osborne by the collar and throwing him to the floor to look up.

"Blast!" Osborne bellowed. "Blast you! I'll kill you for this!"

Lindy jerked one arm behind his back in reply. She felt the gun in his back pocket pressing into her inner thigh; she tore it out, checked the setting, and fired into his shoulder.

Osborne went limp. Lindy sprang off his back and prepared to lunge at Mikel—but Jo had him on his knees in front of the toilet, happily dunking his head into the water. When she pulled him up again, the Xandroan gasped for breath.

"Had enough, creepo?" she shouted.

"Enough!" Mikel gasped. "Enough, I-I beg you!"

Lindy grabbed him by the shoulder and Mikel tumbled onto his back. She jammed her foot into his chest and pointed Osborne's raygun at him.

"Selling your infamous chips, are you?" she demanded. "With Osborne as your middleman?"

Mikel, looking a bit like a half-drowned rat, raised his shaking hands. "Y-y-y-yes…"

"Who's your buyer?"

He gulped, pressed his lips into a trembling line, and shook his head. "I-I can't tell you. He will flay me alive if I tell…"

Lindy removed her foot. "Fine. We'll see how committed you are to your precious secret after the authorities get their hands on you. Truss him, Jo. Show him how lady journalists tie knots."

"Yes, *ma'am*," Jo muttered, flourishing the same necktie that had pinned her hands behind her back. "Let me introduce you to the Meridian Girl Scouts' Triple Knot."

Satisfied, Lindy returned to the still-unconscious Osborne. She tied his wrists just a little tighter than was absolutely necessary before retrieving her comm from his pocket.

"Is he dead?" Jo asked over the spitting water.

"No," Lindy muttered. "I made sure his gun was on stun. But I'm calling the Torxallo police. At this point, we can't handle this alone..."

But before she could finish, the door slammed open. Lindy and Jo sprang up, rayguns at the ready, but quickly lowered the weapons as a dozen police-droids in ray-proof suits and helmets stormed inside. Four of them headed straight for Mikel.

"Mikel Sarkova," one of them droned, "you are under arrest for selling illegal cyberpathic technology to a private, non-Xandroan company and for conspiracy against the People's Republic of Xandroa. You have the right to remain silent—"

"Wait, what's going on here?" Lindy cried.

One of the droids turned to her. "Are you Melinda Tremaine?"

She nodded gingerly; her head still felt thick from the drug and Osborne's slap. "Yes. And this is my photographer, Josephine Camrin."

"Are you in need of medical assistance?" When Lindy shook her head, the droid pointed at the door. "Then please exit the crime scene, Miss Tremaine. You will be questioned in a moment."

Lindy reached for Jo's hand; they followed the droid's gesture into the bedroom. It must've been Mikel's, judging by its finery, but the individuals already waiting for her surprised her more than the extravagance. Senator Ralk sat on an ottoman, fanning his round face with his webbed hand. President Sarkova looked like a feather could knock him over. Lindy almost felt guilty, looking at him. All this long time, MID had suspected *him* of dealing with Osborne. He hadn't been the Sarkova mentioned in all the intel after all.

And I should've picked up on it. I should have. I should've known. I should've guessed!

"Miss Tremaine," President Sarkova said in a soft, quavery voice. "I cannot tell you how deeply sorry I am. If I had known Mr. Osborne and my son would do this to you and Miss Camrin—"

Lindy shook her head. "You couldn't have known, sir. And Miss Camrin and I have had some…self-defense training. We're fine."

Ralk raised his eyebrows. "Your face doesn't look fine."

She glared at him. "I'll live."

Sarkova chuckled, then paused, fixing his gaze on his son as the droids dragged him out of the room. Mikel stared back with cold fury. Once he was gone, the President sighed.

"You should be grateful for a very lucky coincidence, Miss Tremaine," he said. "Our police had just set up a routine inspection checkpoint on the main road when *your* embassy put out an alert for Mr. Osborne. One of the first hovers to arrive at the checkpoint belonged to his men. They tried to speed through it, but the police restrained them in a magnetic field and found the rear hatch full of those blasted chips." Sarkova shook his head. "The Meridians, thank goodness, were not particularly intelligent. They confessed right away."

"And in the meantime," Ralk said, "I'd just realized that you two had gone missing."

Jo rubbed the back of her neck. "Guess we just got caught in the wrong place at the wrong time, huh?"

Lindy glanced at Ralk. When he looked back with meaningful steadiness, she pressed her lips together and nodded. The rescue may have seemed a lucky coincidence to President Sarkova, but she knew better.

The Meridian Intelligence Department had not been idle.

Chapter Four

The party was promptly canceled. Several guests were detained for questioning, and Lindy and Jo soon found themselves in a windowless office at Torxallo Police Headquarters. A medical droid had just finished treating Lindy's bruises when a Xandroan detective walked in.

"Medical droid, dismissed," he ordered. The droid beeped and headed for the door. The detective waited until it was gone before turning to the two women, an elated grin transforming his tough, florid face.

"Good work, ladies," he said, straddling a chair. "Your embassy had been keeping us informed about your MID activities, of course, but when they told us you might be in jeopardy, they hinted we'd find something worth our while. Boy, were they right."

Lindy forced a careful smile; her jaw still hurt. "Well, we're glad we could help. Nobody wants those chips floating around the Star System."

"Yeah, no kidding. Anyway, here's your Interplanetary Crime Prevention report. Your orders are to fill out the form, then head back to your hotel. Your troop commander will meet you there."

Lindy looked up with a start. "Our troop commander?"

"Yes, ma'am. He arrived on the planet about an hour ago."

Lindy shot Jo a worried look, but Jo only shrugged. Lindy swallowed down her questions and bent over the report. The detective wouldn't have the answers she needed anyway. Besides, Meridian was two whole days from Xandroa. Jarvis would've been heading here long before he knew about *this* incident.

With luck, nobody's told him about it yet. We can tell him ourselves. But he'll still lecture us—even if we are *the first to explain what happened.*

Once the report was filed, Senator Ralk himself took Lindy and Jo back to the hotel. The ride was short and awkward, and the Senator didn't stick around. He dropped them off at the door, mumbling a goodbye and mouthing his thanks before his hover shot away.

"If I didn't have a feeling we're being watched," Jo muttered, "I'd be miffed with him for not at least walking us up to our room."

Lindy grunted her agreement. She, too, had spotted a trooper seated on the bench by the front door, reading a shimmering holopaper. To any other observer, he looked like an average Meridian tourist. The MID-issued watch on his wrist, however, identical to her own and Jo's, was a dead give-away. They passed another, far more conspicuous trooper on the way to the elevator: an exotic-looking woman with a raygun displayed boldly on her hip. No one made eye contact, but the closer she and Jo got to their room, the more nervous Lindy felt. Commander Jarvis had obviously brought a large escort with him.

They finally reached their floor, passing yet another trooper duo at one end of the hallway. As Lindy pulled her key out of her purse, she heard voices on the other side of the door.

"We've already got company," she muttered.

"What do you wanna bet they've raided our little kitchen?" Jo asked.

Lindy snorted. She shoved the door open, thoroughly satisfied by the way the three men waiting for them jumped in surprise.

Despite their black suits and crisp neckties, each had made himself quite comfortable. Frank Gridley played a game of holochess at the coffee table. Judging by the commotion in the kitchen, Commander Jarvis himself was the fulfillment of Jo's dire kitchen prophecy. But the man at the window—tall and well-built, with brown hair and a full, boyish face—was the only one Lindy didn't recognize. *Early thirties,* she observed. *Razor burn…big hands… probably works out.* Yet he did seem familiar, and he stared at her with equal curiosity. Lindy turned her attention to Jarvis before it could get too awkward.

"Find something worth eating in there, Chief?" she called.

Commander Benjamin Jarvis—six-foot-five and so broad, she often wondered where he got suits big enough to fit him—shut the fridge with a bottle of soda in his hand. "Well, I found something worth drinking, though I can't say much for your taste in beverages, Lindy."

"At least you'll never catch me drunk on duty, sir."

Redheaded Frank Gridley moved a holographic chess piece. "From the looks of those bruises, Lindy, getting sauced *might* do you a bit of good."

Lindy stiffened. Jarvis twisted the cap off the bottle with a loud snap.

"I understand you required a bit of medical attention today," he said.

Lindy looked away. "Yes, sir."

"The folks at the embassy are still trying to calm down. The way they tell it, they nearly had a collective stroke when they realized the danger you were in."

"We might not have been in any danger if our intel had been sound," Lindy grumbled. "You saw my report?"

"As soon as you submitted it over the MID net."

"Then you know it wasn't *President* Sarkova selling the chips to Osborne. It was *Mikel.* And Osborne was just the middleman. If we can find the actual buyer—"

Jarvis raised his hand. "Hold on. Jo was held at gunpoint and *you* were at the mercy of a man who could've killed you any time he chose. You had no clue if or when help might arrive. Most troopers would've called Operation Kitchingham. That doesn't bother you, Lindy, even a little?"

Lindy drew herself up. "Yes, sir, it does. But Jo and I aren't 'most troopers.' And neither of us would've figured out Mikel was the one involved in the sale if we'd made that choice, so I'd argue it was worth the scare."

"And the bruises," Jo added.

Frank snorted and moved another chess piece. Jarvis raised his eyebrows with a hint of a smile.

"It was quite a risk," he said, "and not one I'd recommend to less experienced troopers. But you've probably halted an extremely hazardous operation, and we can all thank Elyon for that. Now, have a seat. We've got a new mission to discuss."

"Actually," Lindy began—then stopped, noticing the stranger once again. She definitely knew him from somewhere. "Umm…I don't believe we've met?"

"No, ma'am, we haven't," he answered, extending a hand. "Captain Ethan Granger, *MNC Hummingbird*."

"We're partners now," Frank explained, nodding at Granger. "Which means *I* am the brand-spanking-new IT Security Chief aboard the *Hummingbird*. Thank you, everyone, for the hearty congratulations. I'm *really* enjoying my new cover job."

"You double as a Nova Force captain?" Lindy interrupted.

Granger smiled. "Yes, ma'am. Probably not as solid a cover as yours, but I make it work."

"Well, good to meet you." Lindy shook his hand, then sat down beside Jo and faced their boss. "Anyway, Jarvis, I really can't take another assignment right now. I was supposed to be reporting on Xandroan summer fashions at that party today, remember?"

"Of course."

"Well, getting knocked out and slapped around kinda prevented me from getting much of anything. I've got a good excuse for my editor, at least, but I'll have to make up for it. I doubt she'll let me suggest another piece for a while." Lindy hesitated at the look of profound disappointment on his face and kneaded her hands in her lap. "But just in case I *can* pull her strings, what's the new assignment?"

Jarvis shifted on his side of the sofa. "It's a big one. Bigger than any one team can handle. I'd hoped you could work with Frank and Ethan. That's why I let them tag along."

"And I was hoping we could arrange a double date with Jarvis here as the chaperone," Frank added.

Lindy rolled her eyes, Jo turned pink, and Granger chuckled—but Jarvis scowled.

"Frank," he warned.

"Sorry, just kidding. Although *you* two would hit it off, Lindy."

"Cut the jokes, *Francis*. You've kept up with the news from Valya, haven't you, Lindy?"

Lindy's breath caught. Jo noticed and spoke for her. "We've heard a *little*..."

"Then you know the Valyans are finally turning on their former Crown Prince. Turns out he isn't the egalitarian hero they'd hoped for. Surprise, surprise." Jarvis shook his head. "Their planet's a mess. They've got food shortages, inflation, overcrowding, restrictions on everything from education to the worship of Elyon to the press. Their military's the only thing that's stayed in good working order, really."

Lindy said nothing. Jarvis wiped condensation from his bottle.

"This Renegade fellow, though...*he's* gained a lot of traction over the past few years, encouraging the people to protest while he and his guerrillas make trouble. Rael's under a lot of pressure. Which is why..." He paused, looking at each of the troopers. "... the Royal Remnant has decided to offer him another opportunity for a peace conference."

Jo scoffed. "What's their pitch *this* time?"

"Same as usual. If he'll let them come home and rebuild the ariya plantations, *and* if he reinstates the Valyan Parliament, they won't demand any other restoration of their old oligarchy. It'd certainly be better for everyone. The Renegade would lose his influence, Rael would have some checks and balances, and Valya might actually become a respectable society again."

"You think the royals mean it?" Jo asked.

Jarvis shrugged. "I'd be more skeptical if that hotheaded princess was in charge. Thankfully we deal with her old man instead. *Your* grandmother, Lindy, has always trusted his intentions. Maybe Rael does, too, since he's actually agreed to the conference."

"What?!" Jo cried.

Frank laughed. "Didn't see *that* coming, did you?"

"The conference will take place a month from now," Jarvis said. "Our Nova Force will be in charge of security, of course, but you four would function as MID's covert intelligence team. We haven't had a trooper on that planet in nine years—"

"Stop!" Lindy cried. "Please, just *stop*!"

Everyone stared at her. Lindy shuddered and rubbed her arms.

"I can't do it. Even if I *was* free, Jarvis, please don't make me."

"Lindy," Jo murmured.

"Wait, did I miss something here?" Captain Granger asked.

Lindy started to glare at him but quickly remembered: he was a stranger. He didn't know her. But *Jarvis* did. Even Frank knew her better than most. Yet here they were, acting like this was some kind of joyride.

It made her skin crawl. It made her want to scream.

"*I'm* Valyan," she croaked.

Granger's blue eyes widened.

"I can't tell you what my family name was, who my parents were, or what kind of life I had before Rael Navorre decided he was 'the people's champion,'" Lindy went on. "I don't remember any of that. I just know I was supposed to die with my mother and two thousand other people in one night. Sometimes the memories are so horrific, I wish I had died with them. So forgive me, Captain, if I'm not too thrilled about this particular mission. I'll go anywhere else MID sends me, but I'm not going back to Valya—and you're *insane* if you think I ever would."

With that, she sprang to her feet. Jo got up too, but Lindy stormed past her and into the bedroom, slamming the door behind her. She sank to the floor, drew her knees up to her chest, and pressed the ball of her hand into the scar in her shoulder.

"I love you, Lin. I love you so much. Come on, let's say your prayers, all right?"

Lindy drew a shaky breath and squeezed her eyes shut. "Elyon Above, ruler of the stars, blessed be thy holy name. Thy realm…thy realm…"

Her voice cracked. She dropped her forehead on her knees, shuddering under the flood of harrowing memories.

As soon as Lindy Tremaine slammed the door in her friend's face, silence fell in the living room. Ethan Granger stared at Jo Camrin's back as she stood in front of the door, her fist poised to knock. Only when she decided against it and let her arm fall did he figure it was safe to speak.

"She's a *Valyan,*" he said slowly.

Miss Camrin sighed. "Yeah. Don't touch her without giving her a fair warning. She'll speed-read your emotions before you can say 'Hi-how-are-you-how-about-coffee?'"

Under normal circumstances, Ethan might've chuckled at her sarcastic description of the Valyan gift. Instead, he turned to Jarvis. The commander glowered at the coffee table, his square jaw set.

"Why didn't you tell me she was Valyan?" Ethan asked.

Jarvis looked up. "It's not my place. Lindy has always been very private about her origins. I figured she'd tell you if she wanted you to know."

"Did you know she'd react like that?"

Jarvis' silence was answer enough. Miss Camrin turned away, one hand over her mouth.

"Maybe not the smoothest of moves, Jarvis?" Frank suggested.

"Everyone has to face their fears sometime," Jarvis muttered.

"So what, you slam their fears in their face?" Ethan cried. "Come on, Jarvis! You don't have to be a psychiatrist to know that's not how it's done!"

Jarvis glared at him. "You were there after the massacre, weren't you, Captain?"

Ethan froze. Miss Camrin whirled.

"Wait," she said. "*You* were on Valya during the Revolution?"

Ethan cleared his throat. "My, uh…my mother started a relief operation on Valya not long after the Revolution started. I just happened to be with her on that particular visit."

Miss Camrin still looked confused. Ethan sighed, shoving his hands into his pockets.

"My name is Granger, Miss Camrin, but that's not the name my mother goes by. She dropped my dad's name when she went into politics."

Her dark eyes widened. "Oh my gosh. Your mother is—"

"President Stagg. It's all right—our family drama isn't as big a deal as the media makes it out to be." Ethan glanced again at his boss. "This was back when she still ran my dad's real estate business. Since she had assets and contacts on Valya, it was easy for her to pull together an organization and arrange refugee transports. A week or so before the massacre, she decided to go herself. She took me with her only because I begged."

"And you saw the field outside Cor Danem where rebel soldiers mowed down two thousand aristocrats and dissenters, including Rael Navorre's own family?" Jarvis prodded.

"Yes, I saw the field." Ethan paused. "I saw it a few hours after it happened."

Jarvis nodded. "Lindy Tremaine was in that field. Someone found her and dropped her off, alive, at one of your mother's shelters. For all we know, you two may have already met."

Ethan snorted. "You know how many refugee kids I met in my mom's aid stations? I wouldn't remember her unless she gave me some *very* specific identification."

"And she probably couldn't, even if she wanted to," Miss Camrin said softly. "Like she said, she doesn't remember much. She didn't even start talking again until months after Councilor Tremaine adopted her."

Ethan raked a hand through his hair. He'd seen countless children who couldn't—or wouldn't—talk, too. Lindy Tremaine was nothing unusual.

"I never choose my teams haphazardly, Ethan," Jarvis said. "You're a proven leader. You bring out the best in your crew and in other troopers. That woman, however, is the best agent on the force *and* a Valyan. I knew I couldn't bring this up unless I forced her to consider it—"

"It was cruel, Jarvis," Ethan snapped.

"But necessary," Jarvis retorted. "We need her background and her ability to blend in on Valya for this assignment, but she'll need *your* sympathy and shared experience to keep her steady and focused. You'd make a good team—all four of you."

He got to his feet, brushing past Ethan as he tipped the soda back. Miss Camrin frowned.

"What makes you so sure Lindy will accept the assignment, sir?" she asked.

"Because, Jo, *I'm* not the one who requested her addition to the team."

Frank sprang up. "Whoa, whoa, whoa, hold the comm. Who else is pulling these strings?"

Jarvis pulled open the fridge again. His head was deep inside within seconds, but Ethan could still hear the amusement in his voice.

"Councilor Tremaine, of course."

The old nightmare hit Lindy like a storm, ferocious and wild. She heard the terrible screams, the gunfire, and her mother's frantic prayer, and then she felt fire in her shoulder and crumpled to the damp ground. But then the dream shifted from memory to horror: she tumbled into a pit of skeletons, thrashing as she sank deeper into the brittle mass.

When she finally woke with a choking gasp, the sheets had twisted around her legs and her hair clung to her wet cheeks. She scrambled to a seat, gulping for air. *Just a dream. Just the same stupid, awful dream.* She dropped her head between her knees and shuddered.

Once she'd calmed down, she peered at the bed on the other side of the room. Jo slept on, her shock of dark hair all that could be seen over her blankets. Relieved, Lindy swung her legs over the edge of the bed and tiptoed out. It was only five o'clock. She clicked on the lamp, reached for the remote on the coffee table…

And dropped it with a screech as Ethan Granger bolted upright on the couch, tangling himself in the blanket draped over him. Lindy clamped her arms over her chest.

"What are you still doing here?" she hissed. "Don't you have a room of your own?"

"I—" Captain Granger cleared his throat. "Commander Jarvis asked me to stay here and make sure none of Osborne's people decided to pay you a visit. Miss Camrin knows I'm here. She's the one who gave me the blanket."

"Well, she didn't tell *me*."

"Unsurprising, since you were already asleep when we decided to call it a night."

Lindy drew herself up, her arms still tightly folded over her tank top. To his credit, Captain Granger didn't let his eyes wander. He handed her the remote.

"No, don't worry about it," Lindy said, stepping back. "I'll just go back to bed."

"It's your hotel suite. If you want to watch the HV, don't let me stop you."

Lindy bit her lip. The idea of going back to bed *did* make her feel sick.

"All right, fine," she muttered. "Just let me get my bathrobe."

"Do you want me to turn on the coffee pot?" he asked.

"Umm, yes. Thank you."

He nodded, staggering to the kitchen while she darted back into the bedroom, thoroughly mortified. Jo had slept straight through all the commotion, and Lindy was deeply tempted to resent her for it. But by the time she re-emerged in her bathrobe, Captain Granger hadn't just turned on the coffee pot; he'd also occupied himself with the toaster and a stash of bagels. Her stomach growled at the sight. He heard it and raised an eyebrow.

"Hungry?" he asked.

She shrugged sheepishly. "I'm always starving first thing in the morning."

He chuckled, sliding another bagel into the toaster. Anxious for something to do, Lindy opened the fridge and grabbed a stick of butter and a tiny jar of jam. For several minutes they worked in companionable silence. By the time he offered her a warm, toasted, buttered bagel with a sleepy smile, Lindy realized, quite suddenly, that she wasn't miffed with him anymore.

They sat down at opposite ends of the couch. Lindy pulled her comm out of her bathrobe pocket, intending to check her mail, but found herself peeking at him out of the corner of her eye instead. He ate quietly, his blue eyes fixed on the darkened window in front of them. Hints of a beard shadowed his cheeks. His brown hair stuck up rather wildly at the back of his head.

Handsome, Lindy mused, then caught herself and sat up straight. *No, nope…not gonna go there, not even gonna entertain such thoughts.*

"Guess I'd better let my boss know Jo and I couldn't get what we needed for our assignment," she said, breaking the silence.

Granger frowned. "You completed the assignment. You proved Osborne's involvement—"

Lindy shook her head. "No, no, I mean my editor."

He winced. "Sorry. Coffee hasn't gone to my head yet."

"No problem." Lindy typed with her thumbs for a moment, then lowered the comm and tilted her head to the side. "By the way, I do want to apologize for last night. I was tired and caught off guard, but I shouldn't have taken it out on you like that. I'm sorry."

He shook his head. "Not as sorry as I am. I knew about the mission before we got here. I just didn't realize we'd be proposing it to a Valyan refugee. I would've protested if I'd known."

Lindy scoffed. "Like Jarvis would ever listen to *anyone*. He's a great leader, but he's as bullheaded as they come."

Granger shrugged. "I hope he would've at least heard me out."

Lindy sent him a long-suffering look. "How long have you been with MID, Captain?"

"Two years," he replied.

"Well, then…"

"But I've known Benjamin Jarvis since I joined the Nova Force thirteen years ago."

She jerked her head up in surprise. Granger smirked.

"Sometimes MID's business intersects with that of the Nova Force," he explained, taking a big bite of his bagel. "When that happens, they commandeer our ships. The *Hummingbird*'s been a favorite for that sort of mission for a while, probably because she's state-of-the-art."

"Thirteen years, though," Lindy murmured. "How old were you when you two met?"

"Twenty-two, fresh outta the Academy. Jarvis was after a pirate fleet that had been harassing some of our mining outposts. He packed the *Hummingbird* so full of troopers, my old captain was afraid we'd break the occupancy regs."

"Did you?"

Granger laughed. "No, but it was pretty crowded for a few weeks. Jarvis started his campaign to recruit me during that mission. I just wasn't as keen on working for him—at least not until I'd gotten my captaincy."

Lindy set her comm aside. "See, I *always* wanted to work for MID, but I was interested in journalism, too. I had to decide if I'd rather be a fashion journalist and work undercover for MID or write in the field I really preferred."

"Which was?"

"Intergalactic politics. It wouldn't have been a good cover, though. I wouldn't have been able to pull off this innocent airhead act—not to mention everyone would always assume I had a conflict of interest."

"Because of your grandmother?"

Lindy licked a bit of jam off her thumb. "She's not *really* my grandmother, you know."

"And Jarvis isn't really my parent, but he's been there for me when my own mother refused to be," Granger countered. "What's the difference?"

She glanced at him…and sat up with a start. Granger did the same as if bracing himself.

"You're President Stagg's son," she whispered.

He raised his eyebrows. Lindy blinked hard and shook her head.

"Umm…okay. Wow. I'm sorry, I knew I recognized you, but—"

"It's fine—people get confused all the time. She switched back to her maiden name, and I kept my dad's—partly because I prefer *not* being associated with her, partly so I can enjoy reactions like yours."

"Yeah, but she's one of the reasons I'm even alive! Someone dropped me off half-alive at one of her shelters. I might've died if she hadn't taken care of me!"

Granger tilted his head. "Do you want to talk about it?"

"I don't know. Maybe. I probably should?"

"Try. It might help to get it out of your system."

Lindy peered at him. He said it so casually…and yet, what did she have to lose? Nothing but her pride. She drew a breath and leaned back against the couch. When she spoke, her voice held an edge even she hadn't expected.

"I sometimes think it'd be great to figure out who I used to be," she murmured. "I'd have some closure, you know? But then I think about the things I *do* remember, and it scares me so bad I can't see straight. The field, my mother dying…those screams…"

"The Cor Danem Massacre," Granger said softly.

"Yeah." Lindy looked down, tearing her bagel into small pieces without bothering to eat them. "I just can't process that kind of monstrosity. I think it'd drive me crazy if I went back."

"Maybe," Granger said slowly, "it would be easier going with your grandmother."

Lindy shook her head. "Nana is just like Jarvis. She'd be *thrilled* if she knew he asked me to take this assignment. But the more I'm pressured, the more I want to dig in my heels, you know?"

Granger laughed humorlessly. "*Oh,* yes. Mother always wanted me to take over the family business, especially after she became President. 'Make a six-figure paycheck—seven figures would be better!' Sometimes I worry I enlisted in the Nova Force simply because it was the last thing *she* wanted. It's only when I remember how much I love it that I remember that that's not true."

Lindy nodded. He thought for a moment, then gestured at her with the remains of his bagel.

"Here's something for you to think on. I know it's hard, and I know you think it'd drive you crazy, but I'd bet anything you'll get over it one day."

She looked away. "Easy for you to say..."

"I don't mean you'll *forget* it," he said quickly. "You'll never forget it, and you *shouldn't*. But one day, for some reason or another, I bet you'll be able to conquer those memories, because whatever you'll need to do at *that* moment will matter more than whatever it is you're afraid of."

Lindy shot him a wry look. "Like this MID assignment?"

"No, not necessarily. It may be something as simple as...just living bravely."

She blinked. Granger downed the last of his coffee, giving her one last pensive look as he got to his feet.

"Think about it," he said, tossing his plate in the garbage. "We all have to, sometime or another."

Chapter Five

Two weeks later

"'Xandroan fashion, as President Sarkova's daughter Yolande is quick to point out, will always have a touch of the sea about it,'" read Athena Biggweather, editor-in-chief of *The New Harvelle Ladies' Post*. "'The ever-varying shades of blue and green—not to mention the wispy materials used—hearken back to Xandroa's famous oceans.'"

She paused, peering over her horn-rimmed glasses at the reporter seated in the chair in front of her desk. Lindy, aware of the scrutiny, folded her hands in her lap and tried to look both attentive *and* humble. Athena liked it when her reporters acted just a little frightened of her. It made her more likely to take their work seriously.

Satisfied, Athena leaned back in her swivel chair and continued. "'But there's even more nuance within Xandroan couture. Ms. Sarkova, the founder of Rek Harbor Designs, incorporates not only her planet's aquatic culture into her clothing line but also its religion, based as it is on the otherworldly Sacred Manifestations.' Blah blah blah, so on and so forth, et cetera et cetera..."

With that, she threw her glasses and her data tablet onto the desk. Lindy sat up, bracing herself for either rejection or acceptance. You never really knew with Athena.

"Melinda, I'm over the moon," the editor said. "Who would have thought the Sarkovas would hand you *this* treasure on a golden platter after everything that happened? Talk about a peace offering! This is going into next week's issue—no question about that."

Lindy breathed a muted sigh of relief. "Well, I'm just glad you like it."

"'*Like* it?' The *Ladies' Post* hasn't claimed an interview this sensational since we nabbed a piece with that Bosthenian princess—and that was twelve years ago, way before my time. Give yourself some credit, girl. Despite your original assignment getting caught in the crossfire of some crooked scheme, you managed to nab something twice as good."

In more ways than one, Lindy thought, looking down in the hopes Athena wouldn't notice the smirk creeping over her face. The editor put her glasses back on and leaned forward, elbows on her desk.

"I want you and Camrin riding this wave into November," she said. "The next headline I want from you sounds like this: 'Genevieve Stagg: an exclusive interview with Meridian's sweetheart about life, love, and fashion.'"

Lindy looked up with a start. "Genevieve Stagg? But—"

"No buts about it."

"B—" Lindy stopped herself just in time and scooted to the edge of her chair. "Hoadley House isn't exactly friendly to interview requests, Athena. Remember what happened the last time the *Meridian Journal* tried to interview the President? Kermit Swift asked her a question she didn't like, and she wouldn't give him anything more than a monosyllable for an hour!"

Athena raised an eyebrow. "Are you afraid of the President?"

Lindy hesitated. "I'm not *afraid*. Discretion is just a good idea sometimes, that's all."

"Not when it comes to journalism, unless you're covering a battlefield or a terrorist organization—which you're not. Besides, you've practically got an inside track into Hoadley House. Your grandmother's on the Meridian Council. It should be easy for you to get an audience with Miss Stagg."

Lindy flushed. "I'd rather get honest work on my own merits than because of my name. And my grandmother may be a councilor, but that doesn't mean she's on good terms with anybody else on the Council right now—least of all President Stagg."

"So what? You're saying you won't take this assignment?" Athena demanded.

Lindy pursed her lips, her fingers twitching on her knees. *What's happened to your nerve, Melinda?* Two assignments offered in two weeks, one from Jarvis and one from Athena...and she had cold feet over both?

Athena pushed her chair back, tucking her tablet in the crook of her elbow and grabbing a styrofoam coffee cup off the corner of her desk. Lindy stood, too, glad to finally take advantage of her height.

"I want that Genevieve Stagg exclusive, Melinda," the editor said in a tone that brooked no argument. "She's wildly popular, yet she's never been interviewed off the red carpet—and she's *always* on the arm of that mealy-mouthed servant-droid of theirs. I want to know why. It's time to break her out of her mom's cloister, all right?"

Lindy swallowed. "I'll do my best."

Athena nodded sharply and flounced out of the room. As soon as the clear glass door shut behind her, Lindy let out her breath in a whoosh.

Her boss was crazy. Maria Stagg had built a reputation as a ruthless businesswoman long before becoming president, and she'd only solidified it since. When it came to Meridian's interests and security, she was protective to a fault. She was also intensely private. Considering her embarrassingly public break with her son some fifteen years ago, it might've been understandable…if she hadn't been so strangely successful in controlling her daughter's public image and engagements, as well.

Securing an interview with Genevieve *would* be an interesting challenge—especially after meeting Ethan.

It's certainly preferable to sitting around wondering if I should've taken Jarvis up on his *assignment,* Lindy thought. With a deep breath and a squaring of her shoulders, she strode back into the bustling bullpen. A colleague in a nearby cubicle saw her emerge from Athena's office and stopped typing long enough to sneer.

"Well, if it isn't Teacher's Pet, Miss Twice-Lucky," Violet Atwater crooned, leaning back in her chair. "What kind of pat assignment did you talk her into giving you this time? An interview with Councilor Tremaine herself?"

Lindy raised her eyebrows and kept walking. "After my Xandroan debacle, Vi, I'm hardly in a position to demand much. But even if that weren't the case, I *like* challenges. So I'll leave Athena's easier assignments to people of your caliber."

Violet's blood-red lips went slack. Lindy smiled innocently and continued on to Jo's cubicle. She found her friend scowling at her computer screen, trying to fit photos of Yolande Sarkova into the placements she and the magazine's photo editor had agreed upon.

"Heading out for the day," Lindy said, beating a cheerful rhythm on the edge of the cubicle. "Want to come over to the house tonight? Nana and I are ordering pizza."

Jo kept her eyes on the screen, her chin in her palm. "Only if we can have a *Star Chronicles* marathon."

"It's a deal if you promise to help me think of an angle for our next story."

Jo moaned into her hand. "Ugh, Lindy, I've barely recovered from this last one."

"Cool your jets. With luck, it'll be a home-based story…starring Genevieve Stagg."

Jo's head popped up. Lindy shrugged.

"'With luck,' I said. After what happened on Xandroa, I'm not sure I have any worth talking about."

"After snagging a last-minute interview with Yolande, I think you might have too much!" Jo cried. "Genevieve Stagg? Was that your idea?"

"Nope, it was Athena's." Lindy gave the top of the cubicle a final slap and stepped back. "Pizza, ice cream, and *Star Chronicles*. Don't be late."

A few minutes later, Lindy nabbed a window seat on one of New Harvelle's sleek monorails. While the train glided on its winding track above, amid, and occasionally below the capital, Lindy leaned her head back and enjoyed the impressive view of glittering skyscrapers, domed cathedrals, and ribbons of ground traffic.

Eventually, however, the megalopolis yielded to quieter, simpler communities. When the monorail paused in Whitesmith, Lindy stepped out into the late autumn afternoon. Neighbors she'd known for years acknowledged her as she strode out of the train station. Old Mrs. Linsey, walking her yipping dog, smiled and waved. Professor Chittenden roused himself from a pensive examination of his feet and favored Lindy with a nod. Even Mrs. Pocket and her five kids called out enthusiastic greetings as they emerged from the local bookstore, loaded down with curriculum for the new school semester.

Lindy smiled and waved back. It was surreal to think that these good, honest people weren't nearly as safe as they believed themselves to be. It was only thanks to the Nova Force, President Stagg's vigilance, and MID that Meridian was as secure as it was.

They'll never know how much it costs, she thought. *And as long as they* never *have to experience the horrors I did as a child, I don't even mind.*

She turned onto a street full of trees and brick houses, heading for the one with the bay window in front and a sunroom on the side. Finding the door unlocked—*as usual*—she let herself in. The indelible scents of old books and good cooking enveloped her. Lindy shut the door and let her bag drop off her shoulder.

"Nana, I'm home!"

No response. Lindy stepped into the living room. A fat grey-and-white cat blinked at her from the couch.

"Hello, Winston," she cooed, tossing her bag into a chair and scooping him up. "How's my boy this evening, hmm?"

Winston offered a plaintive *meow* and nuzzled his head under her chin. Lindy laughed softly and wandered into the kitchen. Except for the quiet chatter of the cooking channel on Nana's HV, the place was silent. The door to the sunroom, however, was open. So was the door leading out of the sunroom and into the garden.

"Nana?" Lindy called again. "Are you out here, Nana?"

"Melinda, is that you?"

Lindy quickly stepped outside. Nana knelt by her raised flower beds, her sleeves rolled up to her elbows and her trouser legs and gloves stained with grass and soil. At Lindy's approaching footsteps, she twisted awkwardly at the waist and flashed a bright smile.

"I fear you've caught me in a *most* undignified position," Nana remarked, rubbing her cheek with the back of her wrist.

Lindy grinned. "Not as undignified as your reaction when I came home two weeks ago."

"Well, that's what happens when you decide against letting a poor old woman know you're on your way home from an interplanetary assignment," Nana said primly. "You walk in without warning, *I* jump out of my skin."

Lindy laughed and bent to release the squirming Winston. "When did you get home?"

"About an hour ago." Nana spread an extra layer of mulch around her plants. "President Stagg adjourned the Council early. Apparently, we were getting a bit too 'animated' for her tastes."

Great. Lindy knelt beside her adopted grandmother, the lingering damp from yesterday's rain seeping through her slacks. "What was it about this time?"

Nana cut her eyes at her. "You act as if it's a frequent event, Melinda."

"And *you* have a reputation for holding your fellow councilors' feet to the fire."

"Well..." Nana sighed. "I suppose I *may* have ruffled a few delicate feathers when I suggested Meridian had embraced some unrealistic, isolationist positions."

"Mm-hmm."

"You young folks may dismiss it, but I'm telling you and everyone else that that Namarian king is one dangerous player. He's already declared his people 'the superior race,' and now he's hinting he'd like to expand his kingdom to other planets!"

"So *we* march in and put him and his rabble-rousers under lock and key?" Lindy prodded.

Nana scowled. "Don't be ridiculous. I never suggested such a thing."

"*I* know you wouldn't. But the media will sling mud at you at the slightest indication that you're a war hawk—unless you can prove you're looking for the balance between that and isolationism."

Nana hummed in reluctant agreement. "True. Oh, the advantages of having a granddaughter in the media."

"I don't know that I'm giving you much of an advantage," Lindy cautioned, hoisting herself onto the edge of the raised bed. "I just know how reporters think. And you're not helping your reputation by pushing the Valyan issue so noisily."

For the first time since Lindy entered the garden, Nana looked at her with absolute gravity. "*That* is a matter of principle, Melinda. I'll champion the Valyan exiles till I'm dead in the ground—

and I have no intention of dying any time soon. The Council, the President, and Rael Navorre will have to put up with me for a long time yet."

Lindy shrugged and scratched between Winston's ears. Arguing with Nana was pointless when she got this passionate. So when her grandmother pushed herself to her feet—carefully, so she wouldn't tumble backward and repeat the hilarity of two weeks ago—Lindy decided to change the subject.

"Athena wants me to interview Genevieve Stagg for our next issue," she said.

Nana raised her eyebrows. "My, my! She's rather ambitious, isn't she?"

"Yeah. I tried to talk her out of it, but she blew me off."

Nana pulled off her hat and fluffed her white hair. "Well, Maria isn't too set against me these days. The name 'Tremaine' shouldn't sway her against you this week, at least."

"I don't want it to sway her *at all*. I'd rather she just looked at my portfolio and decided I'm a trustworthy professional worthy of interviewing her daughter. It shouldn't depend on whether or not she's mad at you."

Nana laughed ruefully. "Oh, Lindy. Haven't I taught you a thing about politics yet?"

"This isn't about politics!" Lindy cried.

But Nana simply gave her a half-amused, half-skeptical smile, turned on her heel, and strolled back to the house.

That evening Nana, Jo, and Lindy lounged on the couch, pulling pizza slices from the cardboard box on the coffee table. At the same time, the HV projected stunning images of Captain Hudson Thorpe and his gallant, star-running crew. Nana gestured with her pizza crust at the holographic hero.

"He's cute," she declared with great conviction.

"Mmmm!" Jo agreed around a mouthful of food. "Lindy *really* thinks so. Did y'know her trooper code is 'Thorpe?'"

Lindy almost choked. "*Jo!*"

"What? She has top-security clearance—she's allowed to know that!"

"Indeed I am," Nana said. "Although I hope you don't think he's really your type, dear."

Lindy rolled her eyes. Only the chime of the house comm kept her from informing Nana that she'd take Captain Thorpe over half the real-life guys she could name. Nana groaned and heaved herself off the sofa.

"I'll get that. You girls keep watching."

"Okay," Jo said. She waited until Nana was gone before turning to Lindy with a playful grin. "Is it just me, or does Thorpe look like a certain young captain we met on Xandroa?"

Lindy swatted her arm. "Shhh."

"What? He does look like him, doesn't he?"

"Yes, he does, but that's not why I'm shushing you."

"Then why—" Jo stopped. "Oh. You didn't tell Nana about that meeting."

"Nope."

"Why?"

Lindy reached for the last slice of pizza. "I don't want her trying to talk me into changing my mind about that assignment—which she will, the second she hears about it. Besides, if she says anything to President Stagg about it, we'll never get within a mile of—"

"Oh, good heavens!" Nana cried. "Are you sure?"

Jo froze. Lindy grabbed the remote, pausing the HV before Thorpe could stun the monster trying to wrestle him to the ground.

"I'm so sorry," Nana murmured. "Yes, of course I'll come down. Have one of your attendants meet me in the waiting room with the latest news. If I can see him before...oh, yes, of course.

Anything, if it'll put his mind at ease. Yes. All right. I'll be there in a jiffy. Goodbye."

"Who is it?" Jo mouthed. Lindy shrugged, her concern spiking when Nana returned and looked at them both with naked worry and grief.

"That was Mariamne Navorre," Nana said, her voice unsteady. "Her father had a massive heart attack. The doctors don't expect him to survive the night."

"Prince Ilion?" Jo cried.

"The very same. I need to get down to the hospital." Nana rushed to the coat rack in the vestibule. "I've been working with these people for years. Being there is the least I can do."

"Anything we can do to help?" Jo asked.

Nana fumbled at the buttons of her coat, watching Lindy. Something churned in Lindy's gut, and it wasn't the pizza.

"Come with me, Melinda?" Nana asked softly.

Lindy drew her knees up to her chest. "I'd rather not."

Nana pressed her lips together. "All right. Enjoy your show, girls—and don't forget the ice cream, Lindy. I bought cookie dough."

She grabbed her purse and left. As soon as the door closed behind her, Jo sprang up and went into the kitchen. Lindy, however, remained on the couch, her thoughts spinning like a novacraft's soroidium engines. When Jo returned with bowls, spoons, and a pint of ice cream, Lindy looked up.

"Am I a coward, Jo?"

Her friend snorted. "Uh, *no*."

"Are you saying that because you mean it or because it'll make me feel better?"

Jo thrust a bowl and a spoon at her. "Look. You're the one who tackled Christopher Osborne to the floor and then stunned him with his own gun. You are *not* a coward."

"But that's different. It's easier for me to jump into action and just do what needs doing when I don't have a choice than to..."

"To face your past?" Jo shook her head and pried the frosty lid off the ice cream. "You don't want to go back to a planet where your mom's killers are in power. You definitely don't want to trigger the nightmares. I get that. I really do."

"But?" Lindy prodded.

Jo sighed. She dumped a massive scoop of ice cream into Lindy's bowl. The chill leaked through the porcelain. Lindy shivered.

"Y'know," Jo murmured, "if we Meridians still looked at New Harvelle and only thought about the old city that got nuked back in the Dark Ages, we wouldn't be what we are today. We wouldn't have rebuilt anything except a few little villages here and there and *maybe* a sewage system. But that's not what happened. We knew Elyon used the war to discipline us for becoming such a self-obsessed little planet. So we said we were sorry, and we tried to do better. And in five centuries, we've become the happiest, most prosperous planet in the Star System."

Lindy frowned. "What's your point?"

Thunk went an even bigger scoop of ice cream into Jo's bowl. "Well, at the risk of sounding utterly cheesy…if you just wallow around in the past, you're never gonna fly."

She leaned back, her legs tucked underneath her, while Lindy stared at the delectable contents of her bowl. Jo's words rang true —and not just true, but familiar. Captain Granger had said something very similar on Xandroa: *"Whatever you'll need to do at* that *moment will matter more than whatever it is you're afraid of."*

Nana had asked her to go to the hospital. Why? Because she wanted the support…and because she'd always wanted Lindy to break out of her shell and meet some other Valyans. If Lindy *had* met any Valyans in the past twenty-three years, then they were just like her, blending into Meridian society and putting the Revolution's brutality behind them. She'd never wanted anything to do with the refugee communities here on Meridian who wore their nationality on their martyred sleeves.

But would going to the hospital really matter more than the nightmares?

Maybe. It would only be a baby step. But at this point, perhaps that's all that matters.

"If I go," Lindy murmured, "will you promise not to breathe a word about it to Jarvis?"

Jo blinked, surprised, but she raised her spoon to the ceiling. "May all my holocams fall apart and my laptop crash if I breathe a syllable."

Lindy smiled tightly. If Jo was willing to put her computer on the line, she *must* be serious. Lindy dumped her ice cream into Jo's bowl and got up.

"Are you staying the night?" she asked, grabbing her coat off the rack.

Jo grimaced. "I hope so. Otherwise, I have to go to my dad's house."

"Guest room is yours, then." Lindy flung her curls back from her coat collar. "Just leave some ice cream in the carton for me. I'll want some when I get home."

By the time the monorail stopped at Chickering Circus' underground station, Lindy had managed to control her rising panic. Stepping out of the warmth of the subway, she glimpsed the hospital across the street, twenty stories high and checkered with dark and light windows. She swallowed, looked both ways, and crossed.

Stay calm. You're just going to meet the last surviving members of the Valyan royal family. No big deal at all.

When she tiptoed into the waiting room on the fourth floor, she found ordinary Meridians in the seats closest to the door. There was, however, no mistaking the Valyans on the other side of the room: two men—one old, the other young and handsome—and two women—one with snowy hair, the other a plump teenager. The older woman paced, her arms folded and her hair concealing her face from Lindy's view. The girl sat with her knees pressed together beneath a traditional Valyan gown's floor-length skirt.

All four had the rich, umber-colored skin, dark eyes, proud noses, high cheekbones, and broad foreheads of the Valyan race. Lindy gulped. Unique as each face was, she could join them right now and anyone would assume she was one of them.

Well, they would if she was wearing Valyan clothes. Her jeans, sweater, and white peacoat *did* make her stick out like a sore thumb.

Lindy shut the door behind her and walked past the Meridians. The old Valyan kept his eyes closed, his lips moving silently. The white-haired woman continued pacing, but the girl and the younger man looked up.

"Excuse me?" Lindy called.

The woman lifted her head. Lindy's breath caught. She was young—not much older than Lindy, in fact—with flawless dark skin and sharp eyes.

"Yes?" she asked in a distinct, cultured accent. "What do you want?"

"I'm Melinda Tremaine. I'm Councilor Tremaine's granddaughter and…uh…" Lindy glanced nervously at the teenager, who stared at her with friendly interest. "She asked me to come. My grandmother, that is."

The woman frowned, peering at Lindy from the top of her head to the toes of her boots. When she moved to face Lindy head-on, her black skirts rustled against the floor.

"You are the refugee she took in."

Lindy blinked. The woman pursed her lips and shook her head.

"Go home. Councilor Tremaine is with my father. You can do nothing here."

"Is that an order?" Lindy asked.

The woman narrowed her eyes. "I cannot order pretenders like you and expect them to obey."

With that, she resumed her walk. Lindy stared at her, stunned and strangely hurt. "Pretender," indeed. She still shared more genetic code with these people than any dark-skinned Meridian.

It was ironic—and she knew it—but one nasty comment from this Valyan woman did more for her nerve than anything Jo or Nana could've said. Lindy set her teeth, marched forward, and sat with a *thud* in the seat next to the young girl.

The woman stared at her in surprise. When Lindy stared back, thrusting her jaw forward, the woman turned away with a parting glare. Finally, after a tense silence, the teenager beside Lindy cleared her throat.

"Greetings," she whispered.

Lindy jumped; she'd almost forgotten the girl was there. "Hi. Nice to meet you."

The girl inclined her head. "Likewise. My name is Talila...but you may call me 'Tali' if you like."

"*Tali.* I like that. Nobody calls me by my real name either. You can call me 'Lindy.'"

The princess shot them a withering look. Tali winced but seemed to take courage when she saw Lindy remained unfazed. She leaned closer, keeping her voice low.

"That's my cousin, Mariamne," she explained. "That's her husband, Lhoris, and the old one is my uncle's friend, Lord Nhormin."

Lindy frowned. "What's he doing?"

"Praying, probably. My uncle is very ill, you know."

"Yes, I heard. I'm sorry."

Tali cast another cautious glance at her cousin. "You are Valyan, then?"

A familiar, unnerving shiver crept its way up Lindy's spine, but she kept her head up. "Yep. I'm Valyan."

"When did you—"

The waiting room door opened. Mariamne whirled, Prince Lhoris sprang to his feet, and Tali sat up. Nana and an older, heavier Valyan woman entered, eyes on Princess Mariamne as they approached. Her icy sternness crumbled: she brought a hand to her mouth.

"Elyon Above," she gasped.

"He's not dead yet," Nana said quickly. "But he's fading fast. He wants to see you all. *Now.*"

Mariamne gathered her skirts and ran from the room. The older woman with Nana reached for Tali's hand; the girl gave it to her, sending Lindy an apologetic look as they and the men hurried after Mariamne. Within seconds, only Nana and Lindy remained.

"Well," Nana said softly. "You came."

Lindy swallowed hard and clasped her slender hands. "I thought—I mean—Jo said—"

Nana raised her eyebrows. Lindy let out a frustrated breath and closed her eyes.

"I've avoided everything and everyone Valyan for twenty-three years because it was *easier.* When I was a kid it was probably a good idea, but now…now I'm just using it as an excuse to hide. I realized that tonight when you asked me to come."

"So you came and shared a waiting room with Mariamne Navorre," Nana said dryly.

Lindy opened her eyes. "Does that mean I'm even braver than I thought I was?"

Nana smiled. "Oh yes. *I* would certainly say so."

Lindy glanced at the door, still open. "What happens now?"

Nana sighed. "Well, we could pay our respects from a distance. I've been friends with them for so long. I don't think they'd mind if we observed, as long as we remained quiet."

Lindy nodded and rose to her feet, her heart pounding. Nana touched her shoulder just for a moment, then led the way down the corridor.

When they entered the prince's room, they stayed at a careful distance from the grieving family. Lindy's chest tightened. As the younger brother of Valya's murdered king, Prince Ilion had represented the cause of the Valyan refugees for years, rallying support for their eventual return to their planet with his unpretentious yet determined personality. Now he lay motionless in the hospital bed, his broad face hidden by breathing tubes. The heart monitor beeped languidly. Lindy could hear Lord Nhormin's prayers now, his frail old voice rising above the prince's labored breaths.

"Elyon Above, ruler of the stars, blessed be thy holy name."

Lindy jerked her head up at the familiar words. Tali and her mother repeated them softly. Mariamne sat on the edge of her father's bed, tears streaming down her face while she held his hand and choked out a few syllables.

"Thy realm divine our hearts do seek, thy laws our kingdoms follow."

They'd all fled Valya twenty-three years ago, days before the king, his wife and children, and so many others had been butchered. Lindy glanced at Tali. She must've been born here on Meridian. Mariamne, though...Mariamne would remember. She probably remembered more than Lindy could ever dream of recalling.

And now she, Ilion's daughter, would have to lead the refugees. *She* would have to face her rogue cousin and find a compromise—not for the sake of the Navorre dynasty, but for the miserable people back on Valya whose revolution had turned on them so viciously.

Lindy had to hand it to her. *That* was brave.

When the heart monitor flatlined, Mariamne's sobs filled the silence.

Chapter Six

The counter on the punching bag chimed as Ethan Granger's gloved fist collided with the leather. He drew his arm back, pulled in a breath, sent another fist flying. The bag yielded with a heavy thump, the bell rang again, and he gritted his teeth.

Don't think about that video call—DING! *Don't think about what she said to you*—DING!

"I don't know why I even bother asking you to come home for Winterfest," his mother had said, her voice crackling mercilessly through his memory. "I know you'll only make us feel inferior, strutting about in your Nova Force uniform with your security clearance tucked in your breast pocket..."

Ethan grunted, slamming one fist after another into the bag. *Don't think about it, don't let her get to you, why do you* always *let her get to you?*

But the recollection of her accusations never stopped. It was as if he'd memorized them, word for word, as soon as she uttered them.

"You're just like your father. You chase adventure and call it a crusade while the rest of us deal with the more practical realities of society..."

WHAM! Ethan groaned, his knuckles aching even with his protective gloves, and leaned heavily against the bag. His shoulders heaved as he buried his face in the leather and tried to shut his mother—the President of Meridian, possibly the most powerful woman in the Star System—out of his mind.

Amazing how someone so willing to organize relief efforts for any disaster area in the Star System could be so unbelievably hostile to her own son.

Maybe if I'd let her turn me into one of her emasculated stooges, I wouldn't be such a bullseye.

Ethan forced himself to stand up straight; he sniffed, wiped the sweat from his nose with his forearm, and raised his fists again. The hiss of the gym's decompressing door sounded over his resuming punches.

"Is this a bad time?"

Ethan looked over his shoulder at Frank Gridley, officially the *Hummingbird*'s new Chief of IT Security, but also, clandestinely, his new MID partner. Ethan gave the bag one final thump and turned to face him.

"No, of course it isn't a bad time," he panted. "What's up?"

Frank hesitated and glanced at the door, obviously concerned some oblivious crewman might enter. When the door stayed shut, however, he hurried forward, practically quivering with anticipation.

"I hear you got a call from Meridian this morning," he whispered.

Ethan stripped off his gloves. "Hacking the communications system now, are you? That's a blatant abuse of power, Gridley."

"Hey, I'm not *that* devious! I just asked your Comms Chief a few questions, that's all."

"Hmmph. I'm surprised at Lieutenant Cornael. She normally guards confidential information the way a Zathrenalian crackat guards her kits."

"She still does. She wouldn't tell me who it was from, so—taking a wild guess here—I'd say it was about the Valyan mission." Frank rubbed his hands together, grinning like a kid on his birthday. "You know, stuff like itineraries, mission parameters, who's gonna partner with us, the equipment we're gonna use? Come on, man, give me *details!*"

Ethan chuckled, grabbing his uniform blouse off a nearby chair. "Sorry, Frank, but that call had nothing to do with MID whatsoever. Unless you want to call my mother's poor opinion of my career choices 'MID business.'"

Frank winced. "Ah. Bad timing on my part, then."

"It's all right. No harm, no foul."

"Yeah, but still. Sorry." Frank sighed. "I just feel like a guy living during the Meridian Restoration, y'know? We'll be witnessing the reconciliation of Valyan society. It'll be history, right in front of our eyes! And I don't know about you, but I'm chompin' at the bit."

"I wouldn't get my hopes up about that reconciliation if I were you," Ethan warned. "I hear Rael Navorre is a hard nut to crack—as well as an absolute nut."

Frank shrugged. "We've dealt with nuts before. Remember our first mission together in Terithia, with that terrorist holed up in their sewer system?"

Ethan laughed as he tucked his uniform back into his pants. "Ohhh yeah. But here's the difference between that guy and this one: Rael is *intelligent*. Cunning. It's the smart madmen you have to watch out for."

Frank snorted. "Listen to the two-year trooper talking about the psychology of a dictator. Anyone would think you'd been dealing with cutthroats for a decade."

"Trust me, you learn plenty about cutthroats in the Nova Force." *Or when you grow up in the "practical realities of society."* Ethan smoothed his hair and rolled his shoulders. "Come on—my break's over. Time to head back to the bridge."

The *Hummingbird* was a Nova Force Cruiser, large enough for a crew of two hundred, plus up to fifty guests. Only the novacraft of the Destroyer Class surpassed her and her sister ships in size. Where Destroyers went, however, guests weren't keen on visiting. Instead, they patrolled the lengthy border between the Kellan Star System and the as-yet-unexplored Varogen Galaxy, where satellites had picked up subspace chatter in mysterious languages no Kellan understood.

By contrast, patrolling the starfields between Meridian and Valya wasn't nearly as taxing on the adrenaline. Ethan sensed the boredom as soon as he reached the bridge. His helmsmen, communications officer, navigator, first officer, and weapons chief came to attention when he entered with Frank on his heels—but only because it was required, not because they were particularly enthusiastic.

"Captain on the bridge," Weapons Chief Parsons called out automatically.

Ethan smirked. "Wow. Didn't realize I was commanding a crew of droids."

The shot of humor eased the dreary, mind-numbing tedium: laughter rippled through the hexagonal room. Communications Officer Eliva Cornael, a petite Valyan émigré, shot him a grateful smile.

"Captain, *MNC Adamant* is in the area," she said. "Captain Taylor sends his compliments and requests a meet-up at 1900 hours. He says he and his crew could use a break from the monotony of their patrol."

Ethan settled in his seat in the center of the room. "Inform Captain Taylor that if he can catch up with us within the five hours, I'd be more than happy to have him over for dinner. Commander Aeron, how's that soroidium leak?"

Reznor Aeron, a punctilious and handsome Opitheldran, swiveled away from his interactive screen. "The leak is controlled and minor. Engineering still recommends full repairs at our next stop."

Ethan flexed his fingers on the arms of his chair. *Business as usual, then.* "Thank you, Commander."

An alarm suddenly blared from Cornael's station; she jumped, her hands flying over her console. "Receiving interference on the subspace channel, Captain. I can't get through to anything."

Ethan glanced toward the security station. "Frank?"

"I'm on it." Frank slid his chair on its track to the other end of his station. "Okay, it's not our systems. Looks more like someone's purposefully jamming our transmissions."

"How can that be?" Aeron demanded. "There aren't any other ships in the area besides the *Adamant*."

"You're sure it's not coming from them, Cornael?" Ethan asked.

"I'm sure," she replied. "The interference would have a signature I'd recognize."

Ethan leaned forward, elbows on his knees. "Mr. Potter, scan the area for any satellites or space debris. Maybe something's floating around out there and messing with our instruments."

The young navigator at the helm nodded. "Aye, sir."

"Hold on, I've got something," Frank called. "Diagnostics show it's not our systems—but *in* our systems. It's a bit like a virus. I can dig it out, no sweat. Potter can quit his debris scan."

Ethan raised an eyebrow. "Ignore that, Mr. Potter. You keep right on scanning."

The poor navigator nodded again. "Aye-aye, s—"

A shrill wail cut him off as alert messages exploded on every screen. Everyone jerked in alarm, eyes on their stations.

"Aeron, what's going on?" Ethan demanded, deliberately keeping his voice steady.

"It's a—" Aeron stopped short in surprise. "An intruder alert?"

"Should I alert Security, sir?" Parsons cried over the noise.

Ethan thought fast. With alarms going off like this, his crew would already be scrambling to their posts. He'd known them too long to doubt their prompt reaction to an emergency.

But they were in the middle of nowhere. How in blazes could they have an intruder?

Unless…

"Cut off the alarms, Cornael," he ordered. She flipped a lever; the sirens quieted and the screens returned to their standard displays. "Parsons, tell Security to put a guard on Engineering, the arsenal, and the life support systems until we've figured out what's going on."

"Aye, sir."

Ethan reached the IT station in five quick strides. "Frank? Is that virus our intruder?"

"I-I think so. It definitely tripped the security protocol—"

"Did it breach it?"

Frank shook his head fiercely. "*No,* thank Elyon. But here's the thing. When it tripped the alert, it actually drew back…as if it realized it had gone further than it should have."

Ethan laughed. "Wait, are you saying this is a *sentient* virus?"

To his surprise, Frank didn't look amused. He turned back to his station with a scowl and typed in several commands. Ethan gripped the back of Frank's chair and leaned closer.

"What are you saying, Frank?" he asked in a low voice, the kind that his crew knew good and well to never disobey.

Frank pursed his lips. "I don't know yet. But it's pulling itself out of our computer system and I'm not the one chasing it out. It's leaving because it—or whoever put it there—*wants* to."

The security guards never found any flesh-and-blood intruders. Ethan even ordered Dr. Jemima Elliot to scan the ship for unidentified biological prints, but the ship's surgeon pinpointed no more than the usual two hundred crewmen. As for the virus, it had vanished from the computer system, leaving only the evidence of its incredibly sophisticated retreat.

A few hours after the incident, the *Adamant* contacted the *Hummingbird* again.

"Captain Granger?" Cornael called. "Captain Taylor wants to know if you're still up for dinner."

Ethan sank into the extra chair at Frank's station and pulled up a blueprint of the master computer. "Afraid not, Lieutenant. I don't want them docking with us and giving this thing a chance to infect *them*. Just tell him we're under quarantine till we resolve a security issue, and I'll catch up with him next time."

She looked somewhat crestfallen, but Ethan ignored it. As long as the *Hummingbird* remained compromised, her longtime, casual flirtation with Captain Taylor would have to take a back seat.

Frank leaned towards him. "Ethan, we're not getting any answers today. It covered its tracks too well. Give it up for tonight."

Ethan entered a command; the master computer's schematics took holographic form. He raised both hands and spun it around, studying its tentacles, its thrumming kernel, its subdivisions.

"The virus attacked the communications section, right?" he asked.

"Yep. It's the most vulnerable part of the system, even with top-notch security protocols. And this wasn't your typical bug, either, judging by the way the system lost its mind."

"But where would we have picked up something that sophisticated?" Ethan muttered.

Frank shrugged. "The last ship we met was the *Constantia*, and they'd just been to Corea V. You know how shady the info-net is there. They could've picked it up and then passed it to us as soon as we docked together."

Ethan grunted. "Maybe. But Headquarters would've alerted the entire Nova Force if that were the case. Think you can beef up the security protocols in case this thing comes back?"

"I'll do my best. Calling it a day?"

Ethan stood, rubbing his eyes. "Might as well get some shut-eye while I can. Aeron, you have command. I'll be back at 0400, as usual."

"Aye, Captain," Aeron replied quietly. "But if you find you need more rest than that..."

"I'll be here at 0400. Call if you need me."

The Opitheldran nodded and lowered himself into the command seat. Ethan allowed himself one last sweeping glance over the bridge, then strode out.

His cabin was only two decks down and not far from the lift. He put on a show of friendly confidence for the crewmen he passed along the way, but as soon as his cabin door shut behind him, he let his shoulders slump. He unbuttoned his collar and flung himself onto his bunk, not even bothering to remove his boots. Even with his lingering concern over the intruder, his thoughts wandered with sickening inevitability back to his mother.

"Inferior." Is that really how she felt when I decided to join the Nova Force? What if I've become the very thing I hated when I walked away from it all: arrogant, self-obsessed, condescending...and so convinced of my own rightness?

And here's the thing: it'd be easier if it was just me. Then I could ignore every single one of her calls and not even feel guilty about it—except for one thing. She's still got Genevieve.

The computer at his desk chimed. Ethan groaned and propped himself on an elbow.

"Accept call," he ordered. Cornael's sharp, dark features promptly appeared on the screen.

"Sorry to disturb you, sir, but you've received an encrypted video call from Meridian. Do you want me to pipe it to your computer?"

Encrypted? Ethan couldn't see Frank's station, but he could imagine his friend's head whipping around if he'd heard *that* word.

"Yes, thank you, Lieutenant," he said, sitting up. "That'd be fine."

"Do you want me to unwrap the encryption first?"

"*No*. I don't want that virus latching onto it in the transfer. Just pipe it down here and I'll take care of the rest."

By the time he sat down at his desk, the message was ready. He unlocked the encryption and leaned back, arms folded, as Benjamin Jarvis' solid, mustached face appeared.

"Captain Granger," Jarvis said warmly. "Long time, no see."

Ethan forced a smile. "Good to see you too, Commander. What can I do for you?"

"I've got that update on the Valyan mission we've all been waiting for."

"Great. Frank is about to drive me insane about it."

Jarvis chuckled. "How's he doing with his new post? Have your people accepted him?"

"Absolutely. He fits right in on the bridge."

"And nobody suspects he's anything other than a glorified IT technician?"

"As far as I can tell, no. He's good at what he does, so he blends in."

"Excellent. We'll need him on Valya, especially since it looks like we may be expanding your role a bit." Jarvis leaned closer to his screen. "Prince Ilion Navorre. Know the name?"

"Yeah, of course. Leader of the Royal Remnant, younger brother of King Kalen."

"He died an hour ago."

Ethan froze. "You're kidding."

"I wish I were. Apparently, he had a massive heart attack. We probably shouldn't be surprised. The responsibilities he carried would've killed a lesser man a long time ago." Jarvis sighed, rubbed his forehead. "Of course, this means his daughter leads the Remnant now."

"And you don't like her," Ethan said, smirking.

Jarvis rolled his eyes. "She makes President Stagg look like the humblest being in creation."

Ethan snorted. "Enough said, then. But she still wants to have the conference?"

"Oh yeah—she wants to see her cousin taken down a couple of notches. Unbeknownst to her, however, we won't be quite so lenient with her as we would've been with her father." Jarvis paused, looking so sternly at the younger man that Ethan sat up straighter. "You're still the head of our undercover intelligence team, Ethan—don't worry about that. We've simply added Princess Mariamne to your list of individuals who need...monitoring."

Ethan frowned. "'Monitoring?' What's that supposed to mean?"

"Just this. If she gives the slightest indication that she's losing her cool, throwing the negotiations out the window, or, Elyon forbid, forming an alliance with the Renegade, you act first. Place her under arrest, call off the conference, I don't care. But you drag that woman back to Meridian, even if she's kicking and screaming."

Ethan blinked. "Ben..."

"I know, it's not conventional," Jarvis grumbled. "But if Mariamne and Rael go for each other's throats, he *will* win, and then he'll declare war on *us*. We gave the Valyans asylum. It'd be too easy to accuse Meridian of helping Mariamne carry out a coup."

"Whoa whoa whoa! What kind of proof do you have that Mariamne is planning a coup?"

"I'm not at liberty to say. But she never forgave her cousin for his part in the Revolution. That much is certain. She may be motivated by vengeance, not her people's suffering."

"I'll need to see your evidence for that."

Jarvis' weathered face hardened. "I think *you* just need to follow your orders."

"I'm not arresting a woman simply for being angry with the man who killed thousands of her people, Jarvis. If I actually catch her plotting something or acting in a way consistent with evidence that she's planning a coup, that'd be one thing. But you act like I've got to slap handcuffs on her the second her temper flares!"

"It may very well come to that!" Jarvis snapped. "Look, I don't make the rules. The President, the Council, and the MID Generals do. If you have a problem, take it up with them. Otherwise, you follow your orders and do your level best to make sure we don't end up with an interplanetary war on our hands. Do I make myself clear?"

Ethan set his teeth. "Yes, sir. Very clear."

Jarvis held his gaze, his own jaw flexed. But after a long, silent moment, some of the anger faded, replaced by a weariness that made Ethan regret raising his voice at the man who was like a second father to him.

"All right." Jarvis sighed. "Nova Force HQ will call you back to Meridian tomorrow and make the official announcement that you'll take the delegation to Valya. That'll put the *Hummingbird* in New Harvelle on Saturday…and *that* will give me four days to work with you and your team before you leave for Valya."

"Yes, sir," Ethan murmured, then frowned. "You found another team to partner with us?"

Jarvis actually smiled. "Actually, no. I just got a call from Lindy Tremaine. She changed her mind. You and Frank will be teaming up with her and Jo Camrin after all."

Chapter Seven

Four days later

Lindy jogged up the steps to Nana's front door and shifted her library finds into the crook of one arm—not easy, considering she'd packed three massive books all the way from downtown. Her arms quivered from the weight.

It's worth it, though, she thought, fumbling with the doorknob. *I just should've brought a backpack.* Not that she knew where Nana kept any of her old elementary school backpacks or if she *had* kept them. Still, the thought of walking into the New Harvelle Library with a battered pink backpack would be one for the books—pun intended.

"I'm home!" she shouted. "Any calls for me, Jo?"

"We're here in the dining room, dear," Nana answered.

Lindy kicked the door closed with her foot and headed to the dining room. At the sight of her grandmother and Jo still in their pajamas, munching away at fruit and donuts, she stopped short.

"Did you two just get up?" she demanded.

Jo grimaced. "It's Saturday morning. Of course we just got up."

"What time did you leave the house, Lindy?" Nana asked.

"About six-thirty."

Jo glanced at Nana. "Did she *ever* believe in sleeping in?"

"Good gracious, no," Nana said, sipping her tea. "I had to give up my relaxing Saturday mornings as soon as I brought her home."

Lindy snorted. "Or at least until I got old enough to feed and clothe myself. After that, I learned you were quite capable of staying in bed till almost lunchtime."

She set the books on the table with a thud that made the utensils rattle. Nana raised her eyebrows.

"What's all this?"

"These," Lindy said, sliding into the chair opposite her, "are books about Valya. Valyan history, Valyan geography…Valyan fashion." She held up the latter, gesturing at the regal couple in flowing bright robes on the front cover. "It's about Valyan fashion *before* the Revolution, anyway. I take it people don't dress like this anymore."

"The Remnant do, in much darker colors," Nana admitted. "They say Rael and his Dominators still wear traditional clothing on special occasions, too."

"And here I thought they'd totally embraced 'the practical good of an egalitarian citizenry,' " Jo muttered. "By the way, I'm not making that up: I found that phrase in my MID homework last night."

Lindy nodded. "Yeah, I saw that too. I wonder how those protestors in Cor Danem feel about 'the practical good' every time Rael sends his troops after them."

Jo scoffed. Nana said nothing, but when Lindy glanced at her, she caught the gentle, sympathetic pride in her grandmother's bright eyes. Lindy wasn't sure it made her feel better. She looked away and shoved the fashion book aside.

"This one is more recent," she said, taking up the history book. "It has pictures of the Navorres before the Revolution."

"Ooh, let me see," Jo said, scooting closer.

Lindy turned to one of the photos. "Here we go. 'King Kalen, Queen Liliana, and their children: Prince Rael, Princess Cresside, Princess Aneya, Princess Meira, and Princess Alinna.' See, Nana?"

"I saw them with my own eyes when I was the Ambassador, darling," Nana said softly. "I doubt even the finest picture could ever do them justice."

"Look at that baby," Jo whispered. "Isn't she cute?"

Lindy peered at the toddler in the Queen's lap. Alinna had her fat little hands folded, her smile revealing a row of pearly teeth. A huge white bow pulled her dark curls to one side. Her blue dress was a miniature version of her mother's and sisters' gowns.

"'Taken three years before the Revolution,'" Lindy read aloud. "So Rael was fifteen."

"And Cresside about ten," Nana murmured. "She was always the responsible one. Aneya must've been either seven or eight."

Lindy folded her arms on the table. "And what was *she* like?"

Nana laughed. "Oh, she was an imp. I remember one time she caught a frog in her mother's garden, and unbeknownst to us, brought it to teatime."

"Oh gosh," Jo breathed.

"Indeed! Aneya decided it'd be interesting to see what would happen if she released her new friend upon her mother's fine china. I'm sure you can imagine the rest."

"And what about the babies?" Lindy asked. "Meira and Alinna?"

Nana pursed her lips. "Meira was quiet, like Cresside. She would've been four or five in that photo—an absolute angel. And Alinna..."

Her voice trailed off. Lindy frowned and Jo leaned forward, but Nana didn't look at either of them. She drew in a long breath and straightened in her seat.

"Alinna was the only one Rael paid much attention to. He was so moody, even then, and his other sisters irritated him. But I think he liked Alinna, in his own way."

"Not enough to spare her, though?" Lindy prodded.

Nana's eyes hardened. "No. Not enough to spare her."

Lindy looked again at the young prince. He stood behind his seated father, who was himself a tall, broad, short-bearded man in resplendent red. The King flashed a kind smile that reminded Lindy of Prince Ilion, but Rael looked sullen, his head held at a haughty tilt. If a family picture could glow with happiness, this one *did*—except for that one cloudy face.

"They look so content," Lindy said. "Did they have any idea what was coming?"

Nana winced, unsure. "Kalen knew the people were unhappy. Their whole economy depended on that ariya grain. They burned it, ate it, made this beautiful silk out of the recycled stalks—you name it. But after those two decades of blight…"

"They thought getting rid of their aristocracy would solve their problems?" Jo asked.

"It's a bit more complicated than that, dear. Kalen was the first king in a very long time who actually cared about his people. Once he inherited the throne, he devoted what was left of the royal treasury to relief efforts. He championed ecological rehabilitation and encouraged people like Maria Stagg to come in with their resources. But it was too little, too late. There was only so much anyone could do."

"And then the riots started," Lindy said.

"Well, when people have been hungry for twenty years, they don't see too many alternatives." Nana released a frustrated sigh. "And then Rael came home from the university, ranting and raving about how his ancestors were to blame for Valya's suffering."

Jo looked uneasy. "Well, I mean…he wasn't wrong."

"No, not in that regard. Kalen even agreed with him. But then Rael insisted it was time to overturn the old system and establish a new one where 'no one was rich and no one was poor.' Everyone would be equal. Kalen said that was impossible…and Rael said, 'Watch me.' Within weeks he'd whipped the people into such a frenzy of devotion to him and his cause, you could hardly speak a word against him without being killed by some fanatic or forced off Valya altogether."

Nana paused; she fixed her gaze on the photo of the Navorres and beat a tense rhythm on the table with her fingers. "The Council called me home the day Rael and his rabble seized control of Cor Danem. I begged Liliana to take her girls and come with me. She refused, said she wouldn't leave Kalen. Four months later, they were dead. I've spent the last twenty-three years doing everything I can to make sure their people get real justice, one way or another."

Silence fell, broken only by the tick of an antique clock. Jo shivered and rubbed her arms. Lindy lowered her gaze to the Queen's plump, pretty features.

"She kinda looks like what I remember of *my* mother," she murmured. "Just thirty pounds heavier and with a lot more hair."

"Wait, really?" Jo grabbed the book. "Come to think of it, *you* resemble her."

Lindy smirked, incredulous. "Thanks for the compliment, but I really don't."

"You might if *you* were thirty pounds heavier," Jo teased. "But seriously, are you thinking what I'm thinking? Even if you don't remember who your mom was, you do know she died the same night as the Queen, which means *you* must've been aristocratic—maybe even royal!"

"Aristocratic, yes," Nana said, taking another sip of her tea. "Royal? No. All the royals are dead or accounted for, no matter what the Renegade claims."

"Why, what does he claim?"

"That one of the little princesses survived." Nana set down her cup and rubbed at a tiny stain on the tablecloth. "Trust me. If Rael thought any of them had survived, he would've torn up the Star System looking for them a long time ago."

"Oh," Jo said. Lindy said nothing, but she felt a familiar tightening in her chest: the awful, heavy *aloneness* she always got from the nightmare. She shut the book and got to her feet.

"Well, that's enough history for today," she said briskly. "I'm gonna take a shower. Remember, Jo, we need to be out of here by one o'clock."

"Huh?!"

Lindy paused, raising her eyebrows. "Appointment at Hoadley House? Our exclusive interview with Genevieve Stagg, Meridian's Sweetheart? *Remember*?"

Jo's eyes widened. "Ohhhhh, stars and comets…"

"Goodness, Jo, that's a rather significant thing to forget, isn't it?" Nana teased.

Jo responded with a terribly apologetic look, gulped down the last of her coffee, and dashed out of the room. Lindy shook her head with a laugh and gathered up the books.

"Honestly," she whispered, "sometimes I think Jo is the only thing keeping me out of the big black pit of cynicism. If it weren't for her sense of humor—"

"Melinda."

Lindy stopped, looked up. Nana opened her mouth, shut it, and opened it again.

"I—I'm *very* proud of you. You do know that, don't you?"

Lindy frowned. "Of course."

Nana bit her lip. For a moment, she looked as if she wanted to say something else, then decided against it and pulled an uneasy, unconvincing smile instead.

"Go on, then," she said, waving her hand. "One must look one's best for an appointment at Hoadley House."

Genevieve Stagg's secretary had returned Lindy's call the morning after Prince Ilion's death. The woman had sounded just as stunned as Lindy felt, incredulously assuring the journalist that Miss Stagg would be happy to meet with her and offering Saturday afternoon as the best time.

The news had put Athena in an outstanding mood. Surprisingly, so had the announcement from the Meridian Council that Miss Tremaine and Miss Camrin would join the Valyan Conference's press team. Her "best girls," Athena was quite certain, would do the *Ladies' Post* proud. Lindy and Jo, meanwhile, had breathed enormous sighs of relief. So long as their editor stayed happy, the MID assignment would be a cinch.

But as she and Jo left the monorail station in Stanhope, Lindy took in her surroundings with as much caution as if she were walking into hostile territory. Meridian's wealthiest district was lavish and pristine—*too* pristine. New Harvelle lay to the distant southwest, its incessant hum almost nonexistent out here.

"No wonder all these politicians and businessmen seem so out-of-touch," Jo muttered as they strode down the sidewalk. "Stanhope is just a big bubble."

"I guess if you had the money to spare, you'd want to live out here where you're not bombarded by noise and billboards and soroidium pollution," Lindy said. She smoothed her crisp white blouse and picked up her pace. "Jo, I'm nervous."

"About our first official meeting with the Remnant tomorrow? I'm not."

"Of course *you're* not," Lindy teased. "You get to see Frank. Any chance to flirt with him is a treat for you. No, *this* is making me nervous. This interview."

Jo blew a raspberry. "You'll do fine."

"And if the President walks in and doesn't like my tone of voice with her daughter? Or if she thinks I'm getting too nosy? Or if she knows we met her son two weeks ago?"

"Come on, Lin. She doesn't have anything to do with him anymore."

"But she's the President! He's a trooper *and* a Nova Force captain. Technically, he serves at *her* pleasure. She probably knows *we're* troopers—"

"Lindy, stop it," Jo hissed. "You've met her before, she knows you were one of the kids she rescued, *and* she knows you're Margaret Tremaine's adopted granddaughter. She's not gonna bite your head off!"

Lindy snorted. Hoadley House, a sprawling, grey monstrosity surrounded by a cast-iron gate, was just ahead. She began rehearsing a greeting in her head.

"Hello, Miss Stagg. Melinda Tremaine. Thanks for letting us come." Or how about, "Afternoon, Miss Stagg! I'm Lindy Tremaine. Goodness, it's been a long time!"

Well, that's *disgusting.*

"Lindy?" Jo blurted. "You think you'd ever reconsider having that paternity test done? The one the government offered to the Valyan orphans a few years ago? I know you didn't want to do it then, but now that you're, I dunno, warming up to being a Valyan —"

"I can't think of anything I'd rather *not* do," Lindy said, handing her ID to the guard at the mansion gate.

"Okay, but consider this—"

"Your security passes, ladies," the guard droned, handing over two cards. "Give 'em to the butler when you get to the door and he'll show you in."

He hit a button; the gates swung open. Lindy strode through so fast, Jo had to skip to keep up.

"Lindy, listen. What if you took the test and found out you *are* royal?"

Lindy actually laughed. "Come on, Jo! I'm not royal. All the Navorres are either dead or very much accounted for. And just because I'm warming to the idea of being a Valyan doesn't mean

I'm going to start talking or dressing like one! I'm just not as creeped out over the whole thing."

"But don't you want to know who your family might be?"

"No." Lindy seized the brass knocker on the front door. "You and Nana are my family. I'm content to leave it at that."

Ignoring Jo's half-surprised, half-delighted expression, Lindy struck the knocker against the door. When it opened, a pinch-faced butler peered out. Lindy held up the passes.

"Melinda Tremaine, *New Harvelle Ladies' Post*. My photographer and I have an appointment with Miss Stagg."

The butler gave a slow, mechanical nod. It was a sure tip-off: he was a droid. "Yes, of course. Come in, ladies."

They obeyed a bit dubiously. They'd both been to Hoadley House before—just last winter they'd covered President Stagg's third inaugural ball—but they'd never had the house to themselves. Lindy found herself drinking in the magnificent front hall, lined with antique furniture and the portraits of past presidents.

The silent droid led them into a sunroom. Everything was white, down to the wicker furniture and the piano in one corner. Only the autumnal view of the lawn through the tall windows and the young woman reclining on the sofa in the middle of the room shattered the blinding whiteness.

"Miss Stagg," the butler droned. "Miss Melinda Tremaine and Miss Josephine Camrin of the *New Harvelle Ladies' Post*."

Lindy almost dropped a curtsey, the butler's formality was so prim. Genevieve Stagg—small and beautiful, a porcelain teacup personified—glanced up from the book in her lap. She took one look at her visitors and smiled so brilliantly, it settled Lindy's nerves.

Blue eyes, that thick brown hair…yep, she and Captain Granger are definitely siblings.

"Miss Tremaine!" Genevieve's whispery voice brimmed with excitement as she extended a thin hand. "It's been such a long time since we've seen each other. When was it last? The gala for Councilor Throgmorton's birthday, wasn't it?"

Lindy smiled, raised her empathic shields, and clasped Genevieve's hand. "That sounds about right, Miss Stagg. You remember my photographer, Jo Camrin?"

Genevieve nodded eagerly. "I remember your face, Miss Camrin. Not your name, but *definitely* your face."

Jo smirked. "Well, that's an improvement. Usually, people remember the name, not the face."

Genevieve laughed. "Oh good, then I'm not in trouble. You're dismissed, Cephas."

"Shall I bring you any refreshments, Miss Stagg?" the droid asked.

"Perhaps later, thank you."

"Your wheelchair then, Miss Stagg?"

Wheelchair? Lindy glanced at Genevieve, her surprise deepening at the sight of the soft-spoken young woman glaring at the droid.

"No, thank you, Cephas," Genevieve said, her voice holding a stern edge. "Go on—but let me know *as soon* as Mother comes back."

"Yes, Miss Stagg." The droid turned. As soon as he shut the door behind him, Genevieve sighed.

"Please, sit," she said, gesturing at the chairs near the sofa. "I understand you want to interview me about my wardrobe and—how did my secretary put it?—'life as Meridian's sweetheart.'"

"Umm, yes," Lindy said, pulling out her tablet. "And *I* understand this is the first time you've ever been interviewed. I promise these questions won't be intrusive. Our readers are simply interested in your personal sense of style, what you like, what works for you—"

"What if I *want* the questions to be intrusive?"

Lindy stopped. Genevieve raised her eyebrows and smoothed her skirt. Lindy followed the movement of her hands and abruptly realized that while the bodice of Genevieve's pink dress fit her slim torso perfectly, the skirt looked immense, heavy with layers and layers of tulle. Only her slippered feet showed.

"Miss Tremaine," Genevieve murmured, "my mother doesn't know you're here. I intercepted your interview request myself and decided *not* to tell her about it."

Lindy's seat could've transformed into an electric chair, and the shock still wouldn't have been as intense. She stared at Genevieve, then at Jo. Jo's mouth hung open and she shot a furtive glance at the door.

"Miss Stagg," Lindy hissed, "if your mother finds out about this, she'll toss us out—and I'd hardly blame her!"

"Why?" Genevieve asked softly. "I'm twenty-five, not fifteen. Surely I've earned the liberty to make my own decisions by now? If *I* want to be interviewed, if *I* want to tell Meridian what it's like being the daughter of Maria Stagg, don't I have that right?"

"I-I suppose, but..." Lindy cleared her throat. "But I don't think a couple of fashion journalists can do that kind of job for you."

Genevieve smiled. "Oh, don't worry—I'll still talk about fashion. I depend heavily on it. After all, it's the best way to hide *this*."

With that, she pulled her skirts right up to her knees. Lindy brought a hand to her mouth. Jo gasped. Genevieve's legs were long and smooth, but they weren't the kind of legs that made dirty heads turn. They were skeletal, pale, and lifeless, and held in cold steel braces.

"There's plenty about Meridian's sweetheart that Meridian doesn't know," Genevieve said, breaking the stunned silence. "They don't know because Mother doesn't want them to know. But maybe *I'm* tired of the secrecy. Maybe I'm more interested in raising awareness for Davenport's disease than in trying to hide how wretchedly ugly I am under all these clothes."

Lindy shook her head. "You're not ugly, Miss Stagg, not at all. And I think you're incredibly brave."

Genevieve smiled sadly and pushed her skirts down. "I'm not brave, Miss Tremaine. I'm bored and I'm angry. My brother, on the other hand—he's quite brave. Do you remember when he and Mother had their big split? It was in the papers."

Lindy forced herself not to look at Jo. "I remember a little. I was in high school, though. I wasn't in journalism at the time."

"Oh, true. I was young myself. And my mother was always very strict with us. She had definite ideas about what we'd be when we grew up. Ethan was to inherit our father's business, of course...so when he joined the Nova Force, Mother was furious. Her plans had been wrecked, and that was all that mattered. She didn't feel much different after my diagnosis a year later." Genevieve paused, tilted her head to the side. "Take that down, Miss Tremaine."

"Oh!" Lindy scrambled to turn on her tablet. "Umm, Jo, the voice recorder—"

"Whoa whoa whoa, wait," Jo cried. "Are we sure we want to do this, Lindy?"

"I assure you, Miss Camrin," Genevieve said, "this will be newsworthy. Your time won't be wasted here."

"Oh, don't worry, I know that! But this will set all three of us at odds with your mom, and I'm not sure we want to do that at this present juncture, *Melinda*."

Lindy raised her eyebrows. "You weren't worried about that on the way here, *Josephine*."

"Well, I didn't think we were gonna get into the intimate details of the Stagg family life!"

Lindy frowned. Jo had a point. Suppose Maria Stagg found out two undercover troopers had interviewed her sheltered daughter. She could remove them from the Valyan mission altogether—or worse, fire them in a New Harvelle minute. Nobody would be able to gainsay her. It could ruin Lindy and Jo's MID careers forever.

On the other hand, this young woman wanted to stand on her own two feet (figuratively) and not only face the unpleasant truth but speak it, too. Her brother had already paved the way for her. He did seem to have a strangely compelling influence.

"Miss Stagg," Lindy began slowly, "I appreciate your willingness to share your story. I *really* do. It's just that Jo and I have been assigned to the Meridian press pool for the Valyan Conference, and I'd really rather not get on your mom's bad side right now."

Genevieve fingered the embroidery on her skirt. "Of course. I understand."

"Good. That said..."

Genevieve looked up hopefully. Lindy couldn't help but smile.

"That said," she continued, "I'll interview you today as long as we agree to delay the article until we get back from Valya. Would that make you feel better, Jo?"

"Yes," Jo breathed. "Absolutely."

Genevieve beamed. "That would be perfect! What will you tell your editor, though?"

"That we got the interview, but something came up and we couldn't get the photoshoot?" Lindy suggested.

Jo snickered. "Athena will bite your head off."

"Not if I tell her what's *in* the interview. She'll be fine as long as she thinks she's about to blow President Stagg's façade wide open." Lindy shot Genevieve a sheepish look. "Sorry. The world of journalism is a bit ruthless."

Genevieve laughed wryly. "Don't worry. I know how ruthless people can be when they want something bad enough."

By the end of the hour, Lindy wasn't sure if she felt exultant over this unexpected treasure trove of information or miserable. She hadn't even touched Genevieve without her shields, yet her empathy throbbed as Genevieve told them story after story: how her mother insisted she wear the leg braces so she could stand at official functions, how devastated she and her brother were when their father was killed in a hover accident, and how her brother now visited her only when he happened to be on Meridian but their mother was busy elsewhere.

"Where is your mother right now, anyway?" Jo asked.

Genevieve stared at her hands. "Opening a new wing at the hospital…for Davenport's patients, ironically enough. I didn't find out about it until this morning. She didn't tell me."

Lindy looked up. "My grandmother knew I was coming here, and she didn't bother to tell *me* about your condition, either. Does she know? She spends a lot of time here."

"She was one of the first to know," Genevieve admitted. "She and Mother have known each other ever since the Valyan Revolution when they helped all those poor refugees. I hear you're one of them yourself."

Irritation burned Lindy's chest—*how could Nana not at least give me a heads-up about this?!*—but she forced herself to follow Genevieve's change of subject. "Yes, I am. I was five when I came here."

Genevieve's expression grew even softer. "It must be quite a step for you, then, to go back next week."

Lindy forced a smile, but before she could answer, the door behind them opened. She and Jo whirled so fast, the wicker chairs creaked—and at the sight of the intruder, her mouth fell open.

"Captain Granger!" Jo cried.

All the blood rushed to Lindy's face. Ethan Granger stared at Jo, then at her, before he finally turned to his sister.

"Gen?" he asked uneasily. "What's going on?"

Genevieve struggled to sit up straight, her big eyes fixed on him with something close to adoration. "Oh, Ethan, I didn't realize you'd be here today! What happened? I thought—"

"I finished my business at Nova Force Headquarters earlier than I expected. Saw on the HV that Mother was out and about, so I decided I'd run over."

Lindy swallowed. She could hear everything he left unsaid as clearly as if he'd shouted it from the rooftop. *He can't even visit his own sister without having to tiptoe around his mother. What kind of woman does that to her own children? She's known as one of the biggest philanthropists in the Star System, for goodness' sake! Even I owe my life to her…*

"So you three know each other?" Genevieve asked.

Captain Granger's mouth twitched. "You might say that."

Lindy sprang to her feet. "Captain, I swear, it's just a simple interview, *she* accepted *our* request, and it's not going to the presses *until* the delegation gets back from Valya. If I'd known you were coming here, I would've rescheduled or…or something."

Captain Granger raised his eyebrows, amused. "I couldn't care less what your business is with my sister, Miss Tremaine, as long as it's on the up-and-up. I just want to know if *she* is giving you a hard time."

Genevieve laughed. "She and Miss Camrin have been the least nosy reporters I've ever met, Ethan. Come and sit down over here, and I'll get Cephas to bring tea—"

"No," Ethan and Lindy blurted at the same time. Lindy mentally kicked herself and grabbed her bag.

"Actually, we need to start heading back. We've got enough material here to appease my boss until after our Valyan assignment, Miss Stagg. If there's anything else you want to add to it, I'll take it down when Jo and I come back for the photoshoot in a couple of weeks."

"That sounds wonderful, Miss Tremaine." Genevieve smiled and held out her hand again. "I thank you for your time. It's been very…cathartic."

Lindy hesitated just a moment before willing herself to keep her shields down. As soon as she touched Genevieve, she sensed the young woman's genuine gratitude, along with an undercurrent of something solid and assertive that more than compensated for her physical weakness.

"Thank *you,* Miss Stagg," she said. She stepped back as Jo moved to shake Genevieve's hand and looked Ethan in the eye. "Until next time, Captain."

He gave her a small, one-sided smile. "Until next time."

As soon as Lindy and Jo left, Ethan turned to his sister. She gazed pensively at the door as if trying to hear the reporters' retreating footsteps.

"Gen," he said.

She looked up. "Yes, Ethan?"

"Did Mother know they were coming?"

Genevieve looked at him steadily. "No."

Ethan moved his jaw to one side. He unzipped his Nova Force jacket and lowered himself to a seat on the couch by her feet.

Once upon a time, she would've nudged him playfully with her toes. The fact that she didn't told him she *couldn't*.

"You're gonna regret it, Gen," he murmured.

"No, I won't," she said. "What do I have to lose, Ethan? Mother's always been content to live a double life. She shows one thing to the cameras and something else here at home. You didn't want that for yourself and neither do I. This is my chance to show what the real Genevieve Stagg is like—and it may be my last! By Elyon, I'm *not* going to waste it!"

Ethan looked at her. "Your last?"

She blinked, dropped her gaze. Ethan took her hand, every terrible detail he'd ever read about Davenport's disease coming to mind.

"What's going on, Genevieve?" he asked.

She turned her hand over so their fingers could lace. "It's starting to affect my ribs. Once they start breaking, I won't be able to breathe."

Ethan suddenly couldn't breathe himself. He wasn't prone to tears—he hadn't wept since an accident aboard the *Hummingbird* a couple of years ago resulted in the deaths of nine crewmen—but now his eyes stung. Genevieve must've noticed. She squeezed his hand as tightly as she could.

"Don't, Ethan."

He shook his head. "If I could've been with you all these years, Gen…"

"Well, you couldn't. You had to be your own man, not one of those browbeaten milquetoasts who trail after Mother all the time." She paused, thoughtful. "She *is* brilliant. And she knows how to get things done. It's just that she runs roughshod over anyone and everyone. Except for Councilor Tremaine, maybe."

Ethan chuckled weakly. "Watch out, then. From what I've seen of Miss Tremaine, the apple doesn't fall far from the tree."

Genevieve smiled. "You know her well?"

"Not really. We just crossed paths recently."

"Ah. Well, she and Miss Camrin are very kind. Excellent listeners." Her smile turned a little wicked. "They're quite charming, too. Mother told me your ship will take the Councilor and the Royal Remnant to Valya next week. Maybe you can spend some time with one or the other of them and bring me back a new sister-in-law."

Ethan laughed. "Oh-ho-ho, *noooooo.*"

"Why not?"

"Because—" *Because romances between active troopers are absolutely forbidden?* "Because I'm not ready to settle down with anyone yet. And besides, my experiences with women haven't been all that great."

"Oh, Ethan, you can't judge all women by Mother. She's really concerned about this trip, you know. You should hear her go on about what a horrible person Rael Navorre is and how he deserves a sound humbling—but I think she's afraid something will happen."

Ethan frowned. "What kind of 'something?'"

"I don't know. Disasters that look like accidents and really aren't? You know Mother. She's got a talent for thinking up the worst scenarios."

He sighed. "I hate to admit it, but her predictions are usually pretty good."

Genevieve shrugged. "Are you excited?"

"A little. It's an honor for the crew."

"And for you."

He smiled. How well she still knew him. "Well, at least I'll get a chance to enjoy a little shore leave—as long as Mother's predictions don't come true and I don't have to whisk the whole delegation back onto the ship."

Genevieve nodded, rubbing her thumb against the top of his hand. "You'll be careful?"

"Of course. I won't even be involved in the proceedings. I'll just be an observer."

And that, at least, he thought, *is the absolute truth.*

Chapter Eight

Lindy thrust her arms up to her elbows in a sink full of sudsy water and didn't even flinch at the heat. Winston rubbed against her ankles. She ignored him, too busy scrubbing the plates she, Nana, and Jo had left piled up this morning.

She had to remind herself not to scrub too hard. She might take the paint off them altogether.

This hypocrisy stinks. The president of a freedom-loving planet like Meridian—a woman who defied stereotypes for years *with nothing but her wits—who saved hundreds of Valyan kids, myself included—she treats her own children like* that? *And she conceals something like Davenport's disease from the whole planet just for the sake of public image?*

She slammed a clean plate onto the counter. *And on top of all that, I'm a highly-trained intelligence agent! I'm supposed to spot these things. Why didn't I ask myself, "So* why *hasn't Maria Stagg ever let anyone interview her daughter?" Why did I simply assume she was an overprotective mother? I'm* supposed *to think outside the box!*

Although I have to admit, I never would've thought it'd be a disability.

The front door opened and closed; she heard the jangle of jewelry and brisk steps on the wood floor. Lindy gritted her teeth and set a coffee mug on the counter.

"Oh, Lindy!" Nana exclaimed. "I didn't expect you home this early. Where's Jo?"

Lindy didn't turn. She tossed her head, trying to get a strand of hair out of her face without taking her hands out of the water. "She decided to spend the rest of the day with her dad in Wyverstone."

"Ah." Nana set her purse on the kitchen table. "How did the interview go?"

Lindy thrust her jaw forward and stared out the window above the sink. "Why didn't you tell me Genevieve Stagg has Davenport's disease?"

A dead silence fell. Lindy glanced over her shoulder. Nana stood by the table, her hands still on her purse. Her maroon blazer and black skirt looked crisp, professional, dignified—the perfect outfit for a councilor. Her expression, however, was so sheepish, it made Lindy want to throw something.

Not at Nana, of course, but the window would be a nice target.

"Davenport's?" Nana repeated.

"I looked it up when I got home. From what I saw, she's got a bad case." Lindy narrowed her eyes. "Did you also know her mother had *no* idea that Jo and I were coming today?"

Nana lowered her gaze. "No. Although I suspected that might be the case."

"Really." Lindy pressed the small of her back against the counter and folded her arms. "Then you at least had some idea of what Genevieve really wanted to talk about? You didn't think that maybe I could've used a little heads-up?"

"I thought it'd be better if you made the discovery on your own."

Lindy's mouth fell open. "After all these years of you talking with the President almost every day and giving me *ample* opportunities to cross paths with the Staggs, you *never* mentioned it? That poor girl's been forced to hide her handicap since she was thirteen! You didn't think I'd better know that before I started this groundbreaking interview?"

"If I had, would it have changed anything?"

"Of course it would have! I would've been prepared! Emotionally! And I wouldn't have sat there gaping like an idiot!"

Nana said nothing. Lindy put a hand to her forehead and squeezed her eyes shut.

"Why—didn't—you—tell—me?"

"Because it wasn't my place," Nana said, her voice a firm whisper. "Maria has always been desperate to prove she's got everything under control. She has a reputation to uphold, and she's convinced that if she can't keep a tight rein on her own family, it'll reflect badly on *her*. As her friend and a member of the Meridian Council, I have no right to reveal what she prefers to keep under wraps."

Lindy snorted. "Well, it reflects badly on her, all right—just not in the way she thinks."

Nana raised her eyebrows in a way that made Lindy think she agreed. "I admit, I didn't think your request would be accepted. When it was, I suspected Genevieve might risk telling you more than the names of her favorite designers. But *I* couldn't tell you any intimate details ahead of time. Maria would never trust me again if she found out, nor would Genevieve have the satisfaction of telling you her story on her own terms. And *you,* my dear, wouldn't have seen quite as clearly this young woman who faces her fears with such dignity and courage."

Lindy's eyes burned. "This was another lesson, then? Like going to the hospital? Because you think I'm a coward?"

"No, you're no coward. Once you know what must be done, you have no problem doing it." Nana paused."So, did you get the interview?"

Lindy shrugged. "Yes. But I don't dare publish it till we get back from Valya."

"I understand Maria's son will be on your trooper team."

Lindy jerked her head up. "You know he's—?"

"A trooper? Of course I know. So does his mother, although she'll never admit to keeping up with his activities."

"Does she know *I'm* a trooper?"

"The President of Meridian knows who *all* the delegation's MID plants are, Melinda."

Lindy hugged herself tighter. She still hadn't told Nana that she'd met Ethan Granger on Xandroa. She hadn't wanted Nana to tell his mother.

And I'm not gonna tell her now, she thought. *If she can keep her secrets, I can keep mine. At least mine don't matter in the grand scheme of things.*

"I haven't seen him in years," Nana mused aloud. "Maria was furious when he enlisted in the Nova Force. But if he's still the same kind soul I remember, you'll like him."

Not gonna tell her I already know that, *either,* Lindy added mentally.

Nana apparently thought the conversation was over: she slung her purse straps over her elbow and started for the stairs. Lindy unfolded her arms and reached behind her for the edge of the counter.

"I'm sorry, Nana, but I just...I felt *trapped.*"

Nana stopped and turned. Lindy forced herself to look her in the eye.

"I realize you didn't want to betray a trust. But I walked into a situation today that might still end up with me losing both my jobs. You could've at least prepared me, but you didn't. It wasn't right and it wasn't fair...to Genevieve or to me."

Nana sighed, retracing her steps back to the table. "Perhaps you're right. I'm not so enamored with myself that I can't admit to a mistake. But I've found that we don't always need to know everything right away…"

"I'm a trooper before I'm a reporter, Nana!" Lindy exploded. "I've been trained to gather every single scrap of information I can before I make any move, and the idea of someone—anyone—deliberately denying me critical information makes me *sick*! You should've thought of that before you left me in the dark!"

With that, she stormed out of the kitchen, taking the stairs two at a time until she reached her bedroom. She slammed the door behind her and threw herself into the chair in front of her desk. The tab she'd opened earlier on her laptop still showed the webpage she'd been studying.

Davenport's disease is a degenerative bone disease. It usually culminates in a weakening of the legs, ribcage, and breastbone. Asphyxiation is the leading cause of death since breathing becomes increasingly difficult as the disease advances.

Lindy leaned back, a hand at her mouth. She'd have to tell her boss about the interview, promise her it'd be a sensational piece, and then somehow convince her it would be in the paper's best interests if they waited to publish it until after Lindy got back from Valya. Throw in the fib about running out of time for a photoshoot, and there'd be no problem. Except…

The meeting tomorrow. At MID Headquarters.

Lindy leaped to her feet, snatching her comm from where she'd tossed it onto her bed earlier and punching in Jo's number. She started pacing as soon as Jo accepted the call.

"What, you miss me already?" Jo teased.

Lindy ignored the sarcasm. "Where are you?"

"In my dad's kitchen, cleaning up a week's worth of dirty dishes and throwing out—let's see—a dozen beer bottles?"

Lindy stopped. "I thought he was a wine guy."

"He is." Jo's voice dropped to an exasperated whisper. "He just finished off a bottle of that."

Some of the nervous energy drained out of Lindy. If Jo could pinpoint *her* insecurities, Lindy could just as easily identify Jo's—even if they were fewer and farther between.

"Are you all right?" Lindy asked, her voice softer.

"Oh yeah. He's sleeping it off. Honestly, if I weren't so convinced I'm doing the right thing by visiting him once a month like this, I'd ask your grandmother to formally adopt me, too. What's up?"

"President Stagg's gonna be at that meeting tomorrow. At MID Headquarters. She knows we're troopers."

There was a long silence on the other end. "Holy krikalilly."

"I know. If we publish this interview, our MID careers are down the toilet."

"Yeah. And I'd think you were overreacting if I hadn't heard Genevieve's horror stories." Jo paused, then asked, "Did Nana know about Genevieve?"

"Of course she knew," Lindy grumbled.

"Then why didn't she—"

"Because she didn't feel like she had the right. Because she didn't want Maria mad at her. Oh, and here's my favorite: she wanted Genevieve to tell us on her own so I could 'see courage at its finest.'"

"You don't sound convinced."

"I'm *furious!* We've been cornered into something way bigger than ourselves that we did not ask for, and I hate that feeling! It's not fair!"

"Well, don't lose your mind over it. By the time we get back, Nana might be on fabulous terms with the President. She can tell her about the interview ahead of time and soften the blow."

Lindy scoffed. "After what we've learned today, you think she'd appreciate that?"

Jo chuckled. "You're a cynic, you know that?"

"Yeah, well. I'm a trooper. I'm *supposed* to be a cynic."

"You've got a point. Oh wait, I gotta go...Dad's about to roll off the couch."

"Okay. You'll be there on time tomorrow morning?"

"Absolutely. I've got my alarm set and I'll be there at 9 o'clock sharp. I'll talk to you later, okay? Bye."

"Bye," Lindy murmured. She plopped onto her bed, stretching herself on the mattress. What a conundrum she'd gotten herself into. *I'll either break my word to Genevieve and lose my cover job...or do the right thing by Genevieve and risk a dishonorable discharge from MID. Either way, Nana's thrown me under the bus.*

Lindy kicked off her shoes and curled up on her side. Jo was right. She didn't have to decide what to do right now. But the next time she'd let somebody—*anybody*—wrangle her into another corner was the day she really called up Operation Kitchingham.

Frank Gridley always found MID's massive underground facilities disconcerting. What exactly was over his head? A monorail tunnel? The hospital? Or was he still underneath the unassuming four-story that didn't even have an official "MID Headquarters" sign? It was so insulated, New Harvelle could go up in a nuclear inferno and nobody down here would ever know.

Striding down the windowless corridors with Ethan Granger, however, he comforted himself with the thought that Meridian wasn't at war. The only thing he was missing outside right now was a good old-fashioned thunderstorm.

"Stars and comets, this uniform is tight," he muttered, tugging at the collar of his close-fitting black uniform. "I'd like to get my hands on the designer who thought it'd be easy to swallow, let alone *eat* in this thing."

Ethan smirked. "Put on a pound or two since you last wore it, Frank?"

"I'll have you know, Captain *sir*, that I passed my introductory exam in Dr. Elliot's chamber of horrors with flying colors!"

"Not exactly an honest answer to my question, but I guess I'll take it."

Frank grinned. If there was anything he'd learned about Ethan since joining the *Hummingbird* crew, it was that the man maintained an appropriate, benevolent distance with his crew. Here in private, though, and especially in an environment where Nova Force regs didn't apply, they were equals, two troopers on their way to formally accept a brand new mission.

When they reached the conference room, the green light above the closed door told them it was occupied but not yet in lockdown. Ethan squared his shoulders.

"Ready?" he asked, his eyes on the door.

Frank raised his eyebrows. "Are you?"

Ethan let out a huffing breath. "Never been assigned to anything this critical before. I walk in that door, and I'm in the presence of monarchy. *And* my mother."

Frank snorted. "From what I hear, if you can handle your mom, you can handle Princess Mariamne. You'll be fine."

To his relief, Ethan cracked a grin before letting out a more controlled breath and opening the door. The two men stepped inside—and drew up short in surprise.

The Royal Remnant and President Stagg were nowhere to be seen. Jarvis sat at the head of the table in full dress uniform, swiping through files on the table's touchscreen surface. Jo Camrin leaned back in the chair on his left, filing her nails; Lindy Tremaine sat next to her, cradling a tablet in the crook of her elbow and running her fingertip over its screen.

All three glanced up as Ethan and Frank entered. Jo smiled at Frank, much to his delight. Lindy, however, looked straight at Ethan and didn't take her eyes off him.

"Don't tell me all the fun started without us and everyone's gone home!" Frank cried.

Jarvis smiled. "No, I just asked our guests to postpone their arrival by thirty minutes so I could discuss logistics with my troopers. Have a seat. No need for any introductions here, of course."

"No indeed," Frank said, winking at Jo. She turned pink and rolled her eyes. He threw himself into one of the chairs opposite her. Ethan settled into the one opposite Lindy, but Frank noticed she set aside her tablet and turned to Jarvis as if her life depended on it, no longer giving Ethan a smidge of attention.

"I don't need to impress upon you the importance of this mission," Jarvis began. "You'll be the first troopers on Valya in two decades. If you can gather critical information about the planet—its economy, its infrastructure, its military, how the civilian population lives and functions—while making sure the delegation remains safe, then you've pretty much insured the mission's success, regardless of whether or not Rael and Mariamne come up with a treaty."

He tapped the table surface; tiny holographic images of the conference's major players, complete with their names and titles, popped up like chess pieces. Princess Mariamne, her husband Prince Lhoris, her aunt Princess Verrona, Lord Nhormin, and Councilor Tremaine materialized on one side. Rael Navorre, his generals, and his three closest advisors—the Dominators, as they were known on Valya—shimmered on the other.

"All the meetings will be public and held in the State Room at the old Navorre Palace," Jarvis said. "Jo and Lindy, you'll be with the press pool, of course. Ethan, you'll mingle with the civilian audience. You, Frank, will be embedded with our regular security forces. I suggest you download the palace floor plan onto your devices."

With another tap of his finger, the blueprint appeared. Frank leaned forward, studying it. Lindy put her tablet on the table and activated its downloader; Ethan did the same with his comm.

"Now, for your special tech," Jarvis continued. "Jo, you'll record the meetings with a micro-cam and send the videos to MID every evening. Frank, you'll have sensors in your helmet that'll pick up any unauthorized transmissions in the room. Ethan, you'll be in charge of the listening devices in Princess Mariamne's quarters."

"Wait, what?" Lindy blurted.

Jo frowned. "Sorry, Jarvis, but I thought you said 'listening devices.' "

"I did," Jarvis said.

Frank shot a horrified look at Ethan, but the captain only leaned back in his chair with his hand at his mouth, watching Lindy closely.

"We're keeping tabs on the Princess?" she asked in a low voice. "Why?"

"Because MID has reason to believe that Mariamne may have a coup in mind," Jarvis replied.

Lindy laughed harshly. "Jarvis, she buried her father two days ago. Before that, she wasn't even in charge of the Remnant's business. *He* was."

"And Prince Ilion was so single-minded in his quest to bring peace to his planet, he may have missed a few of his daughter's activities." Jarvis jabbed the screen. "Here. Video surveillance of Mariamne from two months ago, leaving her house disguised with head coverings. We tracked her all the way to this building."

Another tap and Frank found himself peering at a grainy video of a slender, veiled figure approaching a ramshackle house that had to be in Manwaring District. Lindy took one look at it and fixed her eyes on Jarvis with more anger than disbelief.

"Did we have a warrant for this surveillance?"

His jaw flexed. "The Navorres are aliens to this planet—"

"Did we have a warrant, Jarvis?" Ethan asked behind his hand.

"That house is a known meeting place for Valyan wannabe-revolutionaries in league with the Renegade," Jarvis snapped.

"For the Princess to meet with them in secret incriminates her in the Renegade's public call for a rebellion against Rael."

"But you don't have enough evidence to confront her about it," Lindy said in a dangerously soft voice. "You can't *prove* that's her because you can't see her face—and even if it is, you have no idea what she said to them. But you can't ask her about it because the legality of your 'surveillance' is as stable as a Xandroan volcano."

Jarvis said nothing. Nobody moved. Frank, however, let his eyes flick between Ethan and Lindy. None of this seemed to have taken Ethan by surprise. As for Lindy, she and Jarvis were now in a literal staring contest. She was the challenger, too angry to look away or even blink.

"We didn't have time to get a warrant," Jarvis admitted. "Nevertheless, this goes all the way up to President Stagg. If you have a problem, you can take it up with her. In the meantime, I'm ordering you not to mention this to Councilor Tremaine or to Mariamne. We have no plans on acting on this information right now. But you *will* keep your eyes and ears open for any suspicious activity on the Princess's part. If you observe any, you will arrest her without hesitation—and you, Trooper Tremaine, will not deviate from that. Understood?"

Lindy leaned back, tossing her hair over her shoulder. "Perfectly."

"Good. The delegation will stay at the Cor Danem Renaissance Hotel. Ethan, as captain of the *Hummingbird* enjoying some well-deserved shore leave, you'll have your own room. Frank, you'll stay with the other security guards. All four of you will come together for your nightly reports. You will be responsible for your own MID tech and tools. Any questions?"

Silence. Jarvis looked at each stony face and folded his arms.

"I understand," he said quietly, "why the idea of spying on Princess Mariamne rubs you the wrong way. But I beg you to remember that this conference is critical to Valya's wellbeing. Those people have suffered and *are* suffering in ways we can't imagine."

Lindy dropped her gaze. Out of the corner of his eye, Frank caught a slight softening of Ethan's posture.

"This conference *must* work for their sakes," Jarvis concluded. "If it doesn't, then we've got to make sure the Valyans don't suffer any more than they have to, and that we get our people back home safely. If that means we have to take unsavory measures, then so be it. I'd rather do the wrong thing for the right reason than watch innocent people die again."

Frank raised a hand. "I guess it's too late for us to pull the 'conscientious objector' card? If we wanted to, that is?"

"Far too late. You leave for Valya in four days—not enough time to assemble a new team."

"How convenient you told us all this today, then," Lindy said icily.

Jarvis raised his bushy eyebrows. "Commander's discretion, trooper. Commander's discretion."

Chapter Nine

Standing with her arms folded and her back against the door-frame of the conference room, Lindy watched Captain Granger disappear into the men's room at the end of the corridor. Jo and Frank chatted quietly at the table; Jarvis studied his tablet. Lindy glanced at her watch. They had ten minutes before Nana, the Valyans, and the President arrived for their first briefing with the troopers.

Time enough for a man-to-man. She looked both ways, making sure Jo and Frank weren't watching. Then she slipped out, crossed the corridor, and threw open the door to the men's room.

As she expected, Granger stood with his back to her at a urinal. He took one look over his shoulder and jerked around again with a startled noise.

"That's all right," she said, crossing her arms. "Finish your business. I'll stay right here."

Granger glared at her over his shoulder, his face flushed with irritation and embarrassment. "Now I know why Frank's been warning me not to underestimate you."

"Because I challenged Jarvis, or because I barged in on you taking a leak? As for the first, it's hardly the first time I've done it. As for the second, I wouldn't have come in if I didn't already know you'd have your back to me. Hope that makes you feel better."

"Oh, well, *thanks*."

He zipped his fly and stormed to the sink. She detected none of the relaxed friendliness he'd displayed in the Xandroan hotel room a few weeks ago. His shoulders were tense, his thick eyebrows knotted. He shut off the water and jerked a paper towel out of the dispenser so fast, it rattled. None of this surprised her, but she had a feeling she wasn't the sole cause.

"How much of Jarvis' news did you already know?" she asked.

Granger dried his hands without looking at her. "I knew he wanted us to arrest her if she made any move to sabotage the conference. I didn't know about the surveillance here on Meridian or her visit to Manwaring. I certainly didn't know we'd be bugging her."

"Do you approve of that?"

He tossed the towel into the disposal bin. "I don't know."

It wasn't the answer she'd wanted to hear. Lindy stepped away from the door. Once she stood right in front of him, she threw her head back and looked him in the eye.

"Listen," she said. "It does look bad if a Valyan princess associates with pro-Renegade groups on Meridian. But she can't take them with her to Valya, and they could never follow her there without us knowing about it. There *has* to be some other reason why she'd meet with them."

Granger mimicked her posture, his hands around his elbows. "What do you think it could be?"

"I don't know. But I'm not bugging that woman without a warrant or better evidence that that was even her. That video wouldn't hold up in a court of law and Jarvis knows it!"

"I know. Believe me, I know. I'm just as frustrated as you are…"

"But you're not going to stand up to him?" Lindy cried.

"I *did* stand up to him! He told me to drag her back to Meridian if she so much as looked at Rael Navorre the wrong way, and I pushed back—and you know what? I was told to shut up and do as I was told. So now I'm far too busy looking for ways to work around that order to waste any more time and energy on noisier resistance."

Lindy blinked in surprise. "I-I'm sorry. I didn't realize. I thought—"

"That just because he's been a good friend to me all these years, I'm Jarvis' 'yes-man'?"

Lindy snapped her mouth shut. Granger gave his head a slight, disappointed shake.

"Okay, look," he muttered. "Your grandmother knows Mariamne better than any of us. Would *she* agree with Jarvis?"

"I don't know," Lindy whispered. "To be honest, I've got my own worries about her. She knew about your sister's condition and didn't give me *any* advance warning. Who knows what kind of info she might have that she's hiding for her own purposes?"

Granger cleared his throat. "Yeah, about Genevieve…"

"Rest easy, Captain. We won't publish anything till we get back."

He sighed. "She's been talking about going to the press for a while. It's not that she wants to embarrass our mother. She just wants to tell the truth for her own sake. But Mother *will* be furious. I hope you're prepared for that."

"Well, at least I'm forewarned now. But I'm a big girl, and so is your sister. She deserves the chance to tell her story."

He smiled. "You have a very black-and-white sense of morality, don't you?"

Lindy shrugged. "Right is right and wrong is wrong. It's that simple and *that* hard."

"Don't I know it. By the way, I had no idea you were there with Genevieve. The droid didn't say a word about any guests when he showed me in."

"Good thing it was you and not your mom," Lindy said. Granger chuckled just as the bathroom door swung open.

"Hey Ethan, the bigwigs have arri—*oh*." Frank froze, staring at Lindy, then at the captain, then back at her. Granger raised his hand with a smirk.

"It's all right, Frank. Miss Tremaine and I were just…talking things over."

"Ah. Right. Well." Frank pointed down the hallway. "Jarvis wants you back in the conference room right away."

"Great. We'll be there in a minute."

"Thanks, Frank," Lindy said.

Frank returned her smile, though he still looked a bit weirded out. When the door shut behind him, Lindy turned back to Granger. He met her gaze.

"We'll figure something out," he said. "We're troopers. We're trained to think outside the box, right?"

Lindy nodded. "Right. And if we can't figure out a way to do our job within the box of legality, we don't deserve the rank."

To her surprise, he grinned. "Agreed. Just one condition, though. From here on out, you call me 'Ethan' or 'Goldhawk,' as the case may be."

Lindy laughed. "Is that your code name?"

"Yep." He opened the door, gesturing for her to go first. Lindy blushed. Captain Granger holding the door for her was considerably more appealing than Senator Ralk of Xandroa performing the same action. She swiveled on her heel as she stepped into the hall.

"Well, then," she said, "it's only fair that you call me 'Lindy' or 'Thorpe,' as the case may be."

"Thorpe? As in 'Captain Thorpe?' "

"Yes! Do you watch *Star Chronicles*?"

He grinned sheepishly. "What kind of Meridian would I be if I didn't?"

The conference room was considerably fuller than it had been when Ethan ducked out to use the restroom. Princess Mariamne, Prince Lhoris, and the older, rounder Grand Princess Verrona were present, along with Margaret Tremaine and Maria Stagg. They had claimed one side of the table; Frank and Jo sat with uncharacteristic decorum on the other side.

The visitors chatted amiably with Jarvis, but as soon as Ethan and Lindy entered, his mother glanced up. When he met her gaze, the corners of her mouth instantly hardened; her folded hands tensed on the table. She looked the same as always: tall, straight-backed, her shoulder-length hair dyed the same dark auburn he remembered from his boyhood. Her crisp green blouse only added to her famous aura of fierce, unabashed confidence.

Which would be fine and dandy if it were tempered by a heart like Genevieve's, Ethan thought, taking the seat beside Lindy's. Her hand nearly brushed his as she grabbed the arms of her chair and scooted forward, but he moved away before she could touch him and feel his resentment.

"Well, now that we're all here," Jarvis said, "let's get started. First, Your Highness, allow me to introduce your MID security team: Ethan Granger, Melinda Tremaine, Frank Gridley, and Jo Camrin. All have outstanding cover jobs outside of MID, which they'll be using on this mission. Ethan, for example, is the captain of the *Hummingbird,* the ship that'll take you to Valya."

Princess Mariamne raised a delicate eyebrow. "Miss Tremaine and I have already met. These are the very best you can offer for our protection, Commander Jarvis?"

"The absolute best, Your Highness," he replied.

"Captain," Prince Lhoris said, his dark eyes bright with interest, "I understand your ship is considered one of the finest in the Meridian Nova Force."

Ethan nodded. "Glad to know she has a good reputation, Your Highness. My crew and I are determined to make your voyage a pleasant one."

"Commander, forgive me, but will these troopers be our *only* security detail?" Princess Verrona asked.

Jarvis chuckled. "No, no. Our Nova Force will provide a squad of fifty fully-trained men and women who'll be charged with your protection. These four, however, are elite agents trained to detect threats even the best soldier might miss."

"'Threats'?" Mariamne repeated, narrowing her eyes. "Specify, Commander."

Jarvis visibly stiffened. "Well, for starters, all four troopers will be observing Citizen Navorre during your daily meetings—"

"Commander," Mariamne interrupted. "While I willingly accept your help, I must demand that you refer to my cousin by his true title. 'Citizen' is a deplorable term—not because it puts him on equal standing with our common man, but because he only *pretends* to be their equal. He was born a prince and remains a prince—a hateful one, no better than our grandfather. I make this demand and no other. Please do not deny me."

Ethan had to bite the inside of his cheek to hide his surprised amusement. Mariamne called the shots today, not Jarvis. Nobody seemed eager to gainsay her, either—not her family, not the President, not even Councilor Tremaine. Jarvis exhaled, schooling his face into submission.

"Very well, Your Highness. The troopers will observe *Prince Rael* from discreet, strategic positions during the meetings. They're also charged with intelligence gathering: monitoring communications, the population, the prince's soldiers and advisors, et cetera. Nothing will slip past them. *Nothing*."

"Which is why I need to ask you a few important questions, Your Highness," Lindy said.

Ethan jumped. Everyone stared at Lindy, but she clicked on her tablet and ignored everyone but Mariamne. President Stagg leaned forward.

"Trooper Tremaine," she said in the authoritative voice Ethan knew so well, "as your Commander-in-Chief, I need to know what you intend to ask the Princess."

"Nothing offensive, ma'am. It's simply a trooper's job to gather all the available information before they make their next move." Lindy glanced at her grandmother, and Ethan could tell she meant it to be a meaningful, pointed look. "I won't be intrusive, I promise. I just want to do my job well."

President Stagg said nothing. Mariamne thought a moment, then drew herself up in her seat.

"Very well," she said. "I have no objections, Miss Tremaine. Ask away."

Lindy nodded. "Thank you. Your father was adamant he only wanted to negotiate peace. He didn't want to lead a military force against your cousin, ally with the Renegade, or split Cor Danem between royal and anti-royal forces. From what I've read, he didn't even want to pull the Meridians into the whole thing at first because he feared it might antagonize Rael."

One corner of Mariamne's mouth twisted. "You *have* done your research."

"And we thank you for your interest in our cause," Princess Verrona said gently.

Lindy smiled, but Ethan noticed she gripped the tablet so tightly, her fingers shook.

"Do you think along the same lines as your father, Princess?" she continued.

Mariamne frowned. "Am I against dividing Cor Danem? Of course. I do not wish for half of my people to be the sole objects of Rael's fury while the other half enjoys the freedom to better themselves. We must strive for the good of all."

"And what about using military force against Rael?"

Jarvis cleared his throat. President Stagg glared at him, but Mariamne only stared at Lindy as if she thought the trooper had lost her mind.

"Rael's Magnificents are too deeply entrenched in Cor Danem. To go against *them* would be disastrous." She paused, her dark eyes flickering over the Meridians in sudden alarm. "Do you not see that? Do you even know what they are?"

Lindy frowned. "Who are you talking about?"

"The Magnificents! They first appeared during the Revolution. At first glance they seem to be ordinary Valyan men, but they've been altered—physically and mentally—and we still don't know how. Somehow, some way, they have lost the Valyan gift."

Ethan shifted in his chair. "You mean they're no longer empaths?"

Mariamne pressed her lips together. Her husband took her hand and shook his head.

"Not anymore," he said. "And the loss of the gift has made them monsters."

"They can't feel their victims' emotions," Lindy murmured.

"Precisely," Mariamne hissed. "They would butcher anyone who tried to join us if we attempted a coup. There are too many of them. I will never risk such a thing…no matter how easy the Renegade makes it sound."

Silence fell. Everyone looked at each other uneasily. Ethan noticed Jarvis had gone pale but showed no signs of antagonism towards Lindy—only sheepish respect. Far more unsettling was the interest with which Ethan's mother peered at Lindy. That rarely meant anything good…at least not in Ethan's experience.

"Now," Mariamne said, her voice softer, "did you have anything else to ask?"

Lindy set her tablet on the table and shook her head. "No. Well, wait—there *is* one more thing. On the way to Valya, could… could one of you teach me how to use my gift?"

The mood abruptly changed. A surprised but undeniably pleased noise burst out of Councilor Tremaine. Princess Verrona raised her eyebrows.

"You speak of your empathy?" she asked.

Lindy nodded. "I can use it, but I block it so often that I'm not very good at it."

Princess Veronna gave a sharp nod and sat back, folding her plump arms. "Come by my quarters once we are aboard the *Hummingbird,* Miss Tremaine, and my daughter Talila and I will train you—with pleasure."

"Aunt," Mariamne murmured.

"You object to one of our own embracing her heritage, Mariamne?" Veronna retorted.

"Especially one with Margaret Tremaine's knack for getting to the bottom of things?" President Stagg interjected.

Mariamne glanced from her aunt to Lindy, blinked, and shut her mouth. Veronna smirked, and this time Ethan couldn't help but grin—both at Mariamne's obvious shock and at Lindy's equally obvious delight.

This was going to be a fascinating trip.

Chapter Ten

"Mama?"

"Shh, Lin, I'm here…I'm here…"

Mama's hand on her cheek. Guards shouting, prisoners whimpering, mud squishing beneath four thousand feet. Swirling fog, damp breeze. People hovering like bees in a swarm.

"I love you, Lin. I love you so much. Come on, let's say your prayers, all right? 'Elyon Above, ruler of the stars, blessed be thy holy name. Thy realm divine—'"

Lindy woke with a gasp, her eyes flying open before the nightmare could reach its usual climax. The horrific field outside Cor Danem's walls faded from her mind as she bolted upright; she was safe in the dark warmth of her bedroom in Whitesmith. Yet she still clapped a hand to her throbbing chest, trying desperately to calm down.

It's all right. It's just another dream, no different than the ones I've had every night since Mariamne told us about those soldiers. It'll get better once we leave tomorrow. It has *to.*

Groaning, Lindy slid out of bed and staggered to the window. After the thunderstorms of the past week, the weathermen had finally predicted a light, late autumn snowfall. Fine, swirling flakes met her gaze when she drew back the curtain. Even the windowpane was icy to the touch.

It felt weird, then, to know that it would be springtime on Valya. The field where Mama and two thousand other people died was probably full of wildflowers by now.

Lindy shivered and let her hand drop away from the curtain. With a weary sigh, she pulled a sweatshirt over her head and tiptoed out of the room. Except for the hum of the heater and Jo's snores in the guest room, the house was quiet. Lindy crept downstairs, avoiding the creaky steps, and had just reached the final one when Winston popped his head around the corner and meowed.

"Hey, sweet boy," she whispered. "Will you miss me while you're staying with the Pockets?"

Winston purred. Lindy scooped him up and wandered into the kitchen, reaching into the cabinet for a glass. As she filled it, she glanced up and caught her reflection in the window.

It startled her. She looked haggard. Hours and hours of preparation, physical training, research, and nightmares could do that to a person. She took a sip of water with a grimace, wondering if maybe, just maybe, this mission simply wasn't worth the emotional turmoil.

"Melinda?"

Lindy almost dropped the glass *and* the cat. Nana stood in the doorway, her hair covered in netting to protect her new perm, her pink night robe shimmering in the dim light. Lindy swallowed the mouthful of water and coughed hard.

"Holy krikalilly, Nana. You scared me."

Nana frowned. "You look terrible, dear. Are you all right?"

The question was so genuinely worried and honest, a sardonic reply seemed petty. Lindy set the glass in the sink and put Winston back on the floor. "I'm fine. It was just a bad dream."

Nana's frown melted. "Another one? Oh, Melinda."

Lindy looked at her bare feet. Nana sighed and stepped further into the kitchen. Lindy lifted her head in surprise as Nana wrapped one arm around her and took her hand.

"Come with me," Nana whispered. "There's something I want to show you."

She led Lindy into her study, Winston on their heels. Scattered tablets and paperwork all over Nana's desk suggested she'd been in here ever since she shooed Lindy and Jo to bed. Lindy gave her a reproachful look.

"You sent Jo and I upstairs, fussing about how we have a big day tomorrow, and *you* haven't gone to bed yourself?"

"Oh, don't be silly," Nana said, releasing Lindy and stepping behind her desk. "I don't need as much rest as two growing girls."

Lindy laughed. "We're twenty-eight years old, and you're—!"

"Not as young as you," Nana interrupted, her eyes twinkling.

Lindy smirked. Nana sat down and opened one of the desk's drawers. Everything about the study—the furniture, the books on the shelves, the lush rug beneath Lindy's feet—was warm, cozy, and comfortingly familiar…unlike the tiny wooden box Nana withdrew from the drawer. Lindy drew closer, curious.

"Before I give this to you," Nana said gravely, "I want you to know that everything I've done for you, I've done because I wanted you to heal as well as you possibly could. I realize that sometimes it seemed like I was rushing you, other times like I was trying to hold you back or even…" She lowered her gaze to the box. "Or even keeping certain information from you."

Before she could stop it, Lindy's observational training kicked in. For a moment, she even felt guilty about it—until she remembered what had happened with Genevieve. She shook the guilt away and took careful note of Nana's downward glance, her hesitant speech, the way she set the box down like it burned her and pushed it towards Lindy. Warily, Lindy took the box and pried the lid open.

Inside lay a gold pendant fashioned in the image of an insect, complete with black stripes and tiny, delicate wings, hanging by a thin golden chain. Lindy's breath caught. The sight made something tingle and writhe in the back of her head as if it was trying to claw itself out of a shallow, smothering grave.

"When someone left you at Maria Stagg's shelter," Nana murmured, "you were wearing that. She and her people thought that someone might be able to use it to identify you. Once it was obvious you couldn't tell them anything about yourself, they zipped it up in a little plastic bag and tucked it into your personal file. When I adopted you, the hospital staff gave it to me."

Lindy stared at her. "And you never showed this to me?"

"I did, once. You'd just started talking again. When I left it on the table with some of your toys, you took one look at it and didn't say a word for the rest of the day. It frightened me. So I decided to keep it safe until you were ready for it."

Lindy swallowed hard and lifted the pendant out of its box. The bee glinted in the light. She set it in her palm and ran her finger over it—then jerked her head up and stared at Nana with wide, eager eyes.

"*Bees!*" she cried. "In the nightmare, the other people in the field crowd around me and my mother, and Dream-Me always thinks they look like a swarm of bees. And then I start remembering something my father said about how swarms operate!"

Nana raised her eyebrows. "Do you think there could be a connection?"

"I don't know, but it's more of a clue than I've ever had. Not that I've ever been looking for clues," Lindy added softly. "But I'm glad to have one now."

Nana said nothing. Lindy clasped the chain around her neck. It was long; the bee lay right in the middle of her chest. On an impulse she couldn't explain, Lindy slipped it beneath her sweatshirt. The pendant felt cold and hard against her skin.

"I think that's a good idea," Nana said. "There's always the possibility someone on Valya might recognize it. Since your parents were likely noble or associated with a noble family, we wouldn't want to cause any trouble. There'll be enough tension to deal with already."

"You're probably right," Lindy said, drawing her hair out from under the chain. She paused, looking hard at the older woman. "Did *you* ever try to find out who my parents were?"

Nana looked straight at her. Lindy took note of it.

"No," Nana said firmly. "I never tried to find out. Are you angry?"

Lindy shook her head. "How could I be when I've never been interested myself?"

Nana relaxed. Lindy walked around the desk, knelt in front of Nana, and took her hands. As she did, she lowered her shields and felt her grandmother's affection pulsing into her own skin.

"Sometimes you make me want to throw things, Nana. But I really do love you so much."

Nana laughed, smoothing Lindy's hair. "Am I really that infuriating?"

"Sometimes. But I don't want you to ever doubt that I love you. Okay?"

Nana cupped her face in both hands. "Okay…as long as you promise never to doubt it on my end, either, my lionhearted girl."

Lindy gripped her grandmother's wrists and nodded. Nana watched her a moment longer, stroking her cheeks with her thumbs before drawing herself up with a nod.

"Now then—off to bed with both of us. The journalists will be out in force in the morning. We certainly don't want to look like death warmed over."

"Well, you weren't kidding about the journalists," Lindy muttered, peering out the dining room window. "I just thought they'd be waiting for us at the novaport."

Nana snorted. "After the role I played in arranging this mess, I'm surprised they weren't camped out last *night.* We can probably thank the snow for that."

"I'm ready!" Jo cried, slamming her suitcase on the bottom stair. "I sure hope the Valyans have some kind of laundry service. If we're there longer than a week, I'm gonna run out of clean clothes."

"Athena's given us an allowance," Lindy said, letting the curtain drop. "If we need to buy any clothes or even extra luggage, we can."

Jo raised an eyebrow. "I'm surprised she gave you more than a pittance after she threw that fit over postponing Genevieve's interview."

Lindy rolled her eyes, but Nana clapped before she could respond. "All right, you two, let me look at you."

Jo threw back her shoulders; Lindy assumed a more relaxed stance beside her. Nana folded her arms over her blue blazer, drumming her fingers and humming her approval.

"Well, you both look very professional, and those peacoats are *adorable.* It's just a shame you're limited to slacks. You both look so lovely in dresses."

"The better to run in an emergency, my dear Councilor!" Jo laughed. "So, are we ready to face the gauntlet? I'm getting antsy."

Nana and Lindy glanced at each other, and Lindy sucked in a breath. *This is it. The second I walk out that door, I'm on my way to Valya.* But for once, the idea didn't paralyze her. She touched the tiny bee, trapped between her red turtleneck and her breastbone, and nodded.

Nana smiled. "Let's show these people what Meridian women are made of," she whispered. She patted both Jo and Lindy's cheeks, seized her own suitcase, and threw open the front door.

The crowd exploded. Lindy flinched. She'd never been on this side of journalism before, and she wasn't sure whether to be amused or insulted by the strange, frantic faces and the microphones and holocams pressing in on them. Nana, however, simply ignored them, holding her head high as she pulled her luggage behind her across the snow-dusted path. The crowd parted, but the roar grew louder.

"Councilor Tremaine, what are your hopes for the Valyan Conference?"

"Councilor, what do you say to those who suggest your involvement gives credence to the accusation that Meridian interferes too much in interplanetary affairs?"

"Councilor, do you think legitimizing the Remnant's cause will embolden other anti-totalitarian movements in the Star System?"

Nana didn't spare them a glance. The hover-taxi driver standing at attention beside his vehicle opened the back door; Nana thanked him and ducked inside. The journalists swarmed around the open door, barring Lindy's way.

"Excuse me!" she shouted. "Excuse me, I need to get through."

The journalists turned on her, jabbing microphones in her face. Lindy reeled, stumbling on Jo's foot.

"Miss Tremaine, how do you feel about accompanying the Councilor to Valya?"

"Can you give us any insight into the Councilor's game plan?"

"What would you say to Councilor Sackville's statement that, quote, 'the inclusion of a fashion journalist in the press attachment isn't just unnecessary, it's also blatant nepotism?'"

"Get off my foot!" Jo hissed. Lindy jerked her foot off Jo's, thrust her jaw forward, and glared at the closest reporter—the one who'd quoted Councilor Sackville, no less.

"I'll say it once, mister," she snapped. "Get out of our way. *Now.*"

Holocams clicked as the surprised reporter and his colleagues slowly obeyed. The exasperated driver took the last of the luggage. Lindy and Jo clambered in after Nana, and Jo slammed the door behind them.

"Good job," Nana said, smoothing her skirt. "Now just pretend they aren't even there."

"I can't believe you let me go into that profession," Lindy grumbled. "You all right, Jo?"

"Except for my poor abused toes, yes."

The taxi pulled away. Whitesmith streaked by, giving way to the highways and overpasses leading into New Harvelle. When they entered the vast novaport complex, they found more journalists and a throng of civilians lining both sides of the route. Lindy peered out the window. Some of the civilians carried placards. One woman, her long, wide-sleeved dress identifying her as a Valyan refugee, held one that read, "JUSTICE FOR VALYA." Another, carried by a Meridian in a business suit, read, "ARE WE OBLIGATED TO SOLVE THE GALAXY'S PROBLEMS?" Lindy glanced at her grandmother, but Nana was too busy scrolling through her mail on her comm to notice.

That, or she doesn't care.

"Councilor?" the driver asked. "You want me to head straight to the *Hummingbird*?"

"Hmm? Oh yes, please. Let's see, here's my security pass. Give it to the guard at the runway, will you? And there—you see it, girls? She's a fine ship, isn't she?"

Lindy leaned forward. Sure enough, a long, dark, sharp-nosed novacraft loomed over the smaller ships on the acres-wide runway. Admiration surged through her at the thought of Ethan Granger in the captain's seat.

As they rounded a corner, however, the driver stopped abruptly. Another larger vehicle had paused in front of the runway's security gate. The protestors gesticulated and shouted at the passengers inside. Even with soundproof walls, Lindy could tell the mood was dark and angry.

"Nana?"

"Yes, I see them." Nana snapped her purse shut and sat up straight. "Do you remember, Lindy, when you asked Mariamne if she would ever take Valya back by force? Well, those are the Manwaring Radicals—Valyans who'd be tickled pink if Mariamne started a war. It's a shame they don't realize what a bloodbath that would be."

Lindy and Jo shared a glance. What was it Jarvis had said? *"For the princess to meet with them in secret incriminates her in the Renegade's public call for a rebellion against Rael."*

"They don't look happy," Jo muttered.

"Why should they be? This conference isn't exactly a great setup for a revolution." Nana craned her neck to the side. "And if I'm not mistaken, that's the Navorres' limo. Poor Mariamne."

Lindy narrowed her eyes and tried to focus on reading the protestors' lips. It wasn't easy—the Valyan accent complicated matters—but she did catch words like "betrayal" and "home" and "monster."

Still, she couldn't help feeling relieved. If Mariamne *had* promised the radicals a revolution, the crowd probably wouldn't be so vitriolic.

Ethan Granger stood at the bottom of the *Hummingbird*'s boarding ramp with his senior officers and tried not to slam his hands into the pockets of his uniform. Any warmth the high-collared green coat and black pants had absorbed while he ironed them smooth this morning had faded away as soon as he headed down the ramp ten minutes ago. His toes tingled inside his gleaming boots; his ears burned beneath the stiff dress hat.

Come on, we're freezing out here, he thought, squinting at the hovers lined up behind the security gate. The foremost one, he knew, probably carried his mother. She loved being the first person on the scene.

Genevieve would be with her, though. Ethan slipped a finger between his collar and his neck and cleared his throat.

"Put on a pound or two since you last wore it, Captain?" Frank Gridley asked.

Ethan cut his eyes at him and at Lieutenant Cornael, who covered her mouth to stifle a giggle. "Should've known that comment would come back to bite me."

Frank chuckled. "I'm just kidding. Miss Tremaine is gonna be very impressed."

"Miss Tremaine?" Commander Aeron repeated. "Is she any relation to the Councilor?"

Ethan frowned. "She's the Councilor's granddaughter. Part of the press pool. Frank, why on earth would she..."

Frank raised his eyebrows. "Oh, come *on*, Captain."

Lieutenant Commander Parsons' craggy face crinkled in a knowing grin. "Ahhhhh..."

"I know, right?" Frank cried.

"Is she pretty?" Cornael whispered.

"Gorgeous," Frank said. "Although, personally, her photographer is more my type."

"What does any of this have to do with my uniform?" Ethan demanded.

Aeron smirked. "I believe Mr. Gridley is implying some kind of attraction between you and Miss Tremaine."

"What?"

"She did walk in on you in the bathroom," Frank said. "On purpose."

"Wait, what?!" Cornael shrieked.

"Okay, okay, that's enough," Ethan snapped. "Stand at attention. The president's hover just got cleared."

Frank and Cornael obeyed with a final snicker, while Aeron and Parsons drew themselves up and adopted remarkably stoic expressions. Ethan fixed his eyes on the approaching hover-limo and hoped, as its landing gear locked onto the tarmac, that his face hadn't turned red. The door slid open, the ramp came down, and President Maria Stagg stepped out.

Ethan tipped his head back. His mother wore a dark red blazer and skirt; black netting draped her upper face from the black fascinator perched on the side of her head. The officers put their fists to their shoulders in a salute. President Stagg smiled and folded her gloved hands at her waist.

"At ease, soldiers," she said smoothly.

They relaxed, Ethan excepted. He was too busy watching the servant-droid as it stepped out of the hover and offered a hand to Genevieve. His mother advanced on him before he could focus too long on the unsteady figure maneuvering herself out of the vehicle.

"Captain Granger," she said. "How lovely to see you."

Ethan forced himself to look at her. "Lady President."

She glanced up at the *Hummingbird*'s massive underbelly. "So this is your ship. I've never seen it this close. Is she everything you dreamed she'd be?"

"That and more."

"Hmm. I've been aboard nova-yachts five times her size. I'm surprised the Nova Force didn't select a ship along those lines, considering you'll have royalty aboard."

Ethan narrowed his eyes. "A yacht doesn't have the necessary defense procedures for guests this important, *Mother*."

Her veneer of cool contempt vanished, turning to irritated embarrassment. Ethan smothered a rush of petty triumph and gestured to his command crew.

"Ma'am, may I present my senior officers? Commander Aeron, first officer; Lieutenant Commander Parsons, weapons chief; Lieutenant Cornael, communications; and Lieutenant Gridley, IT Security Chief."

"Ah, so pleased to meet you," President Stagg said, flashing the famous smile that won so many votes. Ethan stepped back as she shook each officer's hand. By the time she'd finished, the Navorres and their entourage had rolled up in their hovers; within seconds, the tarmac swarmed with elegantly dressed aristocrats, their servants, and the carefully selected press pool.

Ethan, however, slipped off to the side and drifted with exaggerated stealth towards his mother's vehicle. Genevieve grinned and took slow steps towards him on the droid's arm. Ethan took the hand she extended to him, drawing her away from Cephas.

"This is one of your good days, isn't it?" he whispered.

She nodded with a flash of happy pride. "You can tell?"

"Of course I can. You've even got a little spring in your step." He stroked her hand with his thumbs. "You take care of yourself while I'm gone, got it?"

"I will. And *you* have a good time. I'll be watching the news every day to see if I can get a glimpse of you."

Ethan chuckled. "Got any weird requests for a souvenir?"

"I already told you. A sister-in-law would be just fine."

He rolled his eyes. She laughed, then freed her hand and wrapped her arms around him. He returned the hug, his chest aching as he realized how small and thin she felt.

"Stay safe, Ethan," she whispered. "If you need anything, you know where I am."

Ethan rested his cheek against her soft brown hair and said nothing. He held her as tightly as he dared, wishing he could've taken her away with him when he ran away all those years ago.

By the time the local journalists wrapped up one last group photo of the delegation, Lindy wanted to jump out of her skin. If her own interviewees hated sitting for obligatory photo shoots as much as she did, she and Jo would make a concerted effort to speed them up in the future.

"It's gonna be a wide picture," Jo muttered out of the side of her mouth. "I could cross my eyes and nobody would notice until too late."

Lindy snickered. "Don't you dare."

Jo sighed and mustered such a forced smile, she might've looked better if she *had* crossed her eyes. Mariamne wasn't even trying to look pleasant anymore. Only President Stagg acted like she was still enjoying herself, chatting with the reporters and sparring with Nana while she posed and smiled and flattered.

Genevieve and Ethan looked as if simply watching their mother exhausted them. Lindy glanced back and forth between them and the President. What did they see or hear that she couldn't?

She got her answer sooner than she expected. While the Navorres posed with Nana for a final round of pictures, Lindy saw Ethan storming to the far edge of the *Hummingbird*'s grey hulk. His fists were at his sides, his eyes fixed straight ahead, and his mother strode alongside him. Lindy couldn't hear what she said, but when the President grabbed Ethan's sleeve and jabbed a finger under his chin, Lindy's stomach tied itself in a knot.

"Hey," Jo said, coming up beside her. "They want us to start boarding."

"Wait," Lindy whispered.

President Stagg lowered her hand and spun away from her son. Her face was so hard and tight with anger, she barely resembled the pretty, charming stateswoman she'd been just a few minutes ago. Lindy folded her arms and shifted her weight to one leg in a challenging stance, just as the woman who all but saved her life twenty-three years ago happened to glance up.

President Stagg saw her and froze. Lindy narrowed her eyes. The President drew in a shaky breath, clamped her lips, and strode briskly to the hover, scrambling inside beside her daughter. Lindy didn't move until they drove away.

"I suggest," Ethan said quietly behind her, "that the two of you get to your quarters. We'll be lifting off in twenty minutes, tops."

Lindy nodded and gave Jo a gentle pat on her arm. Jo took the hint—but not without a meaningful look at the two of them—and hurried up the ramp. Ethan held out a hand, inviting Lindy to go ahead of him.

"I saw the way she treated you," she whispered. "And I made sure she knew I saw."

Ethan raised his eyebrows. "Not sure what good you thought it would do."

"I'm a journalist. We see a lot, and then we write about it."

His broad forehead crinkled. "You wouldn't."

"No, of course not. I don't even know what you two were talking about. Still..." Lindy patted the messenger bag slung over her shoulder. "There's a lot of power in the *threat* of a fully-functional pen. And we're not even accounting for Genevieve's interview yet."

Ethan smirked. "You're not afraid to throw your weight around, are you?"

Lindy looked at his stern, handsome face, took note of the weariness in his blue eyes...and recalled the way he'd looked in that Xandroan hotel room, with his hair sticking up all over the back of his head while he spread jam on his bagel and encouraged her to face her fears. The thought of anyone tearing down a friend like that made her want to smack somebody.

"I'm *known* for throwing my weight around for my fellow troopers," she said. "And you, sir, are no exception."

Chapter Eleven

"All passengers are aboard, Captain," Lieutenant Cornael announced as Ethan returned to the bridge. "Prince Lhoris sends his compliments from the guest suite, and Princess Mariamne requests extra towels."

Ethan snorted. Cornael might've been a Valyan herself, yet she didn't seem awed by the presence of Valyan royalty. "Trust Mariamne to find fault somewhere. Tell Her Highness we'll see about the towels as soon as we're underway. Engine Room, how're we doing?"

The reply came quickly over the intercom: "Right on schedule, sir. Ready for liftoff in five minutes."

Aeron frowned at Ethan from his station. "Where have you been, sir?"

"Escorting Miss Tremaine and Miss Camrin to their quarters." Ethan leaned back, ignoring the pointed looks his officers—especially Frank—gave each other. "Cornael, inform the novaport we're on schedule and that we request the opening of the orbital gate."

"Aye-aye, sir."

Ethan swiveled his chair towards the window. The view wasn't much to talk about at the moment, just a stretch of concrete with the novaport's central hub off in the distance and smaller ships scattered on the landing pads. But it was still New Harvelle, and he wanted a good look at his home planet before he left it behind again.

Everything would be different once he returned. Genevieve would speak out, and their mother would realize she didn't have nearly the control she thought she did.

"Don't you dare forget you serve at *my* pleasure, no matter which hat you're wearing," she'd hissed right before she stormed back to her hover. "Captain, trooper, son—it doesn't matter. The minute I catch you trying to sway your sister or anyone else against me is the moment you find out who's in charge in this family."

Ethan inhaled and drummed his fingers on the arms of his seat. It obviously never crossed her mind that he and Genevieve never actually wanted to antagonize her. But in her mind, a rejection of her lifestyle and her vision for them had always been a rejection of *her.* She refused to consider an alternative. She didn't *want* to.

And this is why it's probably time to stop worrying about what she thinks.

The thought hit him with the force of a wave. Why worry about something he could never change, no matter what he did? At the end of the day, he answered to Elyon and to Meridian.

And if he ever needed help, at least Lindy Tremaine and Genevieve had his back.

What more could he ask for?

Lindy emerged from the bathroom the following morning to find Jo darting from one end of their cabin to the other, waving one of the lipstick scanners over the walls. Lindy approached warily, rubbing her wet hair in a fluffy towel.

"What in the world are you doing?" she asked.

Jo shot her an irritated look. "Testing our equipment."

Lindy chortled. "What, you think our cabin is bugged?"

Jo said nothing and kept scanning. Lindy frowned and moved closer.

"You know you don't have to worry about that, Jo. Nobody can get in here without our handprint or unless we let them in. Ethan said so. Those biosensors on the door are foolproof."

Again, Jo remained silent. She snapped the top back on the tube and threw herself onto the couch. Lindy sat beside her.

"Talk to me, Trooper."

Jo cut her eyes at her. "You promise you won't laugh?"

"Have I ever laughed at your suspicions?"

"Um, *yeah*. Remember when I was sure that that Terithian tradesman had put poisonous spices on your calamari?"

Lindy grinned. "But did I die?"

Jo snorted and twirled the scanner between her fingers. After a moment in which Lindy maintained a patient silence, she finally sighed and fixed her eyes straight ahead.

"I think Prince Lhoris is spying on us."

"Prince Lhoris?!"

"There, see? I knew you'd think I was crazy!"

"No, no," Lindy said, squeezing Jo's arm. "I don't think you're crazy. Just tell me what you're feeling. Or thinking. Or seeing. Whatever."

Jo exhaled. "Okay. *Okay*. While you were in the shower, I went to the cafeteria for breakfast—they've got doughnuts, by the way, in case you're interested—and Lhoris was in there, talking to the guy from the *Gazette*."

Lindy nodded. "Perry Ambrose. The *Gazette* is pretty pro-Valyan, so I'm not surprised."

"Yeah, well. They were whispering at the bar, and when I walked in, they gave me this long, long look...like they'd been talking about me. I decided to just ignore them and get my breakfast cuz, you know, guys can be weird."

Lindy raised an eyebrow but declined to comment.

"*Anyway,*" Jo went on, "they left before I did. But when I was coming back here, guess who was trying his hand at the biosensor? For *our* cabin?"

Lindy's other eyebrow went up. "Ambrose?"

"No! *Lhoris.* And not only that, but he put his ear to the door like he was listening. Now *you* explain *that.*"

Lindy glanced at the door. "Well...maybe he wanted to discuss the mission with us. And maybe he put his ear to the door because—"

"Because?"

"Because he heard me singing in the shower and decided he'd better not bother me?"

Jo scoffed.

"On the other hand," Lindy muttered, "why would Lhoris be talking about *you* to Perry Ambrose?"

"I don't really know that they were talking about me," Jo admitted.

"But their body language suggested it, and you've gone through too much observational training to make a groundless call." Lindy tossed the towel over her shoulder and stepped into the cabin's narrow front section. Their laptop, linked since last night to the encrypted MID network, sat side-by-side on the workstation. Lindy bent over hers and started typing.

"What are you doing?" Jo asked.

"Requesting any info MID might have on Perry Ambrose. If he's got some kind of connection to Lhoris—or any Valyan faction, for that matter—we should know. And if there is a connection but they're short on details, I may need a surveillance warrant."

"Why contact MID when you're about to go see Princess Verrona for your training?"

Lindy stopped typing. "What do you mean?"

Jo shrugged. "Well, you *did* just up and confront Mariamne about her political views the other day. Why not ask her aunt what Mariamne's husband was doing outside our cabin?"

Lindy shook her head and submitted the request. "Nah. We don't know how long we'll be with these people. I'd rather not get on their bad side. But after I'm finished with Verrona, I *will* have a word with Ethan. Make you feel better?"

"Yeah, I guess." Jo scratched her scalp. "Can I have the shower now?"

"Yep." Lindy fluttered her eyelashes as she sauntered back into the cabin's living section. "Go on, Miss Camrin. Tidy yourself up for your handsome Officer Gridley."

Jo turned bright pink and tried to swat her, but Lindy giggled and leaped out of the way.

When Lindy stepped out of the cabin a few minutes later, she found the corridor empty. She heard the voices of the off-duty crew coming from the cafeteria but saw no sign of Prince Lhoris or any other Valyan anywhere.

I have a hard time thinking the prince would stoop to plain old-fashioned snooping, she thought as she stepped into the lift. *He's more clever than that. Surely he just wanted to discuss the mission.*

But why didn't he just approach Jo? Why would he come to our cabin when he knew I was the only one in there?

Every sordid, ridiculous explanation more appropriate for a tabloid promptly offered itself up for consideration. In the privacy of the lift, Lindy actually snickered. *Head in the game, Trooper. Head in the game.*

The lift opened. Last night Lindy came up here for dinner with Nana, and she'd been so stunned, she had to remind herself to step out. Deck A was finer than anything she would've expected on a patrol ship. There were fewer but much larger cabins than on Deck C, and the walls were all painted a snowy, elegant white. Stepping up to Cabin A-3, she squared her shoulders and put her hand to the biosensor. The door chimed delicately.

"Coming!" someone called. Lindy took a step back. The door opened, and her nervousness melted at the sight of a beaming Princess Talila. *Tali,* Lindy thought, recalling the princess's preferred nickname.

"Good morning, Your Highness," she said, offering an awkward curtsey in her blue jeans.

The teenage princess giggled. "Miss Tremaine," she said as she returned the gesture, her navy-blue skirts pooling on the floor. Then she sprang up and eagerly motioned for Lindy to come inside.

"Mama and I have been so excited about seeing you," she gushed. "You received her message last night, then, about your training?"

"I did," Lindy replied, quickly assessing the white-and-blue room. "I was thrilled she even remembered us talking about it the other day. I didn't want to bother her by asking again."

"Oh no, it wouldn't have bothered her! Your grandmother has been a good friend to us. We'd be happy to do anything for one of her own. And..." Tali shyly lowered her eyes. "You were so nice at the hospital. So kind...and pretty."

Lindy laughed. "Well, thank you—both for the compliment and for being the only one there willing to make friends with me right away."

Tali raised her eyebrows, but before she could reply, a side door opened. Princess Verrona hefted herself out of the sleeper and up into the main room with a groan.

"Oh, my knees. I swear, I wish I hadn't made fun of my old grandmother when she hobbled around..." She glanced up, her round face brightening. "Miss Tremaine! You've come at last!"

Lindy made another attempt at a curtsey. "Your Highness..."

"Oh, enough with the formalities! Tali, did you offer her anything to eat or drink?"

At the sight of Tali's embarrassed wince, Lindy hastily intervened. "I only just got here. She didn't have time to offer—and to be honest, I wasn't expecting refreshments. It's okay."

"But it's an *honor,*" Verrona insisted. "Even the poorest Valyan offers his guest a glass of water. What would you like, my dear?"

Lindy blinked. "A, umm…a glass of water would be fine."

Verrona nodded to her daughter; Tali nodded back and disappeared into the kitchenette. Verrona motioned to one of the couches and sat down, clasping her plump hands in her lap. Lindy sat beside her, but on the very edge.

"Now, let's get down to business," Verrona said. "Tell me what you know of your gift."

"Umm." Lindy cleared her throat, her mind racing. "Well…I know that if I touch someone, I can detect their emotions. And I can raise my shields if I don't want that level of…awareness."

Verrona screwed up her face. "Shields? Wherever did you hear *that* term?"

"The net."

Verrona's eyebrows skyrocketed. Lindy squirmed.

"I was a teenager," she admitted. "My abilities were maturing, I guess, and the emotions were getting more intense if I touched someone. I didn't want that burden all the time."

Verrona sighed. "Well, I can't chide you for it. We've seen this often enough, especially with younger Valyans who simply want to blend in and forget where they came from. But you can't be a chameleon your entire life, can you?"

Lindy looked down and rubbed her hands together. "Some of us try."

Verrona moved a little closer. "Melinda…may I call you that?"

Lindy tried to smile. "I'd rather you called me 'Lindy.' Almost everyone does."

"Very well, Lindy. Margaret told me you survived the Cor Danem Massacre. My brother, Kalen, his wife, and his daughters all died that night...so I *do* know what it's like, to want to forget. But to turn our back on who we are? It makes us no better than Rael or his giftless soldiers."

Lindy drew a shaky breath. "Then what about the...whatever-it's-called?"

"The Shelter?" Verrona smiled like she had a secret. "You should first know what it is like to use the gift *without* it. Here. Give me your hand. Come now! I won't bite."

Lindy's heart pounded. She stretched out a hand. Verrona took it, and Lindy gasped at the explosion of *feeling* inside her chest. Verrona applied pressure. Lindy drew another sharp breath and shut her eyes tight.

She wasn't sure whether to be terrified or ecstatic. The depth of emotion thundering out of the princess and through the pores of her own skin stunned her—and oh, the *colors*! It had to be instinct—Verrona hadn't mentioned it and she certainly didn't remember learning about it—yet she knew, without being told, exactly what the soft purple filling her mind meant. And the pale pinks swirling in and around the purple...*they* meant...

Verrona withdrew her hand. "Well?"

Lindy swallowed, opened her eyes, gasped for breath. "I *saw* it. I saw the feelings."

"In color?"

"Yes! Purple and...and pink!"

"Good, good! Purple would be my concern for you. Red Fear with blue Sadness. The pink is a mix of Fear and white Joy, and it is nothing but curiosity. You have a fascinating Emanation, Lindy. Quite fascinating."

"But the Fear? You're not afraid of me, are you?"

"Oh no, no, not strictly *afraid*. But you are new and different. There's always a certain trepidation over the unknown, isn't there?"

Lindy nodded. "I've never experienced *that* before. I've touched people without the shield—I mean, the Shelter. But..."

"But they've always been Meridians, haven't they?" Verrona chuckled. "They don't have the gift. They can't channel their emotions back to you and theirs aren't nearly as strong as ours—although you will occasionally meet a passionate one who'll surprise you."

Tali returned at that moment with a tray. "I brought water and some of those cookies I found in the cabinet last night. This is a good excuse for a snack, isn't it?"

"As good an excuse as any," Verrona said. "Lindy, would you like one?"

Lindy pressed her lips together and nodded, trying to control her excitement. Tali knelt by the coffee table and tore open the packet, setting the cookies on small white plates. When she held out both a plate and a glass dripping with condensation, Lindy hesitated and glanced at Verrona.

"If our hands brush, will we…you know?" she asked.

Verrona looked at her daughter. Tali's eyes widened.

"Ohhh," she murmured. "Would you rather I used my Shelter? If you do not wish to feel my Emanation, I do not mind."

Shelter! Lindy thought. *It's not a wall or a shield. It's just a safe place. A haven, not a barrier. And there's that word again, too—Emanation.*

"No," Lindy said. "I'd rather feel it. At least this one time."

Tali smiled, relieved. Lindy drew a breath and reached out.

As soon as their hands made contact, yellow-tinged white flooded her head—but Lindy didn't close her eyes this time. She took the plate as calmly as she could and sat back. Tali and Verrona leaned forward.

"What did you see?" Verrona asked.

Lindy grinned at Tali. "Admiration, I think. And just…sheer happiness."

Verrona smirked. "That sounds like my child. And did you feel *her* Emanation, Tali?"

"Oh, yes!"

"What were my colors?" Lindy asked eagerly.

Tali beamed up at her. "White. Just white."

Emotional fingerprints. That, Lindy realized, was the best way to describe Emanations. Verrona's carried good-natured wisdom and dry humor, while Tali's was all sunshine and stubborn optimism. And they sheltered only out of courtesy to strangers. You didn't just go around sharing your Emanation with people you didn't know. That would be rude.

"Valyan families, on the other hand, are like open books with each other," Verrona explained. "I think you'll find, if you spend enough time with us, that we are quite affectionate amongst ourselves. Physical touch is critical to the way we love. It is part of truly knowing another person."

"Which is why," Tali muttered, "you ought *never* to spend too much time with Mariamne and Lhoris at the same time. They will make you sick."

Lindy almost choked on her cookie. "I never would've thought! Mariamne's just so..."

She stopped, not wanting to say anything insulting. Verrona offered her hand.

"Here," she said. "Tell me."

This time, Lindy didn't hesitate. She took Verrona's hand and focused on her memories of Mariamne at the hospital...of Mariamne sneering down at her...of the simmering contempt in Mariamne's voice. Just thinking about it made the blood rush to her face.

Verrona drew her hand back. Lindy opened her eyes, alarmed.

"I'm sorry. She's just..."

"No," Verrona said firmly. "Don't be sorry. If people have no love for Mariamne, it's her own fault. She has not learned to act like a leader."

Before Lindy could reply, the door chimed. Tali scrambled to her feet to answer it. At the sight of Mariamne standing in the doorway, Verrona went stiff as a board.

"Hello, Tali," Mariamne said, her voice unusually warm. She wore a blue dressing gown, an outfit that not only set off the startling whiteness of her hair but made her seem shorter and less… well, intimidating. Lindy stared in wonderment as Mariamne cupped Tali's round cheek in her hand and smiled. "How are you?"

"I-I'm well," Tali stammered. "We have company."

Mariamne took one look at Lindy and her smile went cold. Lindy sat up straighter.

"Have a seat, love," Verrona said calmly. "Tali and I have been explaining the Valyan gift to Lindy all morning. She is an excellent student."

Mariamne looked from Lindy to Verrona; one slender eyebrow climbed as she lowered herself into one of the chairs next to the couch. She leaned back, crossed her legs, and looked so intently at her aunt that Lindy knew she was trying to ignore *her*.

"Lhoris is making good use of the gymnasium," Mariamne said. "By the time we reach Valya, he will have exercised himself into utter weariness."

The gym, Lindy thought. *Good, I'll try to catch him there later.*

"I'm sure he's enjoying himself," Verrona said. "Nhormin told me there's a swimming pool as well. His rheumatism has given him considerable trouble lately, you know. The water apparently brought great relief."

Mariamne snorted. "Perhaps if he's too busy soaking his bones, he'll have no time to lecture me on keeping my head in Rael's presence."

Verrona handed her the cookies. "Never fear. I can deliver that lecture myself, if necessary."

Mariamne smirked but didn't seem surprised or offended. She took a cookie and nibbled at it before turning her dark eyes on Lindy.

"So, Miss Tremaine, I hope you've learned that your gift is nothing to be ashamed of after all."

Verrona and Tali both went very still. Lindy inhaled, looked straight at Mariamne, and smiled.

"I wouldn't say I was ever ashamed of it," she said. "'Wary' might be a better word. But your aunt has been very kind to show me that it really is a gift and not a burden."

"Good," Mariamne said crisply. "Every refugee should know that the key to reclaiming our culture is not by force but by returning to our roots. We will never win our nation back if we come home looking and talking like…aliens."

With that, she raked her gaze over Lindy's Meridian clothes just as she had at the hospital.

"Mariamne!" Verrona hissed. "That is no way to speak of the planet that gave us asylum. If Meridian had not opened its doors to us, to *you*…"

"I would've been slaughtered in the field outside Cor Danem, too?" Mariamne finished, studying her cookie's underside. "Perhaps. Sometimes I think it would have been better if I had been. At least then I would have no reason to be embarrassed by my own people, nor would I be forced to attend a conference that may prove to be an utter waste of time."

Lindy narrowed her eyes. "Sounds like you've already decided it's a hopeless case."

Mariamne sniffed, sweeping crumbs off her robe. "Yes, well. I do not answer to you."

"Actually, you do. I'm here to keep you safe and everyone else on this ship out of trouble. If you're heading to the negotiating table without any real hope of success, why would you even go? I'm sorry, Your Highness, but I need an answer and I need it now."

Mariamne rose, smooth and imperious. "How dare you—"

"How dare *you*?" Lindy snapped, leaping to her feet. "How dare you talk like that about Valyans who found a home and peace and love on Meridian? Do you really resent us for rebuilding our lives instead of feeling sorry for ourselves or wallowing in hatred like you? Let me tell you something. I was there in that field and I hated myself for surviving when my mother didn't—so don't you *dare* talk to me about being ashamed ever again."

Mariamne said nothing; her mouth hung open and her eyes bulged. Lindy marched around the coffee table to the door, but before she hit the exit button, she swiveled on her heel.

"I asked you about the use of force the other day because our people saw you in Manwaring two months ago. I defended you because the surveillance was totally illegal. But if you put this delegation in danger, Captain Granger and I will drag you back to Meridian by the hair if we have to. You got that?"

Mariamne blinked. She started to speak, but Lindy rushed out before anyone could say a word.

Chapter Twelve

"What in the name of all that is good and holy did she mean by that?" Verrona demanded.

Mariamne didn't reply. She sat down slowly, gripping the arms of her chair. No one had ever confronted her like that before. Not that she could remember, anyway.

"Mariamne, speak to me!"

"I—I don't know," Mariamne stammered. "I don't know what she was talking about."

"Why do I find that so hard to believe?" her aunt retorted. "You've grown to hate Rael more than your father ever could, haven't you? If you've aligned yourself with those troublemakers…"

"I haven't!" Mariamne cried. "I swear I haven't!"

"Then what—"

"I don't know! I don't! Now stop it, I beg you, stop it!"

Her aunt obliged her. Mariamne drew a shaky breath and ran a hand through her hair. It had been years since it held a trace of black, and yet black was what filled her now: seething, hate-filled Anger, churning in her gut.

Oh yes, she hated Rael. She hated the Dominators, too, the "advisors" who'd filled her cousin with delusions of power. She hated Maria Stagg and her ships for whisking away the Valyan exiles who should've stayed and fought. She hated *them* and their scandalous Meridian clothes, their adopted customs, and the way they used the Shelter to smother their gift. She hated the Meridian doctors who hadn't saved her baby after they told her they *could*.

Sometimes, Lhoris and Tali were the only ones she couldn't hate.

"You should be ashamed of yourself," Verrona said coldly.

Mariamne jerked her head up. "What? *I* should—?"

"You think you can come waltzing in here and expect everyone to kiss your pretty little feet? Your family may be used to such treatment, dear, but *that* woman is certainly not."

"She disrespected me!"

"You disrespected her first. Did you really think anyone raised by Margaret Tremaine would submit to such contempt as yours? And you forget, too, that she is Valyan. We've never liked being treated as inferiors. The Revolution was proof of that, at the very least."

Mariamne glared at her aunt. "Really? You're legitimizing their cause now?"

"The people always had a cause, Mariamne. Rael only twisted it for his own purposes. If you refuse to acknowledge that, you're no better than the old kings and queens."

"Oh, well!" Mariamne cried, leaping to her feet. "I suppose I should start excusing the conformists next! The ones who've made peace with a foreign culture, telling the rest of the universe that Valyans are content with their lot? No, Aunt. I can *never* forgive them for that."

"Then get out of my sight," Verrona hissed. "I don't want to see you again until I can speak to you without slapping you across your face."

Mariamne blinked. Her aunt never made empty threats, and Mariamne didn't care to test this one. She stormed to the door, but when she reached it, she paused and looked over her shoulder.

"You may think ill of me if you like," she said. "But you may be certain I have not been to Manwaring. Two months ago, I had just lost the baby. The radicals could've rotted in a Meridian jail for all I would've cared."

"Good," Verrona snapped. "But you are the one who must share that with Miss Tremaine. And you'd best do it before you lose our only chance to help our planet."

The lift doors closed behind Lindy. Leaning against the wall, she squeezed her eyes shut, clenched her hands, and let out a furious, closed-lip scream. It felt surprisingly good—certainly preferable to slamming her fist against the wall and maybe breaking her hand.

Oh, I hate *that woman! I can't believe I ever thought she was brave. She's* not. *She's a bully, a coward, and a tyrant! Of course, after throwing the whole surveillance issue in her face, I'm either insubordinate or borderline insane. Probably both.*

Jarvis is gonna kill me…if Ethan doesn't do it first.

"Please choose your destination."

Lindy jumped at the computerized voice. Sniffling, she pressed a button and soon stepped out into the quiet corridors of Deck D. Frank had brought her and Jo down here last night when he gave them a tour of the ship. Most of the crew's quarters were here, along with the gym and the swimming hall. At this time of day, the place was mostly empty. She heard a few voices coming from the cafeteria but none from the gym—which was precisely where she wanted to go.

As soon as the gym door shut behind her, she rolled up her sleeves and pulled on a pair of punching gloves. The bag in the corner hung lazily from a chain. Lindy struck it with her fist. The bag gave a pathetic *thump.*

Gritting her teeth, she hit it again. This time it swayed a bit. Again and again, she slammed it as hard as she could, her breath coming in louder, angrier cries until she was too exhausted to throw another punch. Her chest heaved. Furious tears rolled down her face.

"Lindy?"

She whirled. Ethan Granger stood in the doorway, clad in a white t-shirt and lightweight khaki trousers. He took one look at her and sprang forward, the door hissing shut behind him.

"What happened to you?" he demanded, tossing aside the gloves and a towel he'd tucked under his arm. "What's wrong? Are you all right?"

"Yeah, I'm fine," Lindy lied, peeling off her gloves. "I'll leave…let you do whatever you do in here."

He glanced at the bag. "Well, normally I use *that,* but it looks like you beat me to the punch, so to speak."

Lindy tried to laugh, but her chin quivered and she ducked her head. Ethan put his hands on her shoulders.

"Talk to me, Trooper," he said gently.

She shook her head. "It's nothing."

He was silent. Thanks to the t-shirt, she could tell that he wasn't as heavily built as some of the other male troopers, but his shoulders and arms were still strong…masculine. Before she could stop herself, she wished he'd wrap her up in a warm, safe embrace, only to curl her toes in embarrassment at the very thought.

"We're working together, aren't we?" he prodded.

"Of course."

"Then I need to know what's bothering my friend."

Lindy forced herself to look up. "Mariamne and I…we had a fight."

"A fight?" he repeated.

Lindy inhaled and wound her way back to the beginning. She told him about Jo and Lhoris, about going to see Verrona, about the Emanation and the colors and the Shelter, about Mariamne's insults…and about the surveillance bombshell. Reliving that last part made her conscience feel as if it had been stuck with a red-hot poker.

But Ethan didn't say a word. His thick eyebrows knotted and unknotted as the story went on, but he never interrupted her. When she finished, he let out a long sigh. Lindy held her own breath.

"The Emanation," he muttered. "So you can only detect it by touch, right?"

"Huh?"

"It's not mind-reading or anything like—"

"I don't care about Emanations right now, Ethan! I've just jeopardized this mission by telling the rightful heiress of the Valyan throne to buzz off, *and* I violated a direct order by telling her about that surveillance! What do you want me to—"

Ethan clamped a hand over her mouth. Lindy froze.

"Listen to me," he said. "If your conscience is eating you alive about *that,* okay. Fine. You can feel guilty about that, and I won't try to make you feel better. But I'll bet you are the first person who ever got up in her face and told her, 'This far and no further,' and you are *not* allowed to beat yourself up about that. Not on my ship."

He pulled his hand back. Lindy stared at him. With a smirk, he gave her chin a little tap and her teeth clicked together.

"You were gaping," he explained. "Mouth open, like a fish."

"I—you—you're not going to declare me compromised? Make me sit this one out?"

He shrugged. "I guess I could if I wanted to. But I don't want to. Mariamne might actually toe the line now that she knows you won't take any nonsense from her. And Jarvis doesn't *have* to know that she knows."

"But she'll tell him!" Lindy cried.

"No, she won't," Ethan said, chuckling. "It would be far too incriminating. So here's what we'll do. We'll both go to Mariamne, offer an apology on MID's behalf, and explain that *we,* Tremaine and Granger, refuse to spy on her for the duration of this trip. But we *will* question her about her visit to Manwaring. She'll talk to us. Just watch."

"And if she goes screaming to MID about her privacy being violated anyway?"

Ethan raised his eyebrows. "Remember what you said about sticking your neck out for a fellow trooper? Goes both ways."

Lindy's vision blurred, but before she could thank him, a screeching wail assaulted her ears. Alarmed, Ethan turned away from her, striding to the intercom on the wall. He struck his fist against a button.

"Aeron, what's going on?" he called over the noise.

"The same thing that happened a couple weeks ago, Captain," Aeron replied. "The computer registers an unknown intruder, possibly another virus. Navigation is down and the emergency system has consequently braked us from lightspeed to impulse power."

"Navigation? Please don't tell me we're in the Asteroidea yet."

"Very well, sir. I won't tell you."

Ethan's jaw flexed. "On my way."

"What's going on?" Lindy asked.

He touched her shoulder. "Come with me. We've got a major problem."

If things hadn't been so chaotic, Lindy probably would've frozen on the threshold of the hexagonal bridge in awed delight. She'd done her fair share of traveling, yet she'd never stepped foot inside a novacraft's command center.

Jo would love this, she thought, taking in the computers, scientific instruments, and holographic screens. But then she noticed the alerts on every screen, the tense faces of the crew, and the huge asteroids sailing past the windows. *Nah. Jo doesn't need to be here.*

She and Ethan had kept pace with each other the whole way. Now he broke ahead of her and raced down the steps to the center of the bridge, throwing himself into the empty captain's seat.

"Report, Frank!" he ordered.

Frank spun in his chair at the security station, looking more serious than Lindy had ever seen him. "Basically the same story as last time, Captain. An incoming transmission jammed and then *boom*—intruder alerts all over the place. Only this time, the navigation computer is locked up, and the shields are affected too."

"Any ships in the area, Cornael?" Ethan demanded.

A fair-skinned redhead swiveled at the communications console. "Lieutenant Cornael is off-duty this morning, sir."

Ethan turned in surprise. "Oh! Sorry about that, Lieutenant...?"

"Mockett, sir. There's nobody in the area except for an unmanned, registered freighter six parsecs away, heading at sublight for Opitheldra. The signature from this interference is unrecognizable."

An asteroid bumped the window. The ship rocked; Lindy threw herself against the wall before she could tumble down the steps. Mockett's station erupted in flashing lights.

"The passengers are demanding to know what's going on, sir!" she cried.

"Tell them to stay in their cabins," Ethan snapped. He strode to the helm. "Have you tried punching in the navigation override, Mr. Potter?"

"I've tried, but it won't let me in!" Potter wailed.

"The virus has created a firewall around the whole system, Ethan," Frank called. "Hang on, I'm trying to break in."

Ethan's stern gaze shifted to the levers and columns on the other side of the helm. "Okay. All right, here's what we're gonna do. Ainsworth, you're gonna have to pilot us out of here manually."

"Manually, sir?" Ainsworth squeaked.

Ethan jerked his head up. "*Manually*, Helmsman. Problem?"

"Sir, I—I've only ever flown manually in simulations. Never the real thing."

Lindy couldn't see Ethan's face, but she did hear the tension in his voice. "Frank, shut down the navigation computer."

"I can't! It's taking over everything. Life support, Engineering, the sickbay..."

"Parsons to Bridge!" a terrified voice cried over the intercom. "What the heck is going on up there? I've got weapons powering up here in the arsenal and nobody's touched them!"

"And now I'm getting reports of power surges on all decks," Mockett added.

Ethan all but pushed the helmsman out of the way and gripped the ship's control columns himself, pulling one up and the other to the side. The ship groaned; Lindy felt it shift, then begin a slow, cautious crawl forward. Another chunk of rock scraped against the steel hull.

"Mockett," Ethan said, eerily calm, "tell Engineering to cut off all power to the arsenal."

"Aye, captain," Mockett murmured.

The elevator in the corridor just outside the bridge opened. Lindy turned and saw Jo, all dolled up in a white shirt and red skirt and looking like she'd seen a ghost.

"Lindy, what's going on?" she whispered.

"Some kind of computer virus has taken over the ship."

"I know *that*. Do they know where it's coming from?"

"I don't think so. Why?"

Jo didn't answer. She marched onto the bridge. "Captain Granger, every personal computer connected to the *Hummingbird*'s network is now uploading information to an off-ship address. Only spyware installed through a data port somewhere on this ship could do that—which means you've got a traitor aboard."

Ethan whirled; Frank jerked his head up. Even the officers who had no idea that their captain and IT officer were MID troopers, and who couldn't possibly understand the full implications of Jo's statement, looked like they were on the verge of panic.

"Elyon Above," Frank whispered.

"Cut power to the whole ship," Ethan snapped. "All of it. Cut the whole thing off."

Aeron stared at him. "Captain, if we cut off our life support, we'll only have three hours of oxygen and artificial gravity."

"Tell them to cut it, Mockett!" Ethan roared.

Lindy grabbed Jo's arm. "The laptops?"

Jo nodded. "Right before the sirens went off, they both had a pop-up that just said 'scanning.' I couldn't get rid of it. I unplugged them, I tried turning them off, but they wouldn't let me do anything."

Lindy's stomach flipped. Their laptops were practically open gateways to MID's network. Their links to Headquarters were encrypted, of course, but...

But somebody's trying to get into them anyway. Someone here on the ship is trying to send information to someone off *the ship.*

"Lindy," Ethan said. He had his focus locked on the window, the controls twitching under his hands. Lindy hurried to his side.

"Once the power cuts off, every door in the ship will open," he whispered. "It's a safety measure. That way, nobody gets trapped in their own cabin or the lift during a power outage."

"Okay..."

"You can get around as long as you're willing to climb the lift shafts. But if Jo's right, our traitor will have free range, too." He eased the *Hummingbird* past a massive asteroid and looked up just long enough to meet her gaze. "Open the hatch in the lift floor, climb down to Deck A, and stay with the Navorres until we clear this up. Got it?"

Of course she got it. They were troopers. Lindy squeezed his shoulder.

"I'm on it, Captain," she said.

Chapter Thirteen

"Okay, explain it to me," Lindy said as she and Jo ran to the lift. "Somebody just installed a virus in the *Hummingbird*'s system that affects any computer connected to it, but the virus has shielded itself and there's nothing anyone can do about it?"

"In theory, yes," Jo gasped, trying to keep up with Lindy's longer strides. "Once they cut power, though…"

As if on cue, the corridor went dark. Jo pulled her comm from her pocket. The screen showed a frozen game of solitaire, one card still in the process of moving but locked in time. Lindy pulled her own out of her back pocket and realized, with relief, that she'd had hers turned off.

"Mine's okay," she said. "Should I turn it on?"

"Leave it off for now," Jo said, leading the way by the light of the paralyzed game. "For all we know, it might be the only unaffected tech on the whole ship."

"Shouldn't I call Nana?"

"Hers is probably locked up too. The call wouldn't go through."

Lindy decided to defer to Jo's technological know-how, slipping her comm back into her pocket as they stepped into the lift. Just as Ethan had said, the doors were already open. The balance felt different, though, as if the elevator now depended on a backup mechanical suspension rather than anti-gravs. Lindy hesitated as it shifted beneath her feet.

"Do you have a weapon on you?" she asked, feeling around on her knees for the hatch.

"In my thigh holster," Jo said. "You?"

"Waistband."

"And of course our security dudes are probably scattered all over the place."

"If they've got sense, they're trying to get to the Navorres, too." Lindy opened the hatch and peered into the darkness. The light from Jo's comm illuminated a short platform attached to the underside of the lift, allowing easy access to the ladder stretching along one side of the shaft. Lindy swung her legs over the edge, held her breath, and pushed herself off. As soon as her feet hit the platform, she hurried to the edge, gripped the ladder's rungs, and scurried down as fast as she could. Jo followed close behind, doing her best to hold onto the ladder and keep the comm's light aimed at their next steps.

By the time they reached Deck A's open door, they were sweating, both from climbing and from the noticeable lack of air circulation. The deck was eerily silent. Every cabin looked like a yawning black hole.

"Hello?" Lindy shouted. "Everybody all right?"

She got no reply, not even from the guard who should've been on duty at the other end of the deck. *Dead?* A shiver crawled up Lindy's spine. She pulled out her gun and crept forward, motioning for Jo to get on her right hand.

"Councilor Tremaine!" Lindy called. "Councilor Tremaine? Princess Mariamne?"

Silence.

"Councilor!" she shouted again. She could've kicked herself for the way her voice cracked—until she heard Nana's voice through one of the open doors, shrill with terror.

"Melinda! Oh Melinda, for Elyon's sake, don't—!"

Two huge, shadowy forms sprang out of the cabins on either side of the troopers. Lindy kicked one of the attackers in the gut; with a startled grunt, he crashed to the floor. Jo slammed her knee into the other man's groin and whacked his head with her gun as he crumpled.

"They're Nova Force, Lindy!" she cried.

Lindy didn't reply. She'd realized it, too, by the men's uniforms, but before she could decide what to do, a red beam zipped over their heads from the other end of the corridor. She and Jo crouched low.

"Cover me!" Lindy hissed.

Jo trained her gun on their prisoners. Lindy peered into the dark. The other end of the corridor was lit only by the frozen holographic screen that showed, for the royal guests' benefit, a floor plan of each deck. By that light, she saw a tall, willowy figure, arms outstretched as if aiming a weapon.

"I know you're there," Lindy called, flipping the setting on her gun to heavy stun. It charged with a menacing whir. "Put your weapon down and come forward slow—"

Another beam burst out, this time from a shorter distance. Lindy threw herself against the wall and heard booted feet moving closer. Jo, thank Elyon, had returned her comm to her pocket. Except for the frozen screen, the deck was very dark.

"Stay where you are!" Lindy shouted.

"Or what?" a voice called back…a woman's voice, sharp with venom and desperation.

"Or I'll knock you flat on your back," Lindy snapped. "My authority supersedes that of the Nova Force here, and I'm not afraid to take drastic measures. If you know what's good for you, you stay…where…you…"

A flashlight turned on inside one of the cabins, nearly blinding Lindy and revealing not a security guard as her opponent, but a dark-skinned female in a Nova Force uniform. The woman drew a sharp breath and aimed not at Lindy, but at the figure with the flashlight.

A streak of green sliced straight through her chest before she could fire. She toppled over, her head striking the floor with a sickening crack.

Lindy's mouth fell open as Mariamne Navorre stepped out of the cabin, a flashlight in one hand and a tiny raygun in the other.

Frank shuddered as the power went out. He hadn't realized just how much noise the lights and computers generated. Right now, the engines powered only the main thrust, and Ethan controlled *that* from the helm.

And there's another problem, Frank thought anxiously. *Except for the Meridian sun at our back, he's flying blind.*

Ethan must've had the same concern. "Mockett, get Engineering on the emergency radio and have them turn on the bridge headlights. Then call every deck and tell them to maintain the intruder alert. I want someone on call at all times on every deck."

Within minutes the headlights flashed on. Frank's mouth went dry at the terrifying view. The Asteroidea was a dangerous area even with auto-navigation. Without their shields to protect them from the lumbering asteroids...

Nope. Not gonna let my brain go there. Frank suppressed another shudder and glanced at the rest of the crew. They all looked as scared as he felt. Frank cleared his throat, got to his feet, and planted himself on Ethan's left hand.

"Ethan."

The captain's face twitched in conjunction with the latitude column. "Frank."

"There's a chance that if we start turning the systems back on, one at a time and the less advanced ones first..."

A small asteroid bounced off the *Hummingbird*'s long nose, too far from the bridge for them to feel it but hard enough to shake things up on that end. Ethan winced but said nothing.

"I might be able to narrow down which systems are infected," Frank continued, "*if* they're even infected anymore. The spyware connection would've definitely been severed once we cut power."

Ethan narrowed his eyes and adjusted the controls. For a moment, Frank was worried he hadn't heard him. When Ethan finally did speak, his voice was tense and low.

"Do what you need to do, Frank."

Frank breathed a sigh of relief. "Yes, sir. Lieutenant Mockett, may I use that radio?"

She held out the mouthpiece and offered him her chair. Frank sat down with a grateful nod.

"Bridge to Engineering," he called. "We're gonna do an experiment here. Let's bring the life support back online—but *just* the life support, got it?"

"Got it, Bridge," a female voice called back. The hum of the air circulators immediately came back on; one of the corresponding computers started flickering. Frank leaped away from Mockett's station and attacked the waking console just as it resumed its frantic alert.

"Ohhhhhhh-kay. We still have an intruder alert, which means the spyware is still plugged in somewhere. But it doesn't look like it's really interested in cutting off our life support, so we'll leave that on." He dashed back to the radio. "Bridge to Security. Begin a check of every built-in data port in every cabin. I repeat: check every built-in data port in every cabin—and remove any and every flash drive you can find. Do not hesitate. You see one, you remove it."

"Security to Bridge, acknowledged. Be advised, we've got a team responding to a disturbance on Deck A."

"What kind of disturbance?" Ethan snapped.

"Yeah, what kind of disturbance are we talking about?" Frank bellowed.

"Not sure yet, sir. We'll let you know as soon as we find out."

Frank glanced at Ethan, who spared a look over his shoulder before turning his attention back to the helm. Frank swallowed hard and wiped his sweaty palms, hoping and praying that Lindy and Jo hadn't been too late.

Within minutes of Mariamne firing her gun, the lights came on. Deck A's terrified Valyan occupants leaked out of their cabins to see what had happened. Jo was already sick of the astonished gasps whenever someone saw her and Lindy standing over their cowering prisoners or a shriek whenever they saw the dead woman on the floor.

You'd think they'd never seen a dead person before, Jo thought, tuning them out with a dismissive shake of her head. She focused instead on the murmured conversation taking place between Lindy, Mariamne, Nana, and Verrona. Lindy still had her gun pointed at the man who'd attacked her, never taking her eyes off him while she spoke.

"Did they come up here before or after the lights went out?" she demanded.

"After," Mariamne said. She still refused, Jo noticed, to look at the woman she'd killed. "The lights went out and all the doors flew open. It frightened me, of course, so I went to the door—but then I heard a shot and people coming up the elevator shaft."

"Did you hear them say anything?" Jo asked.

"'Did you get it?'" Nana answered, looking a little shaken. "I heard the woman shout back, 'I have most of it. Find the princess.' One of those men was already in my cabin when you two arrived. He would've found me hiding in the bathroom if he'd stuck around longer."

"I heard the woman give the order as well," Mariamne said. "That was when I retrieved my gun from my trunk. I heard the other man rummaging around until he heard your voice, Miss Tremaine, and he rushed out. I…I thank you for coming when you did."

Jo glanced at Lindy, but her friend was preoccupied with her prisoner, shifting away from his feet and more towards his side. When Jo's captive lifted his head, she slammed her foot into his shoulder.

"Head down!" Jo shouted.

"Hey, lady, you don't have to—"

A sharp yelp from his buddy cut him off. Lindy had kicked the other guy in the ribs.

"What was the officer looking for?" Lindy demanded.

The traitorous guard pulled in a breath through set teeth. "Wouldn't you love to know?"

Lindy dove into a squat and yanked his head back. Mariamne gasped and Verrona's eyes widened, but neither Jo nor Nana even blinked. It was the oldest ploy in the book: make a bad guy think you meant to bash his head into the floor, *then* demand answers.

But Lindy lurched back as if the contact had burned her. The man swore as his forehead harmlessly smacked the floor. Lindy sprang away from him, looking as if she'd seen a ghost.

"What is it?" Jo asked.

Lindy drew a ragged breath. "He's Valyan."

"*What?*" Mariamne blurted.

"I felt his Emanation. I bet they're all Valyan, even *her*."

Mariamne scoffed. "You are probably just exaggerating the strength of his emotions."

"Are you actually gonna argue with me about this?" Lindy snapped.

Mariamne opened her mouth, then shut it so firmly her teeth clicked. When she looked at Verrona, the older woman raised her eyebrows with an *I-told-you-so* look that Jo didn't understand any more than she knew what an Emanation was.

The now-working lift opened and an officer burst in, a dozen men on his heels. He took one look at the crowded deck and moved straight to Lindy and Jo.

"Security Chief Adrian Colt," he said crisply. "Trooper Tremaine, Trooper Camrin. No need to present your IDs—Captain Granger already briefed me about your mission. Which of you killed those two over there?"

Mariamne raised her hand. "I killed the officer. She had already killed the guard."

Colt raised his eyebrows in surprised admiration. "Right. I'll need affidavits from everyone on this deck, of course. Davis, Hastings, take these goons to the brig. Let's see if we can identify this officer..."

He got halfway to the body and froze. When he whirled, Jo was surprised to see the horrified heartbreak on his face.

"Cornael?" he breathed.

"Regular crew?" Nana asked. "Not part of the Special Forces?"

"No. She—she's part of the bridge crew. Comms officer." He turned to Mariamne. "What happened?"

Mariamne actually looked nervous now. "She attempted to kill me, so I...I killed her first."

"It's true," Lindy said. "Both Mariamne and the Councilor heard Cornael order those guards to look for the princess, as well. I suspect they would've killed Mariamne if they'd found her, just like I suspect..."

She holstered her gun and pushed past the whispering nobles to the holographic screen. She probed underneath the console, yanked something out, and held it out to Colt.

"Just like I suspect *this* drive contained the spyware that hijacked every computer on this ship," she finished.

Colt stared at the drive. His Adam's apple bobbed up and down.

"We're gonna have to work together on this one, Chief," Lindy said quietly. "This is bad."

Colt swallowed. "Agreed. It's *very* bad."

As soon as Ethan and Frank could leave the bridge, they raced down to the cargo bay that also held the *Hummingbird*'s brig. Usually, the only occupants were mischief-makers who got too rowdy in the rec rooms on Saturday nights. But now, according to Security, Ethan had two would-be murderers on his hands...and a dead co-conspirator from among his own trusted bridge crew.

And it's Cornael, of all people, he thought bitterly as he sprinted ahead of the shorter, slower Frank. *Kindhearted, cheerful Cornael. Why would she do such a thing?*

As soon as he exited the lift, he saw Security Chief Colt on the far side of the echoing bay, together with the head of the special forces assigned to the delegation, Commander Penderwick. The two men snapped to attention when the captain burst in.

"Tell me what you've got," Ethan ordered.

Penderwick, a big florid-faced man, cleared his throat. "Well, sir, the prisoners are two of my men, I'm afraid. Vorloss was a refugee kid after the Revolution. Devron was born on Meridian to refugee parents."

"Wait, they're Valyans, too?" Frank cried.

"Were you aware of that when you included them on this assignment?" Ethan asked Penderwick.

"Well, yes, of course—but I reckon there are hundreds of Valyans in the Meridian Nova Force these days! I even discussed it with Vorloss before we left New Harvelle. He said it was an honor to escort the princess to Valya, even if he thought she should stay put on Meridian and let bygones be bygones."

Ethan turned to Colt. "What about Cornael?"

Colt ran a finger along the edge of the desk. "We all know her story, sir. Valyan refugee... came to Meridian when she was six years old...totally naturalized. Or, at least, that's what we all thought."

Ethan pursed his lips and turned to the clear-walled cells. Devron, the younger and smaller of the two, lifted tired eyes as he came closer. If looks could kill, however, the thick-necked Vorloss would've been guilty of murder. Ethan stopped in front of his cell and met the Valyan's glare.

"Why?" Ethan asked.

Vorloss clenched his jaw. "You'd never understand."

"Try me."

"Vorloss, just tell him the truth," Devron groaned.

Vorloss shot to his feet. Ethan didn't flinch. If the guard so much as touched the wall, the forcefield would shock him within an inch of his life. Vorloss undoubtedly knew that as well. He only leaned so close and then no further.

"Have you ever found yourself with two evil choices, Captain?" he growled. "You didn't know which to choose, but you had to choose anyway?"

"*Vorloss!*" Devron begged.

"I have," Ethan said coldly. "What's your point?"

Vorloss let out a fuming breath through his nose. "Lieutenant Cornael faced just such a decision. She failed in her mission, but by the walls of Cor Danem, she chose well."

"I don't suppose I could ask you to be any more specific than that?"

Vorloss smirked. "No, you couldn't, Meridian."

Ethan raised his eyebrows. "All right, then. Colt, let me in."

Colt pressed a button on the desk and the cell door slid open. With one meaningful glance at Frank, Ethan stepped over the threshold, making no contact with any part of the enclosure.

"Oh-ho," Vorloss laughed. "What're you gonna do, beat me up or—"

Ethan brought the ball of his hand up so hard and fast, Vorloss' chin flew back with a resounding snap of his teeth. Ethan slammed him onto the nearby cot before he could regain his balance, clamping one hand over the Valyan's neck and drawing the other back in a fist. His knee dug into Vorloss' sternum.

In the other cell, Devron stared in abject terror.

"Was Cornael working for the Valyan radicals on Meridian?" Ethan shouted.

"No," Vorloss groaned.

Ethan pressed his knee harder into the Valyan's chest. "Don't lie to me. Tell me the truth right now, and I'll ask High Command to go a little easier on you at your court-martial. That goes for you too, Devron!"

Devron sprang as close to the wall as he dared. "Cornael was communicating with Rael Navorre!"

A horrified silence fell over the brig. Vorloss went still and closed his eyes, beaten. Ethan didn't dare take his focus off the man, but he suddenly felt as if his own blood had turned to ice.

"You've gotta be kidding me," Frank said shakily.

Devron swallowed so hard, Ethan could hear it. "She said he'd reward all three of us on Valya if we stole the Remnant's files and…and killed the princess. We were going to head to Valya afterwards in an escape pod…"

"What kind of rewards are we talking about?" Ethan prodded.

"Military honors. Lots more money than we could ever make with the Nova Force." Devron's voice rose to a desperate pitch. "But Cornael also said Princess Mariamne was a threat to Valya's stability. If we wanted to protect our people from another civil war, we had to keep things just the way they've been! That's what she said and I believed her—and I think she believed it, too."

Ethan's stomach knotted. Vorloss chose that moment to open his eyes, grimacing as Ethan gripped his collar with both hands and shook him.

"After everything Rael did to his people—*your* people—you'd hire yourself out to him?" Ethan growled. "Elyon Above, I ought to force you to watch footage from the Revolution until we get to Valya!"

"There is no Elyon Above," Vorloss snarled. "And who's to say the Citizen didn't have a cause?"

Ethan flung him away in disgust. The Valyan rubbed his neck with a cough.

"No cause justifies the murder of innocent people," Ethan said. "A refugee like you should've learned that a long time ago."

Vorloss lifted his head and scowled. Ethan stormed out. Colt pressed a button, and the cell door slammed behind him.

Chapter Fourteen

Lindy lifted the thick mattress in the bottom bunk and shone her flashlight into the resulting cavity. She let the mattress rest against her shoulder as she waved the beam slowly along the edge of the bunk, looking for anything remotely suspicious.

Nothing. She wasn't surprised. She and Jo had combed Lieutenant Cornael's cabin from top to bottom for the last hour and hadn't found anything other than toiletries and clothes. At this point, they were retracing their own steps. Lindy put the mattress back and clamped her gloved hands on her waist with a scowl.

"You look mean when you do that," Jo remarked, clattering away at Cornael's laptop.

"I feel more burnt-out than mean," Lindy muttered. "It's been a day."

"Yeah. So I've guessed."

Lindy glanced at her sidelong. Jo still didn't know anything about her visit with Verrona or her conversation with Ethan in the gym. They'd only discussed the three would-be assassins, Mariamne's intervention, and the investigation in which they were now entangled. But Lindy wasn't fooled. Jo might be staring ferociously at that screen and typing like a madwoman, but she was *this* close to begging for details.

Might as well spill now before she practically attacks me for them.

"I knew that guy was Valyan because of something Verrona taught me today," Lindy said.

Jo spun around on her stool and clasped her hands between her knees. Lindy raised her eyebrows with an incredulous laugh.

"Wait a minute, what about that computer?" she demanded.

Jo shrugged. "I'm still waiting on my decryption program to unlock the flash drive. The computer is clean—nothing more than a few letters from home and some Valyan Citizenry propaganda she'd saved from the net. I can afford a break."

In spite of that last part about the pro-Rael material, Lindy smirked. "You're sure?"

"I'm sure. Now start talking."

This time Lindy laughed—but quietly, so that the guards down the hall tearing apart Vorloss' and Devron's cabins wouldn't hear them. Their reactions to Cornael's betrayal and death had varied between infuriated and stricken. Laughter probably wouldn't be appropriate.

"Okay," she said, sitting on the edge of the bunk. "You know how I can sense your emotions if I touch you with my shields down? Between Valyans, it's even more intense and intimate. And we have these emotional fingerprints. Every person's 'Emanation' is different and recognizable, but you're not supposed to share it with everyone, just with people you know. That's where the shields come in—only they don't call it that. They call it 'the Shelter.'"

Jo frowned. "Okay. So you touched Ensign Vorloss and…?"

"He must've been taken off guard and forgot to use the Shelter, so I got the full brunt of everything he was feeling." Lindy laced her fingers and rested her chin on top of them. "He had black Anger and red Fear. Pretty sure that combo gives you Hate."

Jo's eyebrows shot up to her hairline. "Wait, you can see the feelings as colors?"

"That's how Valyans perceive emotion, yeah."

"And what about you and Mariamne? I could've cut the tension between you with a knife."

Lindy sighed and gave Jo a condensed version of their confrontation, following it up with a summary of her conversation with Ethan. By the time she'd finished, Jo's eyes were as big as saucers. She clapped a hand over her mouth.

"Oh my gosh, Lindy."

"I know. Every time I think about it, I want to crawl in a hole and die somewhere..."

"No! No no no, I wasn't talking about the surveillance stuff! I was talking about Ethan!"

Lindy suddenly wondered if someone had kicked up the thermostat, but before she could reply, they heard heavy footsteps in the corridor outside. She sat up as Ethan appeared in the doorway, followed by Frank. Ethan rested a hand on the outside door frame.

"How's it going in here?" he asked.

Jo folded her arms and raised her eyebrows at Lindy, who quickly got to her feet.

"We've torn the place up and put it back together again," she said, rubbing her arms. "Jo hasn't found much on the laptop except some pro-Rael junk. Nothing about any conspiracy, though. Cornael was smart...and very careful."

"What about the spyware drive?" Frank asked, shouldering past Ethan.

"I'm working on decrypting it right now," Jo said.

Frank leaned over Jo's chair. To Lindy's satisfaction, Jo blushed and squirmed a bit.

"Stars and comets, Jo," he exclaimed. "You're still using the Birmingham 6.5 Decryption Cycle?"

"Of course! Isn't that the latest?"

Frank snorted. "Officially, yeah. Here, get up. Let me show you a new trick we technological geniuses are using these days."

Jo sprang up and Frank sat, rolling up his sleeves and wiggling his fingers. Lindy glanced at Ethan. He gave her a tired smile and made a slight gesture with his head. She needed no further invitation: she hurried to him and out into the open.

"I just talked to Jarvis," he murmured, leading her down the corridor. "I told him what happened and what I learned from Vorloss and Devron."

Lindy tried to suppress her alarm at the mention of their commander. "What *did* you learn?"

"The worst possible thing. Cornael was in communication with Rael. He wanted her to steal the Remnant's personal files and kill Mariamne."

Lindy froze in the middle of the corridor. Ethan stopped, too, glancing from side to side to make sure no one was eavesdropping.

"She was in direct contact with Rael?" Lindy whispered. "How…?"

"I don't know, and I don't know for how long. Long enough to convince Vorloss and Devron that they were acting for the good of Valya and that Rael would reward them handsomely."

He paused and rubbed the back of his neck. Concerned, Lindy tilted her head.

"You all right?" she asked.

"Yeah, it's just…" He hesitated, a pained grimace crossing his face. "She was our friend. We trusted her. And now we not only know she meant to kill Mariamne, but that she might've even carried out a trial run the day I learned this assignment was official. What if she found out after hacking the system that day that Frank and I are MID? What if she contacted Rael and told him—"

"You don't know that," Lindy said firmly. "And you won't know until we get into that flash drive and find out what she downloaded and how much she managed to upload before you cut the power. For all we know, none of it reached Valya. We're not gonna make any assumptions just yet."

Ethan chuckled, a low, wry sound. Lindy frowned.

"What?" she asked.

"Listen to yourself. This morning I was telling you not to beat yourself up. Now you're telling *me* not to assume the worst. We'll make a good team before it's all said and done."

Lindy's face warmed as she looked away. "So what did Jarvis say?"

"Just to keep him posted and carry on."

"Really? He doesn't want us turning back?"

Ethan shook his head. "No—not yet, anyway. He was pretty alarmed when I told him Cornael was working for Rael, let me tell you. But he also said Rael likely doesn't know that *we* know. Even if he does suspect that something happened to Cornael, he'll be wondering how much we know and what our next move will be. It puts us at a considerable advantage."

Lindy scowled. "So we rush back if we have the slightest inkling that Mariamne's plotting a coup, but not if we know she practically has a target on her back? Makes total sense."

Ethan sighed. "It *is* risky. But Jarvis may be right. Turning back now would only embolden Rael. He'd know we stopped Cornael, but he'd also assume we're scared of him."

"Maybe we are," Lindy muttered.

"Depends on how you look at it. At least we know where he stands now. We don't have to guess anymore. We might even be able to use it against him."

Lindy nodded slowly, still uneasy, but Jo's voice rang out before she could reply. She and Ethan turned and saw her waving frantically at them. They ran back to the cabin and Lindy shut the door.

"What have you got?" Ethan demanded.

"Well, I broke into the drive," Frank said, "so we can at least see everything the spyware collected for upload before the power died. And since the drive can only contain so much information, she *had* to hone in on specific stuff."

"Is that good or bad?" Lindy asked.

"In one sense it's good," Jo said. "It means she had to be specific about what the program would scan and keep. Our MID stuff isn't even showing up on here, so we don't have to worry about that."

"Then what did it target?" Lindy asked. "And how much of the upload got off the ship?"

Frank grimaced. "To answer the second question, I don't know. As soon as the power went out, the upload self-destructed, too, so I can't see how much of it actually left the *Hummingbird.* But I can tell you that Cornael went for the ship's databanks first and then every personal computer on Deck A."

"The Valyan delegation," Ethan murmured.

"And my grandmother," Lindy added. "Mind if I take a peek, Frank?"

Frank jumped up. Lindy took his seat, peering at folders upon folders of compromised info torn from the *Hummingbird*'s massive system. She scrolled past them to the ones from the computers on Deck A. Personal photos filled this folder, genealogy documents crammed that one, and another even contained someone's credit chip information. It felt wrong, peering into such private information, yet she kept searching for anything related to one specific Valyan. Ethan gripped the back of her chair and leaned over her shoulder.

"What are you looking for?" he whispered.

"You know who I *never* saw on Deck A the whole time we were up there?" Lindy asked.

"No. Who?"

A document entitled "MW NOTES" caught her eye before she could respond. She frowned, clicked it. A page full of text appeared. Lindy glanced through it as fast as she could, and words she hadn't realized she *needed* to see sprang before her eyes. So many things made sense now. She threw herself back in her chair and thrust her palm at the screen.

"Prince Lhoris."

Lindy's stomach twisted as soon as Verrona opened Mariamne's cabin door. It was one thing to see the older princess with the rest of her people after Cornael's attack; it was quite another seeing her in private like this, with the unpleasant memory of what had happened earlier in her cabin hanging between them. Lindy cleared her throat.

"Your Highness..."

Verrona cut her off not with words but by wrapping her arms around Lindy. Lindy froze, keenly aware of Ethan standing behind them, but crept out of her Shelter and let herself feel the white and yellow with hints of pink swirling through the princess's Emanation.

Affection. Worry. Relief. Elyon only knows what she's getting from me. Probably all my jitters.

"I am so glad to see you," Verrona whispered. "I have been worried you would never come back. Are you sure you are all right?"

Lindy drew a shaky breath. "I'm fine. Ethan and I are actually here on business. We need to talk to Princess Mariamne. It's urgent."

Verrona nodded. "Of course. Come in. We were just sitting down to dinner with Councilor Tremaine."

Lindy's anxiety skyrocketed. Nana sat with Mariamne, Lhoris, and Tali at the table beneath the window, her long fingers wrapped around a steaming mug. She met Lindy's startled gaze with more calm and dignity than Mariamne, who looked openly worried, and Tali, who would've leaped out of her chair if her mother hadn't stopped her with a stern look. Lhoris, by contrast, gazed intently at the newcomers. Lindy noticed he spent a strange amount of time looking at *her*.

Ethan's steady voice saved them all from an awkward silence.

"Your Highnesses. Councilor. Sorry to interrupt your dinner, but we need to bring everyone up to speed about the investigation."

Mariamne clasped her hands in her lap. "What have you learned?"

"That my communications officer, Lieutenant Cornael was, at some point, in contact with Rael. She accessed every computer on this deck—at least the ones connected to the *Hummingbird*'s net—and tried to upload specific information to another network outside the ship. We're assuming she was sending it to Rael."

"However, the power outage severed her connection to the outside network," Lindy chimed in. "As a result, we don't know how much was uploaded before the power died, nor can we *confirm* it went to Rael."

At that, Lhoris shifted uneasily. Lindy saw it but kept her mouth shut. Ethan stepped forward.

"Princess Mariamne, Miss Tremaine told me that she told you about MID's surveillance of you," he said, his voice softening. "I promise, she and I knew nothing about it until long after it began. When we did find out, we agreed between ourselves that we wouldn't monitor you any more than is necessary during this trip. Our mission is to keep you safe, not infringe on your privacy."

Mariamne swallowed and gave a slight, uncertain nod.

"That said," Ethan went on, "we couldn't help but see the information Cornael stole from the computers on this deck. There was a lot of it, but we needed to know what she'd taken. We didn't have a choice."

Mariamne nodded again. "You did what you had to. I understand."

"Good. Because we found a memorandum from the pro-Renegade Valyans on Meridian addressed to Prince Lhoris. It was a recap of a meeting they had with him two months ago in Manwaring."

Verrona clapped a hand to her mouth. Nana's eyes widened. Lhoris glowered at Ethan, but the captain met his gaze without flinching.

"Lhoris," Mariamne said, her voice quavering. "Tell me you didn't go to them."

Lhoris turned to her. "I have never lied to you, darling. I won't start now."

Mariamne made a strangled noise and stormed away from the table. Lhoris sprang after her.

"Mariamne, listen to me! Your father and the Meridians did all they could diplomatically, and theirs may still be the right path. But if it's not, what will happen? Even if this conference achieves everything we have hoped for, do you really think Rael will abide by whatever treaty we sign once the Meridians are gone?"

Mariamne whirled. "You'd form an alliance with those troublemakers without telling me?"

"Not in the way you're thinking! Captain, Miss Tremaine—surely you read how I made them promise they'd never attempt any Meridian-based sabotage against Rael *without* the order of the rightful Queen of Valya! Did you see it? Tell her!"

"We saw it," Lindy said. "But we also read that you instructed them to tell the Renegade that Mariamne was coming."

Mariamne turned away, covering her eyes. Lhoris seized her shoulders and made her face him.

"My love, *please*. I am only trying to make certain we have support, no matter what happens. The Renegade wishes to overthrow Rael, yes. But he is also open to returning power to the Navorres if we establish a constitutional monarchy. He has an army of thousands already and even more who support him in secret. The Valyans will rally to him if—"

"Blood will run in the streets, Lhoris!" Mariamne cried. "Rael would rather destroy the planet than give me a single subject to govern! You *know* that!"

"Yes, I do! But must that risk stop us from at least *trying* to do the right thing?"

Mariamne said nothing. Lindy glanced at Nana, and Nana raised an eyebrow.

"I'm not saying we should make the Renegade our ally *now*," Lhoris said. "But Rael is a despot at best and a madman at worst. He will force our hand at some point—maybe not this week, maybe not for years. But when he does, we will need a friend, one with an army that is already prepared and waiting for your command."

Mariamne drew a shuddering breath and turned to her aunt and Nana. Verrona said nothing, but Lindy didn't think she seemed upset; in fact, she looked like she thought Lhoris had a reasonable argument. As for Nana, she raised her palms to the ceiling.

"Mariamne, dear, even the stupidest politicians always have a Plan B. Lhoris is right. It may behoove you to have the Renegade in your corner, especially now that we know Rael has already conspired against you."

"But he is a fool," Mariamne hissed. "He is convinced one of Rael's sisters survived!"

"I never said he wasn't a fool," Nana retorted. "Just that he might be...helpful."

"And if this information from Lhoris' computer *has* gotten into Rael's hands?" Mariamne demanded. "If Rael knows that my husband, the Manwaring Valyans, and the Renegade are all in contact..."

"As we said, we don't know how much of the information got off the ship," Ethan said. "Commander Jarvis recommends we stay on course. He believes we have a tactical advantage over Rael at this point, and I think he's right. That said..." His eyes narrowed. "If *you* think your safety is too compromised, just say the word, and I'll take us straight back to New Harvelle."

Mariamne blinked. "You can do that?"

"I *will* do that. You're the princess. I'm the captain. You and I call the shots out here."

At that, Nana set her mug down with an alarmed *clink*. Mariamne frowned.

"Councilor? You have something to say?"

"I do," Nana blurted. "Jarvis *is* right. Cancel the conference now, and Rael will use it as proof that you aren't committed to the betterment of your people! It'll go to his head and he will never agree to meet with us ever again. It's all about the narrative, Mariamne—and your cousin is very good at narratives."

Verrona snorted. "That boy always was a master manipulator. I doubt he has changed much."

"Then it's settled?" Ethan asked. "We stay on course for Valya?"

Mariamne pressed her lips together, glanced at Lhoris, and sighed. "Yes. Stay on course."

Lhoris smiled and tried to kiss her forehead, but Mariamne jerked away. On her way back to the table, she peered at Lindy.

"You've been rather quiet, Miss Tremaine. What are your thoughts?"

Lindy lifted her head with a start and glanced at Ethan, but his raised eyebrows and their companions' honed interest only echoed the question. She cleared her throat.

"I want to apologize for telling you what I did about MID. I was out of line and said it just to unnerve you. But I still want confirmation that Lhoris *was* the one who visited Manwaring."

"It was," Lhoris said. "Mariamne had only just given birth to our child. She would've been in no condition to make that trip. Verrona and our servants in New Harvelle can confirm that."

Lindy turned to Mariamne, but the princess had her eyes on the floor. "Just one more question, then. Trooper Camrin saw you and Perry Ambrose watching her in the cafeteria this morning, then caught you in front of our cabin. What was that about?"

Lhoris hesitated. Strangely, his gaze skittered to Nana before he answered. "Mr. Ambrose is my contact with the Manwaring

Valyans. He has long suspected you are a Valyan, as well, and I confirmed that for him. But I have *not* told him of your association with MID. I intended to speak with you this morning, hoping that, perhaps, you might be interested in meeting with the Manwaring Valyans at some point. As a fellow refugee, that is, and a voice in the Meridian media."

Lindy grimaced. Perry Ambrose was a no-good snoop if he'd spent that much time pondering her ancestry, and it was more than a little presumptuous of Lhoris to assume she'd throw her support behind a bunch of trigger-happy Valyans.

But then she looked not to Nana, not to Mariamne or Verrona, but to Ethan. He watched her closely without any condemnation or concern—just a steady interest that reminded her abruptly of everything she loved about Meridian: its open-faced honesty and its goodness, even if that goodness was sometimes a little heavy-handed. Lindy drew a breath and realized she knew exactly what she wanted to say.

"I appreciate the thought, Your Highness. But I'm still a Meridian at heart. I doubt I'll ever want to dabble in another planet's politics unless I had no choice."

Lhoris looked intently at her. "I hope you may one day change your mind. But as it is…I thank you for your honesty."

Lindy inclined her head. "And I for yours."

At that, Ethan smiled his kind, one-sided grin. It warmed her down to her toes—but Lhoris didn't take his eyes off her, and Nana lowered her gaze and chewed the corner of her mouth. Lindy found both unnerving, but then Verrona and Tali came up and eagerly invited her back to their cabin first thing in the morning. Between their hustle and bustle, the muted but no longer antagonistic interest in Mariamne's face, and Ethan's approval, she soon forgot about it.

Chapter Fifteen

To Ethan's relief, there were no more alerts and no more attacks on his guests. Knowing that Cornael and the guard she'd murdered were in the ship's morgue made him shudder a few times, but he kept it to himself. If he itched with curiosity when Lindy got clearance to question Vorloss and Devron in the brig, he kept that to himself, too. He didn't want her to think he was hovering or stalking. Besides, he still had a ship to run.

But knowing his ship and the mission had been so easily compromised haunted him. The first night after Cornael's betrayal, he'd lain awake for a long time, wondering what would've happened if she'd succeeded.

What had motivated her to ally herself with Rael Navorre? Ethan couldn't believe it was simply the promise of money or prestige on Valya. Devron had suggested, however, a misplaced desire to protect Valya's people from further bloodshed—and that could've been a powerful motivator for a woman like Cornael. And then there was the former prince's legendary charisma. It had whipped an entire planet into a frenzy twenty-three years ago. Perhaps it could still pull in followers from hundreds of light-years away.

But how could he, Ethan, have missed that shift in loyalty in someone he worked with every single day?

Chalk it up to experience, he'd finally told himself. *And be glad Mariamne was armed.*

For the final evening of the trip, the *Hummingbird*'s senior officers organized a party for the crew and their guests. People milled in and out of the rec rooms, testing the atmosphere and company of each one before settling down somewhere. Cheerful music blared from the intercoms. The journalists, especially, made a dent in the ship's alcohol stash.

When he finally got away from the bridge and entered one of the rec rooms, Ethan found Valyans and Meridians engaged in intelligent conversation at nearly every table. A few couples had even taken advantage of the music to steal a dance or two. With a smile, he settled down at the bar with a shot of Namarian whiskey, content to observe.

"Captain Granger?"

Ethan whirled and saw Councilor Tremaine smiling at him. He set his glass down and extended a hand with a warm grin of his own.

"Councilor, good to see you. I hope you're enjoying your last evening aboard the *Hummingbird.*"

"Yes, indeed," she said, "and hopefully it'll be the last evening for a long while. Not that I think your ship is uncomfortable, but..."

"You're hoping for a long, successful time on Valya. I understand—no need to try and explain that to me. Can I get you a drink?"

"Mm, yes. I'll have some of what you're having."

Ethan nodded and called the bartender. Once she had a shot glass in hand, Councilor Tremaine cast her gaze around the big room.

"You're not in any hurry, are you?" she asked. "I'd like to chat with you if you have the time."

"Not in any rush at all, ma'am. Here, let's grab one of these tables by the window. What's on your mind?"

Councilor Tremaine smiled as she sat down. "My granddaughter, of course."

"Yeah, where is she? I haven't seen her all evening."

"Oh, she and Jo are with Verrona and Talila in the other room down the hall. They'll drift in here eventually." Councilor Tremaine tapped her nails against her glass. "What do you think of her, Captain?"

Ethan drew a breath. "She's...an amazing woman. And I'm not just saying that. I haven't known her long, but I think she's incredibly brave. Honest. Sensitive."

"*Sensitive*—really?"

He folded his arms on the table. "This goes no further than this room?"

Councilor Tremaine made a sweeping motion with her hands. "No further, I swear."

Ethan nodded and dropped his thoughtful gaze to the contents of his glass. "The day of the attack, after she and Mariamne argued, I found her crying in the gym. I think she was afraid she'd blown her one chance of being accepted by the Valyans. It made me realize she's not quite as tough as she'd like us all to think."

"Mmm. And what did *you* do?"

"I comforted her as best I could." He frowned, suddenly curious. "Did she tell you we met on Xandroa?"

The Councilor's smile froze. "*No*. I knew you met at Hoadley House..."

"When she walked into my sister's interview trap?" Ethan chuckled. "I think she may have been keeping a secret or two from *you*, too, ma'am."

Councilor Tremaine shifted. "I suppose she has."

"I mention it only because I found out she was a Valyan on Xandroa. We met her and Jo there to discuss this mission, but she didn't want anything to do with it. I learned later that you had personally asked Jarvis to offer the assignment." He paused, narrowing his eyes. "Did you think she wouldn't fight it?"

The Councilor laughed, but it was a humorless sound. "Oh, I knew she would. I've spent the past twenty-three years alternating between protecting Lindy and urging her to face her fears. And she does have fears. Terrible ones."

"I know," he said softly. "Nightmares."

"Horrendous ones." She sighed, swirling the whiskey and ice in her glass. "I know all about Maria taking you with her on those rescue missions to Valya, too. You must've seen your fair share of tragedy."

Ethan swallowed. Councilor Tremaine laid her hand over his, her blue eyes sympathetic.

"I can already tell you two make a fine team. You both know what it means to face terror with courage. And as her grandmother, albeit an adopted one, I'm just glad she finally has a male friend she can trust."

Finally? Ethan opened his mouth to prod further—but before he could say anything, Councilor Tremaine sat up, her quickening eyes fixed on something behind him. He twisted around just as Frank, Jo, and Lindy walked in. Jo had her arm loosely linked with Frank's, but Lindy came solo in a coral dress with filmy sleeves, her head high and her eyes bright. Her black hair hung loose and straightened, streaming down to her waist.

She was very pretty tonight. Beautiful, even. Ethan looked at Councilor Tremaine and found her smirking.

"Excuse me," he murmured.

"Go right ahead," she cooed.

Ethan got up. Jo saw him first and beamed.

"Hello, Captain!" she cried. "Having fun?"

"Not what Frank would probably call 'fun,' but yes, I think so," Ethan said with a grin. "I've just been chatting with Councilor Tremaine."

Lindy turned from the bar with a tall, slender glass and winced. "I hope she was behaving herself."

Debatable, he thought. His gaze flicked down to her glass, then at her. "I don't suppose you'd be interested in a quick dance, Miss Tremaine?"

Lindy's dark eyes widened. Jo's mouth fell open.

"Why, Captain," Frank drawled. "I didn't know you had it in you."

Jo swatted his arm. "Don't be mean."

Lindy set the glass on the counter. "I'd be happy to dance with you, Captain Granger—if only to show these jokers a thing or two."

All the blood rushed to his face with alarming speed. He offered his hand and she took it, letting him lead her to the middle of the room. He tried not to look at Councilor Tremaine as he laid his free palm against her granddaughter's waist.

"Kick me if I step on your toes," he whispered.

Lindy laughed and curled a light arm around the edge of his shoulder. "I might confront Nova Force captains in the men's room when I'm mad, but I'm not *that* nasty."

He sidestepped in time with the music, drawing her along. She moved confidently and let him twirl her without missing a beat. She was *good.*

"When did you learn how to dance?" she asked as he pulled her back in.

"As a teenager. Genevieve decided she wanted to learn not long before her diagnosis. But I was the only one of us who could 'feel the beat,' so to speak."

"Intuition, then," Lindy said.

He twirled her again. "Sometimes, you just have to trust your gut. Or in this case, your feet-and-ear coordination."

She smiled at that, then glanced off to the side. "Oh gosh, they're watching us..."

"Ignore them." Ethan applied pressure to her waist and gripped her hand a little tighter. "Can't let anyone else's opinion throw you off the beat."

Lindy looked at him, surprised and yet, after a moment, distinctly appreciative. Ethan held her gaze and forced himself to think about nothing else. Not his mother's opinion, not Genevieve's suffering, not the prisoners in the brig...not even the possibility that they were walking into a hornet's nest on Valya.

He only wanted to think about Lindy Tremaine and what her grandmother had said about trust.

The next morning Lindy woke early with a stomach full of butterflies that had nothing to do with the alcohol she'd ingested last night—*a paltry amount, anyway*—or with memories of a certain blue-eyed captain leading her in a smooth, effortless dance. They weren't even the same butterflies she used to have as a kid on the anniversary of her adoption, an event Nana always treated as an alternative to her unknown birthday.

These weren't happy butterflies. These were the "Stars and comets, I'm almost there...please, Elyon, don't let me have a panic attack at the first sight of Valya" sort of butterflies.

Jo pulled the MID equipment out of the secret compartments in their suitcases as soon as they'd dressed. Lindy watched, clenching her hands to keep them from shaking, while Jo calibrated a couple of transparent, touch-activated earbuds.

"Those boys had better be awake," Jo muttered, fitting one of the buds into her own ear. "We said we'd do this at 0630, so they'd better not have forgotten. Testing, Sparks."

Lindy put her earbud in. "Testing, Thorpe."

The earbud crackled. "Testing, Goldhawk."

Lindy glanced at Jo and nodded. Jo frowned.

"You there too, Falcon?" she demanded.

"Testing, Falcon," Frank replied. "Gosh, Jo, you're impatient."

"I wait for no man when I'm in business mode, Falcon. "

"Goldhawk here," Ethan called. "Everybody still clear on the plan?"

"Thorpe here," Lindy said. "We went over it last night before bed. The emergency code is 'Thunder.' Rael is 'Eagle,' Mariamne is 'Stardust,' Lhoris is 'Saber,' the Councilor is 'Tiger.' Goldhawk, we'll see you this evening at the hotel, right?"

"Goldhawk. Correct. I'll monitor the conference opening from the Hummingbird, do my own exploring this afternoon, and meet you three at the hotel at 1800." Ethan paused. "I know this is gonna be tough, Lindy, but you're tougher. Got that?"

Lindy ignored Jo's pointed look and smiled. "Got it. You be careful out there."

Ethan chuckled. "I promise I won't talk to any shady characters. But you've still got the harder job today. I don't think Mariamne will pull any tricks, but don't be afraid to call me if you notice anything suspicious on Rael's end."

Lindy turned slightly away from Jo. "I'm not worried about them, to be honest. I'm way more concerned about Lhoris. If he's still got a plan of his own that Mariamne doesn't know about…"

"We'll pounce before he knows what's up. That's why we're here: to stop a crisis before it happens. We can do that. We've just gotta keep our eyes open."

"Okay, Sparks signing out!" Jo called, dropping her hand from her ear and snapping the suitcases shut. "Ten minutes till we have to be at the exit. Help me with these, Lindy?"

"Yeah, I'm coming. See you later, Ethan."

"Lindy."

"Yeah?"

"Focus, listen, and watch. That's all you have to do. You'll be fine."

Lindy pulled in a shaky breath and dropped her hand without replying. She hurried back to Jo, grabbing one of the suitcases and tucking it under her arm.

"Everything all right?" Jo asked.

"Yeah," Lindy whispered. "Just fine."

Jo grabbed her hand before Lindy could walk past her. Her emotions weren't nearly as intense as Verrona's or Tali's, but they were still there, warm and steadying. Lindy smothered the instinct to dive into her Shelter and instead let the reassurance wash over her like a wave.

"It'll be okay," Jo whispered. "Breathe, Lindy. Just breathe."

Lindy shut her eyes and obeyed. After a moment or two, Jo squeezed her hand.

"Better?"

Lindy opened her eyes. "Yeah. A little, anyway."

"Good," Jo said, letting a mischievous note slip into her voice. "Because now I'd like to take a few minutes to tease you about how much I think Ethan Granger likes you."

As soon as the *Hummingbird*'s boarding ramp hit the runway, the Meridian journalists clambered out, eager to take their first notes on what was, in many ways, an unknown planet. Lindy, however, lingered at the top of the ramp. The air was soft, and a spring breeze skipped over flawless asphalt—but the pristine expanse contrasted sharply with the dilapidated buildings on the other side of the high wall surrounding the novaport. Judging from the size of the buildings, the pungent odor of factory waste, and the dull roar above the ship's idling engines, Cor Danem was as busy and well-populated as it was gloomy and tightly controlled.

Jo nudged her from behind; Lindy gripped her bag and hurried down. She saw two dozen Valyan soldiers already assembled on one side of the ramp, opposite the clustering Meridians. All wore grey uniforms and caps, with black sashes stretching from shoulder to opposite hip. Each carried a rifle. Another group of grim-looking Valyans stood beside them, armed with holocams. They started snapping pictures as soon as the first Meridian set foot on Valyan ground.

Cameras on both sides, however, flashed wildly as the Meridian security forces marched down the ramp. Lindy gave no outward signs of recognition when she glimpsed Frank among them and focused instead on Prince Lhoris. He paused at the top of the ramp, gazing over the runway for a long, tense moment before he held out his hand to someone still inside the ship.

As Mariamne stepped out, Lindy's mouth fell open. The Meridians gasped and the Valyan reporters glared behind their holocams, but the Princess paid them no attention. Instead, she glided down the ramp with her husband, her crimson, gold-hemmed skirts swishing at her feet. Lindy had never seen her dressed in anything so extravagant. She snatched her tablet out of her bag and began scribbling furiously.

Well, at least Jo and I will be sending Athena some fantastic material this evening.

The other nobles followed the Prince and Princess. Nana strode out on Ethan's arm, smiling for the press. They'd all reached the bottom of the ramp when several hover-limos zoomed out of the novaport hangar. A hush fell. Lindy hugged her tablet to her chest and Jo linked their arms as the hovers came to a stop. A Valyan soldier stepped forward. He opened the door of the first hover and stood at attention, one arm bent over his chest and his fist at his shoulder.

"Hail the Magnificent Citizen!" he shouted.

"Hail!" the Valyan soldiers and reporters bellowed. A tall, elegant figure stepped gracefully out of the limo. Lindy's breath caught.

This was him, then. This was Rael Navorre.

My mother's murderer.

Lindy swallowed. He barely resembled the moody young prince she'd seen in that library book she brought home. The receding hairline, the chiseled face, the pleasant smile as he faced the journalists, and the tailored Meridian-style suit all made him appear ridiculously normal. *And yet…*

And yet, something was off. Rael Navorre could've passed for a Meridian politician, but there was something about his steely eyes, the stiff way he held his head, the way his long fingers trembled as they buttoned the front of his suit, and the way he drew an unsteady breath and rolled his shoulders. Could he really be nervous?

Maybe. After all, he hasn't heard from Cornael since her transmission got cut off.

"Mariamne!" he cried, his voice smoother and sweeter than Lindy expected. "It's wonderful to see you again after all this long time, dear cousin."

He held out a hand, his palm facing up. Lindy blinked. The unsettling tension she thought she'd observed had all but vanished. Mariamne raised her eyebrows and laid her palm against his.

"Cousin," she said cautiously. "You honor us with this welcome."

"Anything for you, Mariamne. And Lhoris, my old friend! You were—what—twelve when last we saw each other? Aunt Verrona, wonderful to see *you*. I hear you and Uncle Doras were fruitful and multiplied on Meridian! Where is the old rascal anyway?"

Verrona put an arm around Tali's shoulders. "Your uncle died five years ago on Meridian. You might at least show his memory a little respect."

Lindy glanced at Ethan. He cut his eyes at her—the first time he'd acknowledged her since he got off the *Hummingbird*—but Rael only gave a mellow laugh.

"Sharp-tongued as ever, aren't you, Aunt? That's good. You haven't changed much. And neither have *you*, the famous Margaret Tremaine. You haven't aged a day."

"Why, thank you, Your Highness," Nana said sweetly.

It was as if someone had flipped a switch. The Valyan soldiers and reporters sucked in audible breaths. Rael jerked his head up, all the pleasantness draining out of his face.

"In case you hadn't heard, Councilor," he said, his tone much colder, "I am known as 'Citizen' these days."

"Oh, of course!" Nana laughed, pulling her hand back. "Do forgive an old lady. I tend to be rather forgetful these days."

Rael straightened. "Of course. You are an honored visitor. But I should warn you that my enforcers pay visits to anyone who calls me by any other title, and they tend to be rather…aggressive. I'd rather not have to intervene on your behalf only to find I'm too late."

Lindy gripped her tablet so tightly, her knuckles ached. Nana smiled.

"Don't worry, Citizen," she said. "I rarely make the same mistake twice. Oh, but before we set off, allow me to introduce Captain Ethan Granger. He'll be taking some well-deserved shore leave in Cor Danem while we're here."

Rael peered at Ethan, sizing him up before inclining his head in the barest gesture of respect. Ethan nodded back and looked him straight in the eye.

"Citizen," he said.

"Captain," Rael muttered. He turned to Mariamne. "Are you ready? My people are eager to see what has become of the royal family over the past few years. I've even granted them an early recess from their work to watch our procession."

Mariamne raised an eyebrow. "I am quite eager to see *our* people as well."

Rael clapped his hands. "Then let's be off. Your reporters can pile into this hover. These are for you and your entourage. We will make our way to the Palace this morning as agreed, and then after our opening ceremonies and lunch, we will begin our talks. Is that still agreeable to you all?"

"Quite agreeable," Nana said quickly.

"Good." Rael paused, raking an evaluating gaze over the newcomers before disappearing into his hover. Lindy exhaled for the first time in a while.

"What do you wanna bet Mariamne complies and calls him 'Citizen' the whole time we're here?" Jo deadpanned.

Lindy snorted, remembering how offended Mariamne had been when Jarvis called Rael by that title.

"Do me a favor?" she whispered as they headed towards the press hover. "Just keep the snark buttoned up till tonight. I'd rather not have to bust you out of a 'nasty little place called prison.' "

"Good point," Jo muttered. "Although the temptation might be more than I can bear."

Chapter Sixteen

The initial thrill Frank felt this morning when he donned his Nova Force Security disguise had worn off fast. Every time he caught Commander Penderwick glaring at him from the opposite seat of the hover-limo, he squirmed between the muscular NFS guards on either side of him. Frank guessed they were each a couple hundred pounds while he hovered around a nice, comfortable 150.

Well, as my granny used to say, "It doesn't matter what shoe size you wear, just how big your brain is."

"So this is Cor Danem," the guard on his right murmured.

Frank craned his neck forward—he didn't dare move too much lest the guards encroach on his already-limited personal space—and his eyes widened in surprise. The Valyan citizenry really had turned out to glimpse the exiled royals, lining the narrow streets and making them even more cramped than they already were. Frank tilted his head and peered at the tall, narrow buildings.

"Apartment complexes," he muttered.

"What?" Penderwick grunted.

Frank gestured with his hand. "See all the windows and balconies? The people who work in those factories we've been passing probably live in those apartments. Cram 'em in like sardines at night, and chuck 'em out again every day from nine to five. Well... probably more like five in the morning to nine in the evening."

The guard on Frank's left looked out the window on his side. "What do they make in those factories, anyway?"

Penderwick's scowl deepened. "Valya may be on bad terms with most of the Star System, but I hear they still do plenty of trade with Zathrenal and Namaria. Heavy machinery's their specialty these days—a far cry from the days when the ariya plantations dominated the economy."

"My mother had a wedding dress made of ariya silk," the guard on the right said. "Prettiest thing you ever saw."

The guard on the left snorted. "What, Maycock, you plannin' on wearin' it yourself?"

"Valya pretty much clothed the galaxy once upon a time—and they ate the ariya grain, too," Frank said. "It was a critical industry."

"Exactly," Penderwick said. He glanced over his shoulder at the transparent, soundproof screen separating them from the Navorres and Councilor Tremaine in the front section of the hover. "Which is why we should hope, for these poor folks' sake, that the Councilor can help those royal idiots reach some kind of compromise."

In the journalists' hover, Lindy's keen awareness of the distance between her and the Navorres kept her from becoming too engrossed in her foreign surroundings. Two hovers full of Meridian guards crawled between this one and the royal limo. Frank was with them, she knew, but the unavoidable separation made her nervous.

She scooted closer to the window. She knew the planet was struggling, but she hadn't expected the capital to be quite this grim. The streets were cramped and littered, the air reeked of pollution, and graffiti covered slimy brick walls. Everything looked tired, including the onlookers who crowded the sidewalks, clad in the grey-and-black coveralls of factory workers. Barricades and armored soldiers made sure they stayed well away from the road.

"Magnificents," Jo whispered, nudging Lindy.

Perry Ambrose, sitting across from them, looked up from his tablet. "What?"

"Those guys, the ones in the bulky armor and helmets. Those must be the Magnificent soldiers."

Perry leaned forward, his broad, ruddy face darkening. Lindy remembered uneasily what Lhoris said about Perry being in contact with the Valyan refugees back on Meridian.

"Ah," he whispered. "The real cutthroats, then."

Lindy started to speak, but a scream outside cut her off. Everyone sprang forward in their seats. A cluster of women had leaped over the barricades and now ran towards the motorcade. Lindy and Jo stared at each other in alarm while the other reporters fretted noisily around them.

"What in the name of—"

"What do they think they're doing? They don't look angry, but..."

"They're running for the royal limo!"

Jo nodded at Lindy, eyes wide. Lindy lifted a finger to her ear, prepared to say the word that would bring the *Hummingbird* into the situation.

But the intensifying noise outside exploded in gunfire before she could speak.

"Get down!" Perry bellowed. Jo yanked Lindy to the floor. The reporters swore, shoving each other for space away from the windows. Blood-curdling screams, pounding footsteps, and repeated blasts of concentrated energy engulfed the vulnerable hover. Lindy started to push herself off the floor.

"No, Lindy!" Jo screamed. "Stay down!"

"I love you, Lin. I love you so much. Come on, let's say your prayers, all right?"

The nightmare had flashed alive even though she was wide awake. Lindy jerked herself upright. She heard Jo begging her not to look. She even sensed, without touching anyone, their companions' throbbing horror.

But it all felt and sounded less real than the sight of a dozen Magnificents circling the twitching, smoldering bodies of seven Valyan women.

Lindy touched the window. One of the stricken women lifted her head with an effort, saw her, and reached a shaking arm towards the motorcade.

The nearest Magnificent aimed at her head and fired.

Frank barely heard Penderwick's panicked swearing over the chaos outside. He put one hand to his gun and the other to his ear; the guys on either side of him fumbled for their own weapons.

The shooting, however, stopped before anybody could lock and load. When Frank looked out the window again, he saw the seven women who'd sprinted for the motorcade lying dead in the street. On the other side of the barricades, the terrified crowd bolted away. The Magnificents fired a couple of final shots. Frank shoved his gun back into his holster.

"All clear," he muttered.

"*What?*" the guard on his left cried. "Whaddaya mean, 'all clear'? They gunned those women down!"

Penderwick glowered. "Welcome to Valya, son."

Frank swallowed, but the burning in his throat didn't stop. He peered beyond Penderwick and knew at a glance that nobody in the front of the limo had missed the slaughter. He put a finger to his ear.

"Thunder, Goldhawk," he whispered.

His fellow guards looked at him sharply. Penderwick, who knew more than he let on, just narrowed his eyes. Frank ignored all three. He heard a bit of static, then Ethan's voice.

"Goldhawk. I know—I just talked to Sparks. Is Stardust secure?"

Frank peeked again through the transparent barrier. From his position he could see Mariamne, and he could tell she wasn't using an inside voice.

"Affirmative, Goldhawk."

"Good. But as long as she's safe, we won't have a leg to stand on if we intervene. Stay on the alert and secure the area before she gets out of that hover. Got it?"

"Got it." Frank scooted forward and put his helmet on. Penderwick watched, wondering, no doubt, how a helmet identical to his own could be equipped with state-of-the-art MID tech. Frank continued to ignore him. He activated the hidden transmission interceptor chip with a tap of his finger before he looked Penderwick in the eye.

"New goal, Commander," he said. "We've gotta prevent Mariamne from wringing Rael's neck once we reach the Palace. If we can manage that, we can call it a successful day."

Filthy buildings and grimy people gave way to wider streets, cleaner townhouses, and even a few glassy skyscrapers. The well-dressed, well-fed citizens now lining the streets in the center of town saluted as Rael's vehicle passed. When the royal limo inched by, however, they dropped their hands and glared.

The motorcade halted in front of the old Navorre Palace, a white mansion behind a high black gate. As soon as the vehicles came to a stop, Penderwick's men sprang out. Frank dashed out after them, whirling to face Mariamne…and his heart sank. She was already out, on her way to Rael's hover-limo. *How the heck did she move that fast?!*

A deafening burst of static from the transmission interceptor rattled his helmet. Frank winced and shook his head. The static didn't stop. He turned it off with a frustrated tap of his finger and sprinted after Mariamne.

"Your soldiers shot those women in cold blood!" Mariamne screamed, her voice carrying over the crowd beyond the gate. " What had they done to deserve that, Rael?"

Her cousin stepped out to meet her, placidly fingering the buttons on his suit. "Calm yourself, Mariamne. They were about to storm your limo. You wouldn't have wanted them to succeed, would you?"

"They were unarmed women! What could they have done to me?"

"Umm, your Highness," Frank murmured, coming up behind her. "I think—"

"Tell me, Mariamne, do you want this conference or not?" Rael snapped. "I'm not the one who demanded it, if you recall. Your people did. If the Remnant cannot accept this new Valya, I can just as easily call this entire business off as—"

"As *I* can!"

Frank whirled. Councilor Tremaine stormed toward them, clenching her purse like she might whack Mariamne and Rael over the head with it.

"Now you two listen to *me*," she snapped. "Mariamne, he's right. This isn't the Valya you remember. And Rael, you may be the supreme ruler of this planet…"

"On the contrary—" Rael began.

"Oh, hush. You and your Dominators may talk about 'power for the people,' but everyone in the Star System knows who's really in charge here. It's high time someone cut through all your nonsense. It might as well be me. On that note, let me remind you that this sort of treatment of your own people will do nothing for your popularity on my planet. Am I coming through loud and clear, Citizen?"

Rael set his teeth and clenched his fists. Frank frowned. There was something about the man's demeanor...something agitated and panicky...like a trapped animal with no place to go.

And I've seen that look way too many times on creeps with shorter rap sheets than this guy's.

Frank's hands twitched, one ready to seize his gun, the other to tell Ethan to get his butt on the scene—but before he could do either, Rael blinked. The wild, frantic look faded; he inhaled, rippled his fingers against his thighs, and frowned at the Councilor.

"Very well," he said, quiet and calm. "But if you question my authority ever again, Mariamne..."

"She won't," Councilor Tremaine said.

Mariamne glared in silence. Rael threw his head back.

"Thank you for that assurance, Councilor," he said coldly. "I will be sure to hold you to it."

Despite Rael's promises over the years to free Valya from its past, the Navorre Palace remained extravagant enough for a king. Under normal circumstances, Lindy would've made the observation with withering sarcasm, but she was in no mood for humor. No one was. Words had been few among the Meridian journalists since they saw the Magnificents at work. As they followed a female guide into the building's enormous conference room, their expressions ranged from stony to terrified to furious. Out of the corner of her eye, Lindy caught Jo darting nervous glances at her.

"You all right?" Jo whispered.

Lindy looked around the long room. After counting six rows of seats for the audience and taking note of the stage, the conference table, and the mahogany podium, she finally shook her head. Jo sighed.

"Good," she muttered. "I'd be more worried if you said you were."

Lindy said nothing, distrustful of her own voice, and headed for the front row. Jo claimed a chair beside her and got out her holocam; Lindy produced her tablet and observed the entrance of Rael's chosen audience. Most were wealthy profiteers of his industrialized society; others were in uniform. A few were foreigners, allies from elsewhere in the Star System. Some were obviously ordinary citizens selected to represent Valya's working class. Stiffly dressed in grey, they took their seats with uneasy glances around the room.

The din quieted as two dozen Magnificents marched in, taking their positions along one wall. The Meridian guards came next, planting themselves on the other side of the room. Lindy spotted Frank among them. To her surprise, he suddenly took his helmet off, flushed and visibly frustrated as he inspected its underside. He put it back on as soon as the leading players entered the room, but not without a pained wince.

Then Rael led the way to the conference table, his three advisors and the Remnant filing behind him. The Dominators—the greying, maternal Elva Chevenere, tall and ghoulish Hadrian Daltis, and *his* beautiful daughter Morgarena—all wore trim, dark suits. They seemed to be the most confident and unflustered of the entire group.

Finally, once his companions were seated, Rael strode to the podium. As he gripped it with both hands, the quiet in the room deepened into silence.

"Citizens and guests," he began, his voice rich and low. "We thank you for your presence and for your support of this great planet's future. For the next few days, we will discuss how—and if—we can repair the breach between commoners and aristocrats, the hard-working man and the noble, the haves and the have-nots.

"For years, I have resisted the compromises proposed by the Royal Remnant, fearing they would only embolden those who once oppressed our people." He chuckled sheepishly. "Well, perhaps I was wrong. Perhaps *some* compromises will assuage the trials of the common Valyan and break the power of the insurgents who seek solutions through violence. If so, I will certainly consider it. But I swear that the interests of our citizens are always—*always*—at the forefront of my mind. And so I ask you, my people, to once again trust me with those interests. I may come from royal stock, but I am one with you."

Rael held out his palms. His voice had never faltered, but Lindy noticed a tremor in his hands.

"I promise you," he finished, "your revolution will not be in vain!"

Hadrian Daltis sprang to his feet. "All hail the Magnificent Citizen!"

"Hail the Magnificent Citizen!" most of the audience shouted back. Jo grimaced. Lindy glanced over her shoulder. The Valyans and Rael's allies watched him with everything from interest and adulation to boredom and muted resentment—but the Magnificents' eyes, visible through their visors, remained utterly blank.

What was it Mariamne and Lhoris had both said at MID Headquarters? *"Somehow, someway, they have lost the Valyan gift. The loss of the gift has made them monsters..."*

Rael withdrew from the podium. "Your turn, Cousin."

Mariamne rose. She folded her hands on the podium, inhaled, and looked straight at Lindy. Lindy dared not acknowledge it even with a nod, but she did meet her gaze as steadily as she could. Mariamne pursed her lips, apparently satisfied, and faced the audience.

"Valyans. I am Mariamne, daughter of the man you knew as Prince Ilion, brother of King Kalen. And I have come here with the sole purpose of bringing peace, harmony, and prosperity back to this planet."

Lindy exhaled. The audience murmured.

"I will do everything in my power to come to a mutually beneficial pact with the Citizen, one which will, I hope, bring greater stability to our planet. This can only be good for everyone—for the workers, the economy, and the displaced Valyans on Meridian. They, too, wish to come home. And I assure you that though I am not my father, I will do my best to honor his original purpose for this conference."

She stepped away. A surprised, thoughtful silence hung over the Chamber.

And then, without warning, someone in the back started clapping.

Everyone spun in their seats. Lindy spotted the culprit: a young Valyan wearing the uniform of the palace staff, his face radiant with defiant admiration. When his female companion in a similar uniform took up the applause, the audience turned nervously back towards the stage.

Mariamne seemed uncertain about how she should respond, but Rael looked like a time bomb about to go off. He shot an infuriated look at the Magnificents and at one of them in particular. The soldier stepped forward as if obeying an unspoken command, offered a nod, and turned his head towards the servants.

Lindy didn't stop to think. Her chair scraped the floor as she got to her feet. Rael heard it and locked his gaze on her. She almost quailed, but she set her teeth and slammed her palms together as hard and as fast as she could.

Jo caught on and sprang to her feet, whistling around her fingers. Perry Ambrose leaped up next and roared a wordless cheer. When the rest of the Meridians stood in a swift, simultaneous motion, it sounded like thunder. Their rowdy applause quickly drowned out the servants'.

The rest of the audience maintained an unwavering silence. Lindy looked over her shoulder in time to see the two servants shouldering their way to the nearest exit, breaking into a run as soon as they reached it. Anyone could've stopped them, but guarded respect softened more than one Valyan face—especially among the self-conscious workers who hardly dared move a muscle.

And when she turned back to the stage, she caught the three Dominators exchanging distinctly uncomfortable glances.

Chapter Seventeen

Aboard the *Hummingbird,* Ethan and his officers were riveted to both the live transmission from Valya's only news network and the visual feed from Frank's helmet. When Mariamne finished her speech and the applause began, Ethan slapped his palm against the communications console so hard that Lieutenant Mockett jumped.

"Yes!" he cried. "Yes! Praise Elyon, that's it!"

"Sir?" Mockett asked.

Ethan snatched his jacket off the back of his chair. "We came here assuming the Valyans only saw the Remnant as their last resort. But either Mariamne just made a fantastic first impression, or people have always had a slightly better opinion of the Navorres than Rael wanted us to believe. It's a good start—better than we could've hoped."

"You're still going to assess the city for yourself, then?" Commander Aeron asked.

"I am. That was what we decided yesterday, right?"

"Well, yes. But after that moment of turmoil in the street…"

Ethan nodded. "I'll stay away from the crowds. Take care of my ship, Commander."

Aeron gave him a quiet smile that still held some concern, but the Opitheldran was taciturn and disciplined to a fault. He saluted without further argument.

The hover-taxi Ethan sent for arrived just as he descended the ramp with his suitcase—the one carrying not just his clothes, but the rest of the MID equipment not already tucked away in his fellow troopers' luggage. The pilot, a lanky man with close-cropped hair and hollow cheekbones, didn't get out to take the suitcase. Ethan put it in the back himself and settled in the passenger's seat.

"Where to?" the man asked, his interest visibly growing as he took in Ethan's uniform.

"The Cor Danem Renaissance."

The pilot nodded and put the cab into gear. Except for the restrained answers he gave to Ethan's questions about the factories they passed and how long it would take to reach specific landmarks on foot, he made no conversation. Ethan logged the information into his comm, smiling innocently when the man cast a wary look at the device.

"This is going to be something of a vacation for me," Ethan explained. "I'd rather not get lost on my first day."

"Hmmph," the pilot grunted.

"Have you lived in Cor Danem long?"

The pilot glanced at him sidelong. "What is it to you?"

"Not a thing. Just interested."

The man said nothing. Not until they passed under an archway into the more affluent part of town and Ethan caught sight of the grand, seven-story hotel did he reply.

"I have lived here since I was seven years old," he said. "My father moved us from Relanda, a river village, after the Revolution."

"For work?" Ethan asked.

The pilot maneuvered the cab into a parking spot. "My father was an overseer at one of the ariya plantations. When the nobles fled, the plantations fell apart. So my father had to get a job in a factory."

"I see. He still works here, then?"

With an unnecessarily violent motion, the pilot activated the landing gear. The atmosphere had changed. Ethan found himself keenly aware of the weight of the raygun concealed in his waistband.

"My father," the pilot said slowly, deliberately, "is dead."

"I see," Ethan said again.

"No, you do not 'see.' You foreigners never do. The Magnificents killed him in one of those protests last month."

Oh, Ethan thought. The man continued to glare at him as if demanding an explanation or even an apology. Ethan looked away and got out. He retrieved his luggage from the back. Still the man watched him. Ethan leaned back into the hover and dropped his voice to a whisper.

"I'm sorry about your father. Maybe things will improve after…"

He gestured in the general direction of the Navorre Palace. The man followed the motion and raised his eyebrows, the corner of his mouth turning up in a disparaging smile.

"Hope is for children," he muttered. "That'll be three hundred torrins."

The luggage safely locked in his room, Ethan ventured into Cor Danem. He entered the hotel as an officer of the Meridian Nova

Force; he left it in blue jeans, a black button-down shirt, and a baseball cap.

Makes me only slightly less conspicuous, he thought wryly, tugging the brim of his cap until the micro-cam sewn into the side was nearly level with his eyes. He quickly opted to stay on the main road, not relishing the idea of running into a neighborhood gang, and gave several businesses and offices a closer look. The camera recorded every step and face along the way. The streets, however, were quiet. Everyone had gone back to work after the morning's excitement.

At noon, that changed. Factory whistles blared, uniformed workers returned to the streets, and Ethan found himself borne along a southward wave. He paused at a corner booth where a deaf old woman sold some kind of hearty-smelling, fried vegetable; she gave him a kind, toothless smile as he paid for his share. Teenagers in factory jumpsuits raced past him, yelling and laughing. Ethan decided to follow them, fascinated by their high spirits and appalled to think that kids their age worked in those smoky plants.

His questions sputtered once he realized where they were all heading. Like a purpose-driven swarm of bees, the throng of workers had gone straight to the ancient, crumbling wall on the southernmost boundary of the city. Sprawling green fields lay just beyond the wall. The workers laid out their meals, some of them making seats of the ruins. Ethan ignored the odd stares and hoisted himself atop one of the stones, swinging his legs around so his feet dangled above the grass on the other side.

The air was fresher facing the field. Twenty-three years ago, he knew it had shivered with screams and the throbbing heat of ray-guns.

Lindy and her mother were here, he remembered. *Rael's parents and sisters were here.*

He opened his box of food. The fried vegetable had the filling texture of a potato but tasted more like an onion. He chewed thoughtfully and closed his eyes, remembering the night he and his mother, exhausted after a long day of arranging refugee transports, were woken by a distraught farmer with news of a massacre…

"Sir?"

Ethan jumped, jerking his head over his shoulder. A boy clad in a dark jumpsuit stood below him. He didn't look much older than ten. Ethan cleared his throat and swung his legs around so he faced the boy.

"Yeah? What can I do for you, son?"

The boy flashed an eager, excited grin. "You are a Meridian?"

Ethan chuckled. "I guess I do stick out like a sore thumb, don't I?"

The boy's eyes shone. "I have never met a Meridian. Did you come with the Remnant? Were you in the motorcade?"

"Yes to the first question, actually. But no to the second—sorry."

"Oh. Well. I didn't see it myself, but our supervisors made all the grown-ups stop work to go see it. My father said Princess Mariamne and the Citizen had a fight in front of the Palace." The boy lowered his voice to an anxious whisper. "Is that true?"

Ethan hesitated. How much information should he risk giving this boy? He held out his lunch. "Want some?"

The sparkle in the boy's eyes sharpened. Ethan had seen that look too many times to mistake it for anything other than hunger—so he was surprised when the boy swallowed and shook his head.

"No, thank you," the boy murmured. "I have my lunch."

"Care to sit, then? There's plenty of room here."

Ethan slapped the space on the stone beside him. The boy glanced around; Ethan did the same and saw all the adults nearby watching out of the corners of their eyes. He decided to ignore them, lifting his eyebrows in a welcoming manner. The boy flashed a smile and scrambled up.

"Have a name?" Ethan asked.

The boy opened his lunch tin and nodded. "Avor."

"Nice to meet you, Avor. The name's Ethan." He raised his hand in a Meridian salute. The boy grinned and imitated the gesture before pulling a measly sandwich from his tin.

"What is your uniform for?" he asked.

"Actually, this isn't a uniform. These are my…play clothes." Ethan plucked out another piece of his lunch. "What's *your* uniform for?"

"Grenada Factory A13."

"Ah. What do you do there?"

"I'm on an assembly line. I make sure the rivets are tight on the undersides of hovers."

"Are there any other boys your age working with you?"

"Mmm, yessir." Avor wiped his mouth on his sleeve. "We call ourselves the Grenada Regiment. You should see us! We can tighten rivets faster than a squad of men twice our age."

"I'm sure that wins you points with your 'supervisors.'"

Avor snorted with a cynicism at odds with his age and dove into his sandwich again. "Why are you here?"

Ethan sighed. "Well, my ship is grounded on Valya until—"

"No, no. I mean *here*." Avor lowered his voice. "At the Field."

Ethan looked at him, startled. The boy had said it as if the field, not the wall or the scenic view, was the main attraction. Avor must've noticed his surprise: he squirmed uneasily.

"Foreigners do not normally come here," he said. "They don't like it."

"They don't?"

Avor shook his head. "They say it is haunted."

"Then why…" Ethan gestured with his head at the people perched on the ruins, chatting, eating, or gazing off into the distance. "If it's haunted, why do you come?"

Avor squirmed, gripping his sandwich a little tighter. "Because we have to."

"Because the Citizen says so?"

"Oh, no. My father says if the Citizen knew why we were really here, we'd be in big trouble."

A sharp whistle cut Ethan off before he could respond. He turned and saw the workers wrapping up their picnics and hurrying away.

"Magnificents," Avor breathed. "I've got to go."

"Wait!" Ethan cried. "Here, take this. I'm not hungry anymore."

He held out the box again, still half-full. Avor looked at it, then at Ethan, then back at the food. This time, he snatched it close to his chest, offering a final grin before dashing away. Ethan jumped to the ground just as a cluster of Magnificents burst into the ruins, pushing stragglers around like rag dolls.

"Get out of here," they ordered in eerie, mechanical monotones behind their helmets. "Lunch break is over. Sitting on the ruins is prohibited. Get off of there."

Ethan set his teeth as one of them shoved his rifle butt into a woman's back. She cried out and staggered but didn't fall. Ethan ducked his head and strode away, preferring to avoid a confrontation with Rael's soldiers for a little while yet.

"Why did we have to get a room on the ground floor?" Jo grumbled. "This is crazy. We'll hear every siren in the whole city this close to the street!"

Lindy ignored her. Answering Jo would require too much brainpower already tied up in writing this piece for Athena. She threw herself back in the rickety chair at the desk and raked both hands through her frizzing hair.

"Okay, listen to this. 'Brocade gowns and brighter colors than we're accustomed to from the Royal Remnant and three-piece, pin-striped suits from the Magnificent Citizen and his Dominators certainly made for a fascinating study in contrasts on the first day of the Valyan Peace Conference. The surprises, however, didn't end there. Ordinary Valyans, too, deserve mention, swelling the streets to watch Princess Mariamne's return but dressed without variation in the nondescript uniforms of Cor Danem's sweltering factories...'"

"Athena will cut all that out, Lin," Jo interrupted. "She wants pleasant, pretty stuff—not the nitty-gritty."

"Even when the 'pleasant, pretty stuff' is just a show?" Lindy twisted in her seat. "For the sake of Athena's aesthetic, I have to pretend I didn't see *hordes* of oppressed people today—not to mention a mini-massacre?"

Jo said nothing and continued hanging clothes in the closet. Lindy slumped over the back of the chair.

"Days like this, I wish we'd never chosen fashion journalism as our cover," she muttered.

"Days like this, I'm glad we did. You'd never be able to rein yourself in if we were immersed in intergalactic politics all the time. You're too honest."

In spite of herself, Lindy laughed—just as a burst of static and a quiet voice scratched over their earbuds.

"Goldhawk to Thorpe," Ethan called.

Jo gasped and Lindy sprang out of the chair. "Thorpe to Goldhawk! Where are you?"

Ethan chuckled. "What's the matter, Thorpe? Worried about me?"

"*No*, but we haven't heard from you in hours. Are you in the hotel?"

"Yeah, and Falcon's with me, but we have a problem. This floor is crawling with bellhop droids. I don't like the looks of them. We're gonna come down and meet you in your room."

"Sparks here," Jo said. "You don't think they're surveillance droids, do you?"

"If they are, I don't want to risk them seeing you come up here." Ethan lowered his voice to a whisper. "We're coming downstairs now. What's your room number?"

"12," Lindy said. "Bring your equipment. We can keep it here if we need to."

"Falcon to Thorpe," Frank said. "Equipment on the way. *All* of it."

He sounded sullen, and when Lindy opened the door a few minutes later, she understood why. Poor Frank lugged in a heavy suitcase with both hands, his face pink from the strain. Ethan had an identical suitcase, but either it was lighter, or his height and build made it less of a burden.

"Come in," Lindy whispered. "Jo ordered dinner. She's gone down to the lobby to meet the delivery guy."

"Bless her," Frank gasped, dropping his suitcase. "Now, I'd like to go on record and say this was *not* my idea. We probably looked fishier heaving our stuff downstairs than you would've been coming upstairs—"

"Two women going up with their suitcases and waltzing into a Meridian captain's room would've hardly been inconspicuous, Frank," Ethan said patiently.

Lindy looked from one man to the other. "Do you think you're being watched up there?"

"I don't think *we* are," Ethan replied. "But Frank says the droids knocked on Mariamne's door twice before Commander Penderwick made them go away. Even your grandmother had to kick them out of her room." He paused. "How are you holding up?"

Before she could reply, Lindy heard a knock at the door and hurried to let Jo in. Jo, bearing a flat, warm box, brightened as soon as she saw Ethan and Frank.

"Hey hey hey, guys! Look what I got. The guy called it 'doiya.' It looks and smells like pizza sans the tomato sauce...so it's basically glorified cheese bread."

"You're a dreamboat, Josephine," Frank said, reaching for the box.

Jo snatched it out of reach. "Call me 'Josephine' again, and you won't get any."

Ethan smiled. "Good to know everyone still has their sense of humor. I wasn't sure what I'd find after what happened on the motorcade route."

Lindy and Jo looked at each other, then at the floor. Frank cleared his throat.

"It was hard for everybody, I think," he murmured. "Mariamne was absolutely ballistic there for a few minutes. Rael acted like it wasn't a big deal."

"Are you surprised?" Lindy asked.

"Not really." Frank took a piece of the doiya and enjoyed a satisfying bite before he went on. "I never thought this was gonna be easy, guys, but those two are poles apart in ideology. And they're already making demands that neither one will ever agree to."

Ethan frowned. "Like?"

"Okay, take the ariya plantations. They used to be the bedrock of Valya's economy, right? And Mariamne and Rael both want to rebuild them, minus the old slave labor, of course. The problem is, Mariamne told Rael this afternoon—right after he made us all watch a whole montage of his glorious reign—that she had no intentions of working with him if he didn't reinstate the Parliament."

"To which Rael replied," Jo piped in, deepening her voice and peering at Frank down the end of her nose, "'Well, I want the plantations back, too, but we won't reinstate Parliament unless you agree to help me defeat the Renegade!'"

Ethan smirked at her uncanny impersonation. "How did Mariamne take it?"

"She said she didn't come here to talk about the Renegade," Lindy replied, "and that he becomes irrelevant if she and Rael form an alliance anyway."

"Cue Rael's epic sulk," Frank grumbled.

"Show Ethan the pamphlet, Lindy," Jo urged.

Lindy drew her comm out of her pocket. "Rael presented this as 'evidence' of the Renegade's troublemaking—one of the rebels' most popular pamphlets. It's all over the planet, apparently. I took this screenshot to put in our MID bundle for Jarvis."

She handed the comm to Ethan. He frowned as he read the pamphlet's contents aloud.

"'We ask not for a return to the old days of royal extravagance and the suppression of the poor. We would only be repeating the mistake of the Revolution, exchanging one form of tyranny for another. Rather, we call for the establishment of a new constitution that will effectively protect the rights of all Valyans. Rael Navorre, the Great Usurper...'"

"Catchy," Jo muttered.

"'...has spent the past twenty-three years entrenching himself and his Dominators in the trappings of power. They no more deserve to rule this planet than drunken idlers deserve to be Knights of Elyon.'" Ethan raised his eyebrows. "Doesn't mince words, does he?"

"Nope," Lindy said. "And it's no wonder Rael is so stressed about it. The Renegade has a sizable following, judging from the past months' riots. After what happened today, it might get bigger." She looked anxiously at her partners. "But I'm more worried about Rael than I am about an uprising. He sees Mariamne as a real threat to his regime. He wouldn't have hired Cornael to kill her if he didn't."

"True," Ethan muttered.

"And now she's here, and she's sticking to the Remnant's demands, and the people are clearly intrigued by what she's promising." Lindy shook her head vigorously. "Rael can't afford any sign of weakness on his part. I'm concerned he'll do something rash if he feels like things are closing in on him."

"So how do we move forward?" Frank asked.

"We do exactly what we were assigned to do," Jo answered firmly. "Keep the Remnant safe."

"But if Rael lashes out," Lindy countered, "then our job gets hard, *fast*. Think about it. If the conference fails, if he kicks us and the Remnant out of the Palace one day, then the Valyans who've hoped Mariamne can solve their problems without violence might throw in their lot with the Renegade after all."

"And Valya will disintegrate into civil war," Ethan grumbled. "Again."

"So no matter what Rael does, he's taking some sort of risk," Jo murmured.

"And that makes him ten times more dangerous," Frank said. "I know what bad guys look like when they feel trapped. Rael had that look today, more than once."

Lindy peered at him. "And *you* looked like someone was twisting your ear inside that helmet of yours. What was that about?"

Frank winced. "Something was interfering with the signal. I think I fixed it, but the static nearly blew my eardrums out."

"You don't think it was some kind of shielded transmission, do you?" Ethan asked.

"I don't know. The helmet's supposed to pick up that sort of thing, not act like it wants to self-destruct."

"It could've been the amount of tech in that room," Jo suggested. "We had all those comms and recorders, and all of 'em were connected to goodness knows how many networks."

"Maybe," Ethan muttered. He paused, looking hard at Lindy. "I learned something today about the field where the Cor Danem Massacre happened."

Lindy jerked her head up. He nodded.

"I talked with a kid at the old city wall. There were scores of other Valyans there, most of 'em workers on lunch break. But the boy said something about how they had to go there every day."

"What, you mean by law?" Lindy asked.

"The exact opposite. He said Rael would be furious if he knew about it. Unfortunately, some Magnificents came in ordering everybody back to work before I could ask too many questions. But I can tell you one thing. They weren't there for the scenery."

"You think it's worth investigating?" Lindy asked.

"I do. It may tell us something about what these people are thinking." Ethan hesitated. "Maybe you and I could go down there tomorrow afternoon? Jo and Frank, you could handle things at the Palace without us for an hour, couldn't you?"

Frank shrugged and nodded. Jo frowned at Lindy.

"Can you handle that?" she asked.

Lindy sighed and rubbed her arms. She remembered the women lying dead in the street, the disheartened workers, and the Valyans in the audience who'd mustered enough courage to stay right where they were and let the applauding servants flee. She remembered Mariamne, too, standing proudly behind that podium.

After seeing all that, a little voice in the back of her head whispered, *you'd be a coward if you couldn't drag yourself to that field for just an hour.*

"Yeah," she heard herself say. "Yeah, I think I can handle it."

Chapter Eighteen

When Lindy's alarm went off the next morning, the darkness startled her. She threw off her covers and drew back the window curtain. Rain fell over Cor Danem in great grey sheets.

Jo stirred in her bed. "What's wrong?"

"The heavens have opened." Lindy grabbed her comm and logged onto the Valyan net's weather site. "Look at the radar. We're socked in."

"Ugh, it's too bright," Jo moaned. "Hard on my eyes…"

"There'll be no trip to the wall today," Lindy muttered.

Jo blinked at her over the top of her blankets. "Glad or sad?"

Lindy just sighed and returned to her bed, folding her legs beneath her. Glad or sad? She wasn't quite sure yet. She did feel unusually well-rested, though. She and Rael Navorre had made eye contact yesterday; she'd seen the Magnificents at work; she'd even watched Revolution footage. Yet she hadn't had any nightmares.

Strange.

She checked her mail while Jo staggered into the bathroom. Jarvis hadn't sent any messages during the night, but she did find one from Athena, a reply to last night's article submission. Lindy leaned back against her pillows and thumbed the letter open.

A single sentence awaited her:

You have got to be kidding me.

Lindy raised her eyebrows. Jo had been right, then: Athena hadn't appreciated her observations of Cor Danem. She poised her thumbs above the screen, her dark eyes hardening as she began typing.

A good journalist tells the good, the bad, and the ugly, Athena. We both know the most popular articles on our site have always been the ones that intertwine fashion with real issues. After everything that's happened lately and all the debates we've put up with over the past few years, deviating from that would hardly be fair to our readers.

Thunder rumbled. Lindy paused, waiting until it faded away to continue.

Besides, censoring myself is out of the question. I call it like I see it. Always have, always will. Take it or leave it.

Lightning flashed as she hit "send."

When she told Ethan about the weather, he agreed they couldn't go to the wall today. For one thing, two Meridians heading in such a specific, unusual direction in the pouring rain would be too conspicuous. For another, the idea of getting drenched seemed to make his skin crawl.

Lindy sidled up to him as the journalists, Nana, the Remnant, and the Meridian guards huddled beneath the hotel portico, waiting for the hovers to take them to the Palace.

"What's the matter?" she teased. "Made of sugar?"

Ethan shot her a dry look. He was back in uniform, intending to establish his presence at the conference. He looked rather commanding if she did say so—which, of course, she didn't.

"No, not sugar," he said, pretending to sound offended. "Just a lot of starch."

Lindy laughed. "How much time did you spend ironing that uniform?"

"You don't want to know. Frank already made fun of me."

"So what you're telling me is, we've got the technology to get to the very edge of the Star System, but we *still* haven't invented a rain-proof, wrinkle-proof Nova Force uniform?"

Ethan chuckled. The hovers rolled up; cameras flashed as Nana and the Remnant piled into their vehicle. He leaned a little closer.

"You can be so snarky," he whispered.

Lindy smirked, but her heart fluttered a little too enthusiastically at the twinkle in his eye. She cleared her throat and straightened her face, ignoring the gleeful look Jo shot in their direction.

Valya's infrastructure was even more deficient than anyone outside the planet had suspected. The Renegade and his followers had all but paralyzed transportation, trade, and military activities south of the Great Valyan River. Most government funds went straight to the well-equipped Magnificents and to suspiciously affluent local administrations. The rationing system, however, was strained to the limit, and Valyan money was all but worthless.

Nevertheless, Rael was on his home turf, and he made the most of it over the next four days. Every morning he brought in Valyan families who'd suffered until he came to power, industrialists who used to be dirt-poor and now owned massive factories, and even a few visitors from Namaria and Bosthen who claimed he was a far better diplomatic partner than any of the monarchs before him.

But nobody brought in any of those workers Lindy had glimpsed on the motorcade route. Nobody brought in the families of the women who were gunned down. And nobody applauded Mariamne again.

Over Athena's protests, Lindy made subtle mentions of these incongruities in her daily articles. She and Ethan emphasized them in their reports to Jarvis every night, and the other Meridian journalists brought it up vigorously as well. Jo even found a Valyan news site expressing concern that Citizen Navorre wasn't giving more Valyans the chance to share their views.

Yet Mariamne and the Remnant made no move to capitalize on this glaring weakness of Rael's. They just sat there, listening to Rael's allies in haughty silence. When they had a chance to respond, they simply reiterated their tired old arguments: "The return of the Remnant will bolster the economy. The Remnant swears to never seize control of the government. The Remnant does, however, demand a reinstatement of the Parliament. The Remnant also refuses to raise arms against the Renegade..."

And so on and so on, ad nauseam, Lindy thought, casting her bored gaze over the conference room. For the fifth day in a row, rain lashed the windows. Hadrian Daltis and Prince Lhoris were arguing yet again over whether or not the ariya plantations would return to the nobles who once owned the land. Mariamne studied her fingernails. Verrona, the only royal who showed any outward frustration, looked like she wanted to scream. Nana half-dozed in her seat. Journalists and civilians whispered amongst themselves, their attention lost. Jo shot Lindy a look of pure agony.

This isn't going anywhere, Lindy thought miserably. *And it never will, because deep down, neither party really wants it to.*

"I *told* Mariamne, 'Let Lhoris and Ethan bring in a few of the ordinary folks who know what it's like to live on this planet!'" Nana lamented within the secure confines of Jo and Lindy's room. "'Let them show the Star System the damage Rael has actually done and force everyone to see this is all a big performance!' I begged, I pleaded, I argued till I was blue in the face..."

She paused long enough to sip the coffee Jo offered her. Lindy tried not to tap her foot. She already stood in front of her grandmother with her arms folded in a restless, demanding stance. She didn't want to receive a lecture on the value of patience.

"So what did Mariamne say?" Jo asked, sitting next to Nana on the end of Lindy's bed. "Will she let Lhoris take some initiative?"

Nana made a scornful noise over her cup. "On the contrary, she told me it would be easier said than done and that she didn't want an innocent person to fall foul of Rael's temper."

Lindy clicked her tongue. "Well, she's got a point."

"I thought so, too," Nana muttered, "until she added that she also didn't like the idea of factory workers darkening the door of the Navorres' ancestral home."

Lindy flung her arms down to her sides. "You've got to be kidding me."

Nana sighed. "I wish I was. I thought Verrona might have a heart attack. Poor woman. If *she* were in charge, things would be different, but no. We'll have to suffer through Elyon-knows-how-many-more days of this simply because Mariamne is too proud to ask help from a commoner."

Lindy couldn't stand it. She stomped to the window, tearing a hand through her hair. The rain hammered down on the other side of the closed curtains; she could hear it over the hum of the air conditioner.

"What are we dealing with, Nana?" she asked hoarsely. "A bunch of spoiled brats?"

A knock interrupted Nana's reply. Lindy heard the spring of the mattress as Jo got up, followed by the click of the opening door.

"Hey, Jo," Ethan said. "Is everyone decent in here?"

"Yes, unless you have aversions to seeing an old lady in her bathrobe," Nana grumbled.

Lindy finally turned at the sound of his laugh. He still wore his uniform, but his shoes were wet and his hair was damp. She hadn't seen him so relaxed since he found her in his ship's gym.

"I've been to the *Hummingbird*," he said. "My comms officer says the news waves are full of the conference. So far, the governments of six planets have called on Rael and Mariamne to break the stalemate. Even my mother expressed confidence in your ability to conjure up a deal, Councilor."

Nana snorted. "Sounds more like she's trying to reassure herself."

"Maybe. On the other hand…" He fished around in his pocket. "I printed this letter from my sister. Thought you three might like to hear part of it."

Lindy watched as he unfolded the paper. How he'd tolerated all this maddening arrogance over the past five days without losing his cool, she had no clue. Maybe growing up with his mother's superiority complex had given him a greater tolerance for it.

"'Tell Councilor Tremaine,'" Ethan read aloud, "'she makes Meridian proud every time she stands between the Citizen and the Princess. Tell Miss Tremaine and Miss Camrin, too, that I've been reading their articles every day. But I don't just see all the different fashions they describe. I feel the tension and the fear in that conference room, too. Rael certainly has no friend in Miss Tremaine, and no one who reads her would admire him. I, for one, think that's an excellent thing.'"

Nana gave Lindy and Jo a tired smile. "At least you two are doing your jobs well."

"But it doesn't matter," Lindy snapped. "At the end of the day, Meridians aren't affected by this. The average Valyan, on the other hand, can't express support for Mariamne without staring down the barrel of a gun—and she won't even give them a voice! Honestly, it's enough to make you wish the Renegade comes out on top."

Ethan shrugged. "I don't know. I think you may be selling yourself short. You and the rest of our journalists *are* telling the Star System what the Valyans never could on their own. That's gotta be doing some good."

"Maybe." Lindy rubbed her arms and gave a humorless laugh. "Wouldn't it be hilarious if we did more good as reporters than as troopers this time? We might expose more about Rael's Valya through the *Ladies' Post* than through MID."

"Jarvis might not be as thrilled about that," Jo said wryly.

"Maybe not," Nana said. "But I can tell you one thing: the average Meridian would have a great deal to think about."

On the sixth day, the rain finally slacked off. Elva Chevenere and Morgarena Daltis were conspicuously absent from the morning proceedings. Hadrian Daltis—who, in Lindy's opinion, looked like death warmed over—announced that they had urgent business outside Cor Danem and would be back in a couple of hours.

"A handy excuse," Lindy heard one of the Valyan reporters mutter behind her. She and Jo exchanged questioning looks, but the Valyans kept any explanations to themselves.

By mid-morning, she wished someone would just put her out of her misery. The wizened Lord Nhormin had dragged the audience through his plan to restore the plantations for the past hour, and he wasn't winning any awards for the most entertaining presentation of all time.

"At the height of its profitability," the old nobleman droned, "the Allavonde Plantation produced a tenth of the ariya production on Valya after local scientists invented a synthetic material made from the wheat fibers. Rebuilding their laboratory..."

"Bathroom break," Lindy whispered. "I'll be back."

Jo nodded and tucked her hair behind her ear, subtly assuring Lindy that the micro-cam in her headband was still operating. Satisfied, Lindy crept to the back of the audience. Halfway to the door, she spotted Ethan in his seat; she rolled her eyes and he smothered a grin.

Six Magnificents guarded the silent hallway. Lindy slipped past them and headed for the bathroom reserved for the conference. She wasn't in there long, nor was she about to indulge a childish wish to hide there until the conference broke for lunch. But when she ventured out again, looking both ways to gauge the Magnificents' reaction to her presence, the corridor's priceless collection of paintings and sculptures seized her attention. Lindy hesitated, torn between returning and exploring.

Just for a few minutes...just long enough to psych myself up for the rest of Lord Nhormin's lecture.

With one last wary peek at the Magnificents, she tiptoed to the right. An obsidian figure of a Valyan woman carrying a basket caught her eye, and she moved towards it—only to hear the grand double doors at the end of the hallway creak open.

It could've been a servant—probably someone from the kitchen coming to announce that luncheon was served. Yet for some reason she couldn't explain, Lindy didn't want to be seen. Her hand closed over the nearest doorknob and she slipped into a dimly-lit, musty room just as urgent footsteps burst into the hallway.

"I tell you, Chevenere, if there is any truth to this, we cannot waste time."

At Morgarena Daltis's husky voice, Lindy raised her eyebrows. She bent and put her ear to the old-fashioned keyhole—*just like a little eavesdropping kid,* she thought ruefully.

"The Renegade has been saying this for years," Elva Chevenere replied, low and firm. "There is no need to lose our minds over it right now."

"But if it's confirmed, not even the Magnificents will be able to control the people!"

"And if we act too quickly, we will only make things worse. You're as bad as your father, Morgarena. You'd rather bring down your fist and ask questions later."

"Well, at least *my* father knows how to rule."

"No, your father is drunk with his own power and afraid that any concession to the Remnant will jeopardize it. You'd be put at a disadvantage if that were to happen, too. Do not assume I am unaware of that."

The footsteps abruptly stopped right in front of the door. Lindy held her breath.

You could never write this. Nobody would believe you if you told them you'd eavesdropped on two of the most powerful women on this planet from the vantage point of a storage room.

"You're just jealous," Morgarena sneered. "Time hasn't been as kind to you, has it?"

"Enough has passed for me to be certain Rael's mind is not what it once was," Chevenere shot back. "Don't give me that look. I know him well enough to say it freely, unlike certain women who simply give him…how shall we say it…the *pleasure* he craves."

"How dare you—"

Lindy heard the smack of skin against skin, but it wasn't a slap. Instead, it sounded more like someone catching another's hand *before* the slap.

"What I did, I did for Valya—not for him," Chevenere hissed. "Unlike you, I'm not blinded to his faults, and unlike your father, I do not see him as my pawn. Therefore, I counsel you—strongly—against sharing this discovery with him until we can verify it."

"You counsel me? Or do you order me?"

"I wouldn't presume to give you orders. But take care. Nothing unsettles him more than the possibility that all his efforts have been for nothing."

Morgarena didn't reply, at least not verbally. Lindy heard their footsteps again, followed by the dull, distant thud of the conference room doors. She breathed a sigh of relief and stepped away from the door, resting her head against the wall and closing her eyes.

So Morgarena and Rael are an item. Interesting...and a bit gross. But she and Chevenere are worried about some big news coming out of the Renegade's camp. Who do they think might believe it? The Remnant? The Meridians?

Lindy opened her eyes and looked around. She'd guessed right: she had stumbled into a storage room full of all the things you'd expect. But at the very end of the room, beyond a maze of dust-covered boxes, crates, and old furniture draped in sheets, a huge frame leaned against the wall. Lindy frowned. The painting had faded over the years, damaged by the sunlight coming in through a nearby window. Yet she could still make out the figure of a woman dressed like...

Like a queen.

Lindy took a step forward and then another, picking her way through the clutter until she stood in front of the painting. The tall, plump queen gazed forward in benevolent dignity; her dark skin contrasted beautifully with her rich crimson gown. Lindy leaned forward, hands on her thighs, to read the golden plate at the bottom of the frame.

Queen Liliana. Rael's mother.

"Lindy? Where are you?"

Jo's voice in her ear startled her so badly, Lindy nearly tumbled straight into the painting. She regained her balance and put a finger to her ear. "Jo, what's wrong?"

"Nothing. You've been gone a long time. You sick or something?"

"No, I'm fine. I'll be there in a second, I promise. Where are you?"

"We've been released for lunch. They dismissed us rather abruptly, though. Chevenere and Morgarena Daltis just walked in, and as soon as he saw them, Rael adjourned us early."

"Huh. I may know at least part of the reason why. I'll—"

Lindy's throat suddenly tightened, her gaze locking on the portrait. The earbud crackled.

"Lindy? You okay?"

"Yeah. Yeah, I'm okay. I'll be there in a minute. I gotta go."

Lindy dropped her hand from her ear before Jo could respond. She grabbed one of the nearby boxes, set it in front of the portrait, and climbed on top of it. Her eyes were now level with Queen Liliana's, and she could finally see exactly what hung over the woman's bosom: a golden pendant delicately rendered in the shape of a bee.

Just like mine. Lindy pulled hers out from underneath her blouse. The designs were identical.

"They're looking for a new home, you see, but they have to protect their queen from any birds who might try to eat her up. So they make sure she stays deep inside the swarm where they can keep her warm and hidden…"

Lindy staggered off the box and away from the painting, her heart pounding so hard she was sure everyone in this Elyon-forsaken place could hear it. She returned the box to where she found it and hurried out of the room as fast as she could, but it was too late. Her nightmare—specifically the part where her father's voice penetrated the fear and the chaos—pulsed against her skull like a headache.

Still disoriented, she made her way to the stateroom where Rael's cooks served lunch. Jo, leaning against a wall with a loaded plate, motioned to her.

"Hey, there you are! Come on, taste this. Ethan thinks it's quail."

"No, thanks," Lindy said, her appetite gone. "Where's Nana?"

"Over there with Mariamne. Hopefully, she's convincing her to sign Lord Nhormin up for public speaking lessons when we get back to Meridian." Jo paused. "Are you okay? You look sick."

Lindy didn't reply. Nana had her head close to Mariamne's; the Princess frowned in concentration while Nana gesticulated and gave several sharp, emphatic nods.

Nana was clearly doing her job well. She was giving Mariamne good, sound, honest advice…or was she?

What if none of us know everything we should?

Lindy gulped.

That evening, the possibility of dangerous propaganda from the Renegade got the other troopers' alarmed attention.

"That's just peachy," Frank grumbled as he bit into a slice of doiya—which, unsurprisingly, had become their favorite Valyan dish. "I hate working on shreds of information. We haven't gotten any alerts about hijacked networks, though. That's usually how the Renegade works."

"Well, I'm sorry I couldn't bring you back a dossier," Lindy retorted. "It was the best I could do, considering the circumstances."

"And considering you were hiding in a closet, I'd agree," Ethan teased.

"Want me to pull out some of the listening devices?" Jo asked. "Audio gels? Nano-cams? I might need to bleach my brain afterward, but we might get some juicy information if we eavesdropped on Morgarena and Rael's next romantic tryst."

In spite of herself, Lindy smirked. Ethan chuckled, too, but shook his head.

"I don't think we need to expose ourselves to that just yet, Jo. Getting close enough to a Dominator to apply a bug would be pretty difficult. I don't like the look or sound of Hadrian Daltis, though. As reserved as he seems, it sounds like *he* may be the real power behind the throne."

Jo scoffed. "I think Rael could be pretty bad on his own, thank you very much."

"But maybe Daltis is the one who's always pulled the strings," Lindy murmured. "We've always wondered how a guy could order the executions of his own parents and sisters. What if that idea wasn't his?"

"He still ordered it," Frank said.

"But maybe Daltis was the one who talked him into it."

Frank laughed. "What, are you trying to bail him out or something?"

"No, of course not," Lindy said irritably. "But I think we should take this friction within Rael's core group seriously. Anything's possible at this point—including clashing motivations."

"Should we tell Nana?" Jo asked.

Lindy pursed her lips and snatched another piece of doiya from the box. "No."

"Lindy…" Ethan started.

"*Ethan.*" Lindy looked him in the eye. "I might've learned something else today, something I can't explain to any of you till I know more. But because of what I learned, I *don't* trust my grandmother right now. Not her honesty, not her judgment, and certainly not her agenda—whatever it is. I need you to trust me and wait for *my* call. Can you three do that for me this one time?"

Her companions stared at her with varying degrees of alarm. Frank leaned forward.

"You think your grandmother's compromising us? Or the mission?"

"*No.* I mean…I…"

"Frank," Ethan said. Frank shut up. Lindy struggled to meet Ethan's penetrating gaze.

"I trust you," he said. "But we'll need answers this time tomorrow. That's only fair. In the meantime, the forecast looks clear in the morning. I think you and I should do some scouting—try to see if we can figure out just what this 'rumor' is—and then do our own investigating at the Cor Danem wall like we planned. Deal?"

Lindy swallowed. "Deal."

Long after Jo started snoring, Lindy got up and tiptoed to the desk. She sat down slowly so the chair wouldn't creak and pulled her laptop closer to her.

I have to know. Even if it kills me, I have got to know. It could all be a coincidence. But if it's not…

She pressed her lips together, logged onto Valya's planetary net, and entered *"bees as a symbol of the Navorre dynasty"* into the search engine. The results appeared faster than she expected.

Bees were a symbol of the Navorre Dynasty from the Valyan Year 1917 to the Year of the Revolution (also known as Year 2652 in the old calendar). As a sign of respect for the environment and gratitude for what he called "the diversity of nature," King Kaviol installed beehives in his garden. He instructed his descendants to maintain the tradition to ensure 'the goodwill of nature and the blessing of Elyon."

Lindy swallowed and entered another search: *"King Kalen bees."* This time she rolled her tiny pendant between her fingers while she read.

King Kalen Navorre, the last great tyrant of Valya, was known for his extensive knowledge of beekeeping. While the Magnificent Citizen purged Cor Danem of most outward signs of royal rule, he allowed Kalen's bee hives to remain intact. He has often publicly described their survival as a good omen for his benevolent rule.

So it's something of a family symbol, Lindy realized. *It doesn't necessarily mean I'm a Navorre. I* can't *be—all the princesses died. But it does mean my family was probably closely associated with them...and Nana didn't tell me that.*

She pressed the balls of her hands into her eyes. Two strikes for Nana in the "withholding of critical information" department, then. No doubt she'd call it a "strategic omission."

But why, in the name of all that was good and holy, would *this* be strategic?

Lindy scowled. Perhaps her father had been the royal beekeeper; digging into the Navorre Palace's staff records might be the next logical step. But that would also be a complicated research project, one that would have to wait for another day. She cleared the search and returned to the Valyan government's website, chasing another question that had plagued her ever since this afternoon.

Rael and his cronies clearly thought highly of this site: the network automatically took you there whenever you logged on. The colors, however, were garish, the site crawled with bugs, and the "about" pages were over-the-top. Rael Navorre was, apparently, the Great Liberator, bolstered in all his achievements by Dominators Daltis and Chevenere, "former professors of empathology at the University of Velladon where he first became a supporter of the Citizens' Revolution."

Lindy narrowed her eyes. Why would Rael be drawn to empathologists? Why didn't he find mentors in, say, the history classes? Or meteorology? Or biology, for that matter?

Why make your closest counselors people who specialize in the Valyan gift? How would that help you if you were a dictator?

Lindy smothered a frustrated groan and pressed the balls of her hands to her eyes. The answer was here somewhere, but *where?* She lowered her hands, dug her fingertips into her temples, and glared at her screen.

Oh, Elyon...for the sake of everyone who's suffered under Rael, show me what's going on here. I can't place it. I don't know what it is. But we're missing something. And it's right here with Daltis and Chevenere, isn't it?

She froze, then sat up with a start. The government site shone back at her mockingly, but Lindy squared her shoulders and typed in a new search, following the results with her finger.

Works by Dominator Hadrian Daltis:
—Valyan Empathy and the Power of Thought
—Report From the Velladon Medical School, Volume 1
—Victory or Death: A Biography of the Magnificent Citizen

"Hang it all," Lindy hissed. She cleared the search and entered another.

Works by Dominator Elva Chevenere:
—Report From the Velladon Medical School, Volume 2
—A Case for Empathic Manipulation

Lindy's eyebrows almost reached her hairline. She submitted that last title to the search engine.

RESULT: Not found. Please return to the Official Website of the Government of the Valyan Citizenry.

Lindy leaped out of the chair so fast, it squeaked. She snatched her comm from the nightstand, accessing Meridian's uncensored net through her link to the *Hummingbird,* and frantically typed *"empathic manipulation"* into the search bar. As the results appeared, she sank to a stunned seat on the edge of her bed.

Empathic manipulation: a term used to describe the effects of cyberpathic microchips on Valyan and Opitheldran empathies. Theoretically, empathic manipulation can result in the almost complete control of an individual's emotions by the one controlling the microchip. The first cyberpathic microchip was invented by scientists on Xandroa but condemned by the majority of the Kellan Star System because of the potential for abuse.

Lindy let the comm drop into her lap and tried to catch her breath. *Holy krikalilly. We never did find out who was buying the Xandroan microchips from Mikel Sarkova…or where Christopher Osborne was supposed to deliver them.*

She rushed back to the laptop, logging back into her secure MID connection. After a few clicks, a blank white box addressed to Jarvis popped up on her screen. She positioned her fingers over her keyboard…but then she hesitated, her heart and mind racing.

I may be opening the worst can of worms of this entire mission, she thought. *Maybe the worst of my whole career. And if I'm wrong, my head will be the one that rolls. But if I'm right…*

If she was right, then she'd just unlocked a bigger mystery than anyone ever expected.

Lindy set her jaw to one side and started typing, memories of her all-too-recent adventure on Xandroa thundering through her head.

Jarvis, I think I just cracked the Osborne-Sarkova case.

Chapter Nineteen

10:30 AM

Another day in paradise, Jo thought as she lowered herself into her usual seat the next morning. She pulled her camera bag into her lap and withdrew both her holocam and Lindy's tablet. The camera she set on the floor at her feet, the tablet she laid in her lap.

"Hey, Camrin," the reporter from the *Meridian Advocate* said as he sat down behind her. "Where's Tremaine?"

"Hmm? Oh, she's taking a break today. She'll be back tomorrow."

"Huh," he said, snapping a picture inches from her ear as Rael strode down the aisle in a new black suit. "I would've thought she'd be watching this conference like a hawk, what with her grandmother being front and center."

"Dude." Jo turned her seat, fixing him with a glare. "Ever heard of a monthly? What do *you* think takes front and center: that, or Grandma?"

The lie worked; the poor guy even blushed. Jo smugly faced the conference table again just as Nana and the Remnant followed the Dominators into the room. She slipped the tablet to the side and retrieved her holocam. She was a photographer, not a fashion analyst, yet even she was certain Mariamne's silvery gown with its jet-black embroidered hem was her most regal outfit yet.

What no one noticed—hopefully—was that Jo turned ever-so-slightly to the side, pointing the holocam at the Magnificents standing guard along the wall opposite the Meridian troops. With a twist of her lens, she focused on the expressionless eyes behind their visors.

The tiny electrical current detector she'd installed inside the lens, similar to the one Frank had in his own helmet, clicked softly.

Not that I'll pick up much with all these comms, cameras, and who-knows-what-else in this room, she reasoned. *Still, if Lindy's right and they all have Xandroan microchips in their heads, then they're all controlled by a central network. A whole lot of things are gonna make sense really fast.*

Also, Frank will know why his helmet keeps acting up. The interference must be awful.

Daltis bellowed his daily call to silence: "Order! Order in the chamber! The Magnificent Citizen will open the day's discussions."

Jo leaned back, allowing herself one last peek at Frank before she focused on Rael. To her surprise, his movements were unusually slow as he got to his feet. His hands, fidgeting as they often did with his suit buttons, held a noticeable tremor. He even peered into the audience as if he expected someone to jump out at him.

Hmm. Jo glanced at Nana and Mariamne. They, too, exchanged puzzled looks. Chevenere looked downright alarmed. After what Lindy had overheard, that was unsettling.

What if Morgarena had told Rael the Thing? Whatever it was?

"Yesterday," Rael began in a brittle tone, "we allowed Lord Nhormin to bore us to death with his plans for the reconstruction of the ariya plantations. Today, I offer my rebuttal. I will not be swayed by promises of the prosperity these plans may bring at a cost Lord Nhormin tried to downplay: the cost—of Valyan—equality!"

He brought his fist down on the table with each point of emphasis. Mariamne flinched; Nana narrowed her eyes. A heavy, dread-filled hush fell over the room.

"The Valyan people did not spill gallons of blood," Rael went on angrily, "just for these despots to barge in, claiming they have the good of the common man in mind while they rebuild their lavish houses on the backs of former slaves!"

"With respect, Citizen," Lord Nhormin interjected, "you have always made it clear that you wanted the plantations rebuilt."

Rael drew a shaky breath and stepped back from the podium, looking straight at his aristocratic guests.

"That is true," he said, his voice lower but no steadier. "However, if you think I will let you wield the power you once did, you are a fool."

"Nobody wants that," Mariamne insisted. "It would take decades to achieve the productivity the plantations once had, and we've already sworn we won't return to the old labor system! As for 'lavish houses,' why waste time and resources on those when healthy harvests and the well-being of our workers will be our main focus?"

"But what if it *isn't* your focus?" Rael snapped. "What if you're more interested in getting beyond Cor Danem so you can communicate with the Renegade where I can't keep an eye on you?"

Mariamne's mouth fell open. "I have never spoken with the Renegade."

"But you refuse to fight him."

"Fighting him is not why I want to come back!"

"Enough," Nana said, standing. "Rael, you keep bringing this up, and you keep getting the same answer every time. Mariamne has no interest in the Renegade. She only wants to bring Valyan refugees home and help your planet. Why can't you accept that?"

"Because I now know where the true danger lies," Rael growled, pressing his palms into the table. "My dear cousin and the Renegade plan to ally themselves against me. What better proof do I have than her husband's ties with a certain Valyan faction on Meridian?"

Jo's heart stuttered in her chest. Gasps and startled oaths swept through the audience. Chevenere looked like she might be sick.

"I have no idea what you're talking about," Lhoris said—convincingly, Jo thought.

"Oh, you don't, do you?" Rael shot back. "Morgarena. My tablet, please."

Morgarena produced a tablet from her lap. Rael tapped the screen and held it up.

"My finest technicians have spent days decrypting the files sent to me by my informant within the Meridian Nova Force. At long last, we have evidence of Prince Lhoris' connections with a Valyan group on Meridian. This fringe movement has been in communication with the Renegade for years now, sending him information about the Remnant, Princess Mariamne's activities, and her husband's personal views regarding the Government of the Valyan Citizenry."

Mariamne leaped to her feet, shaking with fury. "How dare you?"

"How dare *I*? *You* have been lying to me." Rael flung the tablet onto the table. "No wonder you won't raise a finger against the Renegade. Your own husband is bound to him. Tell me, Lhoris, are you the one encouraging him to set up a sister of mine in my place?"

Chevenere leaped to her feet. "Citizen, with respect!"

"My cousins are *dead*!" Mariamne cried. "To use them to further any cause is vile. We at least agree on that!"

"Is anyone going to point out what just happened?" Nana asked so sharply, everyone stopped to stare at her. "The Citizen just admitted to using Lieutenant Cornael. Oh yes, Rael...we knew all about that. But we also know that she died trying to fulfill the mission you gave her. You're not just guilty of conspiracy and attempted assassination. You have the blood of yet another Valyan on your hands."

Rael's jaw tightened. "You should have never come, then. You should have turned around."

"Oh, I'm sure you wish we had," Nana said, her blue eyes glinting like ice. "But we weren't about to let you scare us away. And I knew we had leverage if you decided to misbehave. I now have plenty of reason to suspend this conference right now on the grounds of foul play, and I will...right after you answer one question."

"Which one?" Rael hissed.

Nana raised an eyebrow. "Why bring up the possibility of a surviving sister? You could've mentioned any number of possible plots against you and your government, yet this one gets under your skin. Makes me wonder if you're afraid there may be some truth to it."

Rael stared at her, eyes widening to a disturbing size. He pointed a shaking finger at Nana. Jo noticed Frank sliding a gloved hand towards the holster on his hip.

"I did—what I had—*to do!*" Rael cried. "The King was a despot, like his father before him. He would've opposed my government every step of the way!"

"And I suppose your little sisters would've been just as ruthless in opposing their beloved older brother?" Mariamne snapped.

Rael turned on her with such violence, Jo seized the arms of her own chair. "You know nothing of it! You were just as oblivious to the suffering of our people as the rest of our class!"

"And you are a murderer who will never wipe his hands clean of his family's blood!" Mariamne screamed.

Rael whipped aside his suit; his hand came back up with a raygun. Frank and the Meridian troops drew their rifles. The Magnificents sprang from their posts, blasters whirring. Screams erupted from the audience. Jo sprang to her feet and put a hand to her ear.

"Thunder!" she shouted. "Thorpe and Goldhawk, we have a Code Nine-Oh-Ten!"

"Drop the gun, Rael!" Frank shouted.

Journalists and civilians ducked behind their seats. While Verrona shoved Talila beneath the table, Jo pulled her gun from the concealed holster in her belt. Rael had his back to her. From where she stood, she couldn't tell if he had his gun aimed at Mariamne or Lhoris. But he did have about twenty Meridian guns trained on him.

Unfortunately, the Magnificents had *theirs* trained on the Meridians, too.

Elyon Above, Jo thought, her heart pounding. *We're about to have a bloodbath.*

Her earbud crackled. "Thorpe to Sparks! Thorpe to Sparks, what's going on?"

"Rael," Mariamne said, her hands raised. "Put the gun down. Please."

"Jo, talk to me!" Lindy shouted.

"Rael, please," Chevenere gasped. "You fire that gun, and the entire Star System will reject us forever!"

"Do you really think I don't live with it every day?" Rael whispered.

Everyone froze. Jo caught Frank's eye and shook her head; he, in turn, motioned to Commander Penderwick at the other end of the Meridian line. Penderwick nodded. Slowly, the Meridian soldiers lowered their rifles.

Under the rustle and clatter of equipment, Jo flipped the lever on her raygun. It charged with a soft hum.

"Do you really think that I don't lie awake at night telling myself over and over again, 'I did what I had to do?'" Rael demanded. "Do you really think their ghosts don't scream to me, begging me not to pull the trigger? But I pull it anyway. I *have* to stop the screaming. I always pull it anyway."

"Rael, don't do this," Chevenere begged.

"Tell me where my sister is, Lhoris, or I'll kill Mariamne where she stands!" Rael roared.

A horrible silence fell. Jo calculated her chances of incapacitating Rael without sending his soldiers into a frenzy. Lhoris rose to his feet. As he pulled Mariamne behind him, Rael's arm quivered.

"You'll just kill one of us anyway," Lhoris said calmly. "No matter what I say, you're too far gone to listen to reason. But you know the truth, don't you? I see it in your eyes, Rael. You *are* afraid."

"Where—is—she?" Rael hissed.

"Lhoris, what are you doing?" Mariamne cried.

Lhoris ignored her. Jo had never seen him look so peaceful. He even wore a faint smile.

"Long live Her Majesty, Alinna Navorre," he said.

Rael made a horrible sound somewhere between a scream and a sob. He and Jo pulled their triggers at the exact same time.

Half an hour earlier

On the other side of town, Lindy and Ethan sat on a public bench, relaxed and mostly inconspicuous. Ethan couldn't help his Meridian looks, but Lindy, clad in simple black pants and a grey blouse, drew no curious stares. She sat at one end of the bench with a pair of holo-paper conductors, the shimmering blue image covering most of her face. Ethan sat at the other end, pretending to scroll through his comm.

She knew, however, that behind his dark sunglasses, he watched the six Magnificents across the street just as closely as she did. Except for the tinted visors over their helmets, the soldiers looked identical to the guards at the Navorre Palace…which made them the perfect observational experiment.

One soldier shifted. Lindy turned the holo-paper page, bringing the conductors together and pulling them apart again. Ethan caught the signal and tipped the brim of his cap. Lindy, meanwhile, turned the holo-paper towards the soldiers. The faint lines of an electrical current detector quivered over actual headlines. As she leaned back, the Magnificent in the lead detached himself from his buddies and inclined his head to the right.

"Strong electric transmission, consistent with the readings from Frank's helmet," she whispered. "And that incline of the head? It's like he's listening to something."

"And we already ruled out earbuds," Ethan muttered. "Their signal is too weak."

Lindy moved her thumb over the tiny detector chip at the top of the right conductor. The fluctuating line disappeared from the holo-paper altogether. She pulled her thumb away again just before the Magnificent strode down another block. The line reappeared, vanished with his disappearance from view, and skyrocketed when she turned the conductors towards the five remaining soldiers.

"You're recording that?" Ethan whispered.

"Yep." She turned off the conductors and put them in her messenger bag. "We'll send that and your video to Jarvis straightaway. Maybe when he sees it, he'll find it in his heart to forgive me for calling him in the middle of the night, raving about a case I'm no longer attached to."

"Sometimes a trooper just needs to make a gut call," Ethan said. "Jarvis knows that."

Lindy decided not to remind him that that had been the second gut call she'd made in one evening. It had, oddly enough, been easier than her refusal to tell him about the painting of

Queen Liliana. She folded an arm over her chest and tapped her finger on her upper lip.

"Maybe the Renegade's already accused the Dominators of using microchips," she mused, "but now they think *we're* getting wise. Maybe that's what Chevenere and Morgarena were talking about. It would make sense, especially since we busted Osborne and Sarkova last month."

Ethan looked at her with genuine surprise. "Wait, that was just a month ago?"

She smirked. "Seems longer than that since Jo and I got dumped in your lap, huh?"

"I've never regretted meeting you, Lindy," he said kindly.

"Get to know me a little longer, and you might," she teased. "Practical to a fault, bit of a control freak, with an unhealthy preference for pizza and ice cream. Believe me, you'll live to regret it."

"I don't think so," he said. "I have nothing but respect for you. You're great at what you do, you're a loyal friend, and you're honest. If I didn't think highly of you, you'd know it. Just ask my crew how I deal with people who refuse to pull their weight."

"What, you fire them?"

He chuckled. "Let's just say I make it very clear to them that their questionable services are no longer needed on my ship."

Despite an odd flutter in her chest, Lindy laughed. Ethan smiled, glanced at his watch.

"It's after ten. If we want to check out the wall before lunch hour, we'd better get moving."

She nodded, slinging her bag over her shoulder. Ethan stood and looked up and down the street, his vigilant eyes scooping up details with a speed that would've rivaled her own. Lindy, however, just watched him with a mix of fascination and…

And what? Admiration?

On impulse, Lindy reached out. Ethan still peered north towards the Palace, but when her hand slipped into the curve of his elbow, he jumped and stared at her. She smiled shyly.

"Hey...it's crowded, and you're a tourist. It'll look funny if I don't play the part of your Valyan friend."

"I thought Valyans didn't touch people unless they absolutely had to," he murmured.

Lindy just smiled, and thankfully he didn't prod. He led them southward, maneuvering past factory gates, crowded storefronts, and seedy subway stations. When they found a hover-bus bound for the city's extreme south, they boarded and headed for the back. She knew by the way he kept touching the brim of his cap that his micro-cam was preserving this ramshackle side of town for MID's records.

But when they stepped out a few minutes later, Lindy stopped short in surprise. The buildings on the edge of town were even more dilapidated than the ones they'd left. Haggard figures peered through empty windows at the few off-shift workers drifting towards the wall.

"I don't think this area's been touched since the Revolution," Ethan said. "Only the poorest live near a field they all believe might be haunted."

Lindy tightened her grip on his arm. A thin woman appeared in the doorway of one building, a baby on her hip and another small child clinging to her tattered skirt. Lindy's stomach churned.

These people are as poor and oppressed now as they were under the Valyan kings.

Ethan tapped her hand and gestured at the wall in front of them. She drew a shaky breath. Soft, damp moss covered some of the massive stones. A few people sat on or leaned against them. Some of the younger ones climbed up to the higher stones.

Just beyond the wall lay an open field, still wet from yesterday's rain.

"Okay," Ethan said gently. "You're here. How does it feel?"

Lindy exhaled. "I feel…fragile."

"Do we need to go?"

"No, no. Just give me a minute."

Ethan said nothing. Lindy swallowed hard. It had been so dark the last time she'd been here. She hadn't even walked the ground. Mama had carried her.

"I love you, Lin. I love you so much. Come on, let's say your prayers, all right?"

Lindy pursed her lips. She pressed her palms against the stone, jumped, and swung her legs up and over the wall.

"Lindy!" Ethan whispered. She ignored him, landing in the springy grass and rain-sodden dirt. Gripped her bag's strap tightly, she took one step forward…then another…then another.

What do I remember of you, Mama? Who were you? What did you *know about bees?*

She stopped and squatted. The grass came up to her shoulders. Lindy set her bag down, her gaze moving slowly over the grass and the faint outline of the Laronda Mountains to the south, beyond the Great Valyan River. Everything was so quiet…so different from what she remembered. She slid a hand beneath her collar, probing the raised scar on her shoulder. She wondered if Ethan remembered a little girl with a matching wound, unable to move her arm because of the searing pain…

Pain.

Lindy's breath caught, the memory of blinding pain hitting her like a lightning bolt—only this time it didn't give way to a horrific pile of skeletons. Instead, shadowy images that had never once plagued her dreams now streaked through her mind like ghosts. She squeezed her eyes shut with a startled groan and pressed her palms into the damp ground.

Fingernails in the dirt. Clawing. Desperate. Run run run run run…

Can't go any longer.

Collapse.

Waking up in mud and blood. Wrapped in something rough and warm. Turned onto her back.

Cradled.

"What's she doing?"

"Who is she?"

"Her friend is a Meridian. Look at his skin…"

"But she is a Valyan! See how dark she is?"

"Stars and comets, if the Magnificents catch her…"

Anxious whispers swirled around Ethan. He didn't know whether to jump over the wall himself and drag Lindy back or stay where he was. As she knelt in the grass, her long, unbound hair falling in a thick black curtain around her head, he knew he hadn't seen such abject emotional suffering since he was a boy. Not even her tearful rage inside the *Hummingbird* gym had made his chest twist like this.

"Do you know her, Meridian?"

He turned and saw a woman in factory clothes, her hair concealed beneath a shapeless grey cap. Concern filled her thin, dark face. Ethan hesitated only a moment before nodding.

"Yeah. She's a friend of mine."

Her gaze shifted to Lindy. "We are not allowed to enter the field. If she is caught…"

"What? She'll be arrested?"

The woman looked back at Ethan just as a commotion broke out behind them. He glanced over his shoulder, and she gasped. One young Valyan and then another had clambered over the wall. Startled cries filled the air.

"What are they doing?" the woman whimpered. "Dear El—I mean—no no, come back!"

"*Wait,*" Ethan snapped, seizing her by the wrist. She froze, but for once, Ethan didn't care about Valyan customs or sensibilities. "If you're not allowed to go into the field, why do you come?"

The woman looked frantically over her shoulder. More Valyans spilled over the wall, steely, quiet resolve written on their faces. Ethan tightened his grip on the woman's wrist. She winced and swallowed.

"We come to do penance," she whispered.

"Penance? For what?"

She closed her eyes. "There's value in remembering…and in repenting. Please let me go, sir. I must get back to my work."

"But *you* didn't kill those people," Ethan insisted. "Rael did. He ordered the massacre."

Her eyes flew open and she glared tearfully at him. "But we *let* him, didn't we?"

Ethan stared at her. The woman sniffed and tugged her arm. Ethan released her hand. She cradled it against her chest as if he'd burned her.

"I'm sorry," he murmured.

She wouldn't look at him as she jerked her head towards the field. "Show you mean it by getting those people back over the wall. You are a Meridian. They will listen to you."

Cradled? By who?

Lindy dug her fingers in the dirt, trying to focus on the memory, but she couldn't bring up the face of her rescuer. She didn't dare let her brain conjure up any faces she couldn't be absolutely sure of, either.

But that's a memory. It has to be. I crawled away, and then I must've fainted, and then somebody found me. Oh please, please, please don't leave me with this blank!

"Lindy. Lindy, come on, we've got to go."

She lifted her head. Ethan knelt beside her, shaking her gently, but he watched the field with something like panic. She sat up and looked around.

Several dozen Valyans waded through the tall grass. The younger ones gazed around with wide-eyed awe. Those who would've been old enough to remember—who might've even seen the carnage—trudged forward with halting steps. Some were in tears. One man stood alone, eyes closed and fists clenched. Another woman wept, a hand over her mouth as she staggered deeper into the field.

"What are they doing?" Lindy whispered.

Ethan rubbed her shoulder. "I think you gave them the courage to rebel."

She looked at him, bewildered, but Ethan barely had time to force a smile before a burst of static filled their earbuds. He flinched and snatched his hand from her shoulder. Lindy put a finger to her earbud as Jo's screams almost deafened her.

"Thunder! Thorpe and Goldhawk, we have a Code Nine-Oh-Ten!"

Lindy bolted to her feet. "Thorpe to Sparks! Thorpe to Sparks, what's going on?"

Silence. She whirled to face Ethan. He still had a finger at his ear, but his face had drained of all color.

"Code Nine-Oh-Ten," Lindy breathed. "That's—"

Sirens cut her off. She and Ethan spun around just in time to see Magnificents scrambling over the wall, wielding long, heavy rods. The Valyans cried out in confused terror, unsure whether to run back to the city or deeper into the field.

Lindy's blood ran cold as the rods came down and their cries turned into screams.

"Run!" Ethan roared. She clenched her fists and ran as fast as she could back to the wall. One of the soldiers stormed towards her. Lindy whipped her raygun out of her waistband and fired two shots at his chest. The blasts barely dented his armor, but he did reel, giving her a chance to catapult over the wall and into the throng of bleeding, screaming workers. When a hand clamped on her shoulder, she whirled and took aim.

"It's okay, it's okay, it's only me!" Ethan cried. "Are you all right?"

Lindy nodded, too breathless to reply. As they struggled out of the chaos, another burst of static filled their ears. They both froze, recognizing Frank's voice over the noise.

"Code Nine-Oh-Ten! This is Falcon! We are under attack at the Palace! Repeat—we are under attack! Acknowledge, Goldhawk! Acknowledge, Thorpe! Backup requested—"

A horrible burst of static cut him off.

"Frank!" Lindy screamed.

It was no use. The connection was dead.

Chapter Twenty

10:45 AM

"Code Nine-Oh-Ten!" Frank shouted. "This is Falcon! We are under attack at the Palace! Repeat—we are under attack! Acknowledge, Goldhawk! Acknowledge, Thorpe! Backup requested—"

CRACK!

Jo screamed as Frank collapsed, blood trickling from his forehead. The Magnificent who struck him kicked him onto his back. Frank's eyes were closed, his face an unsettling shade of grey. Jo lunged for him, but the soldiers already surrounding her jerked her back.

"Frank!" she cried. "Frank!"

She got no answer. A few of the Meridian guards—bloodied, on their knees, and disarmed—looked morosely in her direction. The reporters and Valyan civilians were on their knees, too, most with their hands behind their heads. There was no discrimination between them while the Magnificents confiscated holocams and comms.

"Destroy the evidence, soldiers," a cold voice ordered behind Jo. "What you have seen you will forget before the day is old."

The Magnificents dropped the equipment and brought their booted feet down with a resounding crash. The reporters winced; a few of them cried out. Jo twisted her head around as far as she could, trying to see who'd given the order.

It was Hadrian Daltis. He saw her watching him and his gaunt face contorted.

"*You,*" he hissed. "You were the one who dared fire upon the Magnificent Citizen."

One of the soldiers seized Jo by the hair and yanked her head back. Her racing heart decided to pick up the pace—not because it hurt (and it did), but because she was afraid her headband and its precious micro-cam might slide off. Daltis gripped the front of her blouse.

"Your name, Meridian," he ordered.

Jo swallowed. The game was up. "Jo Camrin. *Trooper* Jo Camrin…Meridian Intelligence Department."

Daltis' jaw flexed. Jo stifled a whimper as he dragged her to the conference table.

Lhoris was dead; that was horrifically obvious. Chevenere had Mariamne's wrists pinned behind her back. Blood and gore streaked Mariamne's face and clumped in her hair; her eyes were dull and tired. Magnificents surrounded the rest of the quaking nobles. Morgarena Daltis held a glittering knife against Nana's throat.

Jo was so horrified by the sight, she didn't even notice the tall, shaking form storming up to her, clutching his wounded arm. He released it long enough to backhand her. Jo reeled, stumbling into Daltis.

"Who do you think you are?" Rael screamed. "I've killed men for less than this! Look at me, you imbecile!"

"She is with the Meridian Intelligence Department, Citizen—and possibly your most valuable prisoner," Daltis snapped, forcing Jo upright. "I suggest you calm yourself and allow Chevenere to escort you to the hospital."

"Hospital!" Rael let out a shuddering laugh and clamped his hand back over his arm. "If you think I'd allow Valya a glimpse of this, you're mistaken. I won't have it all over the networks that a Meridian woman took a shot at me in the middle of a clean kill."

"Looked more like a lunatic's rampage to me," Jo said.

Rael came closer; Daltis pulled Jo away. Rael tried again, and this time Daltis planted a hand on his chest.

"Rael, *stop*."

"She should die—"

"Oh, you mean like Lhoris?" Jo bellowed. "Just because I said something that rubbed you the wrong way, too? Go on, then! Shoot us all while you're at it! Then everyone will know you're crazy, and you know what else? I hope they blow you to kingdom come and put your sister—whoever she is—on your throne!"

Daltis increased pressure on Rael's chest. "Stand. Down."

Rael clenched his fist—the one attached to the wounded arm—so tightly, it was a wonder he didn't break his own bones. Jo had no problem looking him in the eye now. She was so furious, she could hardly see straight.

"Yes…yes, Rael," Daltis said, his voice dropping so low it was almost a whisper. "She'll die in good time, I can promise you that. But she and the Councilor are far too valuable to do away with now. Think, Rael. Clear your mind."

"Sweep *hers*," Rael hissed. "I want answers before the end of the day. Chevenere!"

The Dominator, who'd kept her eyes down even as she restrained Mariamne, lifted her head. "Yes, Citizen?"

"Inform the prison commander that he'll be receiving every journalist, including ours, until we have this situation under control. And every member of the delegation, too, until I've decided whether they live or die." Rael paused, wincing. "And call my personal physician. Have him meet me upstairs."

Ethan tried to rein in his fearful thoughts while he and Lindy scrambled back to the Palace through alleys and backstreets. Code 9-0-10 was the most dreaded in the MID book: "Mission in jeopardy, request immediate backup." All their worst fears had been realized with Frank's final call.

Then again, Frank hadn't been specific. "We are under attack," he'd said—but did that mean he and Jo had been attacked, or the Royal Remnant...or both? Where was he now? And where was Jo?

Lindy hadn't spoken in a while. She clutched his hand so tightly, it hurt. He knew that if she could sense even a fragment of his emotions, he needed to get them under control.

It'll be okay, he thought deliberately. *It's okay, we're gonna be fine. We just need to get to the Palace, evaluate, and move forward from there. If we need to, we'll head straight for the* Hummingbird *and get in touch with Jarvis. It's okay, it's okay…*

Lindy's grip relaxed. Ethan stopped at the end of a street, looked both ways, then down at her. Her mouth had zipped itself into a hard, thin line, but when she looked up at him, her eyes were large, soft, and dark.

"Thanks," she whispered.

Ethan nodded. "You ready? Once we step out of here, we'll be able to see the Palace."

Lindy slipped her sunglasses down over her eyes. "I'm ready."

"First sign of trouble, we're backing out."

"Okay…"

"And we are *not* revealing ourselves, no matter what happens. We're gonna observe, figure out what happened, come up with a plan…"

"I've been a trooper for six years, Captain. I think I know the proper procedure."

Her voice had gone stern and no-nonsense. He decided to take it as a good sign. He pursed his lips, gripped her hand a little tighter, and strode forward.

But even he stopped short as soon as the Palace came into view.

"Stars and comets," Lindy whispered.

Police and army hovers crammed the street. The civilians and foreigners who lived in this part of town scrambled for spots closest to the Palace gate the way a hungrier, poorer crowd might clamor for bread. Ethan adjusted the brim of his cap.

"Stay back!" a policeman shouted. "Madam, nobody goes past this point, thank you…"

"Will the press pool be released?" someone with a holocam cried.

"We are not authorized to answer any of those questions."

"Is Citizen Navorre injured?"

"What about Princess Mariamne?"

"Here they come!"

The crowd surged. The policemen braced themselves against the gate, but as soon as the Magnificents marching out of the Palace lined up and put their rifles to their shoulders, the mob took a startled step back. Silence fell. Hadrian Daltis appeared, his cold grey eyes taking in the scene. As he glided toward one of the hovers, questions exploded from the crowd.

"Dominator, has the Citizen been harmed? Has the conference been called off? How will you respond to the rumors that the Remnant and the Renegade are considering an alliance?"

"Ethan," Lindy gasped, squeezing his arm. He followed her gaze as more Magnificents exited the Palace, dragging the Meridian soldiers and the journalists between them. The nobles came next, dazed and fragile. Mariamne was covered in blood. Councilor Tremaine staggered along on stockinged feet, her shoes lost somewhere along the way.

"Where's Jo?" Lindy whispered shakily. "Have you seen Jo?"

"Shh," Ethan murmured. "Wait a minute, there she is. Whoa, Lindy..."

He wrapped a firm hand around Lindy's forearm before she could take an impulsive step forward. Jo fought her captors with every step, her short legs dragging as the soldiers tried to force her along. Only her headband kept her hair from straggling in her face.

The crowd jostled, pushing Ethan and Lindy back. From where he stood, her grandmother didn't seem hurt. There was no sign, however, of Frank or Lhoris. He remembered the blood in Mariamne's hair, and his stomach churned.

"Come on," he whispered. "Let's get out of here."

Lindy said nothing, her eyes brimming with tears. Ethan quickly turned her around and led her away as fast as he could.

Lindy felt numb, cold, and ready to break. She had failed. She had failed the very people she was supposed to protect—and for what? So she could probe a threadbare lead and reminisce over an even more threadbare memory?

I left them...I left Nana and Jo at the mercy of that madman...I accomplished nothing at that wall, and I left them alone. Oh, Elyon, what have I done? What have I done?!

"Lindy. Lindy, look at me."

They weren't in the open anymore. Ethan had led her into an alley. Brick walls loomed over them on either side. He gripped her shoulder and snapped his fingers in her face.

"Lindy? Talk to me. Are you all right?"

"I..." She cleared her throat. "*No*. No, I'm not all right. Just give me a minute."

Her head swam. She lurched forward; Ethan caught her before she could tumble into him. She curled her fingers in the front of his shirt and shut her eyes.

"S-sorry."

"No, don't apologize." His arms tightened around her, his hand pressing her head deeper into his shoulder. His chin brushed her forehead with a slight, bristly prickle. He was warm and safe and strong and absolutely rock-hard solid.

"It's all right. It's all right, Lindy. I've got you. Just breathe for a minute."

She pulled in a breath, held it, and let it out again. Ethan stroked her hair, but when his fingertips brushed the place where her forehead and hairline met, her eyes flew open.

The last time a man had touched her this gently, she and Owen were in a coffee shop, each of them working on their own assignments. A few days later, of course, he'd confess that he had no job and that he'd fabricated the details of his latest "assignment." But *that* day, he'd reached over, slid his hand over hers, and laced their fingers. It had warmed Lindy down to her toes.

This was different. Owen's touch had been sweet, but his emotions had barely registered with her gift. Ethan's were almost as vivid as if he were Valyan himself. Only the colors were missing. She still sensed his anger and fear, but there was something else, too...something powerful and protective that she never got from Owen. And she knew somehow that if it had a color, it would be white as Joy, yet burn brighter than a thousand suns.

She lifted her head from his shoulder. Ethan studied her worriedly.

"Are you all right?" he asked.

"Yeah," Lindy breathed. *White as Joy...burning bright...* "Yeah, I'm okay now."

"Good. Then we need to make some kind of a plan.'

"Plan." Lindy cleared her throat and pushed herself away. "Plan. Yes, what's the plan?"

"We need to let Jarvis know what's going on and get some direction. I don't dare go back to the hotel yet. The police might be looking for us, too. Although it ought to be easy to give an alibi..."

"You think they'd care if we had one?"

"Probably not. But we can destroy all our equipment remotely. We won't have to worry about them accessing our laptops." Ethan paused. "You saw Mariamne?"

Lindy gulped. "Yeah. You got all that on the micro-cam?"

"Sure did." He reached for his comm, but when he clicked it on, he turned the screen towards her. Lindy took it and read the notification out loud.

"'Attention! There has been a Planetary Emergency. By order of Dominator Hadrian Daltis, the Valyan Information Network is temporarily suspended until the situation is under control and the Magnificent Citizen's safety assured. Please remain indoors until the all-clear is given. All branches of the military are on standby for any additional emergencies. Long live the Magnificent Citizen!'"

"He's cutting Valya off from the rest of the Star System," Ethan said.

"Not to mention breaking off all communication between the Valyans themselves," Lindy said. "He doesn't want anybody to know or even talk about what might've happened."

Ethan took the comm back. "There's at least one thing he didn't count on, though."

"What's that?"

He shot her a wry look. "MID networks. And Meridian novacraft."

12:00 PM

The guard at the novaport's main entrance looked askance at Ethan and Lindy when they walked up to his station a little over an hour later. The whole city had shut down; getting a taxi had proved impossible. At least the confused, frantic crowds had dissipated. Valyans were obviously good at making themselves scarce when so ordered.

"I need to get to the *Hummingbird*," Ethan barked, releasing Lindy's hand and striding a few steps ahead of her.

The guard frowned. "The novaport is closed. Planetary Emergency Protocol states—"

Ethan shoved his Nova Force ID in the man's face. "I don't care about your protocol. Let me through to my ship, or I'll report you to the novaport authorities so fast it'll make your head spin."

The guard glanced at Lindy. She must've given him a ferocious look because he cleared his throat uncomfortably and pulled a lever. The gate opened.

"All right," he muttered. "But if Novaport Security has an issue…"

"Send it to the *Hummingbird*," Ethan said. "We'll take care of it. Come on, Lindy."

It was a long walk across the wide-open runway. The *Hummingbird*'s boarding ramp was down, but six Meridians stood on either side of it, armed and wary. They snapped to surprised attention when they recognized Ethan.

"Don't take your eyes off that gate," he said, dashing up the ramp ahead of Lindy. "I'm about to send more men down to back you up."

The startled guards gripped their rifles a little tighter.

When Ethan and Lindy reached the bridge, they found Aeron and Lieutenant Mockett at the comms station. He monitored something on the screen; she listened intently to something through her headpiece, jotting it down on a notepad. She saw the newcomers first and gasped. Aeron straightened, open relief on his usually placid face.

"Captain!" he cried. "Thank goodness. We've been trying to contact you for an hour!"

"The planetary net is down," Ethan said, "and I didn't want anyone tracking me through a link to the ship. Listen, I want that security team quadrupled on the boarding ramp. Mockett, establish a live, encrypted comm to MID Commander Jarvis and let him know I need to talk to him as soon as possible. Send the response to my cabin and make sure the encryption is secure."

Aeron frowned. "What's going on, Ethan?"

Ethan paused. Aeron rarely used his first name. He stepped closer and lowered his voice.

"The delegation, the security team, and our journalists have been arrested."

Mockett put a hand to her mouth. Aeron's eyes widened.

"For what reason?" he asked in a similar undertone.

"We don't know yet. But I don't want any Valyan officials aboard this ship until we find out. The *Hummingbird* is still the territory of a neutral power. It should be treated as such."

Aeron nodded firmly. "Yes, sir."

By the time they got to Ethan's cabin, the progress bar on his computer showed that the link with Jarvis was nearly established. Lindy was relieved. She didn't want to be here with Ethan for too long, not after those charged moments in the alley.

Of course, it's not like he'd sense that I *sensed what was going on. But he's pretty sensitive to it. He knows how much a simple touch can mean…*

"Here," he said, turning the swivel chair in front of his desk towards her. "Have a seat."

Lindy frowned. "What about you?"

Ethan shrugged. "I'll stand."

"I don't mind standing. You're the captain."

"And you're the one who almost had a panic attack an hour ago. Sit down."

Lindy bristled, but he didn't sound like he intended to report her for a possible emotional compromise. Tugging her sunglasses out of her hair, she attempted a teasing smile as she sat down.

"If my legs didn't feel like they'd been turned into noodles, I might fight you on this."

Ethan chuckled just as Mockett's voice crackled over the cabin intercom. "Sir, Commander Jarvis is waiting for you on the other end of the commlink."

"Thanks, Lieutenant." Ethan touched a button on the virtual keyboard. The screen blinked, and Jarvis appeared. He smiled with genuine pleasure and leaned forward.

"Well, this is a surprise. I didn't expect to hear from you two until this evening. Any news on Lindy's lead?"

"Sir, this is an emergency comm," Ethan said. "Are you alone?"

The relaxed friendliness drained from Jarvis' eyes. He glanced at someone Lindy couldn't see and gave a crisp nod. After a moment, he shifted even closer to his screen.

"Is this about the microchips?" he asked.

"No sir, though we do have some information on that. We'll forward it to you as soon as possible." Ethan paused. "The delegation's been arrested, Jarvis. Meridians and Valyans alike, along with the security team and all the journalists. We got back to the Palace just in time to see them being forced out, under guard and handcuffed."

Disbelief and then terror streaked across Jarvis' normally stable expression. "What happened?"

"We don't know yet," Lindy said. "Jo sent us a Code 9-0-10. Then Frank followed it up by saying Lhoris and Rael were down and that they were under attack. We saw Jo when we got to the Palace, but not Frank."

"What about the Councilor?"

"Alive," Lindy said quickly. "And unhurt, we think."

"Princess Mariamne?"

"Alive, but..." Lindy shuddered. "We don't think she was hurt, but she had blood all over her. We're assuming it belonged to Lhoris. He and Frank were the only ones we didn't see."

Jarvis pinched the bridge of his nose. "Any idea of what might've happened?"

"None," Ethan said. "I did manage to film what we saw. A sizable crowd witnessed it, too—but the Valyan net is shut down. No information will be getting off the planet any time soon unless it's from the *Hummingbird* or an independent network."

"Which means I can't give President Stagg any more information than what you just told me," Jarvis said.

"Right. And until Rael lifts the netblock, we won't know much more than that, either."

Jarvis sighed. Lindy gritted her teeth, hoping she looked calm, quiet, and in total control of herself and her emotions.

"All right, here's what we'll do," Jarvis finally said. "I'll let the President know there's been a crisis and that the Councilor is in Valyan custody. As for you…*you* stay put."

Lindy gripped the arms of her chair. "Jarvis—"

"I know, I know. It's the last thing you want to hear. But freeing our people is now the top priority, and it'll be a heck of a challenge. Until we know more, all operations on Valya come to a standstill. Understood?"

"Yes, sir," Ethan said. Lindy kept her mouth shut.

"Where's your equipment?" Jarvis asked.

"Still at our hotel," Ethan replied. "We're gonna deactivate it remotely as soon as we get off this call."

"Good. Retrieving it yourself would be too risky."

"Captain?" Mockett called over the intercom again. "Sorry to interrupt, sir, but there's been a breach in the netblock. Someone's piping in a video feed."

"Patch it in, Mockett, and include Commander Jarvis on the channel," Ethan ordered.

The rogue feed appeared next to Jarvis' side of the screen. At the sight of a masked man swathed in navy-blue, seated in front of a grey wall and gripping a long, slender raygun, Lindy covered her mouth. Only his piercing dark eyes showed over the veil, facing her with calm confidence. She shivered and knew, without a doubt, exactly who she was looking at.

"Valyans." The voice was rich and slow. "Rael Navorre may not want you to know what's happened in his Palace—or at least, he's not ready to tell you his monstrous lies about it just yet. But we have the true account from one who saw it all, and we offer you the truth that will set you free.

"Almost two hours ago, your Magnificent Citizen murdered Prince Lhoris Navorre. The prince's only crime? Acknowledging the truth my followers and I have treasured in our hearts all these long years: that a sister of Rael's still lives. Lhoris learned this truth and spoke it boldly, knowing full well that whether he refused to reveal her existence or not, his death at Rael's hand was imminent.

"Rael will undoubtedly present himself as the victim of a horrific plot against him, but know that *he* fired the first shot!" The Renegade raised a gloved hand, index finger to the sky, in emphasis. "Know that *he* threatened an innocent life first! Know that *he* is riddled by guilt for his bloody crimes—and know that *he* fears the presence of his sister, the rightful ruler of Valya. At her name, Valyans all over this Star System will arise and throw him on the ash heap of history where he belongs."

The Renegade leaned forward. Lindy couldn't breathe.

"Your Majesty," he said, his voice soft and pleading. "Come to our aid, wherever you are. Reveal yourself. Rally your people. We'll follow you to the end in the name of our freedom." He sat back again and pounded his fist against his chest. "Long live Queen Alinna Navorre!"

And with that, the screen went black. Ethan leaned forward and hit the intercom.

"Mockett! Mockett, did you record that?"

"Y-yes, sir."

"Then pipe the recording to Commander Jarvis' office."

"Thank you," Jarvis said. "I'll take it with me when I meet with the president."

"What, uh…" Lindy cleared her throat. "What does this mean for us?"

"Nothing until I talk to the President. Stay alert. Rael knows he's got a mole in the Palace now. It may be that he or she comes to you for protection. Be ready to send your crew out at a moment's notice, Ethan."

"In a military capacity?" Ethan asked.

"Maybe." Jarvis pushed his chair back, then stopped, peering at the screen. "This Alinna Navorre, Lindy…what do you think? Do you think she might've survived?"

"I…" Lindy's heart pounded even harder, though she wasn't sure why. "I don't know, sir."

"Hmm." Jarvis nodded thoughtfully and got to his feet. "Well, if she *is* alive, I hope she realizes we're about to have a bloodbath on our hands."

Chapter Twenty-One

3:00 PM

When Jo finally regained consciousness, it felt as if a hundred sledgehammers roared inside her skull. Her tongue lay heavy in her dry mouth. She groaned and flung an arm out to the side.

"Shh, darling. It's all right. Lie still."

Jo forced her eyes open. Through a haze, she saw Nana leaning over her, dabbing something soft and wet against her temple. The yellow light in the background made her wince.

"Where…" She stopped and cleared her throat. "Where's Lindy?"

"I don't know, dear. Somewhere safe, I'm sure. No, no, no, don't get up…"

Jo ignored her. For a minute there, she thought for sure she'd pass out again, but she sat upright, pressing a hand to the side of her throbbing head. Nana sat down beside her with a weary, exasperated sigh.

"Well, at least you're awake," she said. "Verrona was afraid they'd overdosed you."

"Overdosed?" Jo mumbled.

"The Magnificents ended up drugging you. You would've fought them every step of the way if they hadn't." Nana smiled grimly. "I have to admit, I was proud of you."

Jo grunted her thanks and looked around. They were in a small cell lit only by a naked bulb. Verrona and Talila sat on a narrow bench, holding each other. Lord Nhormin slumped in the corner, unconscious; his frail wife stroked his brow fretfully. Mariamne sat on the floor by the cot, staring straight ahead of her and hardly breathing. Jo swallowed at the sight of the dried blood in her hair.

I should've blown Rael's head off. I should've killed him. Why didn't I kill him?

"Do you remember anything?" Nana pleaded.

"Yeah," Jo said slowly. "Not how I got here, but...yeah. I'm sorry, Nana, I'm so sorry."

"Don't be ridiculous. You did your job to the best of your ability."

"But I couldn't save—"

Nana squeezed her hand. "Rael would've killed Mariamne, too, if you hadn't acted. You did what you could. Nobody can blame you for that."

Jo sniffled and lowered her head. "Lindy never came?"

"We were hustled out of the Palace so fast, I doubt she could've gotten there in time—or that she could've done anything about it anyway." Nana dropped her voice to a whisper so soft, she practically mouthed the next words. "Where *was* Lindy?"

Jo hesitated, remembering Lindy's concerns about Nana's integrity. But Lindy *had* overheard the Dominators discussing a "dangerous rumor," and now Jo had a pretty good idea of what it was. *Everybody* did, thanks to Rael. Telling Nana wouldn't make any difference now.

"She and Ethan decided to probe something she overheard Chevenere and Morgarena Daltis talking about yesterday," Jo whispered back, mindful of possible listening bugs. "Lindy suspects the Magnificents are controlled by Xandroan microchips. She thought maybe *that* was what the women were talking about—but now I'll bet it was that rumor about Rael's sister."

Nana said nothing to that. She looked away, kneading her hands.

"Well, at least none of us have been interrogated," she murmured. "They probably don't know what to do with us yet."

Verrona looked up, eyes blazing. "Of course they know what to do. They mean to accuse us of a conspiracy and have us hanged in the city square! Don't underestimate that nephew of mine, Councilor."

"I don't. But I don't underestimate the influence the Dominators have, either. I suspect that Chevenere, at least, knows exactly what the Meridian government would do if any of *our* citizens come to harm. Rael won't touch us. Not yet, anyway."

Jo reached up to rake a hand through her hair and froze. "My headband! Nana—!"

"Hush, child," Nana hissed. She reached into her blazer, and Jo gasped as she pulled out the headband. "As soon as those brutes threw us in here, I took it off. I had a feeling it might be important."

Jo ran her finger over the concealed camera, sighing with relief. Mariamne lifted her head and glared weakly at her.

"Whatever it is will do you no good if you cannot get it off this planet," she whispered. "My aunt is right. Perhaps they will not kill us yet, but Rael will make traitors of us. He will spin such a web of lies around us that by the time we are able to share the truth, no one will believe it."

"Lindy will," Jo said. "And the Meridians would."

Mariamne raised a feeble eyebrow. "If Miss Tremaine cannot free us, it won't matter."

"She and Captain Granger *will* come," Nana said. "What most people would consider a hopeless situation, MID troopers consider a minor inconvenience. But perhaps, Mariamne...perhaps they are not our only means of salvation?"

Mariamne frowned. Lord Nhormin's wife hadn't seemed to be listening, but now she looked hard at Nana.

"What are you saying, Councilor?" she asked.

"I'm saying, my lady, that your people are simmering. They have been for months—and now *this*? This 'rumor' that one of the princesses may still be alive? Add to that the sight of the Remnant arrested and abused, and you have yourselves a witch's cauldron of rebellion."

"Oh, for Elyon's sake," Mariamne groaned. "None of Rael's sisters are alive. That is a fool's hope."

Nana turned to Mariamne, her keen blue eyes glinting.

"And what if I told you it wasn't?" she whispered.

10:00 PM, Meridian time

"The President will see you now," Maria Stagg's butler-droid announced.

Jarvis sprang up from his seat in the hallway and marched into Hoadley House's private sitting room. He knew immediately he'd interrupted a peaceful evening. The President, clad in a crimson dressing gown, sat at a table with paperwork strewn in front of her. Her painfully thin daughter lay on the sofa. Genevieve lowered her book and smiled at him, but President Stagg just kept signing things.

"Good evening, Commander," Genevieve said softly.

"Evening, Miss Stagg," Jarvis said. The President glanced up over her glasses and popped the end of her pen.

"I hope this is important, Jarvis," she muttered. "Genevieve and I were just about to go to bed, so if this could wait till morning..."

"Trust me, Maria, it can't. We have a crisis on Valya."

President Stagg blinked. Alarm flashed briefly across her face.

"What kind of a crisis?" she asked.

"The worst kind. Rael murdered Lhoris in front of the whole conference."

"Oh, dear Elyon," Genevieve gasped.

"The Councilor, the Remnant, our journalists, Jo Camrin, *and* our guards have all been arrested," Jarvis added. He pulled a flash drive out of his pocket and threw it onto the table. "Your son caught the entire thing on video—or, at least, he recorded the Magnificents cramming our people into police hovers."

"Ethan has not been arrested, then," President Stagg murmured.

"No. He and Lindy Tremaine made it back to the *Hummingbird*. Only Frank Gridley remains unaccounted for." Jarvis pressed his palms on the table and loomed over her. "That drive also contains a video transmission from the Renegade, Maria."

"Tell me what it says, then," she snapped. "If what you're saying is true, I don't have time to watch it."

Jarvis yanked a chair back and sat down. "The Renegade has a contact in the Palace. According to his source, Lhoris knew about Alinna. Rael found out and killed him for it."

The President swallowed so hard, Jarvis could hear it. Genevieve shifted on her sofa.

"Who is Alinna?" she asked.

President Stagg set her jaw and didn't answer. She did, however, look Jarvis in the eye.

"Does Alinna know?" she whispered.

Jarvis shook his head. "She's never given me any indication of that."

The President bit her lip. For several moments, she simply clicked the end of her pen over and over again. Jarvis held his breath and tried not to squirm.

"All right." She tossed the pen aside and rose to her feet. "Cephas, comm the Council members. Tell them to come here in their pajamas if they have to. We'll contact Rael, threaten him with military force if he doesn't release our people *and* the Remnant, and in the meantime..."

She hesitated. Jarvis followed her gaze and realized she was looking at a pale and puzzled Genevieve.

"In the meantime," President Stagg whispered, "we move our queen across the board."

Jarvis raised his eyebrows. "Are you sure, Maria?"

"Quite sure." She nodded sharply. "Activate Operation Lionhearted."

4:30 PM, Valyan time

When Lindy put her palm up to the biosensor on Nana's cabin door, the computer recognized her identity and immediately let her in. It had been four hours since she last talked to Jarvis. That meant it was nearly half-past ten at night on Meridian, which also meant it was entirely possible Jarvis was having a hard time jerking the Council—or the President herself—out of bed.

That's four hours we could've spent planning a rescue attempt, she thought bitterly. *If I find out the Meridian Council has spent all this time arguing about whether or not they should still handle Rael with kid gloves...*

She banished the possibility from her mind with a shudder and sank onto Nana's couch. The cabin looked bare: Nana's luggage was still at the hotel. Lindy leaned her elbows on her knees, pressed her clasped hands to her mouth, and shut her eyes.

The Renegade said he's got a contact at the Palace. That's interesting enough. But Lhoris believed Princess Alinna was alive. That *must've been what Chevenere and Morgarena were talking about. They were concerned that someone in the Remnant would capitalize on that possibility, and they were just as worried that Rael would find out and lose his mind.*

But what made Lhoris believe that? He was *in contact with the Manwaring radicals, and they're in touch with the Renegade, who's insisted for years that Alinna survived. But what convinced the Prince?*

The door opened. Ethan strode inside, dressed once more in his captain's uniform. "There you are. I've been looking all over the ship for you."

Lindy shifted her gaze to the low coffee table in front of her. Ethan lowered himself to a seat on it, their bent knees touching.

"The crew's ready?" she asked.

"Yeah. The boarding ramp is up, the ship is sealed, the crew is armed. The mega-cannons are locked and loaded. Even the shuttles are ready for evacuation at a minute's notice."

Lindy looked up, her eyes wide. "Stars and comets, Ethan. What are you expecting?"

He smirked. "Hey, I was a captain long before I was a trooper, remember? If Rael decides to declare war on Meridian and attacks us, we'll be ready. And if Jarvis tells us to attack Cor Danem's prison in a blaze of glory, we'll be ready for that, too."

Lindy grimaced. "I just hope he doesn't keep telling us to stay put."

"It *is* a politically charged situation. The diplomats may need to handle things this time, not the troopers."

"Yeah, as if diplomacy has done us any good," she muttered.

The intercom chimed before he could reply. He gave her a sympathetic look as he got up to answer it. "Granger. What's up?"

"Encrypted comm from MID, sir," Lieutenant Mockett said. "Shall I patch it to your location?"

"Yeah, send it to this room. We'll take it in here."

Lindy got up and joined him at the nearby computer console. It chimed as it received the transmission, but when Jarvis *and* President Stagg's faces came on screen, Ethan actually took a step back. Lindy understood and jumped in before the silence got awkward.

"President Stagg," she said. "Commander Jarvis has brought you up to speed?"

"He has, Trooper," the President said coldly. "And so has my daughter. I hear you intend to publish an interview with her when you return to Meridian."

This time, Lindy went rigid. Ethan stepped forward again.

"Mother, we've got a catastrophe looming over our heads," he growled. "This isn't the time—"

"Hold it." Jarvis held up his hands. "Ethan, this isn't a personal call—she's 'President' for the duration of this conversation, not 'Mother.' As for you, Lady President, I think we'd better hold off on that matter until we've cleared this up. Agreed?"

Ethan sighed. "Agreed."

"Likewise," President Stagg said. "My apologies, Melinda."

Something about the hesitant way she said the name caught Lindy's attention, but Ethan plunged ahead before she could puzzle over it. "All right, what do you have for us?"

"Orders to come home," Jarvis replied.

"What?" Lindy cried. "No, Jarvis! Lhoris has been murdered, we've got nobles, soldiers, reporters, troopers, *and* a Meridian Councilor in prison—and you just want us to *leave*?"

"Leaving now would send Rael a disastrous message, Jarvis," Ethan argued.

"I know," Jarvis said, sounding horribly uncertain. "But we've got a bigger issue on our hands now. Getting Lindy back to Meridian is Priority Number One."

Lindy stared at him. President Stagg leaned forward.

"Melinda," she said, "Rael has reason to believe one of his sisters is alive. The Renegade has been saying it for years, of course.

But Lhoris' Manwaring contacts just confirmed for us that he'd been investigating the possibility for some time."

"You've been in contact with the Manwaring Valyans?" Lindy demanded.

"Open contact began two hours ago," Jarvis said quietly. "No surveillance, no spying."

"Lhoris believed he'd found the missing princess," the President went on. "He communicated his suspicions to the radicals, along with the evidence he and his friend Perry Ambrose had gathered, the day before you left Meridian. The Manwaring Valyans, in turn, forwarded the information to the Renegade. That's why he sounded so confident in his latest transmission. He believes Princess Alinna has been found."

"Okay," Lindy said slowly. "So we need to go back to Meridian and locate this woman?"

Jarvis looked down, cleared his throat, and typed something into his computer. "I'm sending you a classified file: Code Name, Operation Lionhearted. It was put together by Councilor Tremaine and Maria Stagg about a year after the Valyan Revolution. It contains two interviews and a collection of DNA matches. Did you get it?"

Ethan clicked the keyboard. "Got it."

"All right." Jarvis clasped his hands. "Open Margaret Tremaine's interview, please."

Ethan glanced at Lindy; she nodded. He clicked the file, and a shimmering, six-inch hologram appeared on the console shelf where Jarvis and President Stagg could still see it.

Lindy gasped in surprise. It *was* Nana, but she was so young—mid-fifties, probably. She was the same Nana who'd kissed her scraped knees, bought her ice cream, taken her to school, and told her to never, *ever* let anyone tell her she was anything less than a masterpiece.

"Operation Lionhearted, Interview One," Nana said, soft and steady. "I was on Meridian when I heard the news of the Cor Danem Massacre. I was absolutely devastated. My husband had only been dead a few weeks, so to hear that Liliana Navorre and her family had been brutally murdered by her own son was grief beyond imagining."

The hologram paused, folded her hands, took a few steps forward. In spite of herself, Lindy smiled. Nana rarely made a speech without pacing.

"Within hours, I got another call from my friend, Maria Stagg. It was heavily encrypted, so I knew she had something she didn't want the rebel forces to intercept. She'd been on Valya for a week or so, overseeing the relief operations she funded. I believe she'd brought her son along on this particular trip. Poor boy. I can't imagine the things he must've seen."

Lindy touched Ethan's shoulder. He acknowledged it with a tightening of his jaw.

"Maria had been hard at work, comforting royalists who'd witnessed the massacre and were now completely traumatized, when she heard a knock at her door. When she answered it, she found a half-dead child at her feet and a shadowed figure limping away. The child was covered in blood from a wound in her shoulder, and she wore the symbol of the Navorre family around her neck."

Lindy drew in a sharp breath. Ethan looked at her.

"Lindy?" he whispered.

"Maria didn't recognize the child," Nana said. "She'd never been to Valya before. But as soon as I saw the child's picture, I knew exactly who she was. I'd watched her toddling after her sisters countless times. She once gave me a flower for my birthday. I remember she smiled and said, 'Happy birthday, Councilor,' even though she could hardly pronounce my title. She was the apple of her father's eye, her mother's pride and joy, and the only one her brother ever seemed to notice during his moody spells. And now she was the only surviving daughter of King Kalen and Queen Liliana."

Lindy staggered backward. "*No*. Oh no, no, no..."

"Stop the recording," Ethan snapped. He reached for her, cautious and slow. "It's okay, Lindy. Hang on a second, just try to breathe—"

"No!" Lindy screamed, jerking away from him. "No, Ethan! It's *not* okay!"

Ethan stared at her, horror and bewilderment playing all over his face. Lindy spun on her heel, covered her face with her hands, and tried as hard she could to catch her breath and convince herself this was just a new nightmare, as harrowing as the old one.

But it was no use. Her shoulders shook and the tears came—first with a whimper, then a sob, and finally a raw, grinding cry for the father and the sisters she'd forgotten and for the mother she remembered only as a voice cut off in the night.

Chapter Twenty-Two

Ethan could tell his mother and Jarvis didn't know what to do. Lindy's breakdown had been so uncharacteristic of her. Jarvis had probably never seen her fall apart like that, and his mother avoided emotional displays at all cost.

As soon as the worst of her sobbing subsided, however, he followed her to the other side of the room. Lindy still had her back to him, but she didn't push him away when he laid a hand on her shoulder.

"Melinda?" his mother called. "Ethan?"

Ethan ignored her. He pressed his lips to the back of Lindy's head. She sniffled in surprise and spun to face him.

"Shh," he whispered, rubbing her shoulders. "It's all right."

She shivered and shook her head. "I'm sorry. I'm so sorry, I couldn't help it..."

"Ethan," Jarvis called sternly. "Acknowledge us, *please*."

"I'm right here," Ethan snapped.

"Then I need you to come back to the screen."

Jarvis' tone was the kind you obeyed unless you wanted a court-martial. Lindy hugged herself and glared at the computer.

"Go," she croaked. "I'll be there in a second."

It was the last thing Ethan wanted to do, but he had no choice. He returned to the computer.

"Okay, I'm here," he said tersely. "How much is left of that recording?"

"Not much," Jarvis said. "Just that Margaret told Maria to keep the child safe and secret, that the Princess couldn't speak and didn't remember anything once she *could* communicate, and that Margaret re-named her."

"'Melinda,' I'm guessing," Ethan said.

Jarvis nodded lamely. Ethan turned to Lindy, but she'd disappeared into the bathroom.

"Why are you telling us this now?" he hissed. "You do realize she's already had a terrible day?"

"This was hardly planned," his mother snapped. "Margaret intended to keep this a secret unless Melinda's life was in danger!"

"And now it is," Jarvis said. "Thankfully, the Manwaring Valyans assured us that they kept no notes of that final meeting with Lhoris. Whatever Rael may have learned about the Prince's past suspicions, the connection between Alinna and Lindy *wouldn't* have been in the files Lieutenant Cornael sent to him. We're still one step ahead of him."

"And that's why we want you to come home," the President said. "We'll arrange a meeting with the Valyans on Meridian, including the Manwaring group. Melinda can safely declare her identity here and offer Rael a deal for the hostages—"

"No. I'm not doing that."

Ethan whirled and his mother and Jarvis both sat up as Lindy emerged from the bathroom. She looked tired but resolute. President Stagg frowned.

"You have no choice," she said. "You *must* come home, and when you arrive—"

"I'm not leaving, ma'am," Lindy said firmly. "My grandmother and the closest thing I've got to a sister are both in captivity. I'm not leaving them behind. Furthermore, *you* charged us with the protection of Mariamne Navorre and her entourage. If we leave, who'll stop Rael from murdering them, too? And besides *all* that—" She paused, uncertainty flickering in her dark eyes. "Besides that, someone's got to recruit the only ally the Navorres have on this planet."

President Stagg shook her head. "No, you can't—"

"Oh, stars and comets, you're telling me I'm the Queen of Valya!" Lindy exploded. "If that's true, then I've been your pawn, my grandmother's, and my brother's my whole life! No more! *I* make the rules this time!"

The President's mouth fell open, and Jarvis' eyebrows almost reached his hairline. Ethan barely suppressed a proud grin.

"Now," Lindy said, lowering her voice, "the Renegade's fortress is somewhere in the Laronda Mountains, right? The mountains must be patrolled by his people. I can't exactly ring him up without Rael intercepting it, but if I go up there myself, they can't miss me."

"There's the problem of getting past Omstorn without being seen," Jarvis pointed out.

"That's the industrial town on the river, right?" Ethan asked.

"Yes. And the minute anyone notices one of your hovers leaving, the *Hummingbird* will be in big trouble."

"That's no problem," Ethan said. "We'll leave well after nightfall with our lights off and head north, *away* from the novaport. Then we can come back around and head south once the coast is clear."

Lindy looked at him for the first time since she'd returned from the bathroom. "'We'?"

Ethan pulled a face. "You don't really think I'd let you go by yourself?"

The corner of her mouth twitched. President Stagg sighed and held up her hands.

"All right, fine. I get it. A queen outranks a president. Nevertheless, I strongly advise you against reaching out to this…this insurrectionist."

Lindy tipped her head back. "Objection noted. Now let me advise you, President Stagg. Saving my grandmother and my best friend matters a whole lot more to me right now than walking on political eggshells. Don't you dare stand in my way."

6:00 PM, Valyan Time

The cell door opened with a screech. Jo lifted her head off Nana's shoulder, a little surprised she'd managed to fall asleep after hearing the whole whispered truth about Princess Alinna. The Princesses and Lord Nhormin's wife sat up, too, as a Magnificent stomped into the room. His bulky armor made the cell seem even tinier than usual.

"Margaret Tremaine, Josephine Camrin, Mariamne Navorre," he droned.

Nana stood. "Yes? What do you want?"

"The Magnificent Citizen requests your presence at the Palace."

"Oh, well! I hope he knows I'll be protesting our treatment. It's a clear violation of the Kellan Confederation's Declaration of Individual Rights—"

Jo struggled to her feet. "Oh, for Pete's sake, Nana. You like to stir the pot, don't you?"

If Nana wanted a reaction from the Magnificent, she didn't get one. The dark eyes barely visible through his visor held no emotion. Jo reached for Nana's hand. To her relief, Mariamne placed herself on her other side, linking their arms.

"We are ready," Mariamne said calmly. "We will be coming back, won't we?"

"That is for the Magnificent Citizen to decide," the soldier replied.

Within minutes, the Magnificent led them down the long corridor of prison cells. Jo reached up and adjusted her headband. Mariamne noticed and shifted her position, placing a discreet arm around Jo's back and grasping her elbow until Jo clicked on the micro-cam and let her hand drop again.

"Sorry," Jo whispered. "My arms still feel like they each weigh thirty pounds."

"I understand," Mariamne whispered back.

Jo scoffed as they approached an elevator. "You must think I'm a wimp."

"On the contrary, I think you are far braver than I ever thought a Meridian could be."

Nana and Jo glanced at her in surprise. Mariamne looked away and said no more.

Five more soldiers waited for them in the prison lobby; they prodded the women outside and into the dark, stuffy back of a hover-truck. After a short ride, the doors flew open again and the Magnificents yanked them out. Jo blinked in the light and realized they were at the Navorre Palace. No journalists crowded the front hall now; no wide-eyed servants stopped to stare. The Magnificents didn't take them to any of the staterooms, either. As they hurried down unfamiliar hallways, Jo wondered with a start if they were entering far more private quarters.

She knew for sure when they stepped into the most luxurious bedroom she'd ever seen. Rael lay in the bed, his arm in a sling. Elva Chevenere stood on one side of the bed, Hadrian and Morgarena Daltis on the other. Through a tall, narrow window bordered by red curtains, Jo saw beehives standing proud and white in the sunset-dappled garden.

"Bring them closer," Rael said.

The soldier behind Jo gave her a rough push. She stumbled forward. Out of the corner of her eye, she saw Nana stagger. Mariamne alone kept her footing. Rael's handsome face hardened.

"*Closer*."

Another push. Jo's heart raced.

"I want them lined up right here," Rael said, motioning to the edge of the bed.

The Magnificents obeyed again, maneuvering the prisoners until Jo's thighs bumped the mattress. Rael watched in stony silence. He seemed so calm compared to a few hours ago. Maybe they'd drugged him.

"Councilor Tremaine," he said in a low voice. "How does it feel, getting caught?"

Nana peered at him. "How does it feel, knowing *my* security team won't let you get away with murdering a man they swore to protect?"

"Oh, you mean this?" Rael asked, gesturing at his sling. "A mere scratch. I'm just glad your troopers are such poor shots."

Hadrian Daltis smirked ghoulishly at that. Something hot and vicious stirred in Jo's chest.

"You have something to say, Trooper Camrin?" Rael inquired. "Are you sorry you didn't blow *my* brains out? Hmm?"

"Rael, cease this prattle," Mariamne snapped. "I doubt you brought us here simply to insult Trooper Camrin."

"Well, bravo, Cousin. That's a fine deduction. Trooper Camrin certainly interests me, and *you* interest me, and so does Councilor Tremaine—but not because she is a spy, or because you are my rival, or because the Councilor is practically the personification of her busybody planet. No. You interest me because you all knew something I didn't—and because I, unfortunately, lost my temper with your meddlesome husband. I should've kept him alive long enough to give me the information he dangled in front of my nose like a carrot."

"You ordered the hack on the *Hummingbird,*" Jo growled. "You probably got all the information you need."

Rael narrowed his eyes. "You'd think that, wouldn't you? But Lhoris was clever. He only mentioned my sister by her Valyan name in his exchanges with the rebels, *not* by whatever she goes by these days. It was an understandable precaution. A secret like that is best kept within the mind, not a computer. Chevenere?"

The Dominator stepped up without looking at the prisoners and handed him a tablet. With his good hand, Rael clicked it on. "I understand Perry Ambrose, a Meridian reporter attached to your press pool, was one of Lhoris' close friends. What do you know of him, Mariamne?"

"Nothing," Mariamne said softly. "I knew nothing about my husband's contact with—"

"Don't lie to me!" Rael roared. "Your husband was plotting with the Renegade! He knew Alinna was alive and *you* know who she is! Lie to me again, Mariamne, and I swear I will have you tortured until you scream her name and beg me for mercy."

Mariamne's strong jaw flexed. Rael flicked his sharp eyes at Jo.

"You pose as a photographer for the *New Harvelle Ladies' Post,*" he said. "But your colleague, Miss Tremaine, wasn't at the Palace yesterday. Is she a relative of yours, Councilor? Another trooper, perhaps?"

Nana said nothing. Rael swiped the screen and jerked his head at Daltis. The Dominator took up the tablet and held it up. Jo gulped at the sight of Lindy's official photograph for the *Ladies' Post.* She was smiling, her long black hair falling in thick waves around her dark, pretty face. The high Valyan cheekbones were unmistakable.

For the first time, Jo realized she and Rael resembled each other. A lot.

"A Valyan refugee, perhaps, adopted by the Meridian politician who just happened to be good friends with my repulsive mother?" Rael snarled.

Nana tore her gaze from the photo and glared at him. "Your mother loved you, and you had her *butchered* in a field surrounded by strangers."

"She was not alone. She was there with her husband and daughters."

"And you told us yourself that you're still haunted by their screams," Nana hissed. "Do you hear them screaming now? Or are you too obsessed with picking off the lone survivor?"

Daltis shoved the tablet in Nana's face. "Is this Alinna?"

Nana clamped her lips together. Rael yanked off the comforter and swung his long legs over the edge of the bed, glaring at each woman in turn.

"Listen to me. I can make you talk. I can make you *all* talk. And I know how to play my sister's hand. If she is as soft as the rest of you Meridians, she will crack the moment I spill more blood."

"And if she's stronger than you think?" Jo challenged.

"Then she and I will play a nice game of chess, won't we?" Rael snapped. "You, however, are nothing but a Meridian. Malleable as clay. How would you like being like one of *them*?"

He gestured over her head at the Magnificents standing behind them. A chill ran down Jo's spine. Rael smiled.

"They have no secrets," he whispered. "Not from me. The technology that shapes them to my will unveils their minds until they are like open books. Do you know how easy it would be to conquer *your* mind, Trooper Camrin? It would take all of ten minutes...and you don't even have the Valyan Shelter to protect you."

"Rael..." Nana whispered.

"As for *you* and my fair cousin," he interrupted, turning to her, "you will wait while I kill one prisoner at the top of every hour until my sister surrenders herself. If she *is* Melinda Tremaine, then she's still on Valya. The novaport is on lockdown. There is no way for her to escape. She will either give herself up, or she will let you die. Either way, you lose and I win."

Jo tried to swallow, but her mouth was too dry. Rael turned to his advisors.

"Hadrian, return Councilor Tremaine and my cousin to the prison. I'll leave it to you to decide which of our captives will be our first victim. Elva, *you* take Trooper Camrin to our military center. Let us see what happens when another Meridian becomes a Magnificent."

"Another?" Jo blurted. "What do you mean?"

Rael's smile morphed into a sneer. "One of the soldiers we captured…Frank Gridley, I believe his name was? I think he will make a fine soldier. I will be interested to see if you show as much promise."

"Jo!" Nana cried as soon as they were outside again. "Jo, stand strong! Whatever you do, don't let them see you afraid!"

Jo twisted her head, trying to glimpse Nana and Mariamne before the Magnificents and Daltis shoved them into the truck. But Chevenere and the two other soldiers guarding her moved too fast, forcing her in the opposite direction. When Jo tried to resist, Chevenere herself seized her by the elbow and jerked her towards a sleek black hover.

"You two, in the back," Chevenere ordered the soldiers. "I want her up front with me."

The Magnificents obeyed. Chevenere dragged Jo around the front of the hover. This time Jo didn't fight, too busy watching the truck rumble away to care.

Who will Daltis pick first? Oh Elyon, please don't let it be either of them. Surely he won't get rid of their most valuable prisoners first. That's an awful thing to think—they're all *priceless. But surely he won't kill poor Tali! She's all of sixteen…*

BAM! Her head hit the hover's door frame as Chevenere pushed her into the seat. Jo hissed through her teeth and pressed her hand to the bruise. Chevenere slammed the door and marched around to the driver's side. She got in and clicked her seatbelt.

"Ready?" she asked.

Jo shot her the fiercest glare she could manage. Of course she wasn't ready. She would never be prepared to become a human robot, and she would never *be* one.

Operation Kitchingham was just a few hastily-recited numbers away.

Chevenere opened the glove compartment and withdrew a raygun. Jo felt a rush of grim relief. At least a quick, clean shot would save her the trouble.

But then Chevenere twisted and fired four quick shots into the back seat. Jo screamed and covered her ears at the horrible sounds that followed.

"Holy krikallily!" she shrieked. "What are you—?!"

"I asked if you were ready," Chevenere snapped. "Buckle your seatbelt. I have no intentions of following any speed limits."

She tossed the gun into Jo's lap. As Jo buckled up, she saw it was only on the highest stun setting. She turned in her seat as Chevenere sent them flying in the opposite direction of the prison truck.

"But…but they're dead," Jo said shakily. "They're dead, but it's just…it's on stun."

"A well-aimed high-voltage shot to the head, even with the helmet, will cause the cyberpathic microchips to suffer electrical overload. *That* killed them, not the gun."

"Oh. Then you *were* using the microchips."

Chevenere spared her a glance. "Yes. You knew?"

"Um…more like 'suspected.'" Jo cleared her throat. "So why are you kidnapping me?"

"Because Rael Navorre has gone mad."

Jo snorted. "Hate to break it to you, lady, but I'm pretty sure he went loopy a while ago."

"I agree." Chevenere changed gears; the hover zoomed above the street. "But now he will bring the wrath of Meridian upon our heads. I do not care to be on the wrong side of that fury, and I do not want to see Valya suffer any more for Rael's selfish pride."

"Okaaaay. But you do know that if Alinna is alive, she might bring back the monarchy…right?"

Chevenere clenched her teeth and turned a sharp corner. Jo held on for dear life, gasping as she glimpsed the novaport and the sleek, gleaming lines of the *Hummingbird*.

"Even a new queen," Chevenere muttered, "will be better than what I helped raise up."

Chapter Twenty-Three

7:00 PM

Lindy threw a pack of rations into the compartment beneath the back seat of the *Hummingbird*'s tiniest shuttle, on top of the extra blankets, clothes, and first aid kit. She squatted, ran a hand through her hair, and exhaled with satisfaction.

"Okay, that looks good. I've still got space for those rifles. Hand 'em over?"

"Two rifles, coming right up," Ethan said. "Think we should take an extra soroidium canister?"

She hesitated. "I hate to rob from your other shuttles. Especially if the crew ever has to…you know. Evacuate."

He shook his head. "I don't think Rael will attack the *Hummingbird*. Even if he did, it would take a lot to incapacitate her.

We'd be in a lot worse trouble if *we* ran out of fuel. Hang on a second...I'll get it from the shuttle next door."

"Ethan."

He stopped, turning on the shuttle's threshold. "Yeah?"

Lindy blinked. Now that she had his attention, she didn't know what to say—or rather, *how* to say what she wanted to say. She and Ethan had been too busy planning and packing to discuss what had happened in Nana's cabin. It was high time someone acknowledged the elephant in the room.

"I'm sorry I shouted at you back there," she said quietly.

He pulled a kind but incredulous face. "Don't be silly."

"Ethan." Lindy dug her elbows into her thighs and pressed her clasped hands against her forehead. "If it's true...then I'm a *princess.*"

"Pretty sure it's true," Ethan said. "And you're not a princess. You're a queen."

She looked up with a scowl. "Don't make it worse than it is."

He chuckled, then stepped back inside the shuttle and sat down beside her. Lindy stared at the floor.

"Remember how I told you yesterday that I found something that made me question everything Nana ever told me?" she asked.

"Yes..."

"It was a portrait of Queen Liliana. She was wearing a pendant in the shape of a bee." Lindy swallowed. "I did some research right before I discovered the microchip connection. Bees were the symbol of the Navorre dynasty."

She drew the pendant out from underneath her trooper suit, holding it out to him between her thumb and her forefinger. Ethan leaned forward.

"That's the symbol the councilor mentioned in her recording?" he asked.

Lindy nodded, slipping it beneath her collar again. "She didn't tell me what it meant when she gave it to me. But as soon as I saw the Queen's pendant, something clicked in my head."

Ethan nodded. "You started asking yourself, 'What if *I* am a Navorre?'"

"Yeah. But then I talked myself out of it. 'Nah. Your parents were probably just associates or servants. Maybe your dad was the King's beekeeper.'" Lindy snorted. "I'm a trooper and a journalist. My professional life revolves around picking through evidence and reading between the lines…and I missed this. If it had been a snake, it would've bitten me."

Ethan said nothing. Lindy got to her feet and shut the compartment lid.

"Why didn't Nana tell me?" she whispered. "Why?"

"You know why," Ethan said. "She wanted to protect you until the time was right."

"So she deceived me time and time again!"

"Whoa now, hold on," Ethan said, springing to his feet. "You never wanted to know the truth. She respected that, knowing full well you might have to face it one day anyway. She didn't deceive you. She just…withheld the details. Besides, if she *had* told you, how would you have handled it? 'Wow, I can't believe I'm the long-lost princess my own brother tried to annihilate—isn't that awesome?'"

An angry heat flooded her face as she moved to sidestep him. "This isn't funny."

"And I never said it was," he retorted, blocking her way. "I just don't think she's completely to blame. You didn't *want* to know. You should own up to that. Otherwise, you're just making yourself more of a victim than you truly are."

Lindy's mouth fell open. Ethan started to say something else, but she stormed past him and out of the shuttle, heading across the hangar as fast as she could.

If that was the way he felt about it, he could just stay here. She'd find the Renegade herself, bring him back with his army, and tear down Rael's system bit by bit with her bare hands.

But what happens if you can't save Jo and Nana? a small voice in the back of her head countered. *What'll be left for you, hmm? Rael?*

He may be your brother, but he also slaughtered your parents and your sisters. MID? You probably burned that bridge the second you defied Maria Stagg.

You will have nothing if you don't have Ethan.

Lindy stopped, screwed her eyes shut, and turned. Moving far more slowly now, she entered the shuttle just as Ethan lowered himself into the pilot's seat and started checking the instruments.

"You're right," she choked.

Ethan whirled. Lindy rubbed her sweaty palms on her pants and stepped closer.

"Doing the right thing matters more than my fears. But it needs to matter more than my own pride, too. I'm letting *that* get in the way now, and I really can't afford this kind of stupidity on my part at the moment, so…help me? Please, Ethan?"

He said nothing for what felt like a long time. Then he stood, hiked his leg over the stuff between the seats, and approached her. He reached for her hands. Lindy gave them willingly.

"I *want* to help you," he murmured. "But I don't think you really need me."

"Of course I do. Who else will keep me from throwing myself off the nearest cliff if the Renegade decides not to help us after all?"

Ethan smirked. "If you're as good at asserting yourself with him as you were with my mother, you won't have any trouble there."

Lindy rolled her eyes. Ethan chuckled and stroked her hands with his thumbs. The tender gesture triggered her curiosity. She crept out of her Shelter just long enough to get a sense of his emotions, and it hit her again just as it had in the alley—something bright, strong, and fierce, something she would've been able to identify with certainty if he were a Valyan.

"Everything that's ever happened to you has led up to this moment, Lindy," Ethan said. "Your childhood on Meridian, your training, even your writing…it's all been groundwork. You've already got everything you need up here—" He tapped her forehead with his fingertip. "—and here." He pointed at her chest. "And you know what else? I believe in you, and I'm with you every step of the way."

Lindy tried to smile. "That's a lot of faith in a woman who'd just like to go home and curl up with her cat."

"Which is precisely why I'd rather follow you into battle than anybody else. You're not in this for ambition's sake. You just want to do what's right. That sounds to me like a good leader in the making."

This time, Lindy really did smile—a tearful, grateful smile—before dropping her gaze to their clasped hands and squeezing his fingers. He returned the pressure, but before either of them could speak again, the shuttle radio chirped. Ethan reached between the pilot seats for the receiver. "Granger."

"Captain," Commander Aeron said, "a Valyan hover just arrived. Its passengers are begging us to let them aboard, but I won't give them permission without confirmation from you."

"Magnificents?" Ethan asked sharply.

Aeron hesitated. "No, sir. They claim to be Miss Camrin...and one of the Valyan Dominators."

Apparently Jo was hurt, so Aeron directed Lindy and Ethan to Sickbay. When they arrived, they found Jo sitting on the edge of an examination table while Dr. Elliot tended to a nasty bruise on her forehead. Dominator Chevenere maintained a grim, protective stance next to Jo, ignoring the distrustful presence of Security Chief Colt and Commander Aeron. As soon as Jo saw Lindy, she leaped off the table with a cry. Lindy met her halfway, hugging her so tightly that neither of them could breathe.

"Oh, thank Elyon," Lindy whispered. "Are you okay?"

"Yeah." Jo sniffled and rubbed her eyes. "Just a little roughed-up. Are *you* okay?"

"Mm-hmm." Lindy tried to laugh, but it was a strangled sound. "I thought I might never see you again. I've never been so glad to be wrong."

"Same here." Jo gestured at the Dominator. "Elva Chevenere, Lindy Tremaine. Lindy...the Dominator. Don't worry, though. She's on our side."

Lindy narrowed her eyes. "And what does 'on our side' mean, exactly?"

Chevenere held her head high. "It means I wish to help you depose Rael."

"Well, that'll be easier said than done, won't it, no thanks to you?" Lindy snapped, taking a step closer. "I've done my homework. You're an expert in empathic manipulation, which means you almost certainly had a hand in the Magnificent Army program. Right or wrong?"

Chevenere paused a moment, then said calmly, "Right."

"Are they controlled by the Xandroan microchips?" Ethan asked.

She nodded. "Trooper Camrin said you suspected it. What tipped you off?"

"The Xandroans had been selling the chips to an off-planet buyer," Lindy said, "with a Meridian businessman acting as a go-between. We had no idea who the buyer might be until I realized Rael had an expert on empathic manipulation in his inner circle. After that, the rest of the puzzle was a piece of cake."

Chevenere finally dropped her gaze. "It was the most efficient way to control our army. An army without remorse is the most feared army of all, and a frightened populace the most obedient—"

Lindy seized her arm. Jo yelped. Ethan, Dr. Elliot, Aeron, and Colt all sprang forward.

"Stand back!" Lindy shouted, jerking the woman closer. Chevenere clamped her lips together, but Lindy had taken her by surprise. Her vulnerable Emanation brimmed with red Fear.

"Why are you so frightened?" Lindy hissed.

"Because..." The Dominator swallowed hard. "Because no matter who you once were, you are still a Valyan. And if you were on Meridian, then you are a refugee...and if you are a refugee, then you have every cause in the world to wish me dead."

"Oh, that's not even the worst of it. You helped my brother get where he is today. As far as I'm concerned, he isn't the only one with my family's blood on his hands."

"Whoop," Jo murmured. "There it is."

There it was, indeed. Adrenaline surged through Lindy as she uttered the words "my brother" and "my family." It made her feel stronger and more sure of herself than anything the President, Jarvis, or Nana might've said. Chevenere wilted in her grip; Lindy flung her away and turned to Jo.

"Can she help us?"

Jo nodded vigorously. "Oh yeah. But whatever you're planning, you've gotta move fast. Rael's threatening to kill a prisoner every hour if you don't give yourself up. And no, I don't think he's bluffing."

Lindy whirled. Ethan shot her a stern look.

"Don't even think about it," he said.

"About what?"

"Giving yourself up. I won't let you."

"It *would* be a foolish move," Chevenere gasped, rubbing her arm. "The information stolen from this ship did not identify you by your current name. Yes, Rael has deduced that you may be his sister, but he is not certain of it. If you give yourself up now, you will lose your one chance to outmaneuver him."

"And how do I do *that*?" Lindy demanded.

Chevenere hesitated. "If I reveal government secrets to you, and Rael finds out..."

"Don't try to make a deal for yourself," Ethan snapped. "You tell us what you know, or I'll have you thrown into the brig with the two officers who helped Lieutenant Cornael hack our computers."

"Spill, Chevenere," Jo ordered. "You got this far. You might as well go the whole way."

Chevenere still looked doubtful. Lindy took another menacing step forward, however, and she immediately stepped backward.

"Very well," she said, holding up her hands. "Have you wondered how the Renegade knew about the murder in the Palace?"

Lindy frowned. "Yes."

"I am his informant. I have been for two and a half years." Chevenere glanced nervously at the Meridians. "I know every detail of the Magnificent Network. I almost single-handedly constructed it, after all—and I know how to dismantle it. Unless and until that is done, you will have to wade through blood to defeat Rael."

"All right," Lindy said, nodding. "So dismantle it."

"I can't. Not alone. It would require destroying the computers that connect the Magnificents in every major city. And all the computers are protected by force fields..."

"Force fields can be taken down if you focus enough fire on them," Lindy interrupted.

"True, but Valyan orbit is full of our patrol ships. At the first sign of trouble, they will mobilize against you." Chevenere looked at Jo. "Destroying the computer networks will also kill the soldiers. It was a safeguard against rebels who might try to rescue their sons and fathers."

Jo paled. "Frank."

Lindy looked sharply at her. "What about Frank?"

"Rael said..." Jo squeezed her eyes shut and clenched her fists. "He's turned Frank into a Magnificent."

For a moment, no one spoke, too horrified for words. Lindy jumped when Ethan touched her arm.

"I'm gonna call Mother," he said. "Tell her we need reinforcements—as many as she can send."

"But it takes five days for anybody to get here from Meridian!" she cried. "Our people will be dead by then!"

"Not if my mother can pull some strings." Ethan gave her hand a quick squeeze. "I'll be on the bridge if you need me. Aeron, let's go."

With that, he raced out of the sickbay, his first officer on his heels. Lindy stared after him, wondering what in the name of the Holy House of Elyon he might be thinking.

Ethan sensed Aeron's disapproval as soon as the lift doors shut behind them. It made him wish Frank were here—and that, in turn, made his chest clench as he remembered what Jo and Chevenere had said.

Hang on, man. We're gonna save you. Just hold on.

"It's only a matter of time before Rael discovers Chevenere's betrayal," Aeron said, splintering the silence. "When he does, we will be in the center of his attention."

"I know," Ethan said.

"If Rael attacks the *Hummingbird,* it will be an attack on Meridian sovereignty."

"I know that, too. I also know that the second the *Hummingbird* leaves Valya, Rael will have no qualms about killing his prisoners."

Aeron raised his eyebrows. "It doesn't sound as if he has any hesitation about that anyway. Miss Camrin said he's threatening to kill one every hour unless Miss Tremaine…"

He stopped, frowning as the impossibility of the situation dawned on him.

"We can't let *that* happen, either," Ethan said firmly.

Aeron nodded. "No. No, we can't."

The lift opened. They found the bridge in a flurry of activity: officers and midshipmen had crowded around Lieutenant Mockett's station. Worried, Ethan approached.

"What's going on now?" he asked.

Heads bobbed up, every face drawn and fearful. Mockett removed her hand from her earpiece.

"Rael just made a high-priority announcement to the whole planet," she said. "All holovisions were remotely activated. He threatened to kill *our* people, one every hour if his sister doesn't surrender. He says he'll start with Princess Verrona. It doesn't make sense, Captain. I thought he killed all his sisters!"

"Not all," Ethan muttered. "Begin a message to President Stagg and copy it to Commander Jarvis."

Mockett poised her fingers over her keyboard. The crew stared in surprise as Ethan flung open several compartments in the wall; he and Aeron drew out the emergency weapons inside and placed them into shocked but willing hands.

"'President Stagg,'" Ethan dictated. "'Be advised I will not accompany Alinna Navorre on her search for the Renegade. A member of Rael Navorre's government has defected to our side after helping Trooper Camrin escape, but Rael has publicly threatened to murder Meridian citizens and the Remnant one at a time if Alinna doesn't surrender. This is an undeniable act of war. I beg you to send reinforcements as soon as possible—including any troopers or Nova Force crews based on nearby planets.' Emphasis on 'nearby planets,' Mockett."

"Got it, sir."

"'In the meantime, as the only free representative of Meridian on this planet, I will remain with my ship and crew…'"

Ethan paused, his throat tightening. Everything in him wanted to go with Lindy. Before Chevenere came, he could've sneaked off the ship with Lindy and left Aeron in command without a second thought.

But now, grateful as he was for the Dominator's actions, she *had* made his ship a target. It was only a matter of time before Rael sent Magnificents to the novaport.

And I can't let them face that alone.

Ethan set a pistol on Mockett's desk. "'I'll remain with my ship and crew until the Renegade's army arrives or Meridian comes to our rescue. Signed, Ethan Granger, Captain, *MNC Hummingbird.*'"

"You feel a little better about her, then?"

Lindy glanced at Jo as they hurried into the hangar. They'd just left Chevenere in Dr. Elliot's custody after gleaning as much information from her as they could. A slip of paper in Lindy's pocket bore the number for the Renegade's comm channel, as well as the call signs he and his people used to identify themselves. Chevenere had given them to her only after Lindy promised she wouldn't end up in the brig.

"I don't know that I feel better about her," Lindy answered. "But I'm glad she saved your life."

"Well, she saved my sanity, anyway," Jo said softly. "Rael didn't want me dead, at least not yet. He obviously thought it would be more fun to turn Frank and me into his toy soldiers."

Lindy reached for her hand. "We'll do everything we can to save him. I promise."

Jo only nodded. She looked like she was running on empty, and for a moment, Lindy considered talking her into staying behind. But then a new question popped into her head. She paused a yard or so away from the shuttle, and Jo stopped beside her.

"How did you know about Alinna?" Lindy asked.

Jo raised an eyebrow. "How did *you* know?"

"Ethan and I talked to Jarvis and President Stagg. They had a recording of Nana that she made years ago, telling the whole story."

Jo nodded again. "She told me, too. And Mariamne. Verrona and Tali, too."

Lindy grimaced. "I bet Mariamne was thrilled."

"Actually…I think she was, in her own weird, Mariamne-ish way." Jo shifted her weight from one foot to the other. "We were all just relieved that Rael didn't totally win, even back then. *You* lived—and as long as you're alive, there's hope for Valya. Not that I know what a future with you as a queen might look like..."

Lindy let out a half-laugh, half-groan, but she saw Ethan approaching them before she could reply. He sighed and put his hands on his hips.

"I sent a message to my mother," he said, "begging her to send any Nova Force ships in the area to Valya. We've got some small MID bases on Vlinderland and Opitheldra. Vlinderland is only a day away, Opitheldra two. Aeron also located the *MNC Georgiana* about thirty-six hours away in the Lianya Starfield."

"You think she'll send them here?" Lindy asked.

"Well, I told her Rael's threat against our people is basically a declaration of war. But I'm just a Nova Force captain. She's a politician. She might not lift a finger unless he actually makes good on his threat."

"That's madness," Lindy hissed.

"That's politics," Ethan countered. "I copied Jarvis in the message. I'm hoping he'll put pressure on her."

"Great," Jo said. "Then let's get outta here while we can."

She scurried towards the ramp, stopping only when she realized Lindy and Ethan weren't following. "Aren't you coming?"

Lindy swallowed. "Yeah. I'll be there in a minute."

Jo raised an eyebrow, nodded meaningfully, and entered the shuttle. Lindy turned to Ethan. He folded his arms over his chest.

"You're not coming, are you?" she whispered.

He grimaced. "I can't. I wish I could, but if Rael attacks the *Hummingbird*—"

"I know." She touched his arm. "We'll be fine. We both know how to fly a shuttle—you can't even graduate from the MID Academy without at least knowing how to fly a small novacraft—"

"Lindy." He stepped closer, taking her shoulders in both hands. "Rael just made his threat public. He says he'll kill Verrona first."

Lindy froze. Ethan set his jaw.

"I'll try to talk him out of it, but chances are he won't listen to a word I say. You *have* to move fast. It'll take you two hours to get to Omstorn, and I know he's got three dozen or so prisoners, but I don't want to lose any more than I have to. You've *got* to get back here with that rebel army tomorrow morning, all right?"

Lindy released a controlled breath and nodded. "All right."

Ethan smiled, leaned forward, and pressed his lips to her forehead. Lindy closed her eyes. He drew back, tucking her hair behind her ear.

"It's not every man who gets to kiss a queen," he teased.

"Don't push it, Captain."

He chuckled, then released her shoulders and stepped back. With a brave smile, Lindy dashed into the shuttle. Jo, perched in the back seat, turned at the sound of her footsteps.

"Up front," Lindy ordered. "You're my co-pilot."

"Ethan's not coming?"

"No." Lindy sat down in the pilot's seat. "The captain stays with his ship."

A few minutes later, Ethan stood at the window on the other side of the hangar, his hands on the console. At his direction, the interior doors were sealed shut. Nobody could go inside the hangar now. Lindy and Jo were on their own.

"Here we go," Ethan murmured. He pressed another button. The lights in the hangar went off. Another button, and he heard the dull groan of giant gears. He turned on the intercom and connected with the shuttle.

"Wait until the doors are fully opened," he called. "Then turn your lights on the lowest beam. We don't want anyone spotting you."

"Got it," Lindy replied inside the shuttle.

Ethan watched the widening space between the doors. The Valyan night looked brighter than the interior of the hangar. "Okay. Lights on…and go."

The shuttle's dimmed lights flicked on. It rose off its platform, veered drunkenly to one side for one awful moment, and steadied. Ethan clenched his sweating hands as the shuttle slipped out of the *Hummingbird* with a low hum and out into the novaport.

"Shuttle is clear, Captain," Aeron called over from the bridge. "No sign of pursuit."

Ethan sighed. "Make sure the *Hummingbird* is sealed. Maintain battle stations. I'm coming back up to the bridge."

Chapter Twenty-Four

7:50 PM

Lindy's heart was still pounding after her near-collision inside the hangar. She'd managed to steady the tiny ship, however, and now it slipped effortlessly towards the widening hatch.

"Come on, come on, come on," Jo whispered beside her.

Lindy gritted her teeth, accelerated—and they were out. Light rain spattered the windshield. The novaport floodlights and the dim red lights on the *Hummingbird*'s stern filled the cabin. Quickly, Lindy steered to the right and up. The red glare faded, but the floodlight stayed on them with ominous precision. Lindy leaned forward, peering through her side window.

"Jo? I think..."

"So do I," Jo hissed. "We've been spotted."

Lindy changed gears, and they shot forward. The radio crackled.

"Unidentified shuttle, return to your mothership immediately. I repeat, return to your—"

"Shut up," Lindy growled, flipping the radio switch.

"There's a shuttle coming out of the novaport hangar!" Jo cried.

Lindy saw the headlights coming their way and braced herself. "Get to the rear gun."

Jo unbuckled herself and scrambled into the back of the shuttle. The gun probably wasn't *that* powerful, but surely it could match whatever the Valyan ship had to offer.

"Lock onto it," Lindy called. "If it gets too close, I want you to fire."

"I hope you realize Rael will probably take that as an act of war!" Jo shouted.

Good, Lindy thought. *If Maria Stagg won't make her move, I will.*

VROOM! A streak of red fire skirted the shuttle's right side. Lindy gasped and pushed the control columns to their limit as another, even stronger blast barely missed them.

"Jo?"

"Got 'em locked and loaded," Jo called. "That last one was from the *Hummingbird*. I think Ethan's trying to give 'em a warning!"

WHAM! This time the shuttle rocked. An alarm appeared on the screen in the middle of the dashboard. The right rear corner had been hit.

"That was from the Valyan!" Jo screeched.

Lindy dismissed the alarm. Another alert came up: Jo's gun had locked on its target.

"Tell me when!" Jo cried.

"Oh, just use your own discretion, Jo! I can't fly *and* tell you to —"

The whine of the gun cut her off, followed by a crash. Lindy jerked her head over her shoulder in time to see fire rising from the Valyan ship's port bow.

"I got him!" Jo shrieked. "I got him, I got him, *I got him*!"

"Hold on tight!" Lindy shouted. Jo yelped as the shuttle swerved to the south, higher and higher into the clouds. The engine roared. Rain splattered the window, Lindy's ears popped, her teeth rattled…

And they broke through the clouds into a peaceful layer of the Valyan atmosphere where soft flashes of light pulsed beneath them and where there was no rain.

Ethan reached the bridge just as the *Hummingbird* fired a warning shot at Lindy's pursuer. When the beam almost hit her instead, his heart felt as if it had jumped all the way up into his throat.

"Weapons, I'd appreciate it if you didn't hit *our* shuttle!" he bellowed over the intercom.

"The rear gun in Miss Tremaine's shuttle is locked onto the enemy, Captain," Aeron said.

"Weapons, hold your fire!" Ethan cried.

A breathless moment passed in which neither ship exchanged fire. Ethan lowered himself into the command seat and dug his nails into the leather arms. Finally, a red beam burst from the Meridian shuttle. The Valyan ship lurched and hit the ground, flames spewing out of its port nacelle. The officers on the bridge burst into loud cheers. Ethan slumped forward in relief until he heard Mockett's console chime.

"Captain?" she called. "It's Novaport Authority."

Ethan sprang up. An infuriated Valyan woman in a crisp uniform had appeared on Mockett's screen. She jabbed a finger at Ethan when he came into her line of vision.

"You will provide an explanation for that," she screamed, "or you will answer not to me but to the Magnificent Citizen himself!"

Ethan leaned into the screen. "That's not how it works, ma'am. *You* will give an explanation for firing on my shuttle and *you* will answer to Meridian for picking a fight with the strongest Nova Force in the Kellan Star System."

The woman gritted her teeth. "Where is that shuttle going?"

"None of your business."

"No ship is allowed to enter or leave Valyan orbit until—"

"Cut her off," Ethan ordered.

Mockett stared at him, aghast. His last shred of patience wore thin.

"Cut her off!" he thundered.

Mockett obeyed; the bridge went silent. Slightly ashamed of himself, Ethan turned to face his stunned officers. How long could they hold against a concentrated attack? How many Valyan ships were in orbit, anyway? How many in those hangars? Did the Magnificent Army even have the technology to destroy a novacraft as big and powerful as the *Hummingbird*?

More than likely, yes. Rael has funneled nearly all the planet's wealth into his army. We're dealing with state-of-the-art tech here, not a few flimsy rifles.

"We don't take any calls from anyone on this planet unless they're from Miss Tremaine or the Palace itself," he said. "Got it, Lieutenant?"

"Yes, sir," Mockett murmured.

"Good. Send another message to President Stagg and Commander Jarvis telling them *exactly* what just happened, then send another one to the Palace. Tell Rael that if he wants to start killing his prisoners, he'll have to discuss it with *me* first."

Nobody followed the Meridian shuttle into the clouds. Lindy caught her breath and twisted around in her seat.

"Are you okay back there, Jo?" she called.

"Uh-huh," a small voice replied.

"You don't sound all right."

"Just head us in the right direction. I'm not leaving this gun until we're moving *fast*."

Lindy decided not to argue. Jo sounded bad. "Right. Moving fast…in the right direction."

She entered into the computer the coordinates for the circuitous route she and Ethan had planned. Unsurprisingly, she had to wait several nail-biting seconds after hitting "calculate." Computers preferred direct trajectories, and she hadn't provided standard fare.

"See alternate route?" the computer asked hopefully.

"No," Lindy snapped. "Accept original route."

The little ship obediently zipped southeast without leaving the safety of the stratosphere. Lindy unbuckled herself.

"Jo? You can come back up here now."

"Coming." Jo gripped the seats as she made her way to the cockpit. "We've probably got a busted fender, but I don't smell smoke. I don't even think we're listing."

"The computer would've already lost its mind if we were." Lindy closed her eyes and leaned her head back. She heard the cushions sigh as Jo threw herself into the co-pilot's seat.

"They'll come after us, y'know," Jo murmured.

"But we have a head start. And if we don't go straight for Omstorn, it'll throw 'em off track."

"If we're not heading for Omstorn, how will we get to the mountains?"

Lindy lifted her head and rubbed her eyes. "The Larondas are on the other side of the river, due south of Omstorn. If Rael expects us to go to the Renegade, we can't take a direct route. But if we head *southeast*, over pretty-much-empty countryside, we shouldn't run into any patrols until we get back on track at the river. It'll add some time, but I'd rather not get shot down halfway to Omstorn."

"Uh-huh."

"You have a better idea?"

At last, a weary smile crossed Jo's face. "Nope. Just glad one of us knows what we're doing. Oh, by the way…"

She reached for the headband in her hair. For the first time, Lindy remembered the micro-cam. She bolted upright as Jo extended the headband to her.

"That's the whole recording of everything that happened in the Palace," Jo explained, "if you want to watch it for yourself. Sorry I didn't give it to you earlier. Between Chevenere and Dr. Elliot whisking me off to the sickbay, I forgot."

Lindy shook the headband at her. "Don't you dare apologize. I'm the one who's sorry for leaving you at the Palace this morning so Ethan and I could spy on Magnificents."

Jo snorted. "Well, that would be a pretty stupid thing to apologize for since neither of us knew Rael would've gone nuts."

"I guess so," Lindy murmured. "I don't suppose you know where they took Frank?"

Jo's face fell. "Rael told Chevenere to take me to the military center. I'm assuming that's where he is."

"Okay. Ethan and I saw all of you being dragged out of the Palace, but I never did see him. He must've been taken out a different way."

Jo gulped and looked away. Lindy waited a minute before she tried another question.

"Was Nana still okay when you were separated?"

Jo nodded slowly. "Yeah. She was upset, but before that, she'd been smart-mouthing Rael and the guards and rambling on about her rights as a Kellan citizen. In other words, she was the same old Nana."

Lindy winced. "In this case, that's probably not a good thing."

"Hey, as long as she runs circles around them, they'll remain in a perpetual state of confused frustration." Jo paused. "How do you feel about all this? About finally knowing who you are?"

Lindy sighed. "I don't know. Part of me still refuses to believe it. But another part of me feels like I've broken through the clouds for the first time in my life, and everything is clearer than it's ever been."

"Sounds a bit like our view," Jo observed, gesturing at the clear sky above and the roiling clouds below.

"No kidding. But the clarity only goes so far. I know I have to find the Renegade and his army, neutralize the Magnificents, and get our people out of prison—but after that? I have no clue. I don't know anything about being a queen. But if I *am* Alinna and I still don't accept that responsibility…"

"You could always hand it over to Mariamne," Jo suggested.

"But she's turned out to be exactly what the people wanted to get rid of twenty-three years ago. How would that help?"

Jo pressed a button, reclining her chair as far as it would go. "Sounds like you're caught between a rock and a hard place, then."

Lindy snorted, but Jo already lay on her back with her hands folded over her stomach and her eyes closed. Under normal circumstances, Lindy would've forced the seat upright and told Jo she couldn't sleep until she'd talked her out of this unenviable situation. But Jo was still pale and bruised, and her voice had slurred over those last few words anyway. Lindy looked down at the headband and ran her finger over the micro-cam.

She doesn't deserve to relive whatever's on this camera. Not right now.

"Get some rest, Jo," Lindy whispered.

"I intend to," Jo mumbled.

It was the last thing she said for the next hour and a half.

Chapter Twenty-Five

8:45 PM

"Captain!" Lieutenant Mockett cried. "Incoming message from Rael!"

Ethan leaped out of his seat. It had been nearly an hour since Lindy left. If Rael meant to make good on his threat, it was almost time for his first execution—and Ethan's mother still hadn't replied to his last message.

Rael's handsome, canny face appeared on Mockett's screen. She jumped up; Ethan took her seat.

"Citizen Navorre," he said. "Thanks for responding to my invitation to talk things over."

Rael smirked. He sat in a comfortable recliner with his arm in a sling, but judging by the bare stone walls and the harsh lighting, he wasn't in the Palace. "There is nothing to discuss, Captain

Granger. If my sister is alive, she will give herself up. But if she is *not* alive and this is all a figment of warped imaginations, then my enemies will be made irrelevant once and for all."

Ethan clenched his hands. "I'd think twice about that if I were you. If you kill your cousin and the rest of those nobles, you'll cut off your planet from the rest of the Star System, with no hope whatsoever for any economic progress. Worst case scenario, though? Meridian will declare war on you. I've been in the Nova Force my entire adult life. So believe me, you do *not* want to be on its bad side."

Rael looked at Ethan down the length of his nose. "Tell me, Captain...have you ever been so desperate to prove a point, you'd move heaven and earth to do it? Have you ever defied your parents? Teachers? The whole of society, even?"

"As a matter of fact, I have. But it never involved mass murder."

"'Murder' implies the death of innocent victims. I have never been guilty of that."

Ethan leaned closer. "Listen to me. If you so much as lay a finger on your family or on any Meridians, you'll wish you hadn't. Don't wake a sleeping giant if you can avoid it."

For the first time, uncertainty flickered in Rael's face. He bit the corner of his mouth and glanced at someone behind the camera. Ethan held his breath. Perhaps whoever it was had just enough influence to talk sense into the man.

"Captain?" Aeron whispered.

Ethan raised his hand. Rael appeared to be listening to someone intently, as if his life depended on every word being said.

When his jaw set and he returned his defiant gaze to the screen, Ethan's heart sank.

"Meridian will never attack Valya, Captain," Rael said coolly. "I could pick off the entire Remnant one by one—maybe throw a Meridian or two into the mix—and your government will make the customary expressions of outrage. But when it's all said and done, my quarrel is with my sister and with those who've hidden her all these years, not with Meridian itself. Maria Stagg and her Council know that better than anyone."

He waved his free hand, and the camera swiveled away from him. Ethan stiffened at the sight of Princess Verrona on her knees, a Magnificent on either side of her. Her dress was torn, her hair straggled in front of her bloodied face, yet she glared fearlessly at the camera.

The soldiers had their rifles pointed at her head.

"A prisoner an hour until Alinna gives herself up," Rael said offscreen. "And tell her for me that Margaret Tremaine is *not* exempt."

Ethan sprang out of the chair. "Rael! Rael, if you kill that woman, you'll pay a thousandfold! For Elyon's sake, she's your aunt!"

"An aunt for a sister, Captain. And my sister hasn't accepted the bargain."

"Rael!"

Princess Verrona closed her eyes. "Long live Alinna Navorre."

Ethan let out a hoarse "No!" and whirled from the screen a second too late.

10:00 PM

Lindy hadn't been idle while Jo napped. She'd plugged the microcam into the shuttle computer, watched the video, and fled to the back seat for a good cry. But then she'd wiped her eyes, returned to the cockpit, and started fitting the puzzle pieces together in her own mind.

The footage had cleared up several points. For one thing, Lhoris had seemed completely immovable in his conviction that Alinna survived. He had probably been just as sure about her own true identity. Chevenere's devastated reactions put Lindy at ease where *she* was concerned, too. The Dominator had acted exactly like someone who'd tried to play a delicate, dangerous game for a very long time, only for everything to blow up in her face.

Rael's guilt, however, intrigued Lindy the most. Several times she'd replayed the moment when he had the gun aimed at Lhoris and Mariamne.

"Do you really think that I don't lie awake at night telling myself over and over again, 'I did what I had to do?' Do you really think their ghosts don't scream at me, begging me not to pull the trigger? But I pull it anyway. I have to stop the screaming. I always pull it anyway."

Click. Rewind. Play.

"I pull it anyway. I have to stop the screaming. I always pull it anyway."

So he felt guilt, but not necessarily repentance. He might fight to the death under the power of that guilt.

The computer chimed, startling Lindy out of her reverie. "Approaching the Great Valyan River. Omstorn, 25 miles west of current location."

Lindy locked the micro-cam back into the headband. "Jo? Jo, wake up. We're about to cross the river."

"Mmmph?" Jo, curled up in the reclined chair, opened one eye. "Shortest nap ever…"

"I'm sorry. But we're twenty minutes away from the planet's biggest mountain range, and I'd really rather you made the radio calls. I don't want to try handling that while I'm flying."

Jo grunted and fumbled for the button on her chair. Lindy waited until she sat up before handing her the headband. Jo put it on, clumsily arranging her short hair around it.

"You watched it?" she asked. "What do you think?"

"That I'm sorry you had to witness it," Lindy said quietly.

Jo sighed. "I'll have to deal with my trauma later. Give me the frequency code."

Lindy drew Chevenere's notes out of her pocket. Jo reached for the mouthpiece, twisting the radio knobs until she found the right channel. Unfortunately, except for static and an occasional, single *beep*, the channel was silent.

"Whenever you're ready," Jo said grimly.

Lindy nodded. "As soon as we get across. The Magnificents in Omstorn probably monitor that frequency all the time. I don't want them picking up our signal too close."

With that, she initiated a full stop. The shuttle hovered over the clouds. Lindy swallowed hard and punched in a slow, steady descent. The radar was quiet; no one had pursued them since they left Cor Danem. Only the soroidium emissions from Omstorn and the dots and lines representing the river and the mountains showed on the screen.

Within moments land stretched out below them, shrouded in darkness except for a bright cluster of light to the west and a few scattered twinkles. Up ahead, faintly illuminated by Omstorn's lights, lay the river—and beyond it, the mountains. Lindy increased their speed.

"You want me to sit at the gun?" Jo asked.

"Only if something pops out of Omstorn and heads this way."

"Why are we whispering?"

Lindy glanced sheepishly at Jo. "No clue."

Jo giggled. Lindy grinned, grateful for a moment's comic relief. They were halfway across the churning, swollen river when she disengaged the autopilot and turned her lights back on at half-strength.

"All right," she said, gripping the control columns. "Call the Renegade."

Jo cleared her throat and clicked the transmitter. "Farrow-Eagle-Valley-Two. Farrow-Eagle-Valley-Two, this is Liliana—come in, please."

Lindy shot Jo a startled look. "'Liliana?' Are you crazy? Why aren't you using Chevenere's personal code?"

Jo covered the transmitter with her free hand. "It'll get their attention, and if we're lucky, any eavesdroppers will be *thoroughly* bewildered. Trust me. Farrow-Eagle-Valley-Two, this is Liliana—come in, please."

Lindy held her breath, half-expecting the radar to light up with hordes of incoming enemies. Yet they still got only static and the rare, single beep while the shuttle moved closer to the Larondas. Lindy could just make them out now in the ship's dimmed lights: a craggy range covered in sparse forests and snowcaps.

"They're not answering," Jo grumbled. "Maybe we should just land somewhere and hope we run into one of their patrols."

Lindy pursed her lips. "Try one more time."

Jo obeyed, but the channel remained silent. Lindy shifted in her seat. Jo waited a moment, then jammed her thumb against the transmitter.

"Okay, look," she spat. Lindy gasped in horror, but Jo scooted out of her reach. "I know you're there unless your contact in Cor Danem gave me a shoddy channel. To be honest, that kind of backstabbing wouldn't shock me at this point. But if you *are* there, we'd really appreciate it if you just came right out and said so!"

"Jo!" Lindy cried.

"Shh!" Jo hissed. Lindy set her teeth and looked away.

The computer blurted a new message: "Collision imminent—please adjust course." The radar had picked up a new soroidium pulse on the other side of the river, too. Lindy gave the controls a sharp jerk to the right.

"I'm gonna find a landing spot," she muttered. "We can at least shut off the engine until we're sure that blip isn't a patrol coming to check us out—"

"Liliana, this is Farrow-Eagle-Valley-Two."

The rich voice startled Lindy so badly, she lurched back in her seat. Jo's eyes widened.

"That's the voice I heard on the video," Lindy whispered. "That's *him*."

Jo started to reply, but the Renegade interrupted her. "Liliana, you have ventured into Free Valyan territory. Identify yourself and obey every order you receive if you want to live. Otherwise, we will not hesitate to shoot you down."

"Give me the radio," Lindy ordered.

"What?! But you said you didn't want to talk and fly—"

"Just hold it up to my face!"

Jo did so without further argument. Lindy adjusted the controls, her eyes locked on a flat, narrow shelf of rock just up ahead.

"Farrow, you know who I am," she called. "You told me to reveal myself and rally the Valyans—but I can't do that unless I have you and your army on my side. Tell your people to stand down. Brace yourself, Jo!"

Jo gripped the arm of her chair. Lindy activated the landing gear.

"We copy," the Renegade said. "Our nearest patrol will be with you in ten minutes, but I insist that you exit your shuttle unarmed. Do not take any weapons with you. Acknowledge."

"Acknowledged," Jo said shakily. Lindy was too busy trying to avoid hitting the mountain to make her own reply. Sweat trickled down between her shoulder blades. That blip from Omstorn was getting closer.

THUD. The landing gear settled comfortably on flat rock. Lindy shut off the engine, leaned her head back, and closed her eyes. Jo quickly unbuckled herself.

"Come on," she cried. "Don't just sit there!"

"Hang on, give me a minute," Lindy begged. She clutched the arms of her chair, breathing as steadily as she could.

This was it. As soon as she left this shuttle, she'd be stepping into Alinna Navorre's shoes. She would be forming alliances and making policy on her own terms...and she'd be accepting the responsibilities of a queen whether she wanted them or not.

Once she did that, there'd be no turning back.

Five minutes gave them plenty of time to pull out some rations and a couple of Nova Force ponchos. They stepped out of the shuttle better shielded against the mountain chill and ready for their first meal in hours.

"Lantern, check," Jo said as the shuttle locked behind them. "Picnic blanket, check."

"'Midnight picnic' is more like it," Lindy said as she spread the blanket at a safe distance from the drop-off. Jo sat down and set the lantern in the middle of the blanket; Lindy squatted and opened one of the ration packs.

"Go ahead and actually sit down, Lindy," Jo urged. "You look exhausted."

Lindy shook her head. "I don't want to be caught off guard. Not without my gun."

"And if, say, a mountain lion decides to jump us, what good will it do you getting cramps in your calves?" Jo tore a plastic spoon out of her ration pack. "Then again, I doubt there are any mountain lions here. The Renegade and his people probably ate them."

Lindy shot her an incredulous smile. So long as Jo kept making weird comments, her mental state couldn't be that fragile. Lindy eased herself down and sniffed her meal—and something snapped overhead. Jo sat up straight. Lindy bolted to her feet.

"Who's there?" she called.

"Hands above your head," a male voice—not the Renegade's—retorted. "You, on your feet next to your friend. Not a sound from either of you till we get down there."

Jo scrambled to Lindy's side as they lifted their hands level with their heads. Even by the light of the lantern, Lindy couldn't see whoever loomed above them on the outcrop. When five figures clambered down a perilously narrow path she hadn't noticed before, she realized why. They were all dressed in black.

"Raise your hands!" one of them hissed. "Raise them!"

Lindy raised her hands, looking him dead in the eye while he gave her a rough pat-down. One of his companions did the same with Jo while the other three stalked around the shuttle.

"Any weapons in there?" the first soldier asked.

"Just two rifles and our personal, MID-issued weapons," Lindy answered.

He jerked his head towards her. "You're with the Meridian Intelligence Department?"

"We are. I'm Trooper Lindy Tremaine, and this is my partner, Jo Camrin." Lindy held her head a little higher. "I'm here to talk to your leader about Alinna Navorre. I've got to see him as soon as possible. Lives depend on it."

To her dismay, he gave a skeptical snort. "Don't worry. You entered Free Valyan territory when you crossed the river—and nobody on the other side has dared to do that in months. So yes, you will *definitely* be talking to the Renegade."

The men tied rough blindfolds over their eyes and forced them up the mountain path. Lindy couldn't read the emotions of her guide beyond a blur of indistinguishable colors; they were too deeply sheltered. She finally gave up and focused on her feet, hoping to avoid slamming her toes into every rock and root.

The long, upward path, however, was surprisingly unobstructed. These men obviously knew it by heart. The air grew colder and thinner. When Lindy did stumble, it had more to do with her growing exhaustion and breathlessness than anything else.

But after a good half-hour, everything changed. The ground turned smooth; the air warmed; the footsteps took on a new, resounding echo as if they'd entered a tunnel. Then the echoes abruptly swelled into a thunderous chorus of voices, the whir of hovers, and the clang of construction. Lindy's guide stopped and loosened her blindfold. She blinked, looked around, and gasped.

"Oh. My. Worrrrrrrd," Jo breathed.

They stood at the entrance of a monstrous, cylindrical cavern. The walls on every side and all the way up and down twinkled with lights. A wide stone bridge with cold blue railings stretched from one side of the chamber to the other. The roar of construction came from teams of men drilling into the cavern wall.

Rooms, Lindy realized in awed delight. *They're building rooms in the mountain—and maybe not just rooms, but homes. They've got an entire city in here!*

She might've risked a question if a hover hadn't zoomed across the bridge towards them. As soon as the side hatch opened, Lindy and Jo's guides pushed them inside.

"Evrella," the soldier in charge muttered. "Any change to the plan?"

"No, but he's getting impatient." The female driver peered at the prisoners with an especially piercing look in Lindy's direction. "I really don't know what he'll do if he's disappointed. *Again.*"

Lindy clamped her lips and looked away, anxiety curling in her stomach.

The hover shot back across the bridge and down an intermittently lit tunnel before emerging in a smaller cavern with fewer floors and no bridge. Warm light streamed out from behind heavy canvas sheets that served as doors. Once the hover landed, the soldiers led Lindy and Jo to one of the nearest caves. Lindy wiped her sweaty palms on her suit and glanced at her watch.

11:00. About three hours since we left Cor Danem. She drew a shaky breath as one of the soldiers yanked the canvas back and they all stepped inside.

The interior, a mix of primitive furnishings and advanced technology, surprised her. A rough wooden table and benches stood opposite a glowing soroidium heater; shelves on the wall displayed old-fashioned, hardbound books. A huge, broad-shouldered man sat at a large desk, watching several flickering computer screens at once. His posture was as taut as a bowstring.

"My lord," the lead soldier called. "Your visitors are here."

The man sighed. Lindy braced herself as he pushed his chair back, stood, and turned.

For a moment, no one said a word. Lindy narrowed her eyes.

I know him. I've seen him before. Where have I seen him?

The Renegade, handsome and muscular despite the white in his short beard, drew a sharp breath. He reached for his chair. One of the soldiers approached him in alarm, but the Renegade stopped him with a trembling hand. Lindy and Jo shared a worried glance.

"Alinna," the Renegade whispered, his deep voice raw. "You came."

"I..." Lindy blinked and shook her head. "I didn't have a choice. I didn't know I was—I mean—up until yesterday I never thought..."

She broke off, disoriented. The surreal fragility she'd felt in the field outside Cor Danem had returned. The Renegade never took his eyes off her. She took a cautious step closer, trying to place him in her tattered memories.

"You're so sure I'm Alinna," she said. "How do you know me?"

The Renegade smiled sadly, his hand tightening on the chair. "You have your mother's eyes."

"You knew her? Queen Liliana?"

He said nothing, but his eyes shimmered. Lindy frowned harder, her heart racing as she recalled the painting of Queen Liliana and tried once again to figure out why this man felt so familiar...

And then it hit her. Her eyes widened; her mouth fell open. The Renegade raised his eyebrows hopefully as she clapped a hand over her mouth.

"Lindy?" Jo asked, her voice small and worried. "Lindy, what is it?"

Lindy couldn't speak. The history book on Nana's coffee table—the one she'd brought home from the library the day she and

Jo interviewed Genevieve Stagg—the memory of it and the photograph of the Valyan royal family flooded her head.

Everyone had smiled at the camera in that photo except Rael. He had sulked behind his seated, smiling father…a handsome, broad-shouldered, short-bearded man dressed in red with kind, laughing eyes.

"You lived," Lindy breathed. "*You lived.*"

The Renegade's face contorted as if he didn't know whether to laugh or weep.

"So did you, Alinna," he whispered, tears rolling down his face. "So did you."

Chapter Twenty-Six

4:30 AM Meridian Time (11:30 PM Valyan Time)

Genevieve Stagg lay flat on her back in bed, wide-awake and frustrated. Her mother had sent her to bed hours ago before closeting herself with the Meridian Council, the Nova Force generals, and Commander Jarvis. From what Cephas had gathered thanks to some good old-fashioned eavesdropping, they'd been trying to find a way to intervene in the Valyan crisis without inviting criticism or ridicule.

"Unfortunately," the butler-droid had concluded in his maddening monotone, "all possibilities mentioned so far have been dismissed as politically nonviable."

Such a verdict had snapped her last fragile nerve. Genevieve had ordered him downstairs, warning him not to come back unless the Council actually decided something. It had been a relief to raise her voice—and since droids had no feelings, she didn't even have to feel guilty about it.

But now it was nearly dawn, and he hadn't returned. Genevieve sighed and sat up, wincing at the dull ache in her arms as she shifted her weight. When she caught a glimpse of her reflection in her vanity mirror, she shuddered and looked away. Without any cosmetics to fake the color in her cheeks, she looked grey and frail. It scared her.

Worrying over her brother didn't help. Apparently, Rael's soldiers had the *Hummingbird* surrounded in Cor Danem's novaport. If Ethan made a false move, he and his crew would be blown to bits.

But Rael won't attack them, Genevieve tried to console herself. *That would definitely give Mother grounds for war. On the other hand, he can kill as many of the Valyan nobles as he pleases. They're not Meridian citizens, so the Council might decide not to fight for them.*

Genevieve curled her fingers carefully. She didn't want to risk hurting herself, but the sight of a loose but undeniably angry fist was oddly satisfying.

Knock-knock. "Miss Genevieve?"

She lifted her head, relaxing her fingers. "Come in, Cephas."

The droid entered. His sallow face gave no hint of good or bad news. Genevieve folded her hands over her coverlet and tried to look regal, even in her pajamas.

"Well? Did they decide anything?"

"Yes, ma'am. President Stagg has decided she will *not* send the Nova Force to Valya."

Genevieve's heart sank. "In Elyon's name, why?"

"Councilors Throgmorton and Sackville said that such intervention would incur the wrath of the Namarians, who've maintained for the past seven-point-three years that Meridian's influence in the Star System is both imperialistic and expansionist."

"As if they don't have expansionist ambitions themselves! Who cares what *they* think?"

"Councilor Throgmorton and Councilor Sackville," Cephas answered blandly.

Genevieve scoffed. "And my mother, I suppose."

"Ninety-seven percent of the evidence would support that, Miss Genevieve."

She pursed her lips. "And what about the generals? What do they think?"

"They argue that it is only a matter of time before Rael does some harm to his prisoners."

"And Commander Jarvis?"

"He does not believe Miss Tremaine will surrender and therefore concludes the same as the generals."

The clock on the nightstand chimed the bottom of the hour. Genevieve shivered. Her doctor would have a fit if he heard she hadn't slept a wink.

"Will it be on the morning news?" she asked wearily.

"No, ma'am. The President believes it would inflame the Valyan refugees, especially those in Manwaring. She fears they might demand a stronger reaction. The generals of the Nova Force *are* in agreement with her there. They do not want to provoke unrest on Meridian."

Genevieve raised an eyebrow. "Indeed."

Cephas blinked, waiting for her next question. Genevieve bit the corner of her lip, shot a wary look through the open bedroom door, and took as deep a breath as she could with her weakening chest.

"Cephas," she said softly, "shut the door, will you? And get my tablet from my desk. Find out for me which Meridian ships are patrolling near Valya."

Cephas obeyed. "The *Georgiana* is approximately three hours from Valya, ma'am."

"Excellent. Now. You can log into Mother's inbox from my tablet, can't you?"

"It would require her password..."

"Which you know as the highest-ranking droid of Hoadley House, of course."

Cephas's face twitched. "Of course."

"Wonderful. Then log into Mother's inbox, open a new comm-note, and address it to the captain of the *Georgiana*. I'll dictate. Ready?"

Cephas hesitated. "It will take two hours by star relay for the communication to reach the *Georgiana*."

"I don't care. Better late than never. Are you ready?"

If the droid could've sighed, she was sure he would have. "Ready, ma'am."

Genevieve rubbed her thin hands together. She'd be in huge trouble when everyone found out what she'd done—and Meridian probably would be, too. On the other hand, if Rael wanted a fight, he ought to get one. And if Mother wouldn't give it to him…

Then I'm the only one who can. For Ethan's sake, if for no one else's.

"'Top Secret,'" she began. "'To Captain Harold Rogers of the *MNC Georgiana…*'"

Nearly midnight, Valyan time

Whatever lingering doubts Lindy still had about her new identity, they vanished like smoke once the Renegade folded her in his arms. His strong, vivid Emanation met hers without hesitation, and as they wept and clung to each other, their combining emotions nearly overwhelmed them both.

Yet even over her own sobbing, one thought pulsed over and over again through her head: *You're my papa…and you lived…and you know me! YOU KNOW ME!*

As if he could read her mind, he tightened his arms around her and pressed his lips to the side of her head.

"I thought I'd never see you again," he murmured. "All these years, I simply had to trust that you were safe…that Elyon would shield you until the time was right."

Lindy shook her head fiercely against his shoulder. "If Elyon is so good, he'd have let my friend kill Rael this morning and put an end to all this!"

The Renegade gave a soft, patient chuckle and rubbed her back. "How confident you are about that when you only see a piece of the tapestry he's weaving. The moment I crawled to the spot where you and your mother lay in that field, I too saw only a piece…and a hideous piece it seemed to me."

Lindy sniffled, frowned, and lifted her head off his shoulder. That memory of being cradled and lifted out of the mud…those had been *his* arms, then. She loosened her fingers from the front of his vest and took an unsteady backward step, realizing only then that Jo and the soldiers must've crept away to give them some privacy.

"So *you* found me," she said slowly. "And Mama, she…"

"Was dead when I found you." He sank into his chair, leaning his elbows on his massive knees. Lindy noticed he moved with a limp. "It was still dark when I came to. Rael's men were moving through the field, shooting anything that moved. They may have been looking for me."

"Were you hurt?"

He nodded, patting his thigh. "I was shot in the leg. It shattered the bone but missed the artery. Another miracle, no doubt. But as I crawled away as quietly as I could, I…I saw your mother."

Lindy's stomach sank. The Renegade's jaw flexed.

"Judging from her wounds, I don't think she suffered. But you lay nearby, bleeding from your shoulder. I couldn't wake you." Tears sprang into his eyes again. "I couldn't let you die in front of me, Alinna. That would've been more than I could bear."

Lindy exhaled shakily. She reached behind her and unzipped her trooper suit a few inches. The Renegade sat up, watching closely as she tugged the suit to one side and ran her thumb over the raised scar in her shoulder.

"There," she whispered. "There's my proof that I'm that same little girl."

He pointed at the pendant around her neck. "And that would be further proof if I needed any. It was your mother's. I did wonder later if I should've taken it off, in case it was too easily recognized."

"It's probably a good thing you didn't," Lindy said, zipping up her suit. "Did you know who you'd left me with?"

He shook his head. "It was dark. All I cared about was that it wasn't a Magnificents' barrack."

"It was one of Maria Stagg's aid stations. *She* got me off-planet and Margaret Tremaine adopted me. I got a new name and grew up on Meridian—and I knew absolutely *nothing* about myself except that I survived the Cor Danem Massacre."

"Then how..."

"Nana—Margaret—recorded the whole story years ago. I only just watched it a few hours ago." Lindy stepped closer. "You need to understand...I remember the massacre only because I still dream about it. But before that, it's all blank. I don't remember being a princess at all."

A new wave of sorrow washed over his face. "You don't remember going to the sea every summer?"

She blinked. "No."

"You were a fearless little monkey. You'd run straight into the water over your mother's protests. Cresside would have to haul you back, dripping from head to toe." He smiled. "The baby of the family almost always has a spitfire streak."

"I guess that explains a lot of things about myself, then," Lindy teased weakly. "But you haven't told me how you got to be the famous Renegade."

He sighed. "I was certain Rael's men would find me. One of the last royalist groups hiding in the forest a few miles outside the city did instead. From that group, our army grew. We're guerrillas, yes, but we believe it is an honorable way to fight tyranny."

"Do they know who you are?"

"Yes. But at my express command, they do not speak of it."

"Why not?" Lindy cried. "If the Remnant knew, they would've rallied around you!"

His smile turned grim. "I inherited a monarchy based on cruelty and greed. Whether I like it or not, Kalen Navorre will forever be connected to that establishment. If I ever revealed myself, Rael would make it look as if I wanted to overthrow him as he did me and return to the old ways."

"But you don't want that?"

"No. Our planet has suffered enough at the hands of autocrats. I have no desire to be king again."

"But you called *me* 'Queen Alinna' in your transmission."

The Renegade looked at her steadily. "There is such a thing as a constitutional monarchy. A queen raised on Meridian with a healthy regard for the common man would be welcomed on Valya. Trust me: our people resent and despise Rael for betraying their cause. They *will* rally to you."

"And then what?" Lindy demanded. "I don't know how to rule a planet. What if they turn against me the way they've turned against him?"

"They'd only do that if you gave them a reason to," he said firmly.

Lindy frowned. She nodded, slow and thoughtful, and laced her fingers.

"Okay," she whispered. "I still don't know if I'm ready. But if I don't do something, Rael will kill what family we've got left, and my friends, and…and the guy I might be falling in love with."

He raised his eyebrows, amused and surprised. Lindy blushed and decided to ignore it.

"Anyway, that's enough incentive right now," she finished briskly. "I'll cross or burn the rest of my bridges when I get to them."

Jo rejoined them once Lindy and the Renegade stepped out of his quarters. She'd been waiting outside with his soldiers, and as soon as they appeared, she hurried over to them. Lindy understood the eager excitement in her widened eyes and hastened to make proper introductions.

"This is my best friend and my MID partner, Jo Camrin," she said, gesturing between her father and Jo. "Jo, this is...my father."

The Renegade smiled. "I am delighted to meet you, Miss Camrin."

Jo beamed up at him. "Not as delighted as I am to meet you, sir. And that's a *fact*."

The Renegade had laughed a deep, rumbling laugh. Now, as she and Jo followed close on his heels to what he called "the Contact Room," Lindy felt more energetic and hopeful than she had in days.

"Looks like a mining shaft," Jo said as she balanced uneasily in a rocking lift.

"That's precisely what it is," the Renegade replied. "Once upon a time, the people of Omstorn mined for soroidium down here. The mine closed not long after my father died."

"Your dad," Jo mused. "So...Lindy's granddad?"

"Precisely." He paused, looking at Jo kindly. "Alinna says you've been her dearest friend for many years. I am glad she has had such a loyal companion in her exile—and a brave partner in her work."

Jo blushed. "Um, thanks. Did you tell him about Rael's ultimatum, Lindy?"

Lindy nodded. "I told him what Chevenere said about the microchips, too—how we've got to neutralize the Magnificents by shutting down their control centers."

"There are three thousand men and women here who will fight at your command," the Renegade said. "And those are just my trained soldiers. We will have even more friends in the villages and towns once you identify yourself."

"You seem pretty confident about that," Jo said.

He gave her a mysterious look. "We have our ways of knowing things, Miss Camrin. And *that* one we are certain of, beyond a shadow of a doubt."

The lift stopped. The Renegade led them down a low-ceilinged corridor lit only by a few bulbs in the wall. Lindy fought back the claustrophobia until he drew aside one of the canvas "doors" in the left wall and gestured for her to go inside.

She obeyed, cautious—but she and Jo both gasped at the sight of a bustling communications room. Computers and holovisions flashed on all four walls; uniformed men and women monitored the screens and called out radio codes. Every one of them jumped to their feet, however, at the sight of the Renegade. He clasped his hands behind his back and nodded.

"Contact Team," he said sternly. "The rightful Queen of Valya, my daughter Alinna."

Lindy's heart fluttered as everyone stared at her in delighted surprise. She rubbed her fingertips against her palms, tilted her head back, and approached the guy in charge: a wiry young man with ebony skin and eyeglasses. He reminded her of the tech nerds at MID Headquarters.

"Hi," she began. Before she could get any further, the techie bowed so fast and clumsily that he almost hit her with his head.

"Your M-Majesty," he stammered.

Lindy threw up her hands. "Okay, first of all, let's not call me that *just* yet. It makes me want to jump out of my skin, especially since I'm not even wearing a crown."

He looked confused, but he and his companions murmured their assent. Lindy dared not turn around to see the Renegade's reaction. Instead, she pointed at one of the holovisions.

"Is that one connected to the planetary network?"

The techie nodded vigorously. "Yes, Your Ma—uh, *milady*."

"What's playing?"

"At this time of night?" He snorted. "Footage from uh, let's see —"

"Rael's speech at the opening of the Harathella Textile Festival three years ago," one of the girls at the holovision called.

Lindy raised her eyebrows. "Rael airs all his old speeches in the middle of the night?"

The techie nodded. Lindy folded her arms and nodded with amused contempt. "What a windbag."

Startled but genuine laughter rippled through the room. Lindy turned back to the techie. "Can you cut it off and put me on instead?"

He adjusted his glasses. "Yes, with a caveat. The network isn't hard to penetrate, but once it *is*, the officials who monitor it can cut us off easily."

"Fair enough. I don't plan to be on long anyway."

He winced. "There's just one more problem, though? The moment you are on Valyan holovision, they will know you're with us, so…"

"So I lose my advantage of Rael not knowing exactly where I am right now."

"*Right*, yes, thank you."

Lindy shook her head. "I'm more worried about people being sound asleep and missing my message in the first place."

"Oh, but that can be remedied!" a third operator cried from the back, his arm thrust high into the air. "I can hack the Emergency Alert System and wake the entire planet."

"Can you do that in the time we have?" the Renegade demanded.

The young man shrugged. "Depends on how much time I have, my lord."

Lindy glanced at her watch. "You have half an hour."

The young man blinked a couple of times. "Half an hour. I can do it."

"Good. That'll give me time to come up with a speech. Jo, give me your headband."

Jo obeyed. Lindy popped the micro-cam out and pressed it into the first techie's palm. "Can you send messages to Meridian from here?"

He grinned awkwardly. "Oh yes, milady. That's actually a lot easier."

"Fantastic." She pushed him towards the nearest computer. "Send it straight to Hoadley House, and then to MID Headquarters and all your contacts in Manwaring."

"Alinna?" the Renegade called. Lindy whirled and saw him frowning in bewilderment.

"I said nothing to you about our Manwaring contacts," he said. "How did you know we were in communication?"

The irony of the moment was too much. Jo snickered, and Lindy smiled at her father.

"You forget I'm an MID trooper," she said, only half-teasing. "I'm *supposed* to know these things."

Something woke ten-year-old Avor in the middle of the night, and it wasn't thunder.

He *thought* it was thunder, but the rumbling lasted too long and got louder and louder. He sat up in bed. The cracked windowpane in the bedroom he shared with his older sister and little brother rattled. Someone turned on the light downstairs; a faint golden beam appeared between the floor and the bedroom door.

"Ani?" Avor called nervously into the dark. His big sister threw back her blankets in response. Three-year-old Doran began to cry.

"Get downstairs, Avor, quick!" Ani hissed. "Come on, Dor, let's go see Mama."

"Children!" Papa shouted downstairs. "Children, come on down!"

Avor opened the door. Ani dashed out, clutching the sobbing toddler, but Avor didn't follow right away. Curiosity got the better of him: he darted to the window. The pane was so cracked and sooty on the outside, it didn't give him much of a view. He opened it instead, sticking his head outside and craning his neck back.

He glimpsed the source of the noise immediately. A huge dark shape cruised over Cor Danem, red and blue lights blinking from its underbelly as it blocked out the stars.

"A novacraft!" Avor breathed. "Papa, it's—it's a novacraft!"

A strong hand clamped on his shoulder. His father jerked him inside, snatching a glance at the ship before slamming the window shut.

"Is it one of ours?" Avor asked fearfully. "Or…or do you think it belongs to the captain I met the other day?"

His father said nothing and hustled him out and into the bathroom. Avor's sister, mother, and baby brother already huddled in the chipping cast iron tub. The whole house rattled.

"Where was he?" Mama asked.

"Staring out the window," Papa said. "Novacraft should not be flying this low over a city. The magnetic pressure…"

The throbbing roar intensified. Doran wailed. Mama pressed his head against her chest and covered his other ear. An alarm suddenly blared over the thunder.

"Another Planetary Emergency?" Ani shouted. "In a single day?"

Papa frowned. He peered around the door and visibly stiffened. Slowly, he stepped out. Avor followed.

"Avor, no, stay with me!" Mama cried.

He ignored her. Staying just behind his father so he wouldn't be seen, he tiptoed into the living room. Their tiny holovision set had turned on automatically, and Dominator Daltis' ugly face filled the screen. Avor's father folded his arms over his chest.

"Attention, citizens," the Dominator said, his voice stern and gravelly. "Remain indoors, and do not be alarmed. If you are in Cor Danem, Velladon, or Harathella, you may have observed Valyan novacraft flying low over your city. This is a precautionary measure due to hostile forces in Cor Danem, which will soon be neutralized. Again, please remain indoors or take shelter in—"

A terrible screech cut him off. The image on the screen contorted and spliced. Papa took a startled step closer; Avor did the same. The screen turned odd colors and made strange, squeaking noises.

But then it straightened out. No more squeaks, no more weird colors, no more squiggly lines. Everything looked right again. But the Dominator was gone, replaced by a new background and a pretty lady. Papa grabbed the remote, raising the volume. The lady smiled at the camera and threw her head back.

"Valyans." Her voice was clear and steady, but it held a drawl that Avor recognized. The Meridian captain had talked like that. "My name is Alinna Navorre, but for the past twenty-three years, my friends on Meridian have known me as Melinda Tremaine. My brother, the tyrant who's made your lives an absolute misery, tried to murder me when I was only five years old. But now I'm here to tell him, you, and the rest of the Star System that I'm very much alive and that this is the last day you'll have to endure as his slaves."

"Moyra!" Papa shouted, whirling on his heel. Avor froze, but when Papa saw him, his thin face exploded into the biggest smile the boy had seen since Doran was born. Papa grabbed his shoulder and pulled him forward.

"Avor—Avor, sit down—and *listen*. I'm going to get your mother. I'll be right back. Keep listening!"

He dashed away, leaving Avor in the middle of the room. Bewildered but glad, even if he wasn't quite sure why, the boy hoisted himself onto the threadbare couch while the lady continued to speak.

"I need your help. Rael has put this planet in incredible danger. He's killed Prince Lhoris and he's sworn to kill the rest of the Remnant and the Meridian delegation if I don't give myself up. We can't let that happen. We can't risk war with Meridian. But just as importantly, we can't let Rael and the Dominators crush our one chance to bring true, lasting freedom to this planet.

"I know it's terrifying, and I know the Magnificents are dangerous. But I'm not giving myself up—and I *am* coming. As soon as the sun's up, I'll be in Cor Danem. And Rael?"

She jabbed her finger at the screen. Avor sat up straighter as she gritted her teeth and narrowed her eyes.

"You live with it every day? You hear our sisters' ghosts screaming at you? Well, get ready…because your worst nightmare is on her way."

Chapter Twenty-Seven

1 A.M., Valyan time

Lights blinked on all across the planet. Doors flew open; urgent voices echoed in the night. The men seized whatever they could use as weapons: axes, fireplace pokers, wooden planks, wrenches, the odd crowbar. Women followed them into the streets, lighting the soroidium torches everyone used during Valya's all-too-frequent blackouts.

In Cor Danem, Harathella, and the seaside metropolis of Velladon where Rael's insurrection first began, people shook their fists at the menacing novacraft hovering low over their cities. Everywhere the furious cry went up:

"Down with Rael! Down with the Dominators! Long live Alinna Navorre!"

Back at the Cor Danem prison, reclining in a cushioned chair in the main office, Rael studied the names of his captives and tried to assess how valuable each of them might be to his plan. He shifted his position with a grimace. His arm throbbed.

A small price to pay for the advantage I have at the moment, he thought, tossing the list to the side and rubbing his chin. Lord Nhormin's wife had been the most recent to die, a haggard crone who'd probably considered her death a mercy. Her silence and her husband's at their executions had been a welcome change after Verrona and the one-eyed duke who'd followed her. They had been far more defiant, invoking the name of Alinna Navorre even with guns leveled at their heads.

Rael closed his eyes and leaned his head back. Clearly, he'd underestimated the persistent rumors that one of his sisters had escaped. For so long, he'd assumed it was rebel propaganda, a ploy of the Renegade's to gain sympathy for the Remnant's cause.

But then last night, Morgarena had whispered to him about what they'd finally uncovered in Lhoris' stolen files: notes from his meetings with the Manwaring Valyans, hints that he suspected where Alinna was, and promises to the Renegade that he'd do everything in his power to identify her. The news had unnerved him enough to keep him awake all night. As soon as the sun was up, he'd confronted Hadrian Daltis.

But his oldest mentor's reaction—his stony, evasive refusal to deny the possibility that the child *might* have survived—shook him to the core. He had put Daltis in charge of the massacre precisely because of his confidence in the older man's ability to do the job. He'd never questioned Daltis' assurances twenty-three years ago that he'd seen the dead bodies of the royal family with his own eyes.

I should've never trusted him so completely, Rael thought miserably. *I was too young...too desperate...too afraid that if I failed, if one of them survived, they'd make me pay. I should've left no room for doubt. I should've...*

The door opened and Daltis himself appeared. Rael swept his chaotic thoughts and his resentment aside, at least for now.

"Well?" he demanded. "Have we located her yet?"

Daltis' fearsome eyebrows drew together. "No. Not yet."

Rael slammed his good fist on the desk and sprang to his feet. "A shuttle doesn't simply disappear!"

"We are continuing in our efforts to track her. Never fear. We'll find her in good time."

"Or she'll give up and turn herself in," Rael muttered. "Surely she knows I won't hesitate to kill even the Councilor if it comes to that."

Daltis shut the door and stepped closer. "But you haven't taken such drastic measures yet. In fact, you have been remarkably *careful* with your selections. These lesser nobles will carry little to no weight with Alinna, whoever or wherever she is. Perhaps, if you executed a Meridian...the Councilor herself...then perhaps...?"

Rael began pacing, but something twisted in his gut. He hated Margaret Tremaine. Even as a boy, he'd distrusted her scathing wit and those keen blue eyes that seemed to peer right through him. Yet she *was* a prominent politician, respected throughout the Star System, and a close personal friend of President Stagg.

If the Meridians decided to avenge her, could my men withstand such an attack?

"No," he grumbled. "Not the Councilor, not yet. We need to keep her alive for now."

"What about Mariamne?" Daltis prodded. Rael started to reply, but before he could say anything, Morgarena entered.

"Forgive me for intruding," she said, her voice unusually small, "but Alinna has revealed herself."

Rael reached for the back of his chair.

"How did she do it?" Daltis demanded.

"She...she used the Renegade's channel," Morgarena stuttered. "And she penetrated the Emergency Alert System."

Daltis swore. Rael gripped the back of his chair even tighter. Morgarena waited until her father calmed down before she continued.

"Unfortunately, the surveillance ships are keeping everyone awake, so most of the planet saw her message. I put out a bulletin for the Magnificents to remain on full alert, but I can do nothing beyond that. Only one of you can order any stronger action than that now that Chevenere's gone over to the *Hummingbird*." She paused, sullen irritation creeping into her sharp, dark face. "Of course, no one seems to trust *me* with that kind of authority. I'm hardly more than a clerk..."

Rael ignored the jab. "Who is she?"

Morgarena looked him in the eye. "Exactly who we suspected. She's Tremaine's dependent."

Rael clenched his bad fist, ignoring the pain that shot up his arm. Daltis gave him a long, firm look.

"Well?" he asked. "*Now* do you want to keep the Councilor as a bargaining chip? She's harbored Alinna for twenty-three years. If anyone deserves to die, it should be her."

Rael shook his head. "No, Daltis. Killing Margaret Tremaine now will do us no good. But we *can* make her pay for her deceit in other ways. We can make all the Meridians pay."

Ethan paced in front of the bridge window, the reinforced glass reflecting his scowl. The novaport had been lit up for hours. Every hangar door yawned wide open, and every Valyan ship and hover in the compound had the *Hummingbird* surrounded.

They probably have all their guns locked on us, too. And with a dozen more ships in orbit, we'd be under fire in seconds if we tried to make a break for it.

He sighed and rubbed his eyes. The tension was getting to him. He still hadn't gotten any promises from his mother or the Nova Force about backup—but even if the closest Meridian ship did head this way, how would it get past the Valyan orbit patrols? More importantly, how would a Meridian attack affect Rael's execution schedule? So far, he'd already killed four nobles. Ethan had refused to watch the last three.

He glanced over his shoulder at his crew. After the brief triumph of Lindy's spirited message, a tense quiet had fallen over the room. If his crew had reacted so strongly to her rallying cry, what effect had her words had on the soldiers in all those ships surrounding the *Hummingbird*? Surely they'd seen the transmission as well. What were they thinking inside those hunks of grey steel?

Or were they thinking at all? What if Magnificents manned those ships?

Ethan lifted his head with a start. Aeron must've noticed: when Ethan turned, the Opitheldran met his gaze with a questioning look.

"Call Chevenere in here," Ethan ordered. "Tell her I want to ask her something."

Aeron promptly sent the call to Sickbay. Moments later, Chevenere appeared with Dr. Elliot as her escort.

"Captain," she said warmly. "I heard about Miss Tremaine's message to the planet. I'm glad she took that step—and that she obviously found the Renegade."

"Thanks to you," Ethan said. "But now I have a question. Those ships out there? Are they operated by Magnificents?"

Chevenere stepped closer to the window. After a moment, she pointed.

"The hovers most certainly are not," she said. "They are either Cor Danem Police or Novaport Authority. The four novacraft, however, belong to our Nova Force. And yes, *they* are under the umbrella of the Magnificent Army."

"So if we neutralized the crews, we could potentially hijack the ships?"

She looked at him, surprised. "I suppose you could, if you have enough men to spare."

Ethan smirked. "Doesn't take too many men to operate a novacraft. Couple of pilots and a few more guys to fire the cannons? No problem."

"But there is the small matter of actually neutralizing the Magnificents."

"Exactly." Ethan folded his arms. "So tell me what to do."

Chevenere laughed incredulously. "I told you, you need an army for that! The computers connecting the soldiers are too heavily guarded! That is the whole reason why Miss Tremaine went to find the Renegade!"

"Yeah, but here's the thing," Ethan countered, taking a slow step closer to her. "I have a feeling you're not telling me quite everything. You told Lindy that each major city has a protected network connecting the Magnificents. But how does that work within the Nova Force? Is it the same? Is there a computer *we* can destroy?"

Chevenere's expression shifted abruptly from incredulity to alarm. Ethan raised his eyebrows.

"Aeron?" he called. The Opitheldran came closer. Chevenere immediately took a nervous step back.

"As I'm sure you're aware, Opitheldrans are the Star System's resident telepaths," Ethan warned. "They can read your mind without ever touching you. I hear they can even make you *very* aware of their minds invading yours if they want to prove a point…or get the information they need."

Aeron seized Chevenere by the shoulder. She set her teeth, probably trying to resist him from the safety of her Shelter. Valyan empathy, however, proved no match for Opitheldran perception. Her face contorted until she finally whimpered and slumped in Aeron's grip.

"All right, all right!" she cried. "The Nova Force's Magnificents...they're...the computer is in the novaport terminal."

"Where?" Ethan demanded.

Chevenere hesitated. Aeron tightened his fingers, and she flinched.

"Nova Control Room," she gasped.

"Mockett, pull up a floor plan of the novaport terminal," Ethan ordered. "Aeron, organize a team of fifty. Pull out the Class A armor and get Parsons to hand out enough rifles and explosives to blow up a city block."

"Yes, Captain!" Mockett cried. Aeron hurled Chevenere away from him and spun on his heel. Ethan watched as she crumpled to the floor, breathing hard. He didn't feel even a twinge of sympathy.

"Thought that maybe if you didn't give up all your secrets, Rael might forgive you if you found yourself on the losing side?" he asked.

She didn't look at him. Ethan shook his head and turned to the guard who brought her in.

"Take her to the brig—and tell Colt not to let her out of his sight."

Inside the room temporarily assigned to her within the mountain fortress, Lindy pulled on a black tunic. One of her father's female soldiers had given it to her. A yellow sash served as a belt, but she hadn't liked the baggy trousers and opted to keep her trooper uniform's leggings instead. When Jo emerged from the tiny bathroom in a matching outfit, Lindy couldn't help but grin.

"Do I look like a rebel now?" Jo asked, holding up her fists in a fierce pose.

"Oh yeah," Lindy laughed. "How do I look?"

"Fantastic. Yellow and black must be a reference to the Navorre bee, huh?"

"That's what the Renegade says."

Jo raised her eyebrows. "You mean that's what your *father* says."

Lindy smiled, gathering her long curls in a high ponytail. "Yes. My father. He's so confident that I'll be able to rebuild Valya into something new and better."

"If you have the right people helping you, I think he's probably right."

Lindy glanced sidelong at her. "I don't suppose you'd consider being one of those 'right people?'"

Jo snorted. "Well, it's not like I'll ever work undercover again, not after the spectacular way I blew my cover at the Palace. I just wonder if the Valyans will like the idea of a sassy little white girl hanging around you all the time."

"Maybe not initially," Lindy said. "But they'll just have to get used to you."

Jo grinned just as Lindy's comm chirped. The Renegade's techs had connected it to their communication system, so she answered it without hesitation. "Hello?"

"Alinna." The Renegade sounded tense. "Are you nearly ready?"

"Yeah." Lindy made a whirling motion with her finger; Jo nodded and dashed back into the bathroom for her trooper clothes. "Is everything all right?"

"Time is running short if we hope to attack Cor Danem by morning. When you leave your room, instruct the man at your door to take you to the launchpad."

Lindy raised her eyebrows. She'd seen his arsenal, bursting with weapons the rebels had either built themselves or stolen in raids, as well as the huge chamber where the rebels and their families ate in shifts. Her father had made no mention of a launchpad. "We'll be there in just a minute. See you soon."

Sure enough, the soldier assigned to them had a hover ready. Lindy was surprised by how long it took to reach the launchpad, but once they emerged into a wide-open cleft between two mountains, her mouth fell open. Jo bolted upright.

"Wow," she breathed.

The driver chuckled. "You didn't expect that, did you?"

Lindy let out a laughing breath and craned her neck. Floodlights blazed down on a small fleet of novacraft. Most looked as if they were better suited for leisure trips and everyday use than for battles.

"They've been painted to look like rocks from above," the driver explained. "The one time Rael sent scouting ships over the Larondas, they were so fooled, they never came back. So far, they've never found our exact location."

"Where did you get them all?" Jo cried.

The driver shrugged. "A few came with wealthier Valyans who now live among us. A couple we stole from Omstorn. One we cobbled together from a few ruined hovers our scouts found on the abandoned plantations."

Lindy smiled. "Some of you ought to apply for the Meridian Intelligence Department. They could use resourceful people like you."

Men and women hurried to and fro throughout the gorge, guns slung over their shoulders. Commanders shouted orders; soldiers formed ranks. Lindy found her father overseeing the embarkation and hurried to his side.

"You didn't tell me you had a fleet," she said.

He chuckled. "It may be small, but we know how to use it. Often, under cover of darkness, we fly south beyond the mountains where the Magnificents in Omstorn can't observe us and practice maneuvers."

"But you can't pack three thousand soldiers in a dozen ships. What about the rest of them?"

"They'll join us in the hovers," he said, unconcerned. "We'll leave a few behind for the women and children who remain, of course, but the rest will be held within the larger ships' cargo bays —if, of course, that seems a good strategy to *you*."

"My specialty lies more in stealth attacks," Lindy admitted. "Not nova battles."

"That belongs more to the expertise of the man you think you may be falling in love with?" the Renegade asked.

Lindy shot him a look, but something warm and ridiculously happy flared to life inside her at the mischief in the old warrior's eyes. The Renegade was teasing her, just like any good father would.

Ethan crouched near the Hummingbird's main exit, drumming his gloved fingers on the massive rifle in his arms. Three dozen crewmen surrounded him, eyes narrowed behind their visors. He hoped they were all studying the floor plan of the novaport terminal loaded into their helmet interfaces. Their lives, after all, might depend on it.

"Aeron to Granger," his first officer called over the radio. "Shuttlecraft ready to deploy."

Ethan glanced at the clock in his own helmet interface. *Nearly a quarter to two.* Rael had killed yet another noble almost an hour ago: a lady-in-waiting of Mariamne's. He seemed to be saving his biggest prizes for last. Ethan wasn't sure whether or not to be relieved about it.

But you know he'll make good use of them eventually. The longer this drags on, the crazier he's gonna get—which is why I've got to take this risk. Especially if no help comes from home.

Ethan pursed his lips, watching until the seconds ticked into a new minute. As soon as the counter hit *0145*, he barked his order: "Now, Aeron!"

He knew his ship so well, he felt the vibration as the hangar doors on the other side of the ship cranked open. The men around him tensed; he raised a hand, motioning for them to wait.

"The Valyan ships are targeting our hovers!" Aeron bellowed. "Go!"

"Open her up!" Ethan roared.

The man at the cargo bay console pulled a lever; the hatch opened and the ramp extended. Ethan allowed himself a quick upward glance as he and his men hurried outside. The enemy hovers chased six of the *Hummingbird*'s shuttles, spraying red energy beams at the tiny ships. A streak of red snapped the ground inches in front of him.

"Let's go," he hissed. "Double-quick! Let's go, get a move on!"

The men burst into a run, heading straight for the novaport terminal. The fighting shuttles zoomed around and above them. Ethan felt a burst of hot air behind him and heard a strangled cry. He looked over his shoulder in time to see one of his men crumple, a smoldering hole in the center of his helmet.

"Aeron!" Ethan shouted, pressing himself against the terminal wall. "How many guys on the roof?"

"Heat signatures indicate a dozen—three for each corner of the roof. They weren't there when you left the ship. They must have an upstairs passage inside the terminal. We still read about a little under a hundred and fifty Magnificents inside—"

"Captain!" one of the crewmen called. "Valyan hover incoming!"

Ethan peered around the wall. A sleek grey hover zoomed towards them, complete with a mounted raygun manned by three police officers. They aimed the gun at the Meridians.

"Fire at will!" Ethan cried. His men let loose. The Valyans tumbled off their vehicle; the damaged gun sparked and spun on its mount.

"Explosives, Mr. Crane!" Ethan shouted.

The technician and an assistant raced for the terminal doors, the protective cases they carried loaded with fierce little devices. As soon as they returned, the rest of the men instinctively dropped.

BOOM!!! The ground rocked with the explosion. Debris pinged Ethan's helmet; his interface flickered. Right on time, however, steam burst out of the *Hummingbird*'s landing gear. She rose off the runway, ready for battle.

"Captain!" Aeron shouted. "You're clear to enter the terminal!"

"Take care of my ship, Commander!" Ethan bellowed. "All right, boys, let's go!"

With a triumphant cry, the Meridians leaped to their feet. The bombs had done their nasty work: the terminal's huge doors, locked a moment ago by computerized security, had been reduced to twisted chunks of steel. Ethan scrambled into the smoky remains of the front lobby.

"Mockett! Load that floor plan into my helmet again—the debris knocked it out!"

But before Mockett could respond, Magnificents appeared on all sides. Invaders and defenders alike opened fire. Ethan motioned for six of his men to follow him and moved to the nearest wall, only to lurch and stagger as one of the ricocheting beams grazed his upper arm.

"Captain!" one of the Meridians gasped.

"I'm all right…I'm all right." Ethan clamped his hand to the blistering wound and gritted his teeth. "Floor plan, Mockett!"

"Floor plan coming up!" Mockett cried from the *Hummingbird.* The image popped back into Ethan's helmet interface. The control room Chevenere had described lay just above them, nestled between the offices of Rael's ranking generals.

"Upstairs," Ethan gasped. "Come on!"

Guided by the sputtering lights, he and his men bounded up the stairs. When they reached the top, they froze in mingled awe, dread, and interest. The corridor was dark, forebodingly so. Ethan turned on the light attached to his helmet; his men did the same with theirs.

"Interface," he murmured. "Heat signatures on this floor."

The helmet's sensors clicked. "Seven heat signatures in the immediate vicinity. Fifteen additional heat signatures within fifty yards of current position. Forcefield of Magnitude Twelve Strength also contributing to readings."

"Exact locations of those fifteen biological signatures," Ethan ordered. The interface offered the information, and he sucked in a long breath.

"Where, Captain?" one of his men whispered.

"Control Room. Straight ahead." Ethan thought a moment, set his rifle against the wall, and turned to one of his younger soldiers. "Faraday, give me your gun."

The young man obeyed. Ignoring the throbbing pain in his arm, Ethan popped the gun's soroidium charge out of the chamber. He glanced at his men, but no one breathed a word of protest. The bright canister spread a white glow and wavering shadows over the corridor. Ethan held it high. His mouth had gone dry, and it wasn't just from his wound.

"One, two, three." He slammed the canister against the Control Room's door frame. The protective casing shattered and the soroidium reacted immediately, light and heat spilling through the broken canister.

"*Run*!" one of his men hissed. Ethan dropped the canister in front of the door and raced to the other end of the corridor. He'd barely reached his huddled comrades when the door went up in a roar of fire. Within seconds, someone stumbled out of the flames.

"Help me!" the Valyan shrieked. "Help me!"

Ethan nodded to one of his men; the Meridian seized the Valyan and slammed him to the floor, smothering the flames that licked at his clothes. Another figure emerged from the fire, but this one was eerily silent, broad, and bulky with armor. He raised his rifle, but Ethan fired first.

The Magnificent crumpled…just as another stepped out of the flames.

"Let's go! Meridians, to me!" Ethan thundered.

With a cry, the Meridians rushed the imposing figure, firing at his helmet. The Magnificent collapsed and they ran past him and into the room. The computer consoles in the smoke-filled chamber were partly obscured by the shimmer of a forcefield. Just in front of it stood the remaining Magnificents and a general Ethan vaguely recognized from the Palace meetings.

"Step aside," Ethan shouted, "or I'll have no choice but to gun you down!"

The general half-coughed, half-snarled. "Do your worst, Meridian."

The Magnificents—all eleven of them—raised their guns. Seven Meridians did the same.

"Headshots!" Ethan reminded them. "Aim for their heads!"

The raging fire and the burst of raygun energy drowned out his voice. A blast of heat and purple light filled his vision; he cried out, jerking his head to one side and squeezing his eyes shut. Somebody grabbed his shoulder and yanked him to the floor.

When he managed to lift his head, the forcefield was gone. Magnificents sprawled on the floor; most lay still, but a few of them twitched feebly or clawed at their helmets. The general was dead. The unprotected computers smoldered and sparked. Ethan staggered to his feet.

"Captain, no!" one of his men cried. Ethan ignored him, stumbling over bodies until he reached the computers. One fragmenting screen showed the positions of the orbit patrols. Another displayed weather conditions on the planet and ion storms in space.

No no no, it's got *to be here!* Ethan groaned in frustration—but at the sight of a twisting, twitching cluster of tentacles on the third screen, he stopped. Data flittered beneath the cluster, constantly changing. He looked closer. Each piece of information corresponded with a tentacle, and each tentacle had a number rather than a name.

Magnificent 12408A.

Magnificent 24601B.

The dehumanization made Ethan's skin crawl. He ran a gloved finger over the screen, touching the cluster's small, pulsing heart. A tab appeared above it, barely visible as smoke fogged the screen: *Dominator Hadrian Daltis, Supreme Commander of the Valyan Nova Force.*

So the Magnificents within the Nova Force answered to Daltis, not Rael.

Ethan clenched his teeth, stepped back, and fired, destroying the computer with a single shot. At the sudden commotion behind him, he whirled and took aim—but it was only the Magnificents, convulsing violently on the floor. The surviving Meridians jumped back in horror.

"Get out!" Ethan roared. "Quick!"

They didn't need encouragement; the ceiling was beginning to crumble. Ethan followed them, forcing himself not to think about the three Meridians lying dead beside their enemies.

Downstairs, the smoke from the fire mingled with the haze of battle. When Ethan reached the bottom step, he found more Magnificents thrashing on the floor as if they'd been plugged into electrical outlets. The surviving Meridians were already evacuating their casualties out of the compromised building, but one of them stopped Ethan on the way out.

"What happened, sir? One minute they were fighting us, and then they just...collapsed."

"I know. But I think this must've been what the Dominator meant when she said they had to be neutralized." Ethan suppressed a shudder and gestured toward the exit. "Let's go, soldier. We've got a novaport to seize."

Chapter Twenty-Eight

2 AM, Valyan time

"Our orbit ships remain unresponsive," Morgarena said, nervously clicking through the tabs on her tablet. "The novaport terminal is on fire, but the fire brigades can't get past the gates. Every time they try to get through, the *Hummingbird* obliterates them."

"Then send in the *Amiyra*!" Rael screamed.

Morgarena flinched. Her father, leaning over her shoulder to watch the screen himself, lifted steely eyes at the younger man.

"The *Amiyra* is unresponsive," Daltis said coldly. "We cannot contact any ships in orbit, let alone the ones in Omstorn or Harathella. Whatever's happened at the terminal, it has severed my connection with the Magnificents within the Nova Force."

Rael sprang out of his chair. "But there are men within the novaport who are not under Magnificent control!"

Daltis' face set even harder. "True."

"Then why don't *they* contact us? Surely they're not all dead?"

"Perhaps...perhaps they've turned against us?" Morgarena quivered. "Like Chevenere?"

The fear in her voice was infuriating. Rael seized a savage fistful of her short dark hair. She screamed as he yanked her out of her chair and onto her knees.

"Rael!" Daltis roared.

"Stand back," Rael shouted, "or I swear I'll kill you myself!"

Daltis froze. Rael jerked Morgarena's head back. She whimpered. His breath caught at the sound, and for a brief, insane moment, he didn't see *her* at all. He saw...

One of his sisters. *Cresside.*

Morgarena opened her eyes and lifted shaking hands towards him. "Rael, please..."

He flung her away and staggered back to his chair, afraid that his trembling legs might give way if he didn't. Daltis watched coldly, ignoring Morgarena's hasty return to his side.

"Without the Magnificents, I could not have done what I did," Rael rasped. "You told me...you *persuaded* me that I could never lose if I had them on my side..."

"And you still have the ground troops at your command," Daltis snapped. "The *Hummingbird* has a crew of, what? Two hundred? They cannot withstand the full might of your army. All is not lost. Believe that, and you will claim the victory."

Rael drew a shaky breath and glanced at Morgarena. She turned her face away, but not before he saw tears of pain and fury brimming in her eyes.

Did I really try to hurt her? Then again, did I really see Cresside? Did I try to hurt Morgarena because I saw my sister, or did I see my sister because I hurt Morgarena?

I'm going mad. I'm surely going mad...

"Rael!" Daltis hissed. "Pull yourself together!"

Rael clenched his hands. The sharp pain of his nails digging into his palms helped him focus; guilt drained out of him like dirty water, and a surge of cleansing anger filled him instead. He inhaled, drawing himself up to his full height.

"Are we still having disturbances in the cities?" he asked, his voice clearer.

Daltis's mouth twitched at one corner. "Some would-be rebels are trying to stir things up in all four major cities. A most terrifying sight indeed—sarcasm, of course, fully intended."

"Then the Magnificents stationed in each city will have no trouble crushing these demonstrations at once. I don't care how they do it, so long as the rebels are either cowering or dead by sun-up." Rael frowned. "Who's to be executed next among our prisoners, by the way?"

Daltis peered at the tablet. "According to the order you suggested, Perry Ambrose—the reporter with whom Lhoris was corresponding."

Rael nodded. "Good. After the *Hummingbird*'s attack on the novaport, it's time we made better use of our Meridian prisoners."

With a bow, Daltis hurried away. Rael tried to catch Morgarena's eye again, but she only glared at him before following her father. Any other time he would've responded at once, warning her never to look at him like that again. Now, however, even he hesitated at the wrath in her flashing eyes.

It reminded him of his sister's message over the Emergency Alert System.

Alinna had looked just as ferocious.

Orders surged through the Magnificent Network. As the soldiers marched out of their barracks and into the hearts of Valya's four major cities, the citizen rebels found themselves facing their worst nightmare.

In Omstorn, a crowd of civilians hesitated in front of City Hall's marble pillars. Torches flickered, women murmured, men grumbled. The Magnificents halted with a final thunder of boots on the pavement. Their commander stepped out from the head of the line.

"In the name of Rael Navorre," he droned, "I order you to return to your homes at once."

"Or what?" someone screamed from the crowd. "You'll open fire?"

"What will you do when the Queen marches in here and orders *you* to return to *your* homes?" a woman shrieked.

"They don't have homes," another spat. "They're just shells of the honest Valyans they used to be!"

The people growled in angry agreement. The commander returned to his place within the ranks.

"Take aim," he called. The Magnificents lifted their guns. The crowd shifted, half-furious and half-frantic.

"Let's split! Confuse them!"

"No use in dying like cattle!"

The Magnificents didn't give them time to make a decision. The protestors at the front of the crowd crumpled under the withering fire; those behind them took off in a screaming mass.

But the screams weren't frightened or confused. Not in the slightest.

"Flank them!" some of the men roared. "Flank them—take them from the side!"

Like a mighty wave, they rushed through alleys, turned corners, and swarmed back to City Hall. The Magnificents barely had time to react before they hurled themselves into their ranks, snatching away rifles and throwing them off balance. Chaos ruled—until one of the stolen guns roared. One of the soldiers crumpled, his helmet smoking. Everyone froze.

"Their helmets!" the teenager who fired the gun cried. "If you fire at their helmets—"

One of the Magnificents cut him off with a brutal blow; the soldiers regrouped. Unsure of themselves, the civilians staggered backward. The air shivered with the roar of approaching engines.

The people looked up. The Magnificents ignored the sound and marched forward.

"Aim," the commander shouted again—but no one heard it over a sudden, joyful scream.

"Novacraft! From the south! The Renegade is coming!"

Several long novacraft streaked low over the street; their underbellies opened and hovers dropped out, disgorging black-and-yellow-clad passengers. The confused Magnificents tried to shift positions and change targets, but the newcomers moved faster. They stormed into the street, firing into their ranks. The civilians burst into cheers and rushed to join their new allies.

Twenty-three years of waiting and training in the Laronda Mountains had finally paid off.

"Anything from that big ship, the one hanging over the city?" Lindy demanded inside her hover, one of the first to break free of its mothership over Omstorn.

"Not a thing," the pilot replied. "Odd. It's as if the Nova Force has shut down."

"Or something has happened in Cor Danem," the Renegade murmured behind Lindy. "If your friends in Cor Danem have cut them off, then perhaps it is no longer a problem."

Jo folded her arms over her chest with a smug grin. "What do you want to bet Ethan did something really, *really* cool, Lindy?"

Lindy pursed her lips and shot Jo a half-reproving, half-amused glare. The hover zoomed over the Magnificent Headquarters' high stone wall and landed on the main building's flat roof. Another rebel hover followed close behind.

"Open up!" Lindy ordered.

The hatch flew open and thirty rebels spilled out. Lindy drew an eager breath of fresh air as the second hover landed and thirty more of her soldiers emerged.

"Go," she snapped. Five of them raced for the rooftop door; after a few blasts and kicks, they were inside. The rest of the team spilled down the stairs after them. Lindy and Jo waited for the Renegade to join them. His limp was barely noticeable now.

"The building will be guarded," he warned. "You know that."

"We can handle it," Lindy said. She flipped the setting on her gun from stun to kill and gave her father a quick, appraising look. "Better hide your face now."

He smiled and pulled his scarf around his head until only his bright eyes showed. Then he darted down the stairs while Lindy and Jo made the rear.

The staircase was a tight squeeze for sixty armed rebels. When they reached a door on the landing, the soldier in the lead raised a hand and peered through its tiny window. He glanced at the men on either side of him, counted to three, and together they blasted the lock.

Startled shouts immediately echoed on the other side. The Renegade tried to hold Lindy and Jo back, but Lindy broke past him, aiming at the first Magnificent she saw.

She realized too late that he wasn't wearing a helmet. His face was dark, handsome, and devastatingly average. He and his comrades had obviously been on break, and this was a mess hall. Beverages dripped from shattered glasses, food splattered the floor—and none of the men who fell under the rebels' fire were in armor. Lindy reeled in horror.

They're Valyans. They're just like me.

Jo grabbed her arm. "Lindy. Lindy, they've still got chips in their heads. They're no different than the guys who are still wearing helmets, okay? Come on, we gotta move."

But they're still human*! They didn't ask for this!*

"Alinna," the Renegade whispered, suddenly beside her. Lindy looked up. His dark eyes were understanding and regretful. "There is nothing you can do for them. We fight Rael so that this will never happen again to anyone else. Do you hear me, Alinna?"

Lindy shook herself and nodded once. He nodded back, Jo squeezed her arm, and together they raced after their men into the next corridor. This time armored Magnificents burst out of side rooms and an actual fight broke out. Lindy fired, ducked, and ran, staying close on the Renegade's heels.

"Alinna, look!" he shouted.

They stopped at the end of a wider hallway, a few feet from where two parallel staircases led down to the ground floor. The Renegade pointed at a nearby door. Its sign read, in bold letters, "CONTROL ROOM: NO ENTRANCE UNLESS AUTHORIZED." Booted feet and deep voices thundered downstairs. Lindy turned to the men who'd clustered around her.

"Rohm, take your men and secure the ground floor. Marras, you and your men split up—make sure there's nobody in these side rooms. The rest of you, with me."

The Renegade fired at the mechanical lock on the Control Room door. After several blasts, it finally flew open. Lindy stormed in after him and saw exactly what Chevenere told her to expect: a wall of computers behind a floor-to-ceiling forcefield. The three men and two women at the computers looked up. None of them wore armor, but their blank faces told Lindy all she needed to know. She stepped closer.

"Turn off that forcefield," she ordered.

One of the women stood. "We obey only the Citizen. We cannot give you what you—"

Lindy spun on her heel. "Back up to the wall. Concentrate your fire on the forcefield and keep your eyes closed until it collapses."

Her soldiers, Jo, and the Renegade lifted their rifles. Lindy did the same, counted to three, and closed her eyes.

The blinding light still penetrated her eyelids. She twisted her face towards her shoulder with her finger pressed hard against the trigger. When the forcefield finally collapsed with a stinging burst of heat, she staggered. Flames licked at the floor and ceiling. The

Magnificents yanked guns out from underneath their desks. The rebels cut them down before they could fire.

"Okay, let's go!" Lindy cried. "Magnificent Network, Magnificent Network, come on come on come on!"

"There it is!" Jo cried. "Look! 'Magnificent Network of the City of Omstorn.'"

Lindy hurried to where Jo stood at one of the consoles and peered at the screen. A display of writhing, numbered tentacles displayed the activity, status, and location of every Magnificent in the city, all of them answering to a pulsing center. When Lindy touched it, a tab popped up with Rael's name.

"Step back," she ordered. Jo, the Renegade, and their soldiers silently obeyed. But as Lindy pulled out the pistol on her hip, her heart pounded with a strange, fearful grief.

I'm going to kill thousands of Magnificents in one fell swoop, aren't I?

But what was it the Renegade had said? "We fight Rael so that this will never happen again to anyone else." She had no choice. Until someone figured out how to bypass the safeguard Chevenere had imposed on the microchips, she *had* to do this. Stopping Rael—destroying the government that had made this atrocity possible—was the only way to save other Valyans from this horrific fate.

With a ragged breath, Lindy stepped far enough away from the consoles so she wouldn't get a face full of flying glass, and she pulled the trigger. At the exact same moment, thousands of Magnificents all over the city dropped with a crash and the sizzle of overloaded Xandroan microchips.

Inside Omstorn's City Hall, the Lord Mayor and his staff panicked. The old building hadn't seen this kind of chaos since Rael's revolutionaries overran it years ago. Now Rael's officials hurried to destroy their own records. Computers were wiped clean, tablets smashed with hammers, and top-secret papers stuffed into trash cans with a couple of lit matches.

"Don't stop until you've destroyed all sensitive materials!" the Lord Mayor gasped, one hand holding his enormous belly while the other massaged a stitch in his side. "And when you—oof—when you've done all you can—it's every man for himself—"

A nearby window exploded; the tremor and showering glass threw him to the floor. Rebel soldiers in black and yellow streamed through the opening. The Lord Mayor scrambled to his feet, but before he could get away, a tall, fierce-looking young lady seized him. He screamed and decided to go limp.

"Helpful suggestion for the next time you try to get away unnoticed?" she snapped. "Take off that fancy badge. Anyone could've spotted you a mile away."

She ripped off the silver disc pinned to his tunic and tossed it over her shoulder. It landed in the shattered glass with a dull clink. He whimpered as she jerked him even closer.

"Now, listen to me," she said. "You're going to take me straight to your office and comm Rael Navorre. While I talk to him, you're going to order the entire Omstorn Police Force to stand down and surrender their hovers to the Renegade."

At that, the Lord Mayor experienced something new and different for him: courage. He drew himself up. "You must be insane! Surrender to the Renegade? Do you know who I am? And who do you think *you* are?"

"I am Alinna Navorre, and I think *you* are a fat, sniveling coward who'll do exactly as I say unless you want to deal with the Renegade instead." She raised a haughty eyebrow. "I hear you two have had a few run-ins lately. Perhaps you'd prefer a chat with him?"

"No, no, that's fine," he whispered. "I will connect you with the Magnificent Citizen."

"'Rael' will do," she interrupted. "Jo! Come and help me a sec."

"Looks like we got here a little late," Jo muttered as they entered the Lord Mayor's office. Lindy grunted in agreement at the sight of smoking computers and a smoldering wastebasket. She handed her comm to the obese, trembling official.

"You know Rael's personal number?" she asked.

He nodded. "Y-y-yes..."

"Then dial it."

"And no funny business now," Jo added.

The Lord Mayor took the comm, his pudgy hands shaking. Lindy inhaled, trying to calm her own pounding heartbeat. When he returned the comm, he'd established a connection.

"What if he doesn't pick up?" Jo whispered.

Lindy didn't have time to reply: the screen blinked, and Rael's curious, slightly confused face appeared. She held the comm straight out in front of her so he could see her clearly.

"Rael. It's me."

He blinked, his mouth falling open. Lindy shivered a little as she realized that if she had their mother's eyes, he had their father's.

"Alinna," he whispered.

She tilted her head back. "It's time to talk this over like adults."

Rael blinked again, but this time he looked less startled. He leaned back in his chair.

"Adults, yes—but equals?" he mused. "I hope you don't expect *that.*"

"Actually, I do."

"Impossible."

"Is it? I'm in Omstorn's City Hall. I just destroyed the city's Magnificent Network. Your soldiers are either dying or dead, the Renegade and his army are taking control, and we're coming to Cor Danem next." She paused, fury flaring in her chest. "You weren't content to just control them, were you? No, you had to make it so they can't live without that network. As soon as the connection is severed, they go into convulsions. That's on you and your Dominators, not me—just like our mother's and sisters' blood is on *your* hands."

Rael lurched forward. "What do you know about it, you—you imposter?!"

"A lot more than you think I do," Lindy snapped. "I remember when you had us shipped into that field. I remember Mama's fear the moment your soldiers opened fire, and I remember the pain when one of the beams that cut her down hit *me.* Don't ask me what I know about it, because I know you wouldn't be turning your own soldiers on our people and holding our family hostage if you didn't believe I was your sister!"

He stared at her, his eyes shot through with fury. For a moment, she was afraid he'd cut her off, but he only turned the screen away from him towards the center of the room. She frowned, not sure what he was trying to show her—until she saw it. Her stomach flipped.

Six Magnificents stood in the center of Rael's room, carrying rifles and staring blankly ahead. Daltis stood in the background, his bony arms folded, a cruel smile twisting his mouth. But the two unarmored figures standing in the middle of the Magnificents terrified Lindy more than him or the soldiers.

An old woman and a young, fair-skinned, red-headed man.

Faces bloodied and bruised.

Eyes staring, fixed and unseeing, at the screen.

"Oh, Elyon," Lindy whispered.

"What?" Jo demanded. "What is it?"

Rael appeared at the side of the screen, his good hand tucked behind his back, a smug look on his chiseled face. "Well? What do you think of my latest recruits? I'm sure you already knew something about Trooper Gridley, thanks to Chevenere and your other little friend. But don't you think Councilor Tremaine looks far more tranquil as a Magnificent? She's certainly much more tolerable."

Lindy covered her mouth. Rael walked back to the screen and got so close to it, she instinctively held the comm further away from her face.

"You think you can threaten me?" he snarled. "Well, I still have the upper hand. You may take my cities, kill my soldiers… you may even have the support of that mountain rebel. But know this. The moment you destroy the network in Cor Danem, Margaret Tremaine and Trooper Gridley will die—and I won't let any of my prisoners go until you surrender yourself to me."

Chapter Twenty-Nine

3:00 AM

The Cor Danem Novaport belonged to the *Hummingbird*. The terminal was still on fire, but three Valyan ships lay idle on the runway. Nine of the twelve hovers had crashed when their Magnificent pilots were neutralized, while the police and Novaport Authority officers had surrendered after a few fierce skirmishes.

Meridians now piloted the remaining Valyan hovers. Ethan couldn't spare the manpower to operate the bigger ships, but Lindy might need them later on—and she certainly wouldn't be claiming the ones in orbit. They were crashing into each other, and only Aeron's reassuring explanations about how they'd incinerate in the atmosphere long before they reached the planet's surface kept Ethan from getting nervous about it.

He was dizzy, exhausted, and sore. Dr. Elliot had spared only four of her nurses to tend to the wounded among his team, including him; the rest were caring for a few of the Magnificents who had somehow clung to life when their network went down. Apparently, Dr. Elliot had an idea—something involving sedatives and heart synthesizers and "careful removal of the chips and damaged brain tissue"—and she couldn't spare any resources if she could help it.

Meanwhile, Ethan monitored the deteriorating situation beyond the novaport's walls.

"We've got crowds in the industrial district," Mockett called from her station. "One of the factories is on fire. The Magnificents are trying to put it out, but the people keep harassing them."

"Civilians?" Ethan asked.

"Yes, sir. We've got another disturbance in the 4th District—that's mostly residential—and a third mob trying to get into the area around the Palace."

"What's going on at Magnificent Headquarters?"

Aeron turned from his station. "I have a report on that from our surveillance hovers, sir. There is considerable activity surrounding the building. They have a large fleet of hovers, too. They appear to be heavily armed."

Ethan gritted his teeth. "If I weren't so worried about destroying stuff Lindy might need later, I'd just fire our mega-cannon at the building itself."

"'Stuff?'" Aeron repeated. "What 'stuff?'"

"Well, if she wins, she'll need to know exactly what's happened here over the past twenty-three years. I have a feeling plenty of those records are stored up there. And besides, I don't want to blow up a building and risk wiping out any other structures nearby."

"A compassionate strategy...although not necessarily the easiest, most convenient one."

Ethan grimaced. "Whoever said the right way was ever easy or convenient?"

Aeron raised his eyebrows, conceding the point. Mockett's station chimed. She turned to Ethan with big, scared eyes, and he hurried to her.

"What? What is it?"

Mockett gulped. "Daltis. Hadrian, not Morgarena."

Ethan jerked his head. She jumped out of her seat and he sat down, grateful for the opportunity. It had been far too long since he last slept; his bandaged arm ached and his head was starting to feel thick and fuzzy. Still, he accepted the call without hesitation. The Dominator's ghoulish face appeared on the screen.

"Captain Granger," he said. "The Magnificent Citizen demands your surrender."

Ethan laughed. "You're joking, right?"

"Hardly. You cannot hold the novaport by yourself, even with the Magnificents temporarily neutralized."

"Dominator, the Magnificents within your Nova Force are *permanently* neutralized. I've seen them. They're dead or dying. The novacraft in orbit are crashing into each other, and the ships here in the novaport have either crashed or been shut down by my men. They won't be running again until Queen Alinna claims them for her own."

"The Citizen's sister," Daltis snarled, "may not arrive as quickly as you hope. The Citizen just informed her not only of Trooper Gridley's induction into the Magnificent ranks, but Councilor Tremaine's, as well. Alinna may think twice before striking Cor Danem now."

Ethan stared at the hideous old Valyan. Mockett clapped a hand over her mouth.

"Perhaps your surrender no longer seems so unpleasant?" Daltis asked, a satisfied gleam in his eye.

"Unpleasant?" Ethan growled. "It's abhorrent."

"Nevertheless, if you wish to save your crew, you will leave Valya, or you will face attack from the full force of—"

Ethan severed the connection before Daltis could finish and turned to his weapons chief. "Parsons, put your men on full alert.

Mockett, tell Dr. Elliot to secure her patients, and—what is it, Commander?"

Aeron rose from his seat. "Captain...perhaps it would be wiser if we fled the novaport."

"What?"

"We wouldn't necessarily have to leave Valya itself. We could even remain in orbit until Miss Tremaine returns to Cor Danem, but there is no shame in evading a superior enemy—"

"They are *not* superior!" Ethan exploded. "They're *crippled!* And unless Rael starts sending in ships from Harathella or Veladon—which, by the way, will take at least an hour to get here—he can't send anything against us except hovers!"

"But if they have enough of those and carry out a coordinated attack, they could do some serious damage," Parsons murmured. "Even to a ship as large as this one."

Ethan turned on him. "You want to tuck tail and run, Parsons? Is that it? Do you really want to give an inch to a maniac like Rael?"

Parsons said nothing. Ethan clenched his fists and faced his first officer.

"Rael has just done the one thing he never, *ever* should've tried, Aeron. If Daltis is telling the truth, he's all but killed a Meridian ambassador, and *that* is ample cause for war. From this moment on, as far as we're concerned, Meridian is at war with Valya. We are *not* standing down until Lindy gets here with backup. Got it?"

Aeron blinked, glanced down, and nodded. "Aye-aye, Captain."

"Good." Ethan sighed, but despite his brave rhetoric, he felt sick. He'd still heard nothing from Meridian. How long would it take Lindy to secure Omstorn before she headed this way? He didn't dare try to contact her. Rael might intercept it.

For all intents and purposes, the *Hummingbird* was on her own.

The Renegade's personal novacraft rumbled, shifting from where it had hovered for the past hour above Omstorn. Lindy felt the vibration as she sat on a low bench in the main cabin, her head in her hands.

"We will be taking off in a moment or two," the pilot announced over the intercom. "Please find a seat until we have achieved our final altitude."

And where do we go from there? Lindy wondered. *They'll ask me any minute now, and I'll have to give them an answer…except I have no idea what that answer's going to be.*

Her head ached. So far, she hadn't found a single rebel with a stash of coffee. If she weren't so heartsick, she might've joked about coffee imports being her first order of business as Queen of Valya. *But I can't even laugh at myself anymore. All I can think about are those dead Valyans, protestors and Magnificents alike…and Nana. Nana and Frank. Oh Elyon, please, please don't let them die…*

"Lindy."

At the sound of Jo's voice, Lindy lifted her head and blinked hard, trying to get rid of the tears that burned her eyes. If Jo noticed them, she didn't let on. She handed Lindy a paper cup and a protein bar.

"You need to keep your strength up," she said gently. "You've been running on fumes for hours."

"I'm not hungry," Lindy muttered.

"Yeah, well, guess what? I don't care. Here." Jo tore open the protein bar's wrapping and shoved it into Lindy's hand. "Now eat. A cat-nap might do you some good, too."

Lindy gnawed off a chunk of the protein bar. Chewing dutifully, she leaned her head back against the wall. "Every time I close my eyes, I see those Magnificents. The ones without the helmets."

Jo pressed the cup into her other hand. "Then just try and think about those people in Omstorn getting down on one knee the minute you walked out of City Hall. It looked like a movie set, with you as the heroine. It was awesome."

Lindy sighed and tipped the cup back. The icy water felt heavenly on her parched throat.

"More?" Jo asked. Lindy shook her head. Jo set the cup aside and sat down beside her, leaning her elbows on her knees. "So. What are you gonna do?"

Lindy shook her head again, turning the protein bar over and over in her hands. "I don't even know. I was so sure of what I wanted to do until I saw Nana and Frank. I can't win. I'm taking cities, sure. But those chips are electrocuting the Magnificents to death. Can I let that happen to Nana and Frank? Will I be able to live with myself if I lose them like that?"

Jo's chin wobbled and her eyes welled, but before she could respond, the Renegade came in from the cockpit. Compassion and concern both showed in his dark, bearded face as he looked down at the two weary troopers.

"What is our next move, Alinna?" he asked quietly.

Lindy sat up, ignoring Jo's disapproving glare as she slipped the protein bar back into its wrapper. "You're the strategist. You decide."

"And you are the Queen," the Renegade said firmly. "The decision is yours."

Lindy set her teeth at that. *The decision is mine?* What a joke. Less than twenty-four hours ago, she would've been quite content to work as a trooper and a reporter for the rest of her life. A few dangerous missions every year and the odd confrontation with Athena Biggweather would've been more than enough adventure for an otherwise predictable existence.

She hadn't asked for any of this. *I would've* never *asked for any of this.*

"Lindy," Jo said softly. "You may be right. Where Nana and Frank are concerned, there may not be *any* way to win. But... maybe this shouldn't be about Nana and Frank."

"She's my grandmother," Lindy growled. "And *you*—you and Frank—!"

"I know," Jo said, trying to smile. "But if you surrender now, all those people who just swore their allegiance to you will never know what it's like to be free. Nana and Frank would want you to fight, tooth and nail. You know they would! And look...you just asked me if you'll be able to live with yourself if something happens to them. I'm telling you that you'll *never* be able to live with yourself if you let Rael win."

Lindy gulped. A tear rolled down her cheek; she wiped it away quickly, well aware that her father watched her every move.

Nana and Frank would probably die no matter what fork in the road she took. But she had a whole city under her control, an entire Nova Force defeated, and only two hours from here to Cor Danem.

Two hours between her and Ethan.

Two hours between her and Rael.

"Okay," she whispered. "Let's go north."

---

5 AM

Ethan smelled smoke as he strode down the *Hummingbird* ramp, preparing to inspect a twenty-seater hover his men had just captured. He noticed a promising grey smear on the horizon—the first hint of the coming dawn—but it was overshadowed by the far more intense glow of fires in Cor Danem.

"Listen," he whispered as soon as the inspection was over. "You hear that?"

Parsons, who'd come along to check the hover, paused. "I don't hear anything."

Ethan frowned, stepping closer to the *Hummingbird*'s rear. A cool breeze skipped over the runways, carrying not only the acrid smell of smoke but a dull, swelling roar, punctuated by the *THWOOMP-THWOOMP* of raygun blasts.

"The people are still rioting," Ethan murmured. "Cor Danem's being torn apart."

Parsons sighed. "They've rioted before, and they've been stomped down every time. I hope we're not putting our lives on the line for a lost cause, Captain."

"Nothing will ever convince me it was the wrong one, though," Ethan said softly.

To his surprise, Parsons grunted his assent. Ethan clapped a hand on the older man's shoulder as they headed back up the ramp. His comm chimed before they were halfway up, however. He jerked it out of his pocket.

"Granger," he called.

"Captain, where are you?!"

Ethan frowned at Mockett's panicked tone. "I'm coming back aboard. What's wrong?"

Aeron's clipped voice responded. "Captain, Magnificents are approaching the novaport. I expect we will be under attack in a matter of minutes."

Ethan glared at Parsons. "Get the weapons crew ready and put our little 'fleet' on alert."

Parsons sprang ahead of his captain. When Ethan returned to the bridge, he found people running about, shouting orders, manning battle stations. He went straight to Aeron.

"What can you give me on the situation in Cor Danem?" he demanded.

Aeron shook his head gravely. "It is in an uproar. The raygun manufacturing plant is on fire. There's been an explosion at the Revolution Museum and some kind of gathering at the city wall. Approximately half of the Magnificents in Cor Danem are trying to control the riots. The other half are headed this way."

"I just intercepted a transmission between Rael and Magnificent Headquarters!" Mockett cried. "He ordered them to destroy the *Hummingbird*!"

Ethan marched to his seat. "Mr. Potter, Mr. Ainsworth! Lift off and hold in place. Aeron, alert our commandeered ships. I want them running alongside us, weapons at the ready. We won't be sitting ducks if we can help it."

Orders flew from one side of the bridge to the other. The *Hummingbird* roared to life and rose off the runway, her own hovers as well as the captured ones zipping alongside her. Well above the ground like this, Ethan could see the mass of hovers and armored men gathering on the other side of the novaport wall.

Come on, Lindy—come on!

"Incoming message from the Magnificents, Captain," Mockett called.

"Patch it through," Ethan snapped.

A voice crackled over the intercom. "*MNC Hummingbird,* this is the Cor Danem Division of the Magnificent Army. Surrender yourselves to the mercy of the Magnificent Citizen, Rael Navorre."

Ethan slammed his fist into the intercom button. "This is Captain Ethan Granger. Unless your Citizen hands over our people and the Royal Remnant, the *Hummingbird* will neither surrender nor leave this planet. Cut the connection, Mockett."

"What's your plan, sir?" Aeron asked.

"Meet 'em head-on. They asked for a battle. They'll get one." Ethan looked at his senior officers and gave them a single crisp nod. "Fleet, advance."

"Aye-aye, sir!" the officers cried. "Coordinate with our position! Weapons crews, fire on the Captain's signal! Maintain connection on Channel A-R-14! Soroidium levels holding steady on all *Hummingbird* escort ships—"

"Sickbay to Captain!"

The call from the sickbay startled Ethan. "Dr. Elliot?"

"Captain, I think I've figured it out. I've stabilized one of the Magnificents! He's waking up and he's coherent, sir! I think it was a combination of the Thoraginal sedative and—"

"That's fantastic news, Doctor, but we're about to go into battle. Save it until I can give it my full attention, all right? And make sure that solution's foolproof! We may need you to use it on some high-profile victims!"

The *Hummingbird* reached the wall. The enemy hovers rose up to meet her, a few slamming headlong into her massive sides.

"Escorts, fire on those troops!" Ethan shouted. "Arsenal, target the hovers!"

Armored troops spilled over the wall and into the novaport. The *Hummingbird*'s cannons blasted the enemy hovers, but not before they'd concentrated their own weapons on her. Mockett screamed as the ship lurched to one side.

"Parsons, why aren't we hitting those hovers?" Ethan cried, springing to his feet.

"They're fast," Parsons snapped. "And the planet's gravity makes *us* a dead weight!"

The *Hummingbird* swung around. Ethan saw his hovers firing on the ground troops, but the Magnificents fired their own powerful guns straight up at them. The tiny ships scrambled, barely able to regroup before the Magnificents took aim again.

"Aeron, what's that?" Ethan demanded, pointing at a huge cylinder the troops had heaved over the wall. Aeron whirled, but before he could speak, the weapon fired. The *Hummingbird* was struck with such violence, it threw everyone backward. Ethan landed on his back with a raw scream, his bandaged arm slamming the floor. The bridge tilted. Every siren in the ship seemed to go off at once.

"Mega-cannon!" Aeron bellowed. "Fire at that mega—"

BOOM!!! Ethan curled into a fetal position and shielded his head as the window exploded. In frigid, airless space, it would've withstood almost any assault. Down here where gravity bore down on the glass, though…

Ethan staggered to his feet, rushing to Mockett's station. The young woman sat numbly in her seat, held there by her restraints, but blood streamed down her face as she held her shaking hands in front of her. Ethan tore her restraints aside and helped her down to the floor.

"Ship," she whispered, her teeth chattering. "Ship…incoming…"

Ethan looked at her screen, but a glass shard had killed the display. He turned, breathing hard. The *Hummingbird* listed a couple hundred feet above the ground. Potter and Ainsworth crawled out from underneath the helm, shaken and bruised. Parsons clutched a bloody shoulder but kept bellowing orders over the crackling intercom. Aeron slumped over his station, facedown; the blood pooling beneath his head told Ethan all he needed to know. Ignoring his own heartbreak, Ethan limped to the helm.

"We can't risk crashing!" he shouted over the rushing air. "Put us down!"

Ainsworth whirled, his young face white. "But if we're on the ground—"

"Mr. Ainsworth, that's an order!"

Ainsworth scrambled to obey. Ethan returned to Mockett. Her gasps had turned into hysterical sobs. He pulled her into his chest and held her tight.

"Shh," he whispered. "Calm down, breathe. It's just a head wound. Head wounds always bleed more. You're gonna be all right…"

"Don't surrender," she sobbed. "*Please.* I don't want to be turned into a Magnificent…"

Ethan's eyes burned. He tore a strip off the hem of his shirt and pressed the material into the wound. Mockett was just starting to calm down when Parsons called his name.

"What is it?" Ethan asked, hardly caring anymore.

Parsons stood by the helm. They'd almost reached the pavement and their guns had gone silent—yet when Parsons turned, his craggy face wore a smile that looked half-insane with glee. "Sir, I think it's…"

A mega-cannon exploded nearby with a roar that could only come from a novacraft. Instinctively the crew ducked, but Ethan sprinted from Mockett's side just in time to see a sleek grey Meridian ship zoom past them.

The name "*GEORGIANA*" ran in bold letters across her side.

More ships—big ones, and distinctly Valyan—flew in her wake. Hovers flew out of their cargo bays, zipping into formation with the *Hummingbird*'s escorts and spraying the Magnificents with fire.

"Who the dickens are *they*?" Parsons cried.

Ethan let out a gasping laugh. "I think the Renegade and Lindy just arrived."

"Oh no," Lindy breathed as she scrambled down the boarding ramp. "Oh no, no, no, no, *no*!"

"Lindy, wait up!" Jo cried.

Lindy ignored her, running as fast as she could to the *Hummingbird*. The Renegade had talked her into staying aboard his ship until they and the unexpected reinforcements from the *Georgiana* wiped out the last Magnificents still fighting for control of the novaport. But it had been a horrible wait. The *Hummingbird* lay silent on the runway, a shattered hulk of the elegant ship Ethan loved so much.

How many are still alive in there? Please let him be all right, please, please!

Lindy had just darted underneath the *Hummingbird*'s scored, dented wing when she heard a clang overhead. She stopped and looked up. The hatch creaked open. Jo finally caught up with her, seizing her arm with a cry of delight as five crewmen appeared at the widening exit.

"Miss Tremaine!" one of them cried. "Stars and comets, it's Miss Tremaine!"

"Three cheers for Miss Tremaine!"

Lindy smiled, tears of grateful relief blurring her vision. As soon as the ramp hit the ground, more crewmen raced down with rifles in their hands and smiles on their tired faces.

"What happened?" Lindy demanded. "Are you all okay?"

"Most of us are, yeah," one of them replied. "When did you rendezvous with the *Georgiana*?"

"I-I didn't," Lindy stammered, turning to look at the destroyer. To her surprise, its captain approached her at a run as well, surrounded by his officers and a security escort. He saluted her with a grin.

"Captain Rogers at your service, Miss Tremaine. Got a message from President Stagg about three hours ago sayin' our people were in danger and that we were to offer you any and all assistance. What are your orders?"

Lindy glanced at the clustered ships and the last pockets of conflict closer to the novaport wall. "Confer with the Renegade—right over there, the guy with the scarf—and coordinate a patrol over Cor Danem. Once we get control of the airspace, the city will be halfway ours." She turned to the *Hummingbird* men again. "How did you get all those Valyan hovers?"

"Captain Granger disabled the Nova Force," a young woman answered. "He destroyed the Magnificent Network in the terminal!"

"Apparently, there are ships up in orbit crashin' into each other, too," the first crewman added. "It was like a domino effect."

Lindy's chest tightened. "Is he all right? Captain Granger?"

"Of course he is."

She looked up with a start. A tall, broad figure in Nova Force green stood at the top of the ramp. His face was smeared with soot and grime, blood trickled from a gash on his forehead, his brown hair stuck up on end, and he cradled one arm against his chest—but he smiled at her with such pride and relief that Lindy almost laughed. She broke into a run, and the next thing she knew, they were at the bottom of the ramp, hugging each other so tightly that she could hardly breathe.

"You're alive," she gasped. "You're alive, you're alive…"

"You could've called, y'know," he said.

"I would've if I didn't think *he* might've intercepted it. I couldn't risk losing the element of surprise."

"I know, I know…I'm just kidding you." He tucked a strand of hair behind her ear with a tired grin. "But I'll tell you one thing. I've never been so glad to see anybody barge in and take control of a situation."

Chapter Thirty

6:30 AM

The cells were starting to stink. The Magnificents hadn't let the prisoners out to use the restroom, though they'd allowed each cell the use of a bucket. Mariamne smothered her nausea as Tali eased their bucket into the corner, trying to keep the contents from sloshing.

"I'm sorry," the girl whispered. "I tried to move it as little as I could."

Her sad, hopeless tone filled Mariamne with guilt. *She* could handle anything life threw at her and had proved it countless times over. Tali, however, was still just a child.

She does not deserve this. Some of us might, but not her. She was not even born here. Aunt Verrona never should have brought her along.

Mariamne's eyes stung. Verrona had been taken away hours ago. The soldiers who'd come for Lord Nhormin, his wife, and finally Councilor Tremaine never answered Mariamne's panicked demands about her aunt's whereabouts. Even when she'd yanked one soldier's arm and he threw her against the wall like a rag doll, he'd kept his mouth shut.

Of course, maybe they had no idea what had happened to Verrona. If Jo Camrin was right and Rael himself controlled their minds, they were programmed to simply obey their orders and absorb no other information.

It does not matter, anyway. You know what happened to her. It's only a matter of time before it's your turn. Or Tali's.

Mariamne stiffened at the thought. Tali, peering out the tiny window in the door, noticed the subtle movement and looked at her older cousin.

"Come here, Tali," Mariamne said softly.

Tali shook her head. "I want to know when the next one comes. I don't want to be caught off guard."

"They may not even come to this cell. They went to another one last time, remember?" Mariamne patted the space on the cot next to her. "Please, Tali, sit with me a moment. I want to talk to you, and I…I'd rather look you in the eye while I did."

With a sigh, Tali obliged. Mariamne clasped her hand as tightly as she dared without hurting the girl and took a deep breath.

"I have a confession to make," she whispered. "And I'm going to share it with you because I truly believe you are the one who will make it out of here alive."

Tali jerked her hand away. "Don't talk like that!"

"I must. Lindy Tremaine will return long before Rael sets eyes on you. But I don't think he'll let *me* live that long."

Tali's eyes welled. "I don't want to be left alone…"

"Shh," Mariamne soothed. "Calm, Tali, calm. Now listen to me. When they take me away, you will be the last Princess of Valya, which simply means that when Lindy arrives, you must rally the Remnant to her cause."

"But I'm not ready. I'm not old enough."

"Nonsense. King Rhysan was only thirteen when he inherited the throne three hundred years ago. He did all right for himself, didn't he?"

In spite of herself, the young girl smiled. Mariamne cupped Tali's round cheek in her palm. Tali sniffled, then frowned.

"What was your confession?" she asked.

Mariamne bit her lip, tucking a strand of dark hair behind Tali's ear. "Do you remember the night my father died? We were at the hospital, and we met Lindy for the first time."

"Yes..."

"Do you remember how I treated her?"

Tali raised an eyebrow. "You weren't very polite, you know."

"I know. And I could curse myself a thousand times for it because..." Mariamne paused and squeezed her eyes shut. "Because the moment I laid eyes on her, I *knew*."

"What do you mean?"

"There was more to her than met the eye. She felt familiar, even with the Meridian clothes and the accent. There was a dignity, a *fearlessness* there that reminded me of someone." Mariamne rubbed Tali's hand a little faster. "Now I know why. She resembles Aunt Liliana, but she carries herself just like Uncle Kalen did."

"I never knew them," Tali whispered, "so I wouldn't know."

"But you know Lindy," Mariamne said with a sad smile. "And you've been kinder to her and more accepting than I ever was. The two of you will win our people over so quickly. You will be unstoppable."

"But we're going to do it with you," Tali insisted. "You *will* be there to help us! You have to be!"

Mariamne smiled, but just then the door flew open. She drew Tali close as three Magnificents entered the room. Their bulk made the cell seem even tinier.

"You." One of them stretched out an arm, pointing at Mariamne. "And you. Come with us."

Together? Mariamne stood, keeping a firm arm around her trembling cousin. "Where are we going?"

The Magnificent didn't answer. He yanked the princesses apart and pushed Tali out of the cell. Another soldier seized Mariamne; the third slammed the cell door shut behind them all.

Mariamne hoped it was the last she'd ever see of that room.

The Magnificents shoved them into the back of yet another hover, but not before Mariamne noticed a steady, angry rumble in the distance. The cousins held each other through the short, bumpy ride. When a novacraft engine roared overhead, the truck made a sharp turn that nearly threw them off their seat.

"What's going on?" Tali whimpered.

"I think we're taking a detour," Mariamne muttered. "Something is going on in the city."

"Riots, maybe?" Tali whispered. "Like the ones that happened before we came to Valya?"

Mariamne didn't dare speculate as she hugged Tali tighter. The ancient prayer her father used to murmur over her when she was a happy, carefree little princess came to mind. Smoothing the girl's hair, she began in a halting whisper:

"Elyon Above, ruler of the stars, blessed be thy holy name. Thy realm divine our hearts do seek, thy laws our kingdoms follow..."

The hover stopped, the doors opened, and one of the soldiers jerked his hand at them. "Out. Now."

They were back at the Palace. The cool light of dawn filled the empty square; the air smelled of smoke. As Mariamne climbed out, she thought the angry rumble sounded closer.

"Move, move!" the Magnificents ordered, urgency breaking through their usual monotone voices. Alarmed, Mariamne and Tali darted up the Palace's steps just as six grey hovers streaked overhead. The Magnificents weren't supposed to know pain, fear, or regret, but whoever controlled them was clearly unnerved by those hovers.

Once inside, the soldiers led them to Rael's private rooms, taking the same path Mariamne walked twelve hours ago with Councilor Tremaine and Miss Camrin. This time, however, they didn't get as far as his bedroom; they went to the sitting room adjacent to it instead. The brocade curtains were tightly drawn. Magnificents stood at attention along the walls. Daltis paced the room, muttering into a comm, while Morgarena sat at the desk, monitoring several laptops. A general of the Magnificent Army sat in a chair, his head in his hands.

Rael, however, stood at the window, drawing the curtain back just enough so he could look out. Mariamne peered at him, hoping to gauge his mood until her gaze skittered to the left. She seized Tali's wrist. The girl followed her horrified stare and let out a strangled cry.

Rael turned at the sound. "Ah. Good morning, cousins. What do you think of my new troops?"

Mariamne clapped a hand to her mouth. Councilor Tremaine and Trooper Gridley stood ramrod-straight among the Magnificents. Mariamne had never seen the old woman so rigid or her eyes so empty. Trooper Gridley wore a blank expression as well, but the harder lines around his mouth gave him a more dangerous look.

"Dear Elyon," Mariamne breathed. "You've killed them."

"Say that name in my presence again, and I'll kill *you,*" Rael retorted. He clamped his hand on the back of Morgarena's chair. "Well, Mariamne? Are you satisfied?"

"Why should I be?"

Rael shrugged. "My sister and the Renegade have attacked Cor Danem. My Nova Force has been neutralized. Harathella, Omstorn, and even Velladon are overrun by rebels. The old tyranny is about to return...and this time, Meridian will be pulling the strings. What do you say to all that?"

"I think..." Mariamne hesitated, tightening her grip on Tali's hand. "I think I understand everything you've done except for one thing."

"Oh?" Rael sidestepped the desk and approached her. "What quibble do you have with—what will they call it in the Meridian newspapers? My 'reign of terror'?"

Mariamne looked him in the eye. "You should not have touched the Councilor."

"She certainly won't be the first Meridian I've executed today," he said. "Do you think I've limited myself to Valyans over the past twelve hours?"

"No. But you know how much she means to them. If I didn't know better, I'd say these are the actions of a man who *wants* to die."

"More like the actions of a man who wants to prove a point," Rael muttered. Making sure Mariamne and Tali still watched him, he looked directly and deliberately at Trooper Gridley.

The Meridian squared his shoulders as if responding to an order. Before Mariamne could react, he seized her arm and forced her to her knees. Tali shrieked and squirmed as another Magnificent grabbed her by the shoulders. Mariamne tried to get up but froze at the cold, heavy pressure of a raygun against the back of her head.

Councilor Tremaine never moved. She simply watched with a dull, blank stare.

"Move, and you're finished," Rael warned, aiming his finger at Mariamne. "Although I admit, I'd rather keep you alive until Alinna comes barging in. I'd like to see her face when she finds out I still have one or two more cards up my sleeve."

Lindy wasn't sure if it was because she was bone-tired, hungry, anxious, or all three—but studying a map of Cor Danem in the

Georgiana's situation room with her father, Ethan, Captain Rogers, and Jo had to be her most surreal experience yet on this planet.

My first war council, she thought, gazing up at the holographic map. She folded her arms over her chest and forced herself to pay attention to Ethan's briefing.

"The latest reports say the Magnificents have hunkered down in their compound in the center of the capital," he said. "That's good. It means their attempts to quell the riots failed and they're not killing civilians anymore. But it also means that capturing their Headquarters will be a lot trickier than we'd hoped."

"What's the casualty report at this point?" Lindy asked Dr. Elliot.

The surgeon scratched her head. "There *are* dead civilians—unsurprising, given the size of the riots and the fact that the Magnificents never show mercy. The *Georgiana*'s chief surgeon made contact with the Cor Danem hospital, though. Our combined medical resources will be able to provide some help."

"Good," Lindy said. "Hopefully, we'll get more help from the hospitals in Omstorn and the northern cities once we have control of the capital." She paused, looking pleadingly at the doctor. "What about the Magnificents in *your* sickbay?"

Dr. Elliot's eyes brightened. "I was able to save four of them! One has some brain damage, but I'm almost certain he can be rehabilitated. The other three were actually coherent before I sedated them. They acted like they couldn't quite remember what had happened to themselves, but they kept asking if their wives and kids were okay."

"And therein lies the real tragedy," Jo said softly. "All these soldiers we've *had* to kill were probably nice, ordinary guys before they were microchipped."

"I know," Lindy murmured, drumming her fingers on her arms. "But their blood isn't on our hands. It's on Rael's and the Dominators'. We've got to remember that when we make this final attack."

Nobody spoke for a moment. Lindy stepped closer to the map. The Navorre Palace lay in the center of town. Two blocks south of it stood the Magnificent Army Headquarters, once a cathedral dedicated to the worship of Elyon. A block away from that lay the prison.

"MID troopers are trained to use stealth rather than brute force, right?" she asked Ethan.

He smirked. "You've just crashed into Cor Danem with a fleet of ships and a rebel army. I think you've lost the stealth element."

"Yes, but look at that map! Rael knows by now that we neutralized his men in Omstorn. He'll try to prevent us from doing the same thing here because he thinks that as long as he's got men in Cor Danem, he's good to—*oh!*"

Lindy clapped a hand over her mouth. Everyone leaned closer.

"What?" Jo cried. "What is it? What are you thinking?"

Lindy seized her hands, squeezing so hard that Jo yelped and tried to wriggle free. "Jo! We're forgetting! The Magnificents are connected by a network, but for Rael and Daltis to actually give the orders through that network…"

"…Rael and Daltis must have chips as well," Jo breathed.

"If that's the case, why didn't Daltis die when we destroyed the Nova Force network?" Ethan asked. "Why didn't Rael die when you destroyed the one in Omstorn?"

"Perhaps," the Renegade said slowly, "those networks were mere extensions to the main one in Cor Danem. Rael and the Dominators are directly connected to *that* one."

"Which means that when we destroy it, we'll take them out, too," Lindy finished.

"I'll put Chevenere under immediate observation, then," Dr. Elliot said. "If we can stabilize her as soon as you destroy the network, we'll be able to save her without any significant cerebral damage. That's assuming you want to keep her alive, Miss Tremaine."

"I do," Lindy said. "She still has valuable information…and the more you know about minimizing the chips' damage, the better." She paused, looking intently at her friends. "This will have to be timed with absolute precision. Rael expects us to attack Headquarters, so we'll attack the Palace first. Once we draw off his attention, *then* we'll hit Headquarters."

"Diversionary tactics," the Renegade said, smiling. "MID trained you well."

Lindy shook her head. "Even the best tactics in the Star System aren't any good to me if they don't keep my grandmother alive. We can't destroy the network until we've got Dr. Elliot or one of her assistants inside the Palace with eyes on Councilor Tremaine *and* Frank Gridley."

Her father's face softened. "Alinna, remember that you agreed yourself in Omstorn that their survival couldn't dictate—"

"I know what I said. But we didn't know then that Dr. Elliot had figured out how to save these guys from the disconnection." Lindy looked him in the eye, hoping she sounded as confident and commanding as Mariamne whenever *she* made up her mind. "I'm not losing any more of my family if I can help it."

The Renegade said nothing. Lindy sensed everyone in the room—Ethan and Jo especially—holding their breath, waiting to see who'd yield first.

Finally, her father spoke. "I understand…and I don't blame you. Not in the slightest."

7:30 AM

For one very tense hour, Cor Danem made the most of the unofficial ceasefire. Doctors and nurses, Valyan and Meridian, worked frantically to save as many injured civilians as possible. Unscathed townspeople, no longer harassed by ruthless soldiers, struggled to put out fires; at the same time, the Renegade's men rounded up a few Magnificents who hadn't made it back to their Headquarters in time.

The wealthier citizens and foreigners who'd benefitted from Rael Navorre's reign, however, stayed inside, waiting for the hammer to fall. When it did, it was with a roar of novacraft engines that made windows rattle in their panes.

Streaking above the city in tight formation, the rebel ships and the *Georgiana* headed towards the center of Cor Danem. Lindy, sitting in a hover inside the *Georgiana* with Jo, Dr. Elliot, and several of her father's soldiers, watched on the radar as the formation split over the Renaissance Hotel. She touched her earbud.

"Thorpe to Goldhawk," she called. "Keep an eye on my dad, all right?"

The radio crackled. "Goldhawk to Thorpe. The Queen's wish is my command."

Lindy smiled. "You be careful, too, all right?"

Ethan chuckled. "I'll do my best. Stay in touch."

"I will. Thorpe out." She lowered her hand and glanced at Jo. Jo smirked.

"Belinda."

Lindy frowned. "Huh?"

"That's my middle name, in case you two are wondering what to name your first kid."

All the warmth rushed to Lindy's face just as the pilot called over the intercom, "Prepare for engagement!" She barely had time to brace herself. The *Georgiana*'s hangar flew open and the hover streaked free, off towards the Navorre Palace.

In his own hover on the other side of the *Georgiana*'s hangar, Ethan drew a steadying breath. He'd placed the *Hummingbird* and her crew under Parsons' command until he returned. He'd conferred briefly with Captain Rogers, as well, and concluded that President Stagg hadn't been the one to summon the *Georgiana* after all.

Captain Rogers, who'd been as shocked to receive the summons as Ethan had been to see him, had eagerly shared the urgent message from Hoadley House. None of the wording had sounded like Ethan's mother. The postscript even offered a final clue: "Be sure to tell Captain Granger that if he won't ask me for help like I told him to, I'll send it his way whether he likes it or not."

Despite his rising adrenaline, Ethan grinned at the thought of his sister smugly sipping tea in bed while their mother tried to figure out why Captain Rogers had set course for Valya. He stopped smiling when he caught the Renegade watching him. The former king had drawn his scarf over his face; only his keen dark eyes and the bridge of his nose showed.

"Do you love my daughter?" the Renegade asked as the hover shot out of the novacraft.

Ethan blinked. "Sir?"

The Renegade chuckled. "Forgive me. You haven't known her for very long, have you?"

"Long enough to know she's amazing…and that I'm way out of her league."

"Ah, don't sell yourself short, Captain. She thinks very highly of you." The Renegade's eyes softened. "Elyon knows I haven't been able to care for her the way I would've liked. Knowing she has had such loyal friends, however…it puts this old man's mind at ease."

"Well, from what I've seen, you're tougher than most men half your age, sir. I reckon you've got a few years left to love your daughter the way you always wanted."

To his uneasy surprise, the man once known as Kalen Navorre didn't reply. When word came that the Palace was under attack, he merely nodded and took his position in front of Ethan, gripping the railing so tightly that his leather gloves squeaked under the strain.

The six hovers under Lindy's command landed in the square outside the Navorre Palace. As soon as they were on the ground, the *Georgiana* swung up and away towards Magnificent Headquarters. Lindy and Jo faced the empty square, their rifles poised, while their soldiers clambered out of the hovers. Dr. Elliot and one of her trusted nurses made up the rear, rayguns in their hands and medkits on their shoulders.

Then the army of sixty ran up the Palace's front steps as fast as they could.

Magnificents opened fire from the roof. Two of the rebels dropped; the rest dashed underneath the portico and unleashed their weapons on the doors. The overwhelming energy fried any locking mechanisms, and the doors swung open with a groan.

"Go, go, go!" Lindy screamed. Her men needed no prodding. They fired into the Magnificents waiting for them in the front hall, regrouped, and thundered up the marble staircase. Screaming servants ran for cover; the Magnificents holding the second floor crumpled under the rebels' searing fire.

Hang on, Nana, Lindy thought. *Hang on, I'm almost there. Don't give up on me yet.*

As soon as the rebel ships cleared the force field surrounding Magnificent Headquarters, the soldiers inside the compound opened fire. The Renegade waited for a pause in the gunfire, then burst out of the landed hover with a cry. Ethan followed close on his heels, the rest of the rebel soldiers right behind him.

The *Georgiana* and one of the Renegade's larger ships fired their cannons on the lowest setting possible; it sent shockwaves through the compound, confusing the Magnificents and allowing the rebels to gain ground. Between taking cover and firing off several shots of their own, Ethan and the Renegade dashed closer and closer to the old cathedral.

"You're certain this MID technology will get us inside?" the Renegade shouted.

"Absolutely!" Ethan shouted back. "Come on!"

They huddled beside the stone wall just below one of the bell towers. Ethan glanced up and around, then nodded to the Renegade. They lowered their rifles, each yanking a pair of thick gloves out of his back pocket.

"You've got the pads on your boots?" Ethan whispered. "Fine, you're good. Ready?"

The Renegade nodded. "Ready."

Ethan took a deep breath. He'd only ever done this in training, and Jarvis had only authorized the equipment for this trip as a "just in case" measure. He rolled his shoulders, faced the wall, and laid his palms flat against the stone.

He felt the suction immediately. He pressed the top of his foot against the wall and felt it again; he stretched an arm out high above his head and pulled himself up. *Climbing…just like climbing.* He didn't dare look down, but he could tell from the grunts and thuds below him that the Renegade was keeping up.

They didn't stop until they reached the belfry. Ethan hooked one leg over and climbed in underneath the enormous bell. The Renegade tumbled in after him with considerably less grace. Ethan allowed himself one peek down into the compound, approved of what he saw, and opened the door that would take them down into the heart of Rael's brutality.

The diversion outside was obviously working: Ethan and the Renegade left the winding staircase behind and crept into the building's ancient corridors. They moved quickly, following the signs on the stone walls and swiftly taking care of any lone Magnificents they encountered until they finally found the door they were looking for: "NETWORK CONTROL ROOM."

The lock was mechanized, of course. Ethan drew a small explosive from his belt and placed it on the lock.

"Get down, Ethan!" the Renegade roared. Ethan ducked as the Renegade fired on a Magnificent who'd appeared at the end of the long hallway. Two more soldiers immediately took their fallen comrade's place and opened fire. Ethan activated the explosive and pulled the Renegade to the floor just as the Magnificents ran towards them.

Small as it was, the bomb packed a punch; the soldiers got caught in it and hit the ground with a crash. Ethan's ears rang, and his hurt arm throbbed. The Renegade grabbed him by the shoulder.

"Get up!" he shouted. "Get up, Captain!"

"Ethan!" Lindy cried in his earpiece. "Ethan, where are you?"

Coughing and disoriented, Ethan and the Renegade stumbled into the control room. The two Magnificents inside put up a brief fight, but the intruders had the advantage of surprise. Once the room was quiet, Ethan staggered to the computers.

"Ethan!" Lindy called again, static fragmenting her voice. "Ethan, are you there?"

"I'm here," he croaked. "I'm at the computers. Give me the order whenever you're ready."

Lindy was silent. Ethan frowned. The Renegade watched him, his rifle aimed at the damaged, open door.

"Lindy?" Ethan called. "Do you see Rael?"

"He's on the other side of this door." Her words came in a fast, strained whisper. "We're pretty sure he has Nana and Frank with him...Mariamne and Tali, too. This is his last stand, Ethan. He's gonna make it count."

Ethan cocked his pistol. "I'm ready to fire. Just say the word and—"

"They're coming," the Renegade hissed. Ethan jerked his head up, panic and horror washing over him at the sound of dozens of running feet.

"Give me an order, Lindy, and make it fast," he said. "We're about to have company."

"I don't know if I can save them!"

"You won't save anybody unless I fry these computers!" Ethan shouted. "You've *got* to give the order!"

At Ethan's desperate plea, Lindy's breath lodged in her chest. Gripping her gun even tighter, she glanced behind her at her soldiers and friends all crammed in the corridor. They stared back with wide, worried eyes, waiting for her to take the lead.

You're doing this for Mama as much as you're doing it for Nana, you know.

She clamped her lips and shut her eyes, dredging up memories of damp chill, her mother's voice, the frightened crowd, the screams. She felt Mama's fear…heard Mama's voice.

"I love you, Lin. I love you so much. Come on, let's say your prayers, all right?"

Lindy opened her eyes and looked at Jo. Jo looked straight back.

"You can do this," Jo whispered. "I *know* you can do this."

Yes…yes, I can do this. I have *to do this. It's my destiny. My planet. My very life. And all of that is more important than my fear.*

"Ethan?" Lindy called.

"Yeah?"

She nodded at her men, quick and sharp. "Fire away."

With that, she aimed at the door and fired. This wasn't a fortress: the lock melted quickly. She kicked the door open and raced into the room, her men swarming in after her…and froze.

The Magnificents were still on their feet, rifles at the ready, one of them pinning Tali to his chest. Nana stood among them, her expressionless eyes locked on Lindy. Frank held a pistol against a kneeling Mariamne's head. None of them looked even *close* to collapsing under the weight of a destroyed cyberpathic network. Lindy put a shaking finger to her ear.

"Now would be good, Ethan!" she snapped.

Rael rose from a luxurious chair by the window. "Ah! Captain Granger is your brave warrior at Headquarters, is he? How is that counterattack coming, Morgarena?"

Morgarena peered at a laptop screen. "The Magnificents have reached the Control Room, Citizen. Captain Granger is under attack."

"Surrender, Alinna?" Rael asked. "Or will Trooper Gridley have to prove the point?"

Frank flipped a setting on his gun. Mariamne flinched.

"For the love of Elyon, Lindy, do not give in!" she begged.

Lindy staggered backward, lowering her rifle. Rael smiled and moved closer. Morgarena drew a dagger from one of the desk drawers and set the jeweled hilt in his open palm.

"This is the end, little sister," he murmured. "My network is safe. Cor Danem is mine. I win. You lose. Now get on your knees."

"Oh no, Rael," Lindy whispered. "We *both* lose. Because when Meridian sends more ships—and she will—you won't stand a chance. Valya will only suffer more. You'll have the blood of millions on your hands if you don't already."

"That will be my problem, not yours." He shifted his hand around the knife's hilt, the blade now pointing downward towards her. "On. Your. Knees."

"Our father's alive."

Rael froze. Lindy shouldered her rifle with a little more confidence.

"Remember the Renegade?" she asked. "The man who's been a thorn in your side for years? Well, I've had a lot of good conversations with him in the past twelve hours. We caught up on everything that's happened since the Revolution, and it's been *very* educational."

Rael opened his mouth, but no sound came out. Lindy took a bold, firm step towards him.

"I wasn't the only one you missed. You killed our mother and our sisters—but you didn't kill me, and you didn't kill our father. You *failed*. And even if you kill me, you'll still be a failure. Our people know what you really are now, and they will never be deceived by you and your lies ever again."

Rael screamed—and before she could move, he slashed the knife across her face. She reeled, Jo shrieked, Daltis bellowed an order, and the room burst into thunder.

Lindy was on her hands and knees. She *had* to get up—people rushed past her, nearly knocking her down—but blood ran down her face, blinding one eye, and she couldn't catch her breath. The battle raged around her. Someone slammed Frank to the floor; Jo cut Morgarena down with a single shot; Tali screamed and screamed. But Lindy couldn't see Nana or Mariamne. She pulled one hand from her throbbing face and put a finger to her ear.

"Ethan!" she gasped. "Ethan, can you—"

Rael seized her by her ponytail and flung her onto her back. He'd torn his injured arm out of his sling, using that hand to hold his knife. As he clamped his stronger hand over her throat, a wild, suffocating darkness surged into her consciousness.

Anger. Hate. He hates me…hates me with every ounce of his being…

"*I* failed?" he roared. "What do you call this kind of ending for an MID trooper?"

He raised the knife, but Lindy blocked his forearm with her own just in time. The next thing she knew, she had *her* knees rammed into his chest, furiously trying to pin his arm to the floor and snatch the knife away.

When the first Magnificent crumpled with a deafening rattle, she hardly noticed.

When the second one fell, she heard Jo scream, "Way to go, Ethan!"

When the sixth one dropped, Dr. Elliot and her nurse burst in from the corridor. Rael, still flat on his back, went stiff. His eyes popped; he released Lindy's arm and clutched at his head. She pried the knife away and tossed it to the side. He screamed in agony, overwhelmed by spasms.

"Make it stop!" he wailed.

"Trooper Gridley is stabilized!" the nurse cried.

Lindy snatched her pistol out of her belt and pressed the barrel into Rael's forehead. He stopped screaming and stared at her, breathing hard and fast—and Lindy was suddenly and horribly aware of his Emanation. It pulsed with the one blend of color she hadn't expected: a dark blue, so dark it was almost black.

Blue Sadness...and black Anger.

"Surrender, and I'll make it stop," she promised. "Say you surrender!"

Rael pulled in a ragged breath. For an instant, she thought she glimpsed something like sorrow in his eyes...and even now, the faintest trace of guilt.

Which was why when he jerked free, rolled to the side, and grabbed a fallen pistol, she wasn't expecting it.

"Lindy!" Jo screamed.

Lindy flung herself to the side just as Rael pulled the trigger, the beam slamming into the floor. He aimed again, his eyes as wild and full of hate as they'd been when he first lashed out at her with the knife, but this time Lindy didn't hesitate. She screamed with a torment that had absolutely nothing to do with physical pain—and fired.

Rael flew backward and landed with a thud. The whole room went silent. Lindy threw the gun as far as she could, heard it crash against the wall, and pressed both hands over her mouth.

Daltis was dead. Morgarena was dead. The Magnificents were dead or dying.

And Rael, her brother, was dead.

It was all over. Lindy sank to the floor, numb with a terrible, overwhelming grief.

"Lindy! Lindy, come on, quick!"

She was too weary and horrified to move on her own, but Jo managed to get her on her feet and drag her to a far corner of the room. Dr. Elliot bent over a small, frail form in a tattered pantsuit. At the sight, Lindy broke free of Jo's grip and collapsed on her knees.

"Oh no," she groaned, crawling towards Nana. "No, no, no, *no...*"

"It's all right, Miss Tremaine—she's alive!" Dr. Elliot soothed. "She's just sedated. She'll be fine as soon as we get her to the *Hummingbird*—and Trooper Gridley, too. Now, let me see your face..."

But Lindy pushed her away and moved closer to Nana. She took one of her grandmother's hands between her own trembling, bloody palms.

"I love you," she whispered. "I love you, I love you, I love you..."

The cold fingers stirred against her own. Lindy half-gasped, half-sobbed as Nana's blue eyes fluttered open.

"My Lindy," Nana breathed, then fell peacefully back to sleep.

Chapter Thirty-One

A soft, steady beeping woke Lindy. She turned her head slightly to the side and moaned.

"Hey," a deep, familiar voice murmured. "Hey, lie still. You're in the Cor Danem hospital. It's okay. You're safe."

Ethan? Lindy forced her heavy eyelids open. When she saw him standing over her, she threw out a clumsy hand and curled her fingers around his sleeve.

"You're alive," she rasped. "You are, aren't you? Am I dreaming?"

He smiled tiredly. "Not at all. Let me prove it to you."

He pressed a gentle kiss to her forehead, just above her eyebrow. When he drew back, Lindy opened her eyes and smiled back—only to wince, frown, and wince again.

"Ugh. My face..."

"Yeah, it'll be stiff for a while." Ethan traced a diagonal line with his finger over her face. "Dr. Elliot was able to patch you up, but it'll have to finish healing on its own before she can make that scar less noticeable."

Lindy groaned. "Am I hideous?"

"The Queen of Valya couldn't be hideous if she tried."

She let the good-humored compliment slide and swallowed with difficulty. "Are you okay? Morgarena said you were under attack."

Ethan nodded slowly. "Yeah. Yeah, we were."

It took her a moment, but she suddenly realized that he wasn't meeting her gaze anymore. He took her hand and ran his thumb over it, the motion strangely nervous.

"What?" she whispered. "What's wrong?"

When he looked up, the expression on his face made her stomach sink. "Right when you gave the order, the Magnificents started pouring in. I was able to take out the first computer while your dad held his position at the door, but then…he got hit."

Lindy drew a ragged breath and held it. Ethan leaned in close, stroking her hair.

"He's alive, but barely," he whispered. "I think he's holding on for you."

Lindy tried to sit up. Her head throbbed as soon as she lifted it off the pillow, but she ignored it. "I have to see him. Ethan, please, let me see him…"

"Whoa, hold up, don't stand up by yourself!" Ethan wrapped an arm around her shoulders and grasped her elbow, holding her steady. "I'll take you to him. I actually asked Dr. Elliot to bring you out of your sedation. We had a bad feeling…"

That he wouldn't last much longer? Lindy couldn't bring herself to ask if that's what he meant.

Ethan led her past the curtain encircling her bed. She realized then that she was in a large room with beds on either wall. When she saw Mariamne sitting alone beside another occupied bed,

Lindy knew where they were headed. She staggered free of Ethan and sank awkwardly to a seat on the edge of the bed.

"Papa," she whispered, seizing the Renegade's hand. "Papa, it's me."

The Renegade wore an oxygen mask over his bearded face. Bandages covered his stomach, and the monitors hooked up to him offered only dismal readings. At her voice, however, he tilted his head to the side on his pillow, and his eyes fluttered open.

"Alinna," he whispered. The oxygen mask fogged slightly with his breath.

Lindy's eyes filled with tears. She lifted his hand, pressing his palm against her cheek. Mariamne, she saw, gripped his other hand just as tenderly. *Of course*. For years, Mariamne had scoffed at the Renegade and his cause, yet here she was, soothing her uncle. She likely remembered more about him than Lindy ever would.

"I've been telling him all about you," the Princess said softly, as if she'd guessed Lindy's thoughts. "How fierce you are, and how stubborn you can be. I told him you are a true Navorre. And I told him…I *promised* him…that I would follow you wherever you may lead us."

Lindy stared at her, hardly believing her ears. With a weak smile, Mariamne returned her gaze to the former king's face. Lindy gulped and scooted forward, keeping her father's hand against her cheek.

"This is only a piece of the tapestry, isn't it?" she whispered, her chin wobbling with each word. "And it's a hard piece. It's *so* hard. But the threads brought us back together, just for a few hours…and I'll always be grateful for that."

Her father's eyelids drooped. The beeping of the heart monitor slowed.

"I promise." Tears tumbled out of her eyes and into the thin bandages running across her face. "I promise I'll do my best. All those years, you believed in me. I promise I won't let you down, Papa. I love you…I'll always love you…"

The heart monitor flatlined. Lindy burst into tears and pressed her forehead against her father's, careful not to disturb her sutures. She felt Ethan's strong hands on her shoulders, heard him murmuring soft words over her head, and sensed Mariamne hurrying over to her side of the bed. When her cousin gently tugged her into her arms, Lindy clung to her tighter than she ever imagined she would.

"The King is dead," Mariamne whispered, smoothing Lindy's hair. "Long live the Queen."

Sixteen months later

Winter on Valya wasn't much different from winter on Meridian, Lindy decided as she opened the door leading out into the Palace garden. *Although right now, it'll be scorching-hot in New Harvelle. Thank goodness I get to skip* that *this year.*

She closed the door behind her and entered the dormant garden. A crisp breeze skipped in from the north, stirring the shrubs that her brother had kept well-tended during his dictatorship, just as he'd kept the bees. The domed hives were unusually quiet this morning. She stepped off the gravel path and drew up short with a grimace.

"Stupid skirts." She grabbed big fistfuls of the heavy purple material and lifted them distastefully away from her feet. Sometimes she wanted to throw all her new clothes into the biggest furnace she could find—*but hey, when in Cor Danem, do as the Valyans do*. Besides, she *had* to fit in now, to some extent.

Especially today.

A bench sat at a short but safe distance from the hives, placed there long ago by someone who must've wanted to watch the bees without annoying them. Lindy sat down, arranging her skirts with exaggerated dignity. Then she folded her hands, closed her eyes, and breathed.

In…and out. In…and out.

She could do this. Of course she could. She'd managed everything else so far—like sentencing Chevenere to a strict exile on the northern moors, and persuading President Stagg to show her daughter clemency once the President realized who'd forged the *Georgiana*'s orders. Lindy had even cut ties between Valya and Xandroa until President Sarkova finally rooted out all the microchip manufacturers.

There'd been a delicious irony in that. She never would've come this far if she and Jo hadn't had that assignment long ago and far away at President Sarkova's garden party.

Not to mention the fact that you've deported Rael's foreign cronies, abolished the Magnificent Army…and now you're helping the refugees on Meridian come back so they can help rebuild their planet.

What makes you think you can't do this *thing?*

"What are you doing?"

Lindy turned and saw Jo maintaining a wary distance in the gravel path, doubly cautious after an unpleasant experience with the bees a few weeks ago. As she studied her friend's green silk trousers and tunic more closely, Lindy raised her eyebrows in surprised approval.

"How and where did you get an outfit like that?" she demanded eagerly.

"Oh, you know…I cajoled, pleaded, threatened, stomped my foot. No, really, I told your new maid that I wasn't really the dress-wearing type. Thank goodness some of the Valyan ladies from Meridian have come up with this new style. You look awesome, by the way. Quite regal. *Very* traditional."

Lindy snorted. "What I wouldn't give to see Athena's face when we step out in front of all those cameras today. We used to write about trends. Now *we'll* be setting them."

Jo giggled. "No kidding. Has Ethan seen you yet?"

"Not yet. Want to sit with me a minute?"

The caution flooded back into Jo's face. "Are those bees feeling fierce today?"

"No, they're all tucked inside. I don't think they like the cold."

"Oh, okay then." Jo stepped off the path; Lindy bunched her skirts so Jo could sit beside her. For a moment, they sat in companionable silence, watching while a few bees peeked out of the hive before deciding it was still too chilly for their tiny wings.

"Nervous?" Jo asked.

"Oh yeah. Haven't been this nervous since I saw Rael for the first time."

"I'd probably be more nervous if I was getting married or something, but okay."

"Honestly, Jo. You act like opening the Free Valyan Parliament is as simple as ordering a burger meal in New Harvelle. "

"Pretend you *are* ordering a burger meal, then," Jo teased, her eyes sparkling as she pretended to flip a burger. "I'd like a double-decker with extra cheese and a side of fries—leave off the onions—and a chocolate sundae with a cherry on top, thank you very much."

Lindy laughed. "You're awful."

"I know. But seriously, you've rehearsed this speech a million times. Your people *love* you. They're not gonna disown you now."

"I hope not," Lindy murmured. "I know some are worried I'm too Meridian, though. My accent, my friends, my connections…I can see why they think I might be biased."

"Well, not everything about Meridian is bad, and Valya needed a total government overhaul."

"True. I just feel like I've got to reassure them they won't lose their identity."

The garden door opened again. Both Lindy and Jo sprang to their feet when they saw Ethan, Nana, and Frank approaching them, along with two unexpected newcomers.

"Look who's here!" Frank said, jabbing his thumb at the big man beside him.

"Jarvis!" Lindy cried. Her former commander threw his head back with a hearty laugh as she picked up her skirts and ran towards him. "Oh, it's so good to see you! I didn't think you'd be able to come!"

"Well, I was able to pull a few strings with President Stagg. She finally decided she could spare me long enough, especially if I agreed to escort her official representative at your first Parliament."

He gestured at the frail but smiling figure in the wheelchair Ethan proudly pushed along the path. Lindy gently clasped the thin hand Genevieve Stagg held out to her.

"It's so good to see you again, Lindy," Genevieve murmured. "You look beautiful."

"As do you," Lindy said warmly. "I'm so sorry Jo and I never got around to that photoshoot. I hope the substitute photographer Athena sent did the job to your liking."

"Oh, indeed! He wasn't nearly as fun, but that's all right. You two still helped me say my piece. I'll always be thankful to both of you for that."

"And MID?" Lindy asked, glancing up at Jarvis. "Are they willing to…you know…grant me that favor I asked?"

He nodded. "MID has decided, officially, that Troopers Granger, Camrin, and Gridley can be spared for the job of training your new intelligence agency, Your Majesty."

Lindy snorted. "You called me 'Trooper' way too long, Jarvis. You might as well be speaking a different language calling me *that*."

"Don't listen to her, Jarvis!" Nana cried, waving her hands. "It's taken her sixteen months to warm up to the name 'Alinna' on official proclamations and what-not. Just keep calling her 'Your Majesty,' and eventually she'll get used to that, too."

Lindy rolled her eyes, but as she did, she saw Mariamne step outside. The Princess, still looking more like a queen than Lindy suspected *she* ever would, glided towards the little group and curtsied deeply.

"Commander Jarvis…Miss Stagg," she said, eyeing Jarvis with far more respect than she used to show him before turning to Lindy. "The hover is waiting to take us to Parliament. Are you ready?"

Lindy squared her shoulders, her heart fluttering. "Yeah, I think I'm ready. Ethan?"

"I'm ready," he said, handing off his sister's wheelchair to Frank without hesitation and offering Lindy his arm. "And I'm with you every step of the way."

When Lindy emerged from her hover amid camera flashes and cheers, the beauty of the old Parliament Hall caught her eye. Its restoration had been her first tangible public rejection not only of Rael's authoritarianism, but also of the harsh ugliness of life under his rule. Ethan, looking strong and handsome in his Nova Force uniform, once again offered his arm. She was pretty sure she could hear the crowd cheering his name, too. When she glanced up at him, he winked.

"You can do this," he whispered. "*Why* can you do this?"

"Because what I need to do matters more than what I'm afraid of," she whispered back.

He smiled and raised her hand to his lips. The cameras flashed again as shocked murmurs rippled through the crowd. Lindy blushed. She could already guess tomorrow's headlines: "Rumors confirmed: our Queen is in a romantic relationship with the heroic Captain of the *Hummingbird*! Valya has never seen such an open display of affection—and in a place of state, too!"

If Ethan cared, he didn't show it. She knew *she* didn't. He released her hand and stepped back until she stood alone in the doorway. The crowd grew quiet, then silent.

Elyon, give me strength. She clasped her hands at her stomach and stepped inside, focusing on each small step so she could glide like Mariamne down the tiled nave. Valya's new, freely-elected legislators rose from their seats; civilian guests filling the gallery above stood, too, as she approached the simple throne at the head of the room. She mounted the short dais steps and sat down.

Hundreds of earnest, attentive faces watched her from all sides. Mariamne, the Representative of Allavonde Plantation, sat near the throne. When Lindy caught her eye, Mariamne sent her a quiet, subdued smile. Jo, by contrast, started waving in the gallery. Nana forced her hand down and shot Lindy a look of exasperated apology.

Lindy smirked, then composed herself and held her head high. The chamber had gone very quiet. She took a deep breath and looked not at the representatives, but at those seated above her in the gallery.

"People of Valya," she began, her voice clearer than she'd hoped. "Today, we are reopening Valya's Parliament. This is a gathering of elected representatives who've taken oaths to protect and defend the new Constitution *you* approved just a month ago.

"This Constitution declares you are all citizens of equal value before the law. It promises that the Queen—or the King, as the case may be—is little more than a glorified president. She cannot dictate. She cannot demand. She can only advise, authorize the laws that your representatives approve, declare war when we have no other choice, and occasionally veto."

Out of the corner of her eye, she saw Ethan slip into a seat in the gallery between Jarvis and Genevieve. He gave her a thumb's up; she glanced away quickly and went on.

"I know this is something Valya has never experienced. I'm confident it'll work for all of us. But I'm also aware that it's very... Meridian."

The Valyans in the gallery shifted, leaning forward in their seats. The legislators did the same, several of them putting their chins in their hands.

"I'm also aware that *I'm* very Meridian." Lindy hesitated, laughing a little. "Look at me. *Listen* to me. I trip over my skirts half the time, I'm still getting used to the spiciness of our food, and I've got a New Harvelle accent that would put most native-born Meridians to shame!"

To her relief, the hall echoed with laughter, none of it unpleasant.

"So yes," she continued, "I understand your concerns about how I might turn Valya into another Meridian. I have no intention of dismissing any of them. I don't want to make the same mistakes my brother and our ancestors did…the mistakes that brought so much suffering to this planet.

"But this is what I promise you, people of Valya. I am determined to embrace my heritage as much as I possibly can, without denying the influence of those who protected me in my childhood so that I could come back and be with you."

The hall was silent now. Lindy clenched her skirts and blinked hard, willing herself not to get emotional. *Don't think about how much you owe to that woman in the gallery. Don't think about how you once couldn't stand to even look a Valyan in the eye…*

"I can't forget Meridian. I love it, and I hope you'll learn to love it, too, as one of your strongest allies. But Valya is my home now. And I swear to you before Elyon, in whose name we *will* move forward, that until I die, my life is devoted to you."

The silence continued. Lindy's stomach dropped. Despite all her planning, she hadn't expected such a solemn, tight-lipped response. Even a smile would've reassured her, but she didn't get even *that*. She dropped her gaze to her lap and awkwardly smoothed her skirts.

"Well, anyway, that's all I have to say," she mumbled. She shot out of the throne and took her first hasty step off the dais just as Mariamne rose to her feet. Lindy stopped, startled. Mariamne looked her in the eye, lifted her hands…and started clapping as hard as she could.

Lindy's heart started working again. When Mariamne had delivered *her* opening speech at the peace conference, Lindy had burst into applause in order to hide the brave clapping of Rael's servants. Now Mariamne returned the favor. The men on either side of her, encouraged by the Princess' gesture, leaped to their feet and tried to match her vigorous applause. The other representatives followed suit, and then the civilians in the gallery bolted to their feet.

Judging by the growing roar outside, the crowd watching on huge screens had joined in as well.

But more importantly, every face beamed. Through the tears, through the cries of "Alinna! Alinna! Alinna!"—there were great, joyous, welcoming smiles, full of love and acceptance and a willingness to move forward. Lindy covered her mouth, fighting to keep her tears at bay.

Look at how far I've come, Papa, she thought. *Look at how far I've come.*

That night Cor Danem rang with festivities. The Palace square became a huge party area. People ate, chatted, and danced the sunset away, and when darkness fell, fireworks split the night sky with tremendous cracks and whistles.

Lindy watched from the balcony. She could see Frank and Jo whirling and spinning with other dancers in the square. Ethan was in charge of the fireworks with Genevieve as his "assistant." Nana sat in a lounge chair nearby, Winston curled contentedly on her lap. A splash of green and red filled the sky with a loud pop.

"Ooh, I liked that one," Lindy murmured. "Ethan picked some good ones."

"He'll make a wonderful husband for you one day," Nana commented. "I'm sure of it."

Lindy grinned. "Don't tell me you've been planning *that* all along, too."

"I planned a lot less than you seem to think, my dear."

Lindy tore her gaze from the glittering sky and studied her grandmother. Nana had recovered well from her experience as a Magnificent, but Lindy thought she seemed slower these days.

There was a slight but noticeable tremor in her hand as she stroked Winston's thick fur.

"Do you think you'll run for another term as Councilor?" Lindy asked softly.

Nana looked up. "Hmm? Me? Oh, I don't know. After all the mess I dragged her into, Maria Stagg might not want me advising her anymore."

"She won't be in government forever, either."

"That's true." Nana paused, scratching Winston's head. "Perhaps my time as a politician is coming to a close. I've done what needed doing. And retirement doesn't sound so dreadful, now that Winston and I will be visiting Valya more often."

"You're welcome to stay if you want," Lindy said.

Nana smiled, but the expression was small and sad. Lindy knew then that this conversation was no longer going to be light-hearted.

"Do you have any regrets, Lindy?" Nana asked.

An explosion of yellow flared in the sky. Lindy watched it, knowing Ethan had picked it just for her, and shook her head.

"No," she said. "It's been a hard year and a half, though. Just think...we're coming up on two years since that night I sobbed into my pillow over Owen Roth."

Nana rolled her eyes. "Oh, gracious. I'd nearly forgotten about him."

"I tend to forget about him, too," Lindy laughed, folding her arms and leaning against the balcony's stone railing. "Then again, I've had a lot more important things to worry about. And a lot of it's been far, far more painful than anything some boyfriend could've done to me."

"Like the dishonesty of the one person who should've never, *ever* lied to you?"

Another firework whistled and popped, but this time Lindy didn't pay any attention to it. She pushed herself away from the balcony, dropped to her knees, and drew one of Nana's hands off of Winston.

"Nana, look at me," she ordered.

Nana obeyed. Without taking her eyes off her grandmother's face, Lindy kissed her hand.

"I love you," she whispered, her eyes filling with tears she didn't bother to hide. "You've been the most important person in my life. And as hard as it was to realize that you hid things from me, I know why you did it. You wanted to protect me from so much. If you hadn't let me learn it all for myself, who knows what might've happened?"

A tear ran down Nana's cheek. Lindy swallowed and squeezed her grandmother's hand.

"I needed to own it, Nana. I needed to walk through the fire myself—and as much as I wanted to wring your neck sometimes, you let me do that. None of this could've happened any other way. I imagine my parents are very thankful for you. I know I am. Don't ever, *ever* think I'm not."

Nana smiled, sending more tears down her wrinkled face. Gently, she freed her hand and slipped her fingers underneath Lindy's hair, bringing them to rest against the young queen's cheek.

"My lionhearted girl," she murmured.

As if in response, a joyous explosion of yellow and white shattered the Valyan sky.

Acknowledgments

Five years and seven drafts after writing the first chapter of *Operation Lionhearted,* I've finally sent this labor of love out into the world, and thus achieved one of my childhood dreams. But I wouldn't be here without several important and beloved individuals…

Mom: this book wouldn't exist without you. You may insist till the cows come home that you aren't a writer, but the truth is that you can sniff out a good story better than most people—and you're a fantastic editor! Thank you for always encouraging me to pursue my passion for storytelling. I love you so much.

Rachel Gavris: I'll never forget how you comforted me during one of my worst heartbreaks, recommended thrilling novels to take my mind off the pain, and then urged me to chase this story idea. You're one of my very best friends, and I love you!

Rachel L., Gwenna G., Amelie Johnson, and Kimberly French, you are the best beta readers *ever*! The final draft of *Operation Lionhearted* became a tighter, better story, thanks to you. (It might've turned out a bit sadder, too, but I don't consider that a bad thing!)

Emily Betts, Abigail Nicole (AKA "Starfighter"), Wilmer and Betsy Mills, Ken and Cindy Phares, Caroline and Daniel Williams, Lancia E. Smith and the team members (especially you, Jordan Durbin!) of The Cultivating Project, and all my friends from blogging and Twitter: thank you so much for your support over the years! Some of you have been on this journey with me since the very beginning, but all of you have cheered me on and reminded me to trust God's timing.

My cover designer, Joshua Griffin, and my ebook designer, Elisabeth Grace Foley: thank you for all your creativity and your diligent work!

My grandparents (Mimi and Pawpaw, and Mimi and Popsie): I'm sure you thought I'd *never* be finished with this sprawling project, haha—but thank you for all your patience and moral support over the years!

Daddy, TJ, Emily, Anna, Carolyn, Katie, Ben, Lillie, and Joy…I love y'all so much. You put up with me when troublesome scenes made me irritable and when long hours of editing left me wild-eyed—but just as importantly, you've kept me laughing, helped me with proofing and photography, and assured me that *yes*, this story was worth telling. I'm so grateful for your love and friendship.

To God be the glory. This is His doing, and it is marvelous in our eyes.

About the Author

Maribeth Barber is a small-town Southerner captivated by the tales of underdogs, homebodies, and royalty. She is also a contributing writer with *The Cultivating Project* and co-host of *The Movie Score* podcast. When she isn't blogging about movies or writing stories of her own, she's reading, gardening, and collecting figurines of her favorite fictional characters on her family's hobby farm in southeast Louisiana. *Operation Lionhearted* is her debut novel.

Be sure to visit her online at www.maribethbarber.com and sign up for her monthly email newsletter!

Made in the USA
Coppell, TX
03 November 2021